T4-ADP-380

The Postcolonial and Imperial Experience in American Transcendentalism

The Postcolonial and Imperial Experience in American Transcendentalism

Marek Paryz

palgrave
macmillan

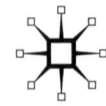

THE POSTCOLONIAL AND IMPERIAL EXPERIENCE IN AMERICAN TRANSCENDENTALISM
Copyright © Marek Paryz, 2012.

All rights reserved.

First published in 2012 by
PALGRAVE MACMILLAN®
in the United States—a division of St. Martin's Press LLC,
175 Fifth Avenue, New York, NY 10010.

Where this book is distributed in the UK, Europe and the rest of the world, this is by Palgrave Macmillan, a division of Macmillan Publishers Limited, registered in England, company number 785998, of Houndmills, Basingstoke, Hampshire RG21 6XS.

Palgrave Macmillan is the global academic imprint of the above companies and has companies and representatives throughout the world.

Palgrave® and Macmillan® are registered trademarks in the United States, the United Kingdom, Europe and other countries.

ISBN: 978–0–230–33874–6

Library of Congress Cataloging-in-Publication Data

Paryz, Marek
   The postcolonial and imperial experience in American transcendentalism / Marek Paryz.
      p. cm.
   Includes bibliographical references and index.
   ISBN 978–0–230–33874–6 (hardback)
   1. Transcendentalism (New England) 2. Postcolonialism in literature.
3. American literature—19th century—History and criticism.
4. Philosophy in literature. I. Title.

PS217.T7P37 2012
810.9′003—dc23   2011029888

A catalogue record of the book is available from the British Library.

Design by Newgen Imaging Systems (P) Ltd., Chennai, India.

First edition: January 2012

10 9 8 7 6 5 4 3 2 1

Printed in the United States of America.

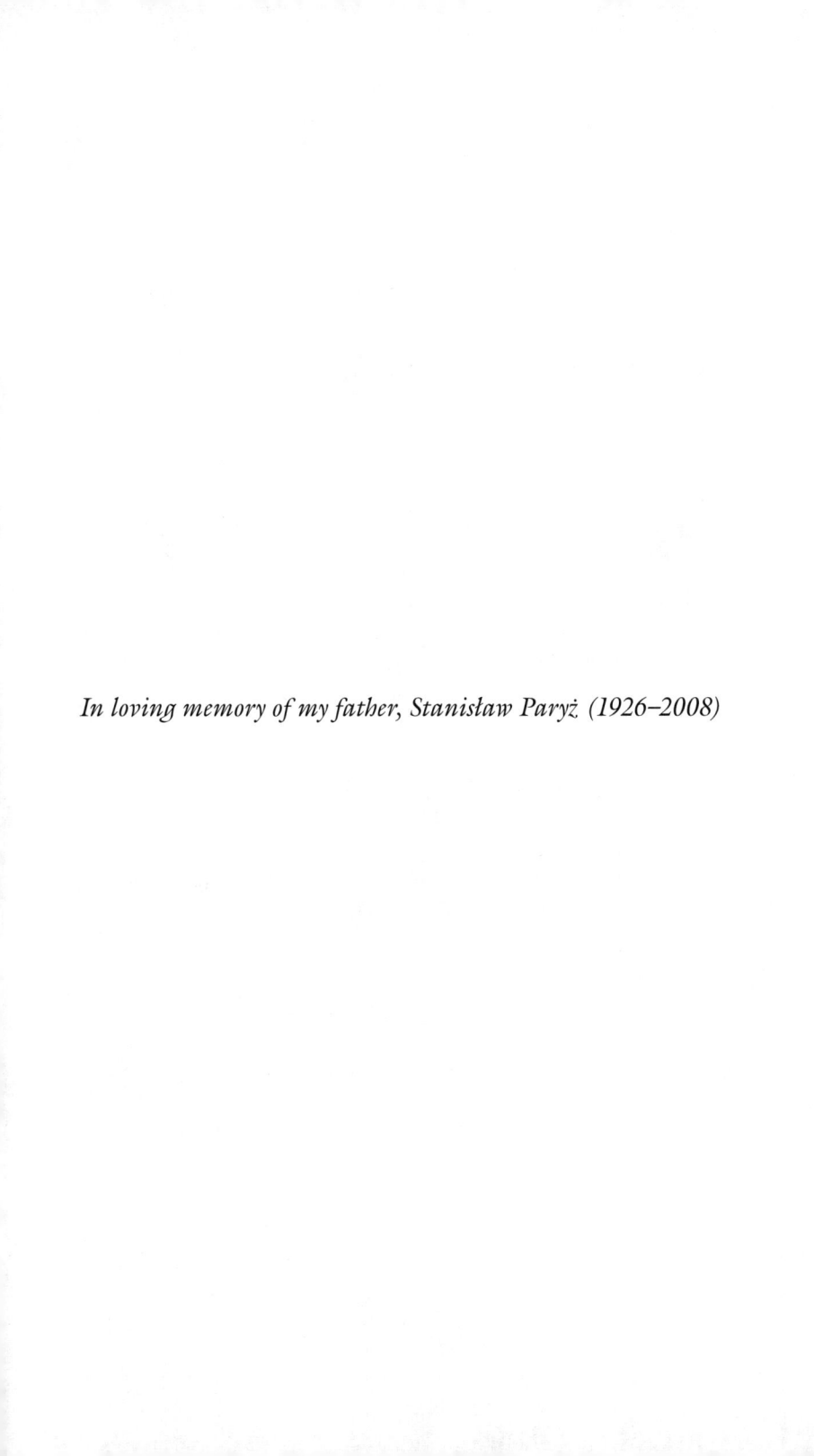

In loving memory of my father, Stanisław Paryż (1926–2008)

Contents

Acknowledgments	ix
Introduction: Mapping the Field	1

Part I   Ralph Waldo Emerson: The Double Figuration

1	Figures of Dependence: Exploring the Postcolonial in Emerson's Selected Texts	25
2	Beyond the Traveler's Testimony: *English Traits* and the Construction of Postcolonial Counter-Discourse	47
3	Emerson, New England, and the Rhetoric of Expansion	75

Part II   Henry David Thoreau: The Imperial Imaginary

4	Thoreau's Imperial Fantasy: *Walden* versus *Robinson Crusoe*	99
5	The Politics of the Genre: Exploration and Ethnography in *The Maine Woods*	123

Part III   Walt Whitman: The National Trajectory

6	Postcolonial Whitman: The Poet and the Nation in the 1855 Preface to *Leaves of Grass*	153
7	Passage to (More Than) India: The Poetics and Politics of Whitman's Textualization of the Orient	179

Conclusion: Representative Men	205
Notes	211
Bibliography	221
Index	237

Acknowledgments

In the course of my work on this book, a number of individuals and institutions have offered me support, which I wish to acknowledge.

I owe the greatest debt to Professor Agata Preis-Smith, former Chair of the Section of American Literature in the Institute of English Studies, University of Warsaw. She has been my guiding star ever since I came to Warsaw for my graduate studies back in the mid-1990s. She represents the professional standard I have always striven to live up to. My gratitude for her encouragement, understanding, enthusiasm, and kindness, is simply inexpressible.

I had a chance to present several parts of my work-in-progress at the meetings of the Section of American Literature; the discussions that followed were immensely enlightening to me. I thank my colleagues in the Section for their interest in my project.

I did the most substantial part of my research during a term as a Fulbright Senior Scholar at the University of Illinois at Chicago. I am grateful to the Polish-U.S. Fulbright Commission in Warsaw, and in particular to Director Andrzej Dakowski, for nominating me for this fellowship. I thank Professor Walter Benn Michaels, former Chair of the English Department UIC, for a kind invitation and a warm welcome to the department. During my stay at UIC, I had the privilege and pleasure to work with Professor Robin Grey and Professor Terence Whalen, who generously shared their time and expertise with me. Specifically, I am indebted to Professor Grey for her invaluable last-minute help in collecting the missing bibliography. Professor Lawrence Buell, whom I had the honor to meet at Harvard University, expressed keen interest in my book-in-progress and suggested the ways of streamlining my argument. It goes without saying that Professor Buell's pioneering scholarship on the postcolonial implications of the American Renaissance writing informed my project at every stage of preparation. I thank him for the work without which this book would never have been written. Professor Josie Campbell and Professor John Leo, my great friends at the University of Rhode Island at Kingston, invited me to lecture on a subject related to my project and offered the kind of academic appreciation that is always more than welcome. My other friends and colleagues in the U.S.—Dr. Agnieszka Bedingfield in Boston, Professor Holli Levitsky in LA, and Professor Monika Adamczyk-Garbowska, then in Washington, DC—invited me to their places, making my American experience as exciting as it only could be. Last but not least, I wish to express my gratitude to Carol Rigmark and Tom Byrnes, residents of Northbrook, IL, for allowing me to use their townhouse during my term at UIC.

* * *

Several chapters of this book have appeared as articles prior to the present publication. Chapter Two was published in *ATQ* 20.3 (September 2006); Chapter Four in *Mosaics of Words. Essays on the American and Canadian Literary Imagination in Memory of Professor Nancy Burke*, ed. Agata Preis-Smith, Ewa Luczak, and Marek Paryz (Warsaw: Institute of English Studies, University of Warsaw, 2006); Chapter Six in *Community and Nearness. Readings in English and American Literature and Culture*, ed. Ilona Dobosiewicz and Jacek Gutorow (Opole: University of Opole Press, 2007); and Chapter Seven in *The Poetics of America. Explorations in the Literature and Culture of the United States*, ed. Agata Preis-Smith and Marek Paryz (Warsaw: Institute of English Studies, University of Warsaw, 2004).

Introduction: Mapping the Field

This study has been designed as an analysis of the literary representations of the American experience in selected works of Ralph Waldo Emerson, Henry David Thoreau, and Walt Whitman with regard to the fundamental ambivalence that, in the writers' time, underlay the cultural and political development of the United States as a former colony with only a recent history of independence, on the one hand, and as a burgeoning imperial power, on the other. It aims to reach beneath the surface of the political allegiances declared by these authors or the ideological stances contested by them, and thus to explore symbolic literary structures revolving around the figurations of dependence and expansion. The termination of colonial dependence and the later continental expansion were historical and political processes that determined the shaping of American nationhood in the nineteenth century. The discourses that were forged around the time of the Revolution and in the course of subsequent decades provided the framework for the articulation of the American experience. This experience was commonly defined in terms of emergence and prospect. These two related notions, apparently suggesting a national teleology, concealed a great historical and cultural paradox, which consisted in the parallelism of two discourses: the one dwelling on the national emergence and expressing America's postcolonial condition, the other proclaiming the grand national prospect and articulating America's undeniable imperial potential. In Emerson's time, those Americans who were engaged in the public debate often expressed the awareness of their national lineage, which was reflected in the literary redefinitions of America's cultural debt to Europe. At the same time, Emerson's contemporaries were exposed to the appealing ideology of expansionism, which can be seen as a specific American variant of imperialism. It must be emphasized that political ideas function on the level of individual and collective consciousness, as much as they leave an imprint in the individual and collective subconscious. This is important to remember, since the fact of ideological influence does not have to entail a direct reaction of support or rejection; quite on the contrary, it inspires interests and poses dilemmas whose connection to ideological issues is not always evident. In literature, such interests and dilemmas manifest themselves through rhetorical and thematic tropes, generic and stylistic structures, topoi and figurations, which are the primary subject of analysis in the present work. The identification of, so to speak, political sediments in a literary text can only be accomplished through the examination of the strategies of representation. Accordingly, representation is a category emerging at the intersection of the esthetic and the political; moreover, it has a certain existential function, as it serves to mediate the complexity of human experience. For instance, Emerson's American scholar, Thoreau's autobiographical persona, or Whitman's poet are highly imaginative figures, infused with historical and political significance and epitomizing particular existential priorities. The study of literary representation results in the recognition of multiple configurations of interdependence between experience, politics, and aesthetics, with rhetorical constructions as the medium that binds these three domains. The process of translating experience, which is inseparable from historical circumstances, into literary representation, which depends on the existing forms of aesthetic production, invariably involves the work of imagination. Now, imagination is a notion that has a certain vagueness about it insofar as it names the faculty of the mind that evades the controlling effect of rationalization. However, it is precisely this vagueness that accounts for the presence of literary categories that signify on their own terms, and not in strict conformity with political categories. It must be added that imagination is not only an individual feature, but also a sort of cultural value, as it helps to delimit the horizons of expectations within which the author and the audience function. Imagination is a realm where the semantic boundaries of ideas dissolve and the ideas themselves are subjected to interrogation or reinvention. It is a realm where fears or wishes become potentialities and where such potentialities acquire the shape of linguistic utterances. The use of imaginative constructions characterizes not only literary texts, but also ideological doctrines, especially discursive forms such as programs, manifestos, or declarations, setting the aims to be achieved in the future and therefore evoking the reality that does not exist yet. It is worth mentioning that numerous texts, endorsing the doctrine of Manifest Destiny, inspired among Americans the most bizarre fantasies of conquest.

This study focuses on the specificity of the writing produced during the period in American history that can be described as concomitantly postcolonial and imperial. Critics who look at nineteenth-century

American literature through analogous lenses often tend to emphasize either the former or the latter aspect of the historical context; this project aims to combine the interpretative perspectives that hinge on the recognition of America's postcolonial situation, on the one hand, and of the nation's imperial design, on the other. Such a convergence of stances and methods helps to explore the complex course of history and the tensions among its varied aesthetic renderings. For a better part of the nineteenth century, if not throughout the century, the postcolonial phase and the imperial phase coincided, giving rise to essential ambiguities and contradictions in American culture. Such coincidence was connected with the continuous nature of postcolonial cultural processes; namely, the postcolonial phase, in principle, has relatively definable beginnings (once the meaning of "the postcolonial" has been decided upon), but the moment of its conclusion is virtually impossible to determine, because the cultural process initiated at the onset of the phase continues to affect multiple spheres of human experience and artistic production in spite of political changes. As Peter Hulme puts it aptly:

> "Postcolonial"...should not be used as if it were an adjective describing a condition that is automatically and for all time assumed once a formal colonial status has been left behind, any more than it should be taken for granted that the change in *formal* status automatically implies that the psychological, economic, and cultural effects of being a colony can be sloughed off like a snake's skin....We should have no difficulty in saying that the United States was once "postcolonial" in one meaningful sense, but at some point (1898?) it ceases to be useful to describe it as such. If such a label can make Charles Brockden Brown more interesting to read, then that it something else to be said in favour of the term "postcolonial." The same argument applies to almost all of the countries of Central and South America. And because "postcolonial" should not be used as a merit badge, the adjective implies nothing about a postcolonial country's behaviour. As a postcolonial nation, the United States continued to colonize North America, completing the genocide of the native population begun by the Spanish and British. Or, to use a more recent example, "postcolonial" is not a description that should be awarded Indonesia when it became independent from The Netherlands and taken away when it invaded East Timor: a country can be postcolonial and colonizing at the same time. (121–122)

The spectacular career of the term "postcolonial" or "post-colonial" began in the late 1950s when it was first used in a typically descriptive sense to characterize the transformation of India after the British colonial rule had come to an end. It was readily adopted by those historians and political scientists who wrote about the countries in Asia and Africa that became independent states in the 1950s and 1960s (Walder 3). The late 1970s witnessed the first uses of the term by literary critics who were interested in probing "the various cultural effects of colonization"; the initial scope of application of the term in the analysis of culture was rather limited, as it referred primarily to "cultural interactions within colonial societies in literary circles" (Ashcroft, Griffiths, and Tiffin, *Key Concepts* 186). The work of fundamental significance in this early development of postcolonial studies was Edward Said's *Orientalism*, published in 1978, but the grounds for this kind of critique had been laid even earlier with the appearance of Franz Fanon's *The Wretched of the Earth* (1961) and Albert Memmi's *The Colonizer and the Colonized* (1965). In the course of time, especially from the early 1990s onward, the scope of applications has been broadened to an impressive extent, not only substantiating innovative analyses of literary and cultural phenomena, but also provoking a great theoretical debate about the aims and strategies of postcolonialism as a form of cultural intervention. Nowadays, it is next to impossible to contain postcolonialism within any complete critical model; one can only try to compose catalogues of thematic fields, contextual variants, and interpretative tools, while themes, contexts, and procedures may converge in a considerable degree, may have limited mutual equivalence, or may be altogether discrepant:

> "Post-colonialism/postcolonialism" is now used in wide and diverse ways to include the study and analysis of European territorial conquests, the various institutions of European colonialisms, the discursive operations of empire, the subtleties of subject construction in colonial discourse and the resistance of those subjects, and, most importantly perhaps, the differing responses to such incursions and their contemporary colonial legacies in both pre- and post-independence nations and communities. While its use has tended to focus on the cultural production of such communities, it is becoming widely used in historical, political, sociological and economic analyses, as these disciplines continue to engage with the impact of European imperialism upon world societies. (Ashcroft, Griffiths, and Tiffin, *Key Concepts* 187)

A good example of the complications involved in the use of postcolonialism is the dispute about the meaning of "the postcolonial" in reference to the chronological moment that it designates. Some critics define "the postcolonial" as "coming after colonialism and imperialism, in their original meaning of direct rule-domination, but still positioned within imperialism in its later sense of the global system of hegemonic economic power" (Young 57). Others claim that it signifies the time "after the imprint of colonialism"; "In this sense, post-colonialism began the moment the colonizer established his presence on foreign soil and continues through to today" (Piper 19). Paradoxically, both these competing definitions are valid because they identify two turning points in the formation of practically every postcolonial society and in the development of its culture.

It seems that the explanation for such a complicated state of things in the field of postcolonial studies lies in the primary subject of analysis, that is imperialism with its varied manifestations and multifarious consequences. In his seminal book *Culture and Imperialism*, Edward Said formulates his definitions of imperialism and colonialism: "'imperialism' means the practice, the theory, and the attitudes of a dominating metropolitan centre ruling a distant territory; 'colonialism,' which is almost always a consequence of imperialism, is the implementing of settlements on distant territory." The critic goes on to say that both imperialism and colonialism "are supported and perhaps even impelled by impressive ideological formations that include notions that certain territories and people *require* and beseech domination, as well as forms of knowledge affiliated with domination" (8). The "ideological formations" and the "forms of knowledge" exist as a body of discourses that perpetually oscillate between different areas of human activity and linguistic production, such as politics, economy, pedagogy, religion, art, entertainment et cetera. In a sense, discursive formations replicate themselves as they change contexts, for instance religious ideas often played an important part in the theories of racial superiority that, in turn, helped to justify the necessity of the economic exploitation of colonies. Said emphatically states that there was much more to "the expansion of the great Western empires" than just "profit and hope of further profit":

> There was a commitment to them over and above profit, a commitment in constant circulation and recirculation, which, on the one hand, allowed decent men and women to accept the notion that distant territories and their native peoples *should* be subjugated, and, on the other, replenished metropolitan energies so that these decent men and women could think of the *imperium* as a protracted, almost metaphysical obligation to rule subordinate, inferior, or less advanced peoples. (10)

Thus, Said's definition of imperialism, initially predicated on the geopolitical relations between the metropolis and the colony, expands in such a way as to pay attention to the ways that "decent people" felt about the imperial design. In other words, the critic proceeds from the discussion of a geopolitical structure to the recognition of a type of mind-set; he talks about the process whereby the dissemination of knowledge elicited emotional reactions, shaped intellectual attitudes, and determined existential decisions. One can risk a thesis that while geopolitical structures differ radically across contexts, the types of mind-set reveal important parallels.

The multilayered critique of imperialism accounts for the emergence of a political agenda in postcolonialism, because such critique represents, in Robert J. C. Young's words, "a theoretical and political position which embodies an active concept of intervention within…oppressive circumstances." Symptomatically, Young puts emphasis on the political charge of postcolonialism, juxtaposing it to the concepts of "colonialism," "imperialism," and "neocolonialism," which "adopt only a critical relation to the oppressive regimes and practices that they delineate." Unlike the procedures relying on these three concepts, postcolonialism "is both contestatory and committed towards political ideals of transnational social justice." It does not merely offer an analysis of, but it virtually "attacks the status quo of hegemonic economic imperialism, and the history of colonialism and imperialism." Young compares postcolonialism to Marxism and feminism on the grounds that these three critical stances have developed the domains for "an activist engagement with positive political positions and new forms of political identity." He maintains that postcolonialism offers "an interventionist methodology developed for the analysis of the subjective and material conditions of the postcolonial era articulated with active transformative practices" (57–58). Young's discussion sounds somewhat radical, which is understandable in the light of the fact that he takes interest in relatively recent, mostly twentieth-century, models of domination, liberation, and transformation, and in the continuing effects of imperialism visible in the contemporary world. Young's observations have rather limited relevance for the study of nineteenth-century American literature, but there is one important aspect of his argument that illuminates this particular context; namely, in highlighting the role of political activism in postcolonial critique, Young establishes a certain relation of equivalence between imperialism and postcolonialism as realms of discourse and as spheres of praxis.

Postcolonialism is one of the most hotly debated issues in contemporary literary and cultural studies; the discussion of this debate lies beyond the scope of this project.[1] Notwithstanding certain traps that the employment of postcolonial reading procedures may entail, such as a suggestion of a homogenized view of diverse national experiences and cultural outputs, postcolonialism is useful in the analysis of nineteenth-century American literature for two reasons: first, it is a tool of historical diagnosis that illuminates the ambivalence of the formation of American nationhood, and second, it is an interpretative model that examines the functions of a literary text within the framework of ideological formations, the functions reflecting a broad spectrum of textual variants, delimited by the extremes of endorsement and contestation. The paradoxical coexistence of postcolonial and imperial tropes in American political rhetoric and literary writing resulted, to a great extent, from the nation's origin as a settler colony. Contrary to the colonies of occupation, "where indigenous people remained in the majority but were administered by a foreign power," in settler colonies, "the invading Europeans (or their descendants) annihilated, displaced and/or marginalized the indegenes to become a majority non-indigenous population" (Ashcroft, Griffiths, and Tiffin, *Key Concepts* 210). The authors of *Key Concepts in Post-Colonial Studies* provide the following examples of settler colonies where this process of marginalization of the indigene by the people of European background had taken place: Argentina, Australia, Canada, and the United States. The specificity of the settler experience results from the fact that settlers established their identity in relation to the colonizing nation and culture from which they had been alienated, on the one hand, and in relation to the colonized people, whom they had helped to subdue. The point is that their identity hinges on the recognition of the concomitant difference from and closeness to the colonizers and the colonized alike. The essential predicament of the settler is that in the face of such representatives of the empire as, for instance, the administrators, he embodies an inferior human category, and begins to feel as if he were a colonial subject himself. As Ashcroft, Griffiths, and Tiffin put it, settlers "are simultaneously both colonized and colonizer" (211). The critics point out that the most important consequence of such in-betweenness is the forging of "a distinctive and unique culture that is neither that of the metropolitan culture from which they [settlers] stem, nor that of the 'native' cultures they have displaced in their early colonizing phase" (212).

The study of settler culture alone is a complicated task, as it involves the investigation of class divisions, economic practices, administrative standards, intercultural contacts, spatial configurations, and, last but not least, mental states. And this is only one from among a number of fields of research that postcolonial studies comprises. Therefore postcolonialism as a way of reading must be flexible; as Young claims, it is not a theory in the strict sense of the word, because it does not constitute "an abstract model" that rests on "a number of axioms" and applies to "empirical descriptions": "There is no single methodology which must be adhered to; rather, there are shared political and psychological perceptions, together with specific social and cultural objectives, which draw on a common range of theories and employ a constellation of theoretical insights" (64). Thanks to this diversity of theoretical and interpretative frames, postcolonialism offers equally valid insights into texts that remain oppositional toward the imperial rhetoric and into those that reproduce it. In general, postcolonialism presupposes a fundamentally dialogical nature of a literary text, because it sees textuality as a site of resistance. The text destabilizes the dominant rhetoric through reworking its tropes; such tropological modifications result from the convergence of themes and the divergence of aesthetic strategies. In other words, by multiplying the variants of representation, the literary text breaks the monopoly of highly ideologized representations. At the same time, postcolonialism proves to be equally useful in the analysis of texts that partake of the discourses of imperialism. Namely, literary texts tend to interrogate the doctrines that they apparently subscribe to, because they expand the field of signification and thus attest to the mutability of rhetoric by way of the incorporation of new tropes. Postcolonialism looks closely at intertextual connections across literary and nonliterary discourses; this is, ineluctably, "politicized intertextuality," to use Francis Barker and Peter Hulme's term (128).

One of the most interesting issues in postcolonial studies is the place of the United States in this model of critical analysis. Probably the most important early attempt to situate America in the conceptual framework of postcolonialism is the recognition of the development of American literature as a specific paradigm of cultural emergence of a postcolonial society in the seminal *The Empire Writes Back* by Ashcroft, Griffiths, and Tiffin, one of the first books that identified and synthesized a variety of postcolonial critical practices. In fact, the authors regard the United States as "the first post-colonial society to develop a 'national' literature" (16). The literature of the United States serves as an illustration of the national model of analysis, the other models being regional, comparative, "Black writing," hybridity, and syncreticity. The critics emphasize the fact that the ideas of literary sovereignty in the late-eighteenth-century United States accelerated "the optimistic progression to nationhood," because it allowed the people to articulate their sense of difference from Britain. Ashcroft, Griffiths, and Tiffin claim that "the American experience and its attempts to produce a new kind of literature can be seen to be the model for all later post-colonial writing" (16). However, in the aftermath of the American Revolution, the economic and political changes preceded unique cultural achievements, especially that Americans were used to thinking of their cultural production as secondary to British and accepted the fact that their culture was "an offshoot of the 'parent-tree.'" The crucial factor in the growth of cultural sovereignty of the United States was the ability to develop literary characteristics that differed from British standards, as a result of which "the concept of national literary differences 'within' English writing became established." Without clearly defining the time of this fundamental process, the critics conclude that: "The eventual consequence of this has been that 'newer' literatures from countries such as Nigeria, Australia, and India could also be discussed as discrete national formations rather than as 'branches' of the tree" (*Empire Writes Back* 16–17).

Characteristically, while Ashcroft, Griffiths, and Tiffin treat the literature of the United States as one of the primary models for postcolonial writing, in the course of their discussion they seem to minimize this aspect and do not use any American examples of the more recent politics of representation. Perhaps this is one of the reasons why those Americanists, who acknowledge the necessity to locate some fields of interest in American studies within the framework of postcolonialism, have found the theoretical proposition formulated in *The Empire Writes Back* far from satisfactory. For example, Deborah L. Madsen claims that the view presented by Ashcroft, Griffiths, and Tiffin excludes a large body of American writing from the postcolonial critical paradigm, because they "describe the postcolonial as being identical with the former British Empire" (4). In other words, they concentrate on the historical emergence of national literature in the United States and ignore the later forms of cultural hegemony visibly reminiscent of colonial domination. Essentially, Madsen speaks of the growth of the white Anglo-American canon and the accompanying marginalization of ethnic writing, and she puts stress on the postcolonial status of the latter literary category:

> Only in a comparative framework can the colonial and post-colonial condition of ethnic communities within the borders of the United States, communities such as the Native American tribes, Chicano/as, Afro-Hispanic and African American communities, be recognized for precisely what they are. In comparison with the post-colonial expression

of Australian Aboriginal writers, Canadian First Nation writers, the work of American Indian writers assumes a new set of significances that is derived from a matrix of indigenous experience and not from the stifling paradigm of sophisticated metropolitan center versus primitive post-colonial margin. (10–11)

Likewise, Karen Piper, in her critique of the politics of multiculturalism, takes it for granted that postcolonial models apply primarily, if not exclusively, to ethnic literatures of the United States (14–28). Amritjit Singh and Peter Schmidt, the editors of an important anthology *Postcolonial Theory and the United States: Race, Ethnicity, and Literature*, include in their volume contributions that, with one or two exceptions, address a plethora of issues related to ethnic studies. The proponents of what they call "the Borders School" in American studies, Singh and Schmidt delineate the following areas where postcolonial reading procedures can be used with particular adequacy: diaspora and immigration studies, transnational studies, whiteness studies, and globalization theory (3–69).

Those critical uses of postcolonialism in American studies that rely on the evidence of ethnic cultures and literatures usually disregard other possibilities of employing this interpretative apparatus, in particular its applicability in the study of American culture in the colonial era and in the postcolonial period after the Revolution. Paradoxically, it is as if in postulating specific reading procedures the scholars working in the field of ethnic studies attempted to marginalize other critical perspectives with which theirs share certain sources and precepts. This becomes visible when critics like Deborah Madsen dismiss the historical description of the American cultural emergence presented in *The Empire Writes Back* as simplistic or irrelevant. Perhaps the explanation why this kind of dismissal has taken place is that the exponents of postcolonialism in American ethnic studies suspect that the recognition of the postcolonial status of the works of nineteenth-century white, male, Anglo-Saxon literary masters would lead to the reconstitution of the old canon, which is itself, indeed, a domain where certain acts of colonization have been performed. Such critics tend to deny the idea that, as Lawrence Buell puts it, "the canonical U.S. white male writers might have experienced a phase of cultural subalternity in any meaningful sense of the word" ("Postcolonial Anxiety" 214, n. 2), or that, as Geoffrey Sanborn has said it, these writers were "early articulators of a postcolonial sensibility" (14). In consequence, it becomes risky to trace the possible correspondences between differing postcolonial models that apply to American contexts. It so happens, however, that the term most adequately naming the cultural and political condition that is the focus of this study appears in an article that has hardly anything to do with the American nineteenth century. The term in question is "postcolonial imperialism," used by Susie O'Brien to denote the shifting patterns of U.S. national mythologies in the age of globalization (159–183). The historical origins of American postcolonial imperialism (albeit such a term does not appear in the discussion itself) are analyzed by Peter S. Onuf, who claims that "the American Revolution precipitated epochal constitutional and conceptual changes reflected in controversy over the implications of territorial expansion for the future of the American union." Onuf concentrates on the political conflict between the Federalist antiexpansionists who believed that expansion would hamper the solidification of the nation and weaken its position "in a dangerous world," and Jeffersonian expansionists who claimed that the centralization of power should be avoided because it could cause the nation's collapse, just as it had led to the collapse of the British empire (303). Admittedly, this historical debate showed the symptomatic mutual entanglement of postcolonial and imperial notions and tropes. It is also worth mentioning that Timothy Powell considers the emergence of the Monroe Doctrine as a moment defining American "*postcolonial colonialism*" (original italics):

> [P]*ost*colonial in the sense that, as Monroe formulated the doctrine, it applied only to those nations in the Western Hemisphere that had "declared their independence" from the European colonial powers, yet still a form of colonialism in that the doctrine gave the United States a loosely defined economic/political sovereignty over the Western Hemisphere that would come to be used, many times over, to justify America's imperial intervention. Monroe defines the "right" of the United States to establish not colonies... but capitalist/imperialist spheres of influence. These spheres of influence served the nation's conflicted sense of itself as a postcolonial superpower well in that they allowed America to intervene on foreign soil without entitling the subjects of these "postcolonial colonies" to any democratic rights as American citizens or, more important, given the nation's deep-seated nativist anxieties, to the right of return.(351–352)

In recent years, the use of postcolonialism in the study of eighteenth- and nineteenth-century American culture has received considerable enhancement from the rapidly growing field of transatlantic and transnational studies. This approach has stimulated a new interest in the cultural relations between the United States and Europe, the interest that did not develop earlier despite the appearance of a number of important books with a transatlantic focus in the 1980s. In *Transatlantic Insurrections*, Paul Giles proposes a methodology that helps to demonstrate "how the emergence of autonomous and separate political identities during this era [the eighteenth and nineteenth centuries] can be seen as intertwined with a play of opposites, a series of reciprocal attractions and repulsions between opposing national situations" (1). Giles postulates a comparative approach in order to show that "American culture at the turn of the nineteenth century was not simply 'anti-colonial' in the sense of seeking to resist a hegemonic British power, but rather embodied many of the internal contradictions of a settler culture" (2). John Carlos Rowe, another leading proponent of a transnational approach to the postrevolutionary and nineteenth-century United States, claims that American politics of that time was based, to a great extent, on the ideas extracted from British colonialism:

> The post-revolutionary United States emerged as a coherent nation in many respects as a consequence of its colonial imaginary and the latter's deployment of a wide range of symbolic instruments. Culture was from the very outset fantastically conceived as unified in order to legitimate the indisputable fiction of the union of states previously held together primarily by means of British colonial foreign policies and laws, many of which varied drastically to regulate different regions and economies in British North America. It is possible to speak of early United States nationalism as itself a colonial project, insofar as the formations of the nation depended crucially on the transformation of British colonialism into national institutions and practices in a rapid defensive manner. ("Nineteenth-Century United States" 80)

It is important to mention that, in Rowe's view, American imperialism as articulated in the doctrine of Manifest Destiny was a sign of colonial legacy insofar as "the expansion of the national border functions as one means of controlling threats within an unstable, new and contrived nation by projecting them outside or beyond that nation" (80).

This study is, in part, transatlantic in its scope, using as basic literary evidence the topoi, genres, and figurations that came into existence or underwent transformation in the "contact zones" between American and European cultures. However, the transatlantic issues, albeit significant, should not exclude the domestic affairs from view. In the nineteenth century, American culture was shaped in a unique political environment, where the expansionist nation, striving to build the famous "empire for liberty," created quasi-colonial, and at times openly colonial, forms of dependence between regions, races, and classes, as if it had forgotten the lesson of colonization from its recent history. Possibly, the colonial past represents the repressed in the discourse of the nation; if this is the case, it is certainly worth probing the multiple layers of literary discourse in order to trace the strategies of the linguistic repression of burdensome memory as well as to identify the discursive contexts wherein the repressed surfaced as linguistic utterance. Admittedly, postcolonialism has developed an apparatus allowing one to adequately recognize and analyze various representations of dependence, subjugation, resistance, liberation, expansion, hegemony, and so on. This project takes a specific stance regarding the relevance of postcolonialism in American studies, and it does so without contesting other readings that derive from postcolonial methodologies. It aims to extend the scope of scholarship on nineteenth-century American imperial/postcolonial literary culture, treating the existing body of criticism as a valid point of departure.

Although the study of cultural relations across the Atlantic in the Romantic era in general, and of literary influences in particular, has quite a long tradition in American criticism, the contemporary tendencies to "reconsider" the American Renaissance have resulted in the appearance of new, groundbreaking theses, such as the thesis about the postcolonial beginnings of the U.S. national literature. It was first put forward with utmost directness by Lawrence Buell in his 1992 influential and controversial article "American Literary Emergence as a Postcolonial Phenomenon," subsequently revised and published under the title "Postcolonial Anxiety in Classic U.S. Literature" in 2000.[2] The point of departure in the article is the incontestable historical fact that America was the first colony to win independence, which allows one to infer that America provides a model of cultural emergence for the countries with a colonial past that became independent in later epochs. In his discussion, Buell highlights two factors underlying the tensions between America and Europe in the postcolonial phase: on the one hand, the formation of the patterns of cultural critique, informing a vast majority of British texts about America, and on the other, the production of American texts predicated on the necessity to disprove European representations of the United States and thus to establish new prisms of the nation's self-perception and self-understanding. Buell speaks about the general tendency among the British to dismiss

American literature as worthless, and he specifically concentrates on the prejudices that had been codified in British literary discourse, most notably in travel writing. Namely, there is more than ample literary evidence that the British in principle looked down upon the United States, having in mind a set of ideas founded on the conviction of cultural superiority. These ideas constituted the ideological framework for the British accounts of America, while the terms of presentation in such accounts were heavily reminiscent of colonial discourse, as they emphasized the exotic and barbarian metonymic qualities of the country and the people. Buell points to the corresponding tropes of the descent into "darkness" in Charles Dickens's *Martin Chuzzlewit* and Joseph Conrad's *Heart of Darkness,* or to analogous kinds of sensitivity to unacceptable, revolting local habits, expressed in Frances Trollope's *Domestic Manners of the Americans* and V. S. Naipaul's books about India. The individual experiences and observations of British travelers confirmed the general beliefs about the degraded condition of American people ("Postcolonial Anxiety" 199–202).

Buell's central argument hinges on the assumption—considered objectionable by a few critics who responded to Buell in a polemical spirit—that there exist hints of parallelism between the aesthetic as much as political choices made by the writers of the American Renaissance and the motivation behind the literary strategies of the writers from postcolonial countries in the twentieth century. Notwithstanding the radically different historical circumstances, writers from both these groups had to face the consequences of the earlier cultural hegemony. In general, the writer in a postcolonial context cannot create new art in isolation from the aesthetic models that usually had predominated for long periods of time in the colonial phase. One of the most serious matters that the writers from the former French and British colonies in Asia and Africa had to settle with themselves was the choice of language; not accidentally, many of them decided to write in the language of the colonizer, which had a powerful effect leading to the interrogation of the models of representation previously enforced in the course of the hegemonic rule. In other words, the manifest signs of colonial legacy, primarily the language, were used to compromise this legacy. Obviously, the writers of the American Renaissance did not have to make any decisions regarding the choice of language, but they certainly shared the awareness that new models of literary creation would have to be developed from the existing ones, given America's inevitable debt to European culture. Buell gives several examples of how American writers meaningfully reworked European tropes, styles, and genres; thus, he claims that "what Whitman has done is to make grotesque a trope from the Eurocentric repertoire, the *translatio studii*—the transfer of art and learning from Old World to New; a trope that had been invoked to underwrite colonization efforts and subsequently the hegemony of the late colonial gentry." Another case of a literary strategy aimed at displacing a dominant paradigm is James Fenimore Cooper's fashioning of Natty Bumppo as a "vernacular hero," modeled on the British literary type of "the genteel protagonist cum vernacular sidekick." Buell's third example is Emerson's "The American Scholar"; this time, however, the critic comments on the belated appearance of ideas that would facilitate the national formation: "the valorization of the humble and the familiar" and "the renewed respect accorded to the individual person." The point is that Whitman's and Cooper's reworking of European tropes as well as Emerson's continuous search for American terms of conceptualizing ideas become signs of the same postcolonial cultural condition (202–205).

Lawrence Buell maps out several fields of aesthetic and ideological investigation where important commonalities between the American Renaissance literary culture and the twentieth-century literary cultures of postcolonial countries can be found. First, he speaks of "the semi-Americanization of the English language" as a case of "linguistic indigenization," the phenomenon that in the twentieth century manifested itself on a large scale in texts written by postcolonial writers in the language of the former colonizer. Such texts reflect the nature and the extent of the institutionalization of English in different colonial contexts and illustrate one of the characteristic strategies in postcolonial writing that consists in the blending of the colonizer's language with the vernacular. Such a linguistic amalgam, in turn, is targeted at the centripetal model of cultural hegemony. Second, Buell claims that classic U.S. literary works yield the effect of "cultural hybridization"; his examples are: "Whitman's composite persona, Thoreau's hovering between the traditions of Puritan, Greco-Roman, Native American, and Oriental mythographies in *A Week* and *Walden*; Melville's multimythic elaboration of the whale symbol in tandem with presenting the *Pequod* as a kind of global village; Cooper's heteroglossic tapestry of six or seven different nationalities in *The Pioneers*." All these literary qualities are signs of what might be called the politics of heteroglossia, which also plays a central role in the writings of contemporary authors from former colonies. Third, Buell comments on the ambivalence that surrounds the writer's function in the postcolonial phase as a result of "the expectation that artists be responsible agents for achieving national liberation"; this ambivalence revolves around the dialectic of the artistic and the political, problematizing the status of art as a compromise between the artist's sense of creative autonomy and of public duty. Fourth, the critic pays attention to the existence of what he calls "alien genres," which can be seen as markers of cultural difference. These were the genres that, having undergone thorough modifications in the colonial era, helped sustain European cultural prominence, and in the postcolonial times, they were used to interrogate the European patterns of representation. Fifth, Buell emphasizes the role of the pastoral as a genre that was developed in colonialism as a tool in the discursive construction of alien space and which was later reworked, most notably, by African authors who presented "a preurban, precolonial ideal order as a badge of distinctiveness." Sixth and last, Buell ponders the notion of "belatedness," a reflection of European fantasies about colonial space bespeaking a sense of nostalgia (208–212).

This study is greatly indebted to Lawrence Buell's pioneering scholarship on the postcolonial underpinnings of classic nineteenth-century American literary texts; in a way, this project takes off where Buell's argument comes to conclusion. Namely, his article ends with a handful of observations about the convergence of the postcolonial and imperial stages in the nineteenth-century United States. The writings of the authors discussed by Buell provide ample evidence that the writer can "play" either "the (post)colonial" or "the imperialist." This is precisely the central premise of the present study. Buell points out that the roots of the U.S. imperial design can be found in the nation's colonial history: "In the case of the U.S., the dream of what might meaningfully be called empire as opposed to colony dates from the colonial period itself, and the self-conception of many American colonists including future founding fathers like Benjamin Franklin of participating in the consolidation of a greater British America" (213). John Carlos Rowe seems to make an analogous point when he says that "U.S. imperialism extends the established practices of European exploration, conquest, and colonization against which the United States struggled in its own anti-colonial revolution" (*Literary Culture* 11). While this study derives its methodological basis from Buell's pioneering description of the literary culture of the American Renaissance as a postcolonial phenomenon, it is equally indebted to the critical discussions of the cultural work of American imperialism, such as Amy Kaplan's analysis of various literary and extraliterary contexts, both domestic and foreign, showing the extent in which imperial imaginings shaped the consciousness of

American people and infused their rhetoric from the mid-nineteenth to the beginning of the twentieth century (*Anarchy of Empire*). After Lawrence Buell's article, a number of academic publications have appeared, drawing from postcolonial criticism; such reading procedures are no longer extraordinary in the study of classic American literature, but at the same time, they are far from being some kind of standard.[3] For example, Edward Watts, in his monograph, explores the processes of decolonizing the American scene of writing and reading in the early Republic on the basis of books by Hugh Henry Brackenridge, Judith Sargent Murray, Royal Tyler, Charles Brockden Brown, George Watterston, and Washington Irving (*Writing and Postcolonialism*). The nineteenth-century American writer whose work has proved to be the most inspiring for critics inclined toward postcolonialism is, predictably enough, Herman Melville, to whom Geoffrey Sanborn devoted his book *The Sign of the Cannibal: Melville and the Making of a Postcolonial Reader*. Sanborn looks at Melville as a writer excessively preoccupied with the idea of "newness," which is a defining aspect of the colonial encounter. Using Homi Bhabha's concepts, Sanborn reads "newness" as a sign of epistemological impasse, conditioned by the momentary absence of "the recognizable object" in the colonial encounter, which generates a "phantasmatic quality" in the stereotypes of the colonialist and of the native. The ultimate consequence of the interplay of stereotypes is the hybrid character of the colonial encounter: "In every such encounter, the colonialist must come into being by way of a postulated native, and the native must come into being by way of a postulated colonialist" (9). At present, a considerable proportion of Melville criticism is, in one way or another, indebted to the achievement of postcolonial studies. A completely different example of reading nineteenth-century American literature along the lines of postcolonialism is Robert Weisbuch's article "Post-Colonial Emerson and the Erasure of Europe." Weisbuch sheds light on Emerson's postcolonial situation by arguing that "his ambivalence toward Europe tends to resolve itself negatively because the crucial necessity to dignify the New World and Europe as idea or trope for Emerson overwhelms the Europe of mere fact" (194). Importantly, the critic identifies a set of what he calls "post-colonial generalities" that apply not only to Emerson's work, but also to the nineteenth-century American cultural context on the whole: "the monopolizing of prestige by imported models of high culture; the encouraging of third-rate imitations of these models; and thus a long lag between political independence and its cultural counterpart" (195). Analogically to Weisbuch, Mark A. R. Kemp probes

"American postcolonial ambivalence" in relation to Europe in his article on Nathaniel Hawthorne's *The Marble Faun* where he discovers "a nostalgia for colonial origins and the dependency complex this nostalgia generates." Unlike Weisbuch, however, Kemp goes as far as to consider the complications that this national condition determines for the emergent imperial design: "Nostalgia and dependence are in tension with the underlying faith in the ideological rightness of American exceptionalism and ascendancy in the world" (210–211). Last but not least, postcolonialism seems to be the major theoretical foundation for the important recent criticism locating the literature of the American Renaissance in the transamerican context.[4]

While sharing certain assumptions with the above-mentioned sources, this study differs from them in method and in scope. It develops the idea that most of those critics of classic American literature, who use postcolonial methodologies, usually articulate, but treat it in a cursory manner; namely, that the fundamental ideological dilemma that writers from Charles Brockden Brown to Henry James faced was the profoundly ambivalent political legacy of the United States as a former colony with unique prospects for national growth, which resulted in the emergence of expansionist policies within decades after the Revolution. Since this study concentrates on the processes whereby literary discourses reformulate ideological issues, it seems that the most relevant method for such a scrutiny is tropological analysis. According to Hayden White:

> Tropology centers attention on the turns in a discourse: turns from one level of generalization to another, from one phase of a sequence to another, from a description to an analysis or the reverse, from a figure to a ground or from an event to its context, from the conventions of one genre to those of another within a single discourse, and so on. (10–11)

Furthermore, White claims that

> [Tropology] does not suggest that everything is language, speech, discourse, text, only that linguistic referentiality and representation are much more complicated matters than the older, literalist notions of language and discourse made out. Tropology stresses the metalinguistic over the referential function of discourse because it is concerned more with codes than with whatever contingent messages can be transmitted by specific uses of them. Insofar as codes are themselves message-contents in their own right, tropology expands the notion of message itself and alerts us to the performance, as well as the communicative, aspect of discourse. (17)

As a tropological analysis, this study explores the ways in which rhetorical operations lead to the establishment of orders of signification. One of the specific interests pursued in the present work is the functioning of figurative language and the purposes that such language serves. Admittedly, the texts by the three writers discussed here are characterized by close attention paid to the real circumstances—hence Emerson's existential formulas, Thoreau's scholarly passion, or Whitman's identification with the commonplace—and a concomitant dissatisfaction with the literal. Essentially, their reliance on figurative structures has to do with the necessity to relate to America as an idea. By no means is it accidental that they all invented the types of protagonists—like Emerson's scholar, Thoreau's explorer, and Whitman's poet—who, despite their uniqueness as authorial projections, should be seen as epitomes of the national experience as envisaged by the three writers. The frames within which such protagonists appear are constituted by, among others, topoi and genres. Topoi and genres are formulas that undergo alterations with every new deployment, but they invariably establish intertextual connections. In consequence, they have the power to transfer not only structural configurations, but also ideological notions from one context to another. This study deals with a variety of subjects and problems, among others race, class, transatlantic relations, constructions of space and time, and inventions of nationhood, so as to combine them within the frames of a balanced argument, without giving priority to any single aspect. Unless relevant for the portrayals of literary protagonists, issues of gender, prominent as they are in contemporary scholarship on nineteenth-century American literature, have been excluded from the scope of the present work because their inclusion would require a fundamental reformulation of the thesis and altogether a new argument. Such an argument definitely deserves to have a book on its own instead of being just a part of a larger argumentative structure that perhaps would not do justice to it.

This study focuses on the writings by the leading literary representatives of American transcendentalism; of course, Whitman did not belong to the transcendentalist movement in the formal sense, nevertheless his literary and intellectual debt to Emerson is self-evident. As David S. Reynolds observes:

> Whitman's...poetry had elements of Transcendentalism on the one hand and working class and frontier expression on the other. Whitman's interest in yoking together disparate cultural levels made his poetry far more distinctive and wide-ranging than that of any of

the previous prose-poets. The Transcendentalists...provided precedent for Whitman's organic rhythms, aesthetic sensibility, and belief in the saving power of poetry. (*Walt Whitman's America* 316–317)

Perhaps the most predictable answer to the question about the choice of transcendentalism for analysis would be that the ideas propounded by transcendentalism were, in Lawrence Buell's words, both "native" and "imported" ("Transcendentalists" 369), and therefore they illustrate the cultural ambivalence which is the primary subject of this book. Indeed, transcendentalism was immersed in European Romantic philosophies, and at the same time it addressed strictly American matters, which is best seen in the reformatory doctrines that evolved from it. However, this is a less significant part of the answer. The basic reason for choosing transcendentalism is the discursive aspect. Essentially, transcendentalism is treated here not so much as an intellectual movement, but as discourse, that is an extensive body of texts with common rules of utterance. These rules have to do with the terms of representation, such as the creation of style or the use of imagery, on the one hand, and with epistemological forms, which involve the transactions between ideology and aesthetics, on the other. The thesis about the fundamental role of the postcolonial / imperial dichotomy in the formation of American nationhood and the rise of American culture could well be developed on the basis of different literary evidence. The point is, however, that the discourse of transcendentalism comprises a body of texts that are concomitantly varied and related in terms of stylistic structures, thematic concerns, or ideological allegiances; this combination of diversity and commonality accounts for a unique insight into the dynamics of the dichotomy in question.

The first part of this book discusses several texts by Ralph Waldo Emerson, in significant ways an emblematic author in the articulation of American postcolonial sensibility. His redefinition of the concept of history, alongside his metaphorization of the American experience in "The American Scholar" and "Self-Reliance," can be seen as a postcolonial gesture of relegating the burdensome legacy of colonization to the sphere of figurations, where the anxieties experienced by the young nation, epitomized in the figures of its imaginary delegates, should be resolved. Furthermore, Emerson embodies a kind of postcolonial syndrome, which manifests itself in the writer's inability to express America on its own special terms and in his search for certain auxiliary principles of representation. Thus, in his essayistic travel book *English Traits* the American experience is refracted through the depiction of the phenomena that characterize the British way of life. At the same time, against the background of nineteenth-century Anglo-American travel writing, *English Traits* appears to be a paramount example of postcolonial counter-discourse insofar as it undermines prejudicial European representations of the United States. Emerson felt profoundly troubled by the nation's colonial past, but he also experienced a sort of anxiety about American expansionism. His texts from the early 1840s suggest that he apparently supported expansionist policies without being fully convinced as to whether this was the proper course for the nation. Characteristically, the resulting ambivalence is resolved through the interplay of concrete and figurative imagery.

The second part demonstrates how ideology works through topoi and genres, that is, through vehicles for imaginative structures, on the basis of selected works by Henry David Thoreau. Admittedly, Thoreau is a paradoxical case; he manifestly opposed American imperialism, but created literary forms that were fairly attuned to the rhetoric of empire. Thus, *Walden* can be read as a reconfiguration of the colonial topos established in Daniel Defoe's *Robinson Crusoe*. Thoreau finds Defoe's model of protagonist useful in shaping a specific self-portrait; however, what complicates the authorial self-presentation in *Walden* is that Robinson Crusoe is an emanation of a certain ideological subtext that enters Thoreau's work. Essentially, just like Robinson on the desert island, Thoreau on the pond in a forest remains a man with his own cultural allegiances that shaped his consciousness. The paradox of the writer's mind-set becomes even more apparent in *The Maine Woods*, a record of how his innermost convictions had been tested in the harsh conditions of the New England wilderness. Thoreau's observations about the natural landscape and its native inhabitants reveal the extent to which his ideas had been influenced by the imperial design.

The third part concentrates on Walt Whitman's selected texts, representing different stages in his development as a writer. The Preface to the first edition of *Leaves of Grass*, which Michael J. Hoffman has called "the most representative Transcendentalist document in American prose" (58), is a postcolonial text addressing the issue of the responsibilities of an artist in a new nation. The dialectic of unity and separation defines the central ambivalence of the artist's position. Nevertheless, Whitman's poet aims to set the criteria for the recognition of the nation's unique situation. The Preface stands out in the context of Whitman's writing because it conveyed a clear postcolonial message at the time when the author openly endorsed American expansionism. Whitman's view of the potential of American people for achieving global leadership evolved with the passage of time. After the Civil War, he became rather disenchanted with real politics and he subsequently reinvented the American imperial design as a primarily imaginative project. "Passage to India" illustrates the shifting modes of political engagement in Whitman's poetic writing.

Part I

Ralph Waldo Emerson: The Double Figuration

CHAPTER 1

Figures of Dependence: Exploring the Postcolonial in Emerson's Selected Texts

In his seminal book, *Literary Transcendentalism: Style and Vision in the American Renaissance*, Lawrence Buell emphasizes the presence of paradoxes and contradictions in Ralph Waldo Emerson's discourse. The critic attributes this stylistic and conceptual quality to the transitions that the author of "Self-Reliance" constantly makes between two forms of communication valued by the Transcendentalists: the conversation, itself thematically varied and irregular in structure, and the moral essay, characterized as "a short unsystematic meditation on a given abstract issue, often marked by curtness, lack of transition, and aphoristic statement" (101). Elsewhere in the book, Buell adds: "in Emerson's essays there is generally an implicit framework, which is continually blurred and defied by improvisation and diffuseness" (161). This chapter extends Buell's perspective in such a way as to highlight certain political ambiguities the symptoms of which can be found, precisely, in linguistic ambivalence. Accordingly, structural inconsistency and generic vagueness as well as the strategies of figuration and the choice of thematic spectrum will be seen here as manifestations of Emerson's attempts to make his statement about American historical legacy less obvious and, in a sense, less obliging. The question that such an assumption immediately provokes is why the writer who authored a number of politically influential texts should have doubts about expressing his stance with respect to American history.

The gist of argument in this chapter is that Emerson cannot envisage his nation reaching the stage of maturity, and that his America is in the process of transition the conclusion of which he can present only in terms of speculation and prophecy, if not wishful thinking. In other words, Emerson's America, just like his discourse, is continually in process. The writer apparently feels at home with America as an amorphous cultural and political entity. Such amorphousness, in turn, can be seen as symptomatic of a kind of postcolonial condition that seems to exist between the time of liberation and the time of the solidification of the new state establishment. This is the period when hope most successfully conceals apprehension. Representing the generation that succeeded the revolutionary founders of America, Emerson finds himself, so to speak, at the crossroads of history. He does not have his own memories of the time of America's dependence and of the fight for freedom, nevertheless he turns out to be unable to establish a necessary distance toward the past, which would facilitate both his reassessment of the historical legacy and his examination of the present course of America. Emerson's acute awareness of the essential inseparability of the past and the present, the awareness surfacing in such figurative constructions as the metaphor of America's youthfulness, apparently testifies to his acknowledgment of the significance of history, though simultaneously it suggests that the thinker feels trapped by history, hence his reconsiderations of this very concept.

Lawrence Buell thus defines "the Emersonian paradox":

> The Emersonian paradox...—a pertinacious insistence on the benefits of one's own time and place versus an anxiously eclectic quest for conceptual models far afield is—of course a "postcolonial" condition, a mark of the hopeful anxiety of the intellectual in a new nation aware that "our American letters are in the optative mood"...and determined to remedy that lack by an independent-minded ransacking of all available traditions that will not succumb to any form of traditionalism and least of all to provincialism. ("Emerson in His Cultural Context " 58)

This paradox corresponds to the fact that America constitutes a very problematic subject in Emerson's writings. He explicitly declares his willingness to talk about the unique qualities of America, the special attributes of its exemplary citizens, in the very titles of such addresses as "The American Scholar" and "The Young American." However, these are texts that bewilder the reader who expects to acquire a thorough knowledge of Emerson's views of his nation, of its past and present, because no uniform vision of America emerges from them. The features of the model American and of the universal being become impossible to distinguish. An analogous situation characterizes Walt Whitman's poems, but the fundamental difference is that for Whitman the universal being is recognized in the American and such a recognition hints at the poet's imperialist stance insofar as it posits the American as the natural "global" leader, while for Emerson the universal being should be presented in such a way as to obviate the need to specifically define the American; to put it briefly, the Emersonian American dissolves into the universal being.

Characteristically, critics dealing with Emerson's oeuvre differ in their assessments of the crystallization of his vision of America. For example, Sacvan Bercovitch writes: "'I dedicate this book to the Spirit of America,' Emerson wrote at the start of his journal on July 11th, 1822. He might have begun all his works this way" (*American Jeremiad* 182). It seems surprising that the critic, who is so extremely conscious of the ubiquity of symbolic constructions in American culture, takes Emerson's words about "the Spirit of America" for what they are, without delving into the very rhetoricity of such a statement. Bercovitch aims to prove that the writer was unsurpassed in his ability to reconcile differences: "Of all symbols of identity, only America has united nationality and universality, civic and spiritual selfhood, secular and redemptive history, the country's past and paradise to be, in a single synthetic ideal" (176). Mary Kupiec Cayton, who claims that "he [Emerson] has assumed the mythic status as the firstborn American democratic philosopher and the advocate of the unlimited possibilities of the common man" (x), would undoubtedly subscribe to Bercovitch's opinion. However, there are critics who discern dichotomy where others see convergence; for example, Clarence Ghodes writes: "The groundwork of Emerson's conception of democracy is firmly rooted in idealistic philosophy, not in societal externals" (13). In the like vein, Alfred Kazin observes: "As it would turn out, America was not an idea in Emerson's mind. His difficulty was with the application of his favorite ideal. The 'active soul' was not easy to fit in with so much aggressive self-interest" (45–46). Stephen E. Whicher, in a somewhat aphoristic manner, points to dualism as an inherent feature of Emerson's life and vision: "He taught self-reliance and felt self-distrust, worshiped reality and knew illusion, proclaimed freedom and submitted to faith. No one has expected more of man; few have found him less competent" (224). John Carlos Rowe and Lawrence Buell explicate the intrinsic ambivalence of Emerson's discourse in ideological terms; the former remarks that "Emerson's political writings from 1844 to 1863 remain so profoundly divided internally between transcendentalist values and practical politics as to be practically useless, except as far as the value of their political rhetoric might be measured" (*At Emerson's Tomb* 22). Buell writes:

> Emerson imagines a discourse that encloses the British within itself as a part of a syncretistic assimilation of disparate cultural voices and values, a discourse that will simultaneously preserve and decenter by making Anglo-American letters more global, a discourse that is forever disrupting the literary order by moving in the direction of a lower style...and forever challenging the cultural order by acknowledging the need to transcend its Anglo- and Euro-centrism. (*New England Literary Culture* 161)

This chapter is concerned with what may be called a fragmentary articulation of America in Emerson's writings. The shifts toward metaphoric representation, alongside digressiveness, thematic changeability, and generic hybridity, are seen as clues to Emerson's incertitude about the vision of America. The question that the vagueness of Emerson's enunciations provokes is whether the implied reader or addressee of his essays and speeches must be American or not necessarily; and, if the latter is the case, how would the existence of the implied "universal" reader modify the sense of Emerson's appeals. In any case, the writer aspires to address problems that the entire human kind faces. This chapter reiterates Lawrence Buell's question from his book on Emerson: "How American was Emerson's 'American Scholar'?" (*Emerson* 43).

In his well-known essay "DissemiNation: Time, Narrative, and the Margins of the Modern Nation," Homi Bhabha stresses the problematic status of the discourse of modern nationhood in the light of the inevitable metaphorization of the nation. Bhabha makes it explicit that his intention is to work out "the complex strategies of cultural identification and discursive address that function in the name of 'the people' and 'the nation' and make them the immanent subjects and objects of a range of social and literary narratives" (*Location of Culture* 140). The critic detects discontinuities between the subject of representation, that is the nation, and the discursive terms of the representation itself. He comes up with the term "metaphoric movement," which denotes the proliferation and dissemination of the discourses of the nation: "We need another time of *writing* that will be able to inscribe the ambivalent and chiasmatic intersections of time and place that constitute the problematic 'modern' experience of the western nation." In the face of "the *metaphoricity* of the peoples of imagined communities," "the space of the modern nation-people is never simply horizontal." Horizontality implies "centred casual logic" and homogeneity that are displaced as a result of the metaphoric movement in language (141). In other words, linguistic representations remodel spatial attributes of the perceived reality of the nation or, as Bhabha puts it elsewhere in the essay, of the "finitude of the nation" (151). The dissolution of the distinct boundaries of "nation-space" in metaphor is accompanied by a corresponding temporal complication, which the author of "DissemiNation" describes using Derrida's words: "the present is no longer a mother-form [read mother tongue or motherland] around which are gathered and differentiated the future (present) and the past (present)...a present of which the past and the future would be but modifications" (141).

Bhabha talks about "the finitude of the nation" as an impossible "expressive totality" and about "the liminality of the representation of the people." These concepts correspond to two aspects of the representation of the modern nation: "the pedagogical" and "the performative." The former notion is connected with the existence of a nation as "an *a priori* historical presence," whereas the latter indicates narrative constructions of the nation, "its enunciatory 'present' marked in the repetition and pulsation of the national sign." Bhabha writes:

> The pedagogical founds its narrative authority in a tradition of a people, described by Poulatnzas as a moment of becoming designated by *itself*, encapsulated in a succession of historical moments that represent an eternity produced by self-generation. The performative intervenes in the sovereignty of the nation's *self-generation* by casting a shadow between the people as 'image' and its signification as a differentiating sign of self, distinct from the Other or the Outside...
> ...The boundary that marks the nation's selfhood interrupts the self-generating time of national production with a space of representation that threatens binary division with its difference. The barred Nation *It/Self*, alienated from its eternal self-generation, becomes a liminal form of social representation, a space that is *internally* marked by cultural difference and the heterogeneous histories of contending peoples, antagonistic authorities, and tense cultural locations. (147–148, original italics)

Homi Bhabha's notions of "the pedagogical," "the performative," and "the metaphoric movement" can help illuminate the ambivalence of Ralph Waldo Emerson's idea of America. First of all, it seems that in Emerson's writings, from which no coherent view of the history of the United States emerges, "the pedagogical," associated with "historicism where narrative is only the agency of the event, or the medium of a naturalistic continuity of Community and Tradition" (Bhabha 151), is extremely problematic, because it is constituted by hints, as if smuggled into serious treatises that address matters of universal importance and applicability. There are two possible, mutually exclusive, explanations for the indeterminate character of "the pedagogical" in Emerson's discourse. On the one hand, he may take "the pedagogical" of his nation for granted and thus feel no need to articulate it, which would imply, however, that he did not share his contemporaries' growing interest in America's past, reflected for instance in the contents of the mid-nineteenth century oratories. On the other hand, he may feel baffled by the fact that "the pedagogical" of America is part and parcel of "the pedagogical" of Europe; for someone who talks so much about the necessity of ultimate freedom, this is a frustrating realization. It does not mean that history as "an event" is completely erased or radically marginalized in Emerson's essays and lectures; the ambivalence of history results from the author's particular perception of what Bhabha calls "the eternal visibility of a past" (151). Namely, the frame of historical references in Emerson's texts is constituted by signifiers that have rather little to do with the origins and the historical development of America. To put it more precisely, Emerson feels much more at home with ancient Greeks than with contemporary Americans.

Homi Bhabha writes that "the borders of the nation are...constantly faced with a double temporality: the process of identity constituted by historical sedimentation (the pedagogical); and the loss of identity in the signifying process of cultural identification (the performative)" (153).[1] In Emerson's writings, this inevitable "loss of identity" in the process of constructing metaphors of the nation is illustrated by the constant thematic oscillation between the features and values that are typically American and the features and values that are admittedly universal. Significantly, the former often remain in the sphere of implication, while the latter are recognized with utmost conviction.

Discursive fluctuations that characterize formations of the performative and that erode the "horizontality" of history can be traced in Emerson's essay "History" (1841) the text representative of, in Robert D. Richardson's words, "the period in which Emerson most actively sought to break with tradition, to rethink the problem afresh" ("Emerson on History" 50). Emerson's redefinition of history consists in purifying this notion of all possible connotations of burden; he achieves this through undermining unequivocal relations of importance between various epochs, events, processes, spheres of human activity whose development reveals historical continuity. His reconsiderations enable him to overcome historical determinism; as Joel Porte puts it: "He did not step out of history but into it, deciding to make it rather than be made by it" (*Consciousness and Culture* 59). "History" abounds in references to the past, arranged quite randomly, and these references constitute the frame for Emerson's examination of subjects that transcend the conceptual boundaries delineated by the notion of history. In Olaf Hansen's words, "Emerson retranslates the idea of history into the shape of a narrative, stressing the fluidity over and against the harsh, institutionalized structure of history seen as a series of factual events" (86). What is symptomatic is that the writer creates apparent continuums wherein he includes phenomena that lack mutual equivalence: "This life of ours is stuck round with Egypt, Greece, Gaul, England, War, Colonization, Church, Court and Commerce, as with so many flowers and wild ornaments grave and gay" (Emerson, *Essays and Lectures* 240). Elsewhere in the essay, he writes:

> A man shall be the Temple of Fame.... I shall find in him the Foreworld; in his childhood the Age of Gold; the Apples of Knowledge; the Argonautic Expedition; the calling of Abraham; the building of the temple; the Advent of Christ; Dark Ages; the Revival of Letters; the Reformation; the discovery of new lands, the opening of new sciences and new regions in man. (255)

The stylistic device of cataloguing, used in these two passages, establishes the relation of parity between heroic deeds and adventures known from the Bible and the Greek mythology, epochs ("Dark Ages"), processes like colonization, and finally the enigmatic "opening [of] new regions in man." Emerson broadens, and thus modifies, the original meaning of such signifiers as names of heroes, events or places, to the extent of its ultimate dissolution. It is interesting to notice that in both passages Emerson evokes colonial contexts: "Colonization" in the former, and "the discovery of new lands" in the latter. Inscribed in the common legacy of mankind, the fact of colonization has the same meaning for an American citizen as, say, for a British subject. As Sacvan Bercovitch puts it succinctly, "[Emerson's] vision annihilated division" ("Emerson the Prophet" 15).

In "History," Emerson undoes the national perspective of perceiving history, the perspective that he purportedly establishes in "The American Scholar." Emerson willingly dwells upon ancient history, which substantiates the largest number of allusions. It is worth remarking that one of the few specific references to American history, if not indeed the only one, is "a Salem hanging of witches," after which the writer mentions a fad of his own day, "the Animal Magnetism in Paris, or in Providence" (241), which implies his distrust of the idea of history as a hierarchical arrangement of different events or influences. In a sense, "History" projects the eponymous concept as a timeless fusion of the past, the present, and the future.

History requires justification and derives it from the fact that history functions as a record of the transcendent human mind: "This human mind wrote history and this must read it.... If the whole of history is in one man, it is all to be explained from individual experience" (237); "All history becomes subjective; in other words, there is properly no History; only Biography. Every soul must know the whole lesson for itself—must go over the whole ground. What it does not see, what it does not live, it will not know" (240). Emerson made these statements at a time when historiography flourished in New England. There seems to exist a striking dissimilarity between Emerson's discursive procedure and the one found in the writings of nineteenth-century New England historians, about whom Lawrence Buell says that they "set the contemporary standard of scholarly rigor, assembled, preserved, and at times mutilated an immense amount of data still assiduously mined today," and "provided the key sources for the historical portions of period oratory and historical literature" (*New England Literary Culture* 214).

This subordination of history to the human mind and experience[2] is a redeeming state, in which history does not signify difference, but sameness. Such a view of history sheds light on Emerson's postcolonial position. Namely, the emphasis on difference is a crucial feature of both colonialist and anticolonial discourses, on the one hand strengthening the sense of superiority in the colonizer, and on the other shaping attitudes of resistance in the colonized subject. In his stress on sameness, Emerson undermines polarity conditioned by the presence of differences and assumes a detached stance, freeing himself from the need to consider troubling historical or political facts. In other words, while challenging the colonizer's way of reasoning, he does not have to admit to his own identification with the colonized. The contexts in which Emerson recognizes difference are also quite symptomatic, for example when he seeks justification for American reforms in improper European manners. His rethinking of the connections between America and Europe, inherent in his definition of history, can be described in terms of a dialectic of explicit continuation and implicit alteration. Elleke Boehmer, who discusses twentieth-century postcolonial literatures, makes a remark that quite adequately characterizes Emerson's revisions:

> To disavow dominant colonial myths and languages, the colonized had in the first place to inhabit them. European conceptual traditions in history, philosophy, literature, and so on, which downgraded that which was non-European, had first to be displaced by an act of repetition, even 'slavish' copying. Success lay in camouflage and subterfuge. (171)

In his pioneering article entitled "The Post-Colonial Emerson and the Erasure of Europe," Robert Weisbuch asserts that "History" is a central text in the writer's oeuvre because it develops ideas upon which "all of Emerson's thought rests." The critic argues that in contrast with such writers as Washington Irving or James Fenimore Cooper, who invent "an American history to satisfy the European demand for one, Emerson refuses the rivalry and substitutes for history the vertical time of the present moment that, rightly seized, leads to overwhelming truth and a nature of transparent magnificence" (206). Weisbuch interprets Emerson's rejection of the admittedly European dialectic of the past and the present as a significant element of his plan to "erase" Europe and coins the term "American actualism" to describe the condition that Emerson envisages for his countrymen. Such a stance entails "the demand that the writer live out in every moment of his social being, on the very surface of life, his deepest delvings, that the writer must become her or his most visionary ideas" (203). When confronted with Europe, America might appear to be "secondary" (197). It is as if Emerson put the past, associated with Europe, and the present, connected with America, on the scales to check the weight of which would be greater. Certainly, he knows the answer in advance; convinced about the essentially timeless nature of human experience, Emerson refuses to acknowledge the possible merits of the European, "horizontal" notion of history. Accordingly, when he treats particular ideas as axioms, it is not merely a sign of his authorial presumption, but primarily a political gesture, and possibly a defensive one.

The uniqueness of Emerson's idea of history in the contemporary context becomes visible when his perspective is compared, for example, with the historical awareness that informs Daniel Webster's oratories, fairly representative of New England historiography of the first half of the nineteenth century. Webster was a major figure in American politics from the early 1820s, when he was first elected to Congress, till 1852, when he retired from his position as Secretary of State. The history of the United States constitutes a central theme in Webster's speeches, many of which belong to the canon of the nineteenth-century American oratory. Among his most important statements about the course of American history, there are two speeches delivered in 1825 and 1843 at the Bunker Hill Monument to commemorate one of the first battles of the Revolutionary War.

In Webster's first Bunker Hill address, there appear observations suggesting that he would agree with Emerson in seeing history as "the universal remembrance of mankind" and in appreciating "imagination and sentiment" (Webster 22), which, in Emerson's view, would signify the biographical imprint in history. Further on, Webster declares: "We consecrate our work to the spirit of national independence, and we wish that the light of peace may rest upon it forever" and "We come, as Americans, to mark a spot which must forever be dear to us and our posterity" (22). Emerson is proud of the entire human kind, while Webster is proud of America; this crucial difference sheds light on the fact that in Emerson's other texts the recognition of America's power is invariably conditional, because he still discerns tests that America should undergo, or obstacles that it should overcome. Even though, analogically to Emerson, Webster talks about America's greatness as a future condition, he indicates that the course of development has been clearly defined:

> We see before us a probable train of great events; we know that our own fortunes have been happily cast; and it is natural, therefore, that we should be moved by the contemplation of occurrences which have guided our destiny before many of us were born, and settled the condition in which we should pass that portion of our existence which God allows to men on earth. (20)

In other words, the greatness of America's past anticipates, even guarantees, the greatness of its future. Therefore it comes as no surprise that the considerations following this assertion focus on the three momentous events in the history of the United States: the discovery of the new continent by Columbus, the settlement of New

England, and the Revolutionary War. Perhaps Webster adheres to the European notion of historical continuity, but he fills it with specifically American content and rejects the Eurocentric vantage point, whereas Emerson rethinks the very concept of history, yet he finds no relevant American content for it. In consequence, Webster turns out to be more logical in his explanation why Americans are destined for "great things."

Emerson's conviction of the necessity to put an end to American dependence on Europe can sound appealing, but he does not clarify the terms of such cultural divergence. Webster, in turn, discusses various particular issues that facilitate the recognition of the significance of Europe for the formation of America, highlighting both continuities and discontinuities in American and European politics, societies, and cultures. For instance, Webster pays a lot of attention to the differences between the revolutionary movements in colonial America, Europe (the French Revolution), and South America, emphasizing the fact that the exceptional American character had been shaped in such a way that the Revolutionary War did not result in the abuse of power:

> The possession of power did not turn the heads of the American people, for they had long been in the habit of exercising a great degree of self-control. Although the paramount authority of the parent state existed over them, yet a large field of legislation had always been open to our colonial assemblies.... The character of our countrymen, moreover, was sober, moral and religious, and there was little in the change to shock their feelings of justice and humanity, or even to disturb an honest prejudice. We had no domestic throne to overturn, no privileged orders to cast down, no violent changes of property to encounter. In the American Revolution, no man sought or wished for more than to defend and enjoy his own. (36)

The clue to Webster's elucidation of the exceptional character of the American Revolution, and of Americans in general, can be found in his second Bunker Hill speech, where he examines the differences between the British colonization of America and the Spanish colonization of South America, inferring that: "The distinctive characteristic of their settlement [Plymouth and Massachusetts] is the introduction of the civilization of Europe into a wilderness, without bringing with it the political institutions of Europe" (64). In the earlier Bunker Hill address, Webster categorically asserts that "at this moment the dominion of European power in this continent, from the place where we stand to the south pole, is annihilated forever," and immediately adds that: "In the mean time, both in Europe and America, such has been the general progress of knowledge, such the improvement in legislation, in commerce, in the arts, in letters, and, above all, in liberal ideas and the general spirit of the age, that the whole world seems changed" (24), thus unequivocally identifying Europe and America, on equal terms, as the driving forces of the world's development. It seems that the metaphor of the umbilical cord aptly describes the ways in which Webster and Emerson envisage America's indebtedness to Europe: Webster believes that this umbilical cord has already been severed, while Emerson implies that it is high time to cut it, which means that it still exists.

In *Visionary Compacts*, Donald E. Pease suggests that Emerson's notion of history can be related to his doctrine of self-reliance through a reference to the concept of memory. The critic says that "Individual self-reliance disabled the work of human memory." His argument revolves around the opposition between individual memory and collective memory, and he uses the writings of Emerson and Hawthorne as illustrations of how individual and collective memory functions. He claims that the central theme of Hawthorne's fiction is "commemorative perception": "the ability to perceive a person as at once himself and a communally sustained account of him." Essentially, in Hawthorne's texts memory fulfils a socializing function, because it secures "a shared human context for a person's movement through time." Emersonian self-reliance, in turn, does away with memory: "Memory put a person in mind of what he had done; self-reliance put a person in mind of what he could do." Pease goes on to say that in contrast with Hawthorne, who regarded memory as "a beleaguered servant," Emerson saw it as "a tyrant" and, accordingly, he disapproved of the retrospective spirit of his epoch (206–207). The critic concludes:

> But Emerson could not overthrow the faculty of memory without putting another in its place. Self-reliance usurped at least part of the work usually assigned to the faculty of memory: it acknowledged previous cultural achievements but only the better to separate the power (whether physical, perceptual, intellectual, moral, or emotional) leading to the achievement from the achievement itself. Self-reliance produced an enabling amnesia. (207)

The way the influence of history should be understood is among central issues discussed in "The American Scholar" (1837), an address that illustrates how a text's structuring conceals—or reveals—its political motivation. In this work, described by Gustaaf Van Cromphout as "an eloquent plea for man's advancing liberation from intellectual conformity and spiritual rigidity, a liberation without which no escape from time and the grip of history is possible" (64), the political subtext is constituted not only by a handful of clearly political pronouncements, at times almost bordering on propaganda, but, more significantly, it can be traced in the writer's characteristic movement away from tangible political issues toward abstractions. One can distinguish three parts in "The American Scholar": the introduction, covering several opening paragraphs, in which Emerson defines the subject of his considerations, the essential part, exploring the major influences that the scholar should take into account, and the conclusion, where the writer refers his general observations to the tangible American context. It is precisely Emerson's meanderings between philosophical divagations and political appeals that undermine the meaning of the memorable words about American independence in the closing part of the address. Robert E. Burkholder writes: "a process of translation of concern for specific social and political problems into the realm of ideas is typical of much of Emerson's writing, but it is nowhere so apparent as in 'The American Scholar,' a work whose historical context suggests a plausible rationale for the ideology expressed in it" ("Radical Emerson" 46).[3]

The opening and the conclusion of "The American Scholar," the parts wherein Emerson is most straightforward about a recognizable political situation and its causes, provide a frame for the central musings that cannot be anchored in any specific temporal and spatial reality and thus harmonize with the Emersonian notion of history. It goes without saying that the structure of any text determines the terms for the presentation of ideas; the structure of "The American Scholar" suggests that the examination of the American reality gives Emerson a pretext for probing some universal concepts that he is more eager to explore. The address does contain unequivocal statements sounding like elements of the national program that, however, has been formulated very generally, and therefore vaguely: "Our day of dependence, our long apprenticeship to the learning of other lands, draws to a close. The millions that around us are rushing into life, cannot always be fed on the sere remains of foreign harvests" (*Essays and Lectures* 53); "We have listened to long to the courtly muses of Europe" (70); "We will walk on our own feet; we will work with our own hands; we will speak our own minds" (71). Burkholder claims that "in their expression of the conventional idea of *translatio studii*—the classical theory of the westward movement of civilization—these memorable nationalistic phrases represent the most hackneyed thoughts in the entire oration" (44). However, Emerson creates a discursive context that displaces politics; for example, the first sentence from among those quoted above appears in the paragraph opening with words apparently emphasizing the uniqueness of the speaker's and the auditors' situation, but possibly causing the audience's confusion because of the rhetorical device that comprises a chain of negative association: "We do not meet for games of strength or skill, for the recitation of histories, tragedies and odes, like the ancient Greeks; for parliaments of love and poesy, like the Troubadours; nor for the advancement of science, like our contemporaries in the British and European capitals" (76). In general, this statement seems to be characteristic of Emerson's strategy of deferment. The two sentences issuing a call for intellectual independence, in turn, are included in the longish last paragraph, which among a plethora of observations contains, for instance, this remark: "'I learned,' said the melancholy Pestalozzi, 'that no man in God's wide earth is either willing or able to help any other man'" (70). It is possible that such a comment somehow pertains to what Emerson has to say about America, still it complicates the recognition of specific historical and political problems, events, or contexts through establishing a redundant frame of reference. Buell contends that "the whole literary nationalist theme, as 'The American Scholar' handles it, is so comparatively muted and so belated" and ironically adds that:

> Perhaps because he was addressing one of the most Anglophile audiences in America, but more likely because he himself was too cosmopolitan (and too honest) to restrict the scholar solely to American influences or to exerting a solely American influence, Emerson kept his cultural nationalist rhetoric to a minimum: a few mandatory flourishes at start and close. Self-reliance clearly interested Emerson far more than national self-sufficiency. ("American Literary Emergence" 600)[4]

Emerson expresses convictions that are the most heavily charged with the national rhetoric only at the end of "The American Scholar." There are two possible explanations for such a structural development: on the one hand, understandably, the conclusion functions as the narrative climax and therefore should recapitulate the most crucial arguments and observations presented earlier. On the other, Emerson may be delaying the articulation of ideas about which he does not feel at ease, but which he feels obliged to relate to. In other words, his utterances about Americans speaking their own minds can be infused with hope and confidence or, conversely, with anxiety and incertitude. As Pamela Schirmeister observes: "Despite the apparent literary nationalism of Emerson's address, he is not responding to an aesthetic problem per se, but according to the opening fable, to a crisis in subjectivity both private and public that apparently can only be presented at all in a literary form, and that must perhaps be solved on literary grounds" (45). The writer himself is aware of his tendency to concentrate for too long on matters of limited interest to his auditors or readers: "But I have dwelt perhaps tediously upon this abstraction of the Scholar. I ought not to delay longer what I have to say, of nearer reference to the time and to this country" (67). In the light of the words that follow, it is arguable whether Emerson fulfils this promise, as he says: "Historically, there is thought to be a difference in the ideas that predominate over successive epochs, and there are data for marking the Genius of the Classic, of the Romantic, and now of the Reflective or Philosophical Age"; then he remarks that: "I believe each individual passes through all three. The boy is a Greek; the youth, romantic; the adult, reflective" (67). Thus, a potential subject of "nearer reference" gives way to yet another digression. Emerson's procrastination throws an ambivalent light on his final political pronouncements.

The pivotal opposition in Emerson's argument presented in "The American Scholar" is dependence versus independence. When in the beginning he speaks about Americans' "long apprenticeship to the learning of other lands" (53), he does not give any specific reasons for such a state of things other than the general weakness of human nature. The very concept of "the American scholar" possesses a historical sense, which Emerson undermines when he extensively discusses the ahistorical dilemmas that "Man" faced in various epochs. Moreover, even "the American scholar" proves to be too particular a category for the writer, who more willingly describes the qualities of "Man Thinking." Of course, the notions of "the American scholar" and "Man Thinking,"[5] in Emerson's argument, possess a certain mutual equivalence, nevertheless the fact remains that their respective signifieds differ. This partial convergence of the two crucial terms produces the effect of narrative bifurcation. The American scholar, in Homi Bhabha's terms, is a metaphor of the nation, in other words an emblem of its "performative." What Emerson does in his famous address is construct the figure, which is "Man Thinking," of a metaphor, that is "the American scholar." Such a strategy of double metaphorization, of producing "figures of figuration" (Dauber 239), results in the shaping of a discourse that may easily preclude expressions endowed with concrete political meanings.[6]

Perry Miller observes that "[t]he American scholar is a student but all the while a rebel against study. The point was—and still is—that the American independence had to be achieved *through* dependence. This is how America perforce stands in relation to the past" (400, original italics). Given the frequency with which Emerson talks about various manifestations of dependence, such as following somebody else's instructions, mendicant reading, conformity with the rules of social conduct, adherence do one's own earlier choices, it is fully justified to treat colonization as a metaphor for different negative conditions of existence described by Emerson. Thus, Albert J. Von Frank associates the threat of colonization with "the external requirements of family, church, social position, and political party" (109). Indeed, it would be impossible to imagine the entire Emersonian semiotics without configurations of dependence and liberation. Emerson's "partial man" lives in a state that may be called the colonization of the mind, the state characterized by the renunciation of intellectual aspirations in the face of a daunting outside power; this means that the writer translates a pressing political problem connected with the existence of mental obstacles deferring the formation of national identity into a more easily controllable metaphor rendering a general human condition.

Symptomatically, the ideas of "the complete man" and "the partial man" also illustrate the parallelism of imperial and postcolonial discursive tropes, because while the partial man reveals many weaknesses typical of the colonized, the complete man is, even if only for himself, an emperor. What emerges from Emerson's writing is, to use Quentin Anderson's influential term, "the imperial self" (17–18). The Emersonian complete man decides about his own aims and ways of achieving them; he challenges commonplace preferences and assumptions, establishing an autonomous domain outside them. In this case, too, Emerson finds a safe equivalent for a particular political situation, this time associated with Americans' booming expansionist aspirations, in the realm of abstract concepts. While the author of "The American Scholar" can consider political imperialism as a flawed project, he must nevertheless reckon with his fellow citizens' aspirations. Consequently, he discerns a redeeming force in the individual who builds his own empire outside collective social formations. The central paradox of Emerson's discourse is that imperialism, just like colonization, is present in it, so to speak, "under the skin" and never comes to the surface. The figurative treatment of the postcolonial legacy signals the escapist quality of Emerson's writings, escapist in the sense that the dialectic of metaphors replaces the dialectic of historical processes.

Kerry Larson remarks that Emerson's texts abound in "metaphors of possessions, entitlement, and emancipation" ("Individualism" 996). With regard to the presence of such figurations, "Self-Reliance" (1841), in many ways, corresponds with "The American Scholar". Indeed, in "Self-Reliance," Emerson examines those spheres of life wherein the individual is most likely to face the danger of some kind of colonization. In a tone of muted lament, Emerson talks about a common tendency to seek an excuse for one's existence in an identification with collective establishments, like religious sects, institutions, and communities. Believing that the well-being of a larger group guarantees one's own peace of mind, a timid, "colonized" individual refuses to recognize the personal cost that he incurs. Namely, the individual expense to be paid for the deceptive sense of safety in a collective body is submission and renunciation of free will. The ultimate consequence is the erasure of unique selfhood.

In Emerson's vision of the existence in compliance with or at variance with society, one can easily distinguish certain semiotic features of the colonial situation. First of all, society as a colonizing force imposes upon an individual a set of values that is not subject to any negotiation. Analogically to the colonialist strategies aimed at presenting indigenous creations in the negative light as barbarian, obsolete, or at best inadequate, society works in such a way as to eliminate individual initiatives, that have a subversive potential and, consequently, should be viewed as culpable. In addition, just like a colonial power, society conceals its hegemonic power in the declarations of common good. The assumption that society should "protect" an individual resembles the colonialist project of enlightening the colonized. Exploring the subtle mechanisms of colonial hegemony, the authors of *Key Concepts in Post-Colonial Studies* use the word "patronage," that describes adequately situations evoked in "Self-Reliance":

> The patronage system may even, in one sense, be said to be the whole society, in so far as a specific society may recognize and endorse some kinds of cultural activities and not others. This is especially true in colonial situations where the great difference between the colonizing and the colonized societies means that some forms of cultural activity crucial to the cultural identity of the colonized, and so highly valued by them, may simply be unrecognizable or, if recognized at all, grossly undervalued by the dominant colonial system. (43–44)

In his essay "On National Culture," Franz Fanon makes a corresponding observation: "the total result looked for by colonial domination was indeed to convince the natives that colonialism came to lighten their darkness" and to prevent them from "fall[ing] back into barbarism, degradation, and bestiality" (*Wretched* 210–211). In Emerson's essay, the fear of returning to the state of degradation and bestiality is replaced by the fear of facing society's anger; in both contexts, though, fear turns out to be a crucial motivation.

An interesting aspect of Emerson's construction of the figures of dependence is the use of discourse that imitates the language of medicine and thus enables the writer to "diagnose" the condition which may be called "intellectual colonization" as one resembling an organic affliction. He writes about this mental state in such a way as if he were describing its quasi-medical symptoms: "Their works are done as an apology or extenuation of their living in the world, as invalids and the insane pay a high board" (*Essays and Lectures* 263); "If you maintain a dead church, contribute to a dead Bible society, vote with a great party either for the Government or against it, spread your table like base housekeepers—under all these screens I have difficulty to detect the precise man you are" (263); "He is a retained attorney, and these airs of the bench are the emptiest affectation. Well, most men have bound their eyes with one or another handkerchief, and attached themselves to some one of these communities of opinion" (264). Thus, Emerson, speaking here in his characteristic tone of unwavering self-confidence, compares the condition of colonization, no matter which sphere of life its symptoms manifest themselves in, to disability, insanity, death, blindness, and emotional desiccation. This is a narrative strategy that helps him to make a virtually imperceptible mental process of yielding to outside influences more palpable by translating it into the terms well-known in popular medicine. In Emerson's time, medicine was developing rapidly and new discoveries were often familiar not only to specialists, but also to average people, therefore medical references, in his writings, appear to be recognizable, adequate and convincing. The discourse of medicine is also a useful linguistic tool for awakening the reader's consciousness; it is no coincidence that the writer mentions such bodily conditions that signify hopelessness and irreversibility: madness, blindness, demise. The use of the language that imitates medical statements also illustrates the way in which the author of "Self-Reliance" creates the narrative authority in his texts through the reworking of influential discourses of the day. However, there is a double edge to such an operation because while enhancing his narrative authority by means of weaving a specific discursive strand into his text, Emerson makes his political position more ambivalent, introducing a superfluous frame of reference.

A somewhat analogous discursive intermixture can be found in Emerson's method of endowing some ideas with spatial significance. Toward the end of "Self-Reliance," the author mentions certain contemporary fashions and attitudes that attest to the absence of self-reliance; his most memorable comments concern traveling and prayers. For instance, this is what he writes about the habits of praying: "Prayer looks abroad and asks for some foreign addition to come through some foreign virtue, and loses itself in endless mazes of natural and supernatural, and mediatorial and miraculous" (275). Such words as "abroad" and "foreign" do not refer here to physical space; rather, they indicate the existence of some kind of the inside and some kind of the outside as well as the distance between them, the distance that enables one to see how the outside predominates over the inside. The unfolding of Emerson's argument about false prayers is symptomatic insofar as the writer proceeds to juxtapose the person who prays in an improper manner, expressing regrets and requests, to the idealized "self-helping man":

> Welcome evermore to gods and men is the self-helping man. For him all doors are flung wide. Him all tongues greet, all honors crown, all eyes follow with desire. Our love goes out to him and embraces him, because he did not need it. We solicitously and apologetically caress and celebrate him, because he held on his way and scorned our disapprobation. The gods love him because men hated him. (276)

The "self-helping man" replaces society as a source of authority and inspiration. In contrast to the stealthy influence exerted by society, conspiring against man, his power is easier to recognize because he acts openly. If this replacement were to be translated into the semiotics of the colonial situation, one might say that the ruthless colonizer (society) has been defeated by the element that has not been conquered (the self-helping man). Additionally, the passage illustrates how smoothly Emerson makes a transition from the figuration of dependence and subordination to the figuration of expansiveness.[7]

While negative habits of thinking are made to appear more striking when Emerson creates certain spatial configurations and emphasizes the detrimental influence of forces coming from the outside, existing geographical locations signify not only as physical places, but primarily as projections of the deficiencies of the colonized mind. When in "Self-Reliance" Emerson enumerates the places that the American traveler feels obliged to visit, he associates the craze of travel with idolatry: "the superstition of Travelling, whose the idols are Italy,

England, Egypt" (277). In other words, he defines a contemporary fashion of traveling using a word that has unequivocally negative religious connotations and which corresponds very well to the metaphor of blindness. Idolatry implies religious narrow-mindedness and a strong identification with an outside power, therefore it stands in sheer opposition to the Emersonian idea of man's spiritual independence. It comes as no surprise, then, that the soul is defined as "no traveler." Another meaningful context in which names of geographical locations appear evokes the notion of ruination and defeat: "He who travels to be amused, or to get somewhat which he does not carry, travels away from himself, and grows old even in youth among old things. In Thebes, in Palmyra, his will and mind have become old and dilapidated as they. He carries ruins to ruins" (278). Finally, foreign places enhance one's sense of loss and discontent, instead of filling one with delight: "I pack my trunk...and at last wake up in Naples, and there beside me is the stern fact, the sad self, unrelenting, identical, that I fled from" (278).

Another manifestation of internal colonization is inordinate reverence for the printed word. In "Self-Reliance," Emerson observes that "[o]ur reading is mendicant and sycophantic" (268), which immediately brings to mind "The American Scholar" with its extensive critique of improper ways of reading. In "The American Scholar," the reading of books is inextricably connected with the study of the past. Emerson regards the past, "in whatever form, whether of literature, of art, of institutions," as one of the "great influence[s] into the spirit of the scholar" (56), alongside nature and action. However, while he has no misgivings whatsoever about the influence of nature and action, his acknowledgement of the significance of the past as well as of its literary medium seems to be conditional; thus, as the source of inspiration, books should be used with care: "The sacredness which attaches to the act of creation—the act of thought,—is transferred to the record. The poet chanting was felt to be a divine man: henceforth the chant is divine also.... Instantly, the book becomes noxious; the guide is a tyrant" (57); "instead of Man Thinking, we have the bookworm" (57); "Books are the best of things, well used; abused, among the worst" (57); "I had better never see a book, than to be warped by its attraction clean of my own orbit, and made a satellite instead of a system" (57). Emerson suggests that books may serve to spread somebody else's mesmerizing power; hence his readiness to renounce the use of books if they pose any threat to his own integrity. Indeed, he writes about the influence of books in such a way as if he wanted to discourage the reader from treating them as a valid source of guidance. He regards the reservation about other people's writings as a very natural attitude. Thus, in his consideration of the importance of books, there surfaces a familiar opposition of imposition and resistance. The negative consequences of slavish book-reading can be counterbalanced by the redeeming influence of action. As Merton S. Sealts observes, in Emerson's view, action leads to "intellection" and "utterance," or, more precisely, "intellection" and "utterance" are integrated into action (106). The author of "The American Scholar" writes: "life is our dictionary. Years are well spent in country labors...to the one end of mastering in all their facts a language by which to illustrate and embody our perceptions" (61–62). Unlike the rigid language of books, which defends old meanings, the newly forged language of the American scholar, the language that crowns action, is constantly in process so that it can embrace ever new experiences and perceptions. It is symptomatic that Emerson talks about "a language," granting the individual the freedom to shape it. There may be situations where language proves to be an inadequate invention; on such occasions, one should be ready to renounce it altogether: "A great soul will be strong to live, as well as strong to think. Does he lack organ or medium to impart his truths? He can still fall back on this elemental force of living them. This is a total act" (62). The view of language as secondary to action obviates for Emerson the need to define the American political program in specific, obliging, and final terms; the formulation of such a program would precede resulting actions, which would be out of keeping with Emerson's logic of action. Any form of American politics should be tentative, and Americans should have confidence in the "natural" course of events. For Emerson, who does not want to be mistaken in his assessment of America's goals, this is a convenient view of politics.

Emerson's strategies of constructing the narrative authority, on the one hand, and his indications of the ultimate tentativeness of language, on the other, attest to the central ambivalence of his discourse: namely, he creates an autonomous language that, he hopes, will inspire his contemporaries as well as subsequent generations and which therefore must be characterized by a notable degree of referentiality, while he concomitantly fears that language anchored in tangible referents instantly becomes irrelevant, obsolete, since it describes the reality that is permanently in process. Striving to overcome this short-livedness of language, Emerson ends up only confirming it: his language is a liminal construction temporarily coming into existence on the boundary between utter abstraction and historical contingency.

The liminality of Emerson's discourse corresponds very closely to his fragmentary vision of America, where, in Sacvan Bercovitch's words, "'America'...is a rhetorical battleground, a symbol that has been made to stand for diverse and sometimes mutually contradictory outlooks" (*Rites of Assent* 355). One of the themes that recur in his texts is the idea that America is on the threshold of its true greatness and that Americans, endowed with the most natural gift of leadership, will inaugurate a new era. However, this vital gift still remains undeveloped and America's leading role in the world rather belongs to the sphere of speculation. It seems that it is precisely in this aspect of Emerson's writings that the dialectic of postcolonial apprehensions and imperial aspirations best manifests itself: the current political vision is uncertain, but nevertheless the future is booming.

Chapter 2

Beyond the Traveler's Testimony: *English Traits* and the Construction of Postcolonial Counter-Discourse

Contrary to what Emerson's well-known statement in "Self-Reliance" that "Traveling is a fool's paradise" (278) seems to imply with regard to his reservation about this particular fashion of the day, the writer traveled quite extensively. Aside from going on lecture tours in America, he took advantage of the opportunities to travel to Europe several times. Emerson began his first visit to the Old World early in 1833, his itinerary including Italy and England. This journey helped Emerson recover his health and spirits after a series of depressing experiences: the death of his first wife, the resignation from ministry, and a serious illness. Needless to say, it also gave him a strong intellectual impulse, as he could appreciate European art and became personally acquainted with several leading figures of English literary and intellectual life: Coleridge, Wordsworth, and Carlyle. Emerson's second trip to Europe took place in the years 1847 and 1848 and was practically limited to England, with a brief sojourn in Paris. The literary result of this journey was the publication of *English Traits* in 1856; the book was a study of the exceptional qualities of the British nation or "race," as Emerson has it, and proved to be quite a big publishing success on both sides of the Atlantic. Merton Sealts writes that about fifty reviews of *English Traits* appeared in America and England in 1856 and 1857, most of them extolling Emerson's percipience and sound judgment; however, there were English reviewers who questioned the validity of Emerson's observations, doubted his good will, and discerned bias in his remarks (224–225).[1] That was an early attestation to the possible controversial content of *English Traits*. Finally, between October 1872 and April 1873, Emerson visited Europe once more, accompanied by his daughter Ellen. Beside the usual European attractions, such as England, France, and Italy, the itinerary of his third voyage overseas also included Egypt, the country becoming increasingly popular with European and American travelers.

This chapter looks at *English Traits* as an ambiguous instance of the Emersonian project of giving testimony to the growing power and significance of America and, less evidently, to the continuous maturation of American national consciousness; this time, Emerson is not manifestly concerned with America, he rather reserves the subtext for it. Characteristically, just like in "The American Scholar," where he defines the American through a reference to the intermediary, figurative category of "Man Complete," in *English Traits* his vision of America is encoded in the multifaceted presentation of England. It is as if Emerson first needed to work out the way of talking about England, the former colonizer, in order to construct the discourse about America. Thus, *English Traits* proves that the colonial legacy is still troubling for Emerson, in a sense, setting limits to his imagination and to his language. What underlies his writings is the compulsion to produce, so to speak, oppositional texts that find paradoxical justification in the ideas that they critique. In *English Traits*, specifically, the inception of the discourse about America parallels the modification of the existing discursive model of travel writing, therefore the meta-discourse of Anglo-American travel writing constitutes an appropriate context for analyzing Emerson's work.[2]

There are three intertwined aspects of the traveler's discourse in *English Traits* that account for the novel quality of Emerson's narrative and have crucial political implications. First, *English Traits* is a unique text in generic terms. Emerson does not compose a typical travelogue that would focus on the author's impressions from a foreign country; instead, he probes the limits of the genre, using the narrative structure of the travelogue as a pre-text. Such a reworking of the recognizable narrative paradigm can be accomplished, for example, through changing the proportions between the constitutive elements of the genre. Second, Emerson redefines the position of the traveler-persona, perceiving travel as much more of an intellectual activity. It can be assumed that in a representative travelogue, perhaps even regardless of the time of composition, the author—the narrator and the experiencer—is the central presence and the central concern; his personal testimony guarantees the authenticity of the narrative, whereas his authority, as the one who tells the truth, extends onto the literary artifact. In *English Traits*, interestingly, Emerson creates the impression that there is a mutual enhancement of the author's evidence by the evidence of the text alone, especially by scientific discourse employed in it, and vice versa; this is a paradoxical endorsement that leads to the marginalization of the author-traveler in most chapters. It is as if Emerson wanted to sustain the authority guaranteed by the traveler's firsthand experience and concomitantly to remove the inevitable personal imprint from the account. Third, quite predictably, the reconfigurations in the generic paradigm as well as in the positioning of the author-traveler influence in the ways of presenting the subject matter.

In this chapter, *English Traits* is seen as an example of what renowned postcolonial scholar Helen Tiffin calls "post-colonial counter-discourse." Tiffin remarks that "Decolonization is process, not arrival; it invokes an ongoing dialectic between hegemonic centrist systems and peripheral subversion of them; between European or British discourses and their post-colonial dis/mantling." She goes on to say that since "national or regional formations" that emerged in the process of decolonization cannot possibly escape "their historical implication in the European colonial enterprise," the essential project of postcolonial literatures has been the interrogation of "European discourses and discursive strategies from a privileged position within (and between) two worlds." Furthermore, "the rereading and rewriting of the European historical and fictional records are vital and inescapable tasks"; the revision of the colonial discourse being the primary concern of postcolonial writers, their strategies of interrogation should be regarded as "counter-discursive rather than homologous practices" (95–96). Simultaneously, as Diane Macdonell rightly notices, the notion of counter-discourse presupposes "a reversal of, rather than a radical departure from" existing discursive models (89). In her article, Tiffin concentrates on what she calls "canonical counter-discourse," taking a closer look at texts that visibly engage in a critical dialogue with particular narratives produced in the colonial era, for example Jean Rhys's *Wide Sargasso Sea*, a response to Charlotte Brontë's *Jane Eyre*, or J. M. Coetzee's *Foe*, a polemic with Daniel Defoe's writings. It seems that a corresponding critical analysis can be applied to well-established colonial literary genres; Tiffin indicates such a direction of inquiry when she writes that "European texts captured those worlds, 'reading' their alterity assimilatively in terms of their cognitive codes. Explorers' journals, drama, fiction, historical accounts, 'mapping,' enabled conquest and colonization and the capture and/or vilification of alterity" (96–97). Emerson's *English Traits* clearly shows that the reconfiguration of a certain generic paradigm reveals its political underpinnings.

Travel accounts constituted an important segment of colonial writing and shared the characteristics of this specific discourse of power. One of the most crucial premises of colonial discourse and one that primarily informed travel writing was the logic of binarism. In general, the travelogue foregrounds two figures: the traveler himself, that is his background, perspective, and perception, and the traveler's Other, seen as a metonymic amalgam of individual features, communal properties, territorial conditions, local customs, and so on. In Eric J. Leed's opinion, the persistence of antagonism has been an unchanging characteristic of travel writing across centuries (291). In a sense, a colonial travel account performs reductive discursive operations insofar as it posits the Other in such a way as to enhance the ultimate validity of the traveler's cultural allegiances. In her important book *Imperial Eyes: Travel Writing and Transculturation*, Mary Louise Pratt emphasizes one of the fundamental functions of colonial travel writing that was to produce "Europe's differentiated conceptions of itself in relation to something it became possible to call 'the rest of the world'" (5). Simply, travel writing expressed the biases as well as the pretensions of the colonizer. It is also significant to point out that travel literature written in the era of colonization provides an interesting illustration of how official colonial discourse, fed by politics and propaganda, administrative procedures, projects of exploration and mapmaking, spread through various contemporary popular discourses, making the colonial enterprise appeal to people who were not directly concerned about it.[3]

Lawrence Buell discusses demeaning, oversimplified opinions that British visitors uttered with regard to America in the mid-nineteenth century. He writes: "During what is now called our literary renaissance, America remained for many foreign commentators (especially the British), albeit diminishingly, the unvoiced 'other'—with the predictable connotations of exoticism, barbarism, unstructuredness" ("Postcolonial Anxiety" 200). In principle, British commentators assumed a superior stance, resulting directly from the preconceptions of colonial politics, even though they were aware of the impressive progress that Americans made in legislature and economy. To some extent, what aggravated the tension between American citizens and British travelers was the Americans' sensitiveness to criticism, a weakness that Buell calls "proverbial." Predictably, major criticism expressed by British travelers was targeted at the American lack of refinement, the harshness of manners, the evidence of which the British found virtually at every step. Commonly, if British travelers acknowledged America's success in certain spheres, they balanced their positive assessments with remarks about how evidently Americans lagged behind in other areas ("Postcolonial Anxiety" (200–201). Similarly to Buell, Joyce Appleby identifies the patterns of cultural critique that emerge from the accounts written by foreigners visiting the United States:

> Foreigners—many of whom published travel journals—frequently converged on the same repellent qualities in their American travels: the promiscuous mixing of social classes, the confident forwardness of American women, and the crassness of incessant money-making, all testifying to the distance white Americans have moved from their Old World origins. (252)

It is also interesting to add that European travelers who came from different national backgrounds and professed different political views converged in their critiques of America: "Both aristocrats and romantics, conservatives and radicals, looked down on a middle-class republic that was certainly not their idea of utopia" (Rubin and Rubin 42).

In the first half of the nineteenth century, there were divergent developments in British and American travel writing, shedding light on the historically determined perceptions of the former colony by the former colonizing power and vice versa. Texts created by American travelers in Europe quite successfully counterbalanced the critique emerging from English accounts of America and, moreover, implied that American travelers excelled their British counterparts in their readiness to make adjustments in their preconceptions about the other nation. As Christopher Mulvey claims, American travelers were open-minded and flexible in their judgments; they did not adhere to the opinions formed prior to the journey, and they verified their secondhand knowledge, if they discovered that the state of things in Europe differed from what they had expected it to be. The critic makes a meaningful comment that Englishmen came to America in search for England, whereas Americans journeyed to England to explore that country. In a sense, Americans were intellectually better prepared for transatlantic travel than Englishmen, who frequently reacted to America with bewilderment: "the English suffered from a kind of perceptual impoverishment that was quite the reverse of the enriched, imaginatively organized vision that the American brought to his looking at England." While the American in England would sooner or later discover the familiar there, the Englishman in America, faced with the enormous and boundless landscape, would feel estranged and apprehensive (*Anglo-American Landscapes* 11).

Comparative readings of nineteenth-century British travel accounts of the United States reveal close correspondences between different narratives and attest to the existence of patterns of cultural critique that was formulated by English writers. Robert B. Downs enumerates several thematic aspects that the foreign authors of travel accounts repeatedly addressed and which thus provided the grounds for the critique the travelers expressed: manners and customs, women and family, agriculture and industry, slavery, religion, education and literature, Indians, and government (6–16). One of the favorite concerns of English visitors was also the degraded condition of American institutions (Conrad 30–60). Considerations of the unpleasant sides of the American ways of living recurred in English travel accounts with unfaltering frequency, as if the English felt that they should observe certain internal obligations in this respect. As a rule, British travelers talked about America and Americans patronizingly, not infrequently condescendingly, and they composed their narratives in such a way as to demonstrate that there were good reasons for cultural criticism. For instance, perhaps the most repulsive, and therefore memorable, image that appears in English accounts of America and functions as a kind of emblem of an inferior culture is that of pigs in the streets of American towns. For example, Frances Trollope writes in her *Domestic Manners of the Americans* (1832) about the hygienic work that pigs do in Cincinnati:

> In truth the pigs are constantly seen doing Herculean service in this way through every quarter of the city; and though it is not very agreeable to live surrounded by herds of these unsavoury animals, it is well they are so numerous, and so active in their capacity of scavengers, for without them the streets would soon be choked up with all sorts of substances in every stage of decomposition. (23)

The fact that pigs help to sustain proper hygienic order in Cincinnati indicates that the inhabitants of that town, and implicitly Americans in general, are not capable of this on their own. Likewise, in *American Notes* (1842), Charles Dickens, writing about pigs in Broadway, goes as far as to personalize them as the citizens of New York: "Here is a solitary swine lounging homeward by himself....He leaves his lodgings every morning at a certain hour, throws himself upon the town, gets through his day in some manner...and regularly appears at the door of his own house at night" (133). Dickens craftily fashions this description to shock British readers through showing something completely unthinkable to them as American normalcy.[4] When talking about American manners, British travelers are bound to comment with disgust on the common habit of tobacco chewing and spitting. Thus, Isaac Holmes, in his book entitled *An Account of the United States of America* (1823), says: "It is, however, of no consequence, let it be tessellated marble pavement, Turkey carpet, or any thing even more valuable, those who chew, which nearly all do, discharge the saliva wherever they are....I have frequently seen spitting boxes before them, and they have turned to spit on the carpet" (343). Almost identical passages can be found in Trollope's and Dickens's books. A symptomatic common feature of English travelogues is the conditional recognition of American assets, whether these might be the achievements of individual people or entire communities, the good functioning of institutions, or the beauty of landscapes. Frances Trollope, even when admiring the great American scenery, expresses her doubts about the profundity of its effect on people.[5]

The figure that is virtually indispensable in English travel books is that of the backwoods settler, whom writers invariably present with a sense of disquiet, if not altogether fright, suggesting that he is a human being of a different breed, whose beastlike features have been shaped by the adverse conditions of living in the wilderness. Isaac Holmes remarks that "In some of the back settlements, the people are very brutal, being almost free from all restraint of law" (344). Dickens uses metonymy to stress the connection between the desolation of the landscape and the barrenness of the life there. The sad image of the American pioneer that Dickens remembers is that of "the settler lean[ing] upon his axe or hammer, and look[ing] wistfully at the people from the world" (244). Interestingly, this observation made by Dickens acquires additional cultural significance in the light of the writer's eulogy of the dignity and indefatigability of Canadian settlers, "far from home, houseless, indigent, wandering, weary with travel and hard living" (320), elsewhere in *American Notes*.[6] In turn, Frances Trollope is stricken with awe and overwhelmed with pity at the sight of the woodcutters living on the bank of the Mississippi; they are "miserable" as well as "dreadful," have "squalid look" and "wear...the same ghastly hue." No wonder, the traveling English lady concludes that she "never witnessed human nature reduced so low" (10). Christopher

Mulvey, in his book *Transatlantic Manners*, discusses British travelers' fondness for distinguishing various regional human types in America, the most representative of which was the "Western man," named so by Richard Burton in *The City of the Saints, and Across the Rocky Mountains to California* (1862). Burton recognized two classes of the Western man: one was "like an Indian in temperament; he lived by hunting, he hated labour and he loved tall stories," while the other was, in Burton's own words, "the offscouring and refuse of the Eastern cities, compelled by want, fatuity, or crime" (45).

For crucial reasons, the American backwoods settler is a necessary figure for English travel writers, enabling them to articulate cultural difference and to justify their sense of superiority. Those Americans who lived in Eastern cities could not fulfill this role because, more often than not, their similarity to the English was more visible than their difference from them. Dickens's praise of the inhabitants of Boston convincingly illustrates this. Importantly, the backwoods settler had numerous counterparts in colonial discourse; as Ania Loomba observes: "Despite the enormous differences between the colonial enterprises of various European nations, they seem to generate fairly similar stereotypes of 'outsiders'—both those outsiders who roamed far away on the edges of the world, and those who (like the Irish) lurked uncomfortably nearer home" (106–107).

The sphere wherein the difference between English and American people could be felt most immediately was language, therefore it comes as no surprise that British travelers were extremely sensitive to the oddities of American English. For example, Charles Dickens marvels at how many things Americans can express using a single word "fix" (223), while Isaac Holmes is astonished at the frequency with which the phrase "I guess" appears in American common speech and explains to readers, clearly his fellow Englishmen, how this phrase modifies the meaning of whole sentences (374). Thus, the former talks about the impoverishment of the English language in America, whereas the latter comments on funny superfluities, both suggesting that peculiar, "impure" linguistic forms are manifestations of cultural degradation. Probably the most symptomatic assessment of the way Americans spoke English can be found in Holmes's account, where we read that "The English language in the United States is well spoken and there is not that variety of dialect as in Great Britain." Holmes goes on to say that an American person would not understand the dialect of the lower classes of Yorkshire, in this way upgrading English dialect in treating it as a measure of the command of English and denying American English the status of a legitimate linguistic variant. Holmes concludes his observations on the nature of American English with the sentence: "There are some other trifling peculiarities, but certainly the language may be said to be well spoken throughout the Union" (375), in which the initial phrase "is well spoken" has been replaced by a less appreciative one: "may be said to be well spoken." Altogether, he talks about English in America as if it were a foreign language.

It is interesting to see that English travelers in America often composed their accounts with the awareness that their texts would have public significance in England and would provoke anxious responses in America. In other words, they treated travel writing as a forum for cultural debate and, accordingly, they felt obliged to take sides in it. Isaac Holmes, who on the opening pages of his book expresses his downright disappointment with America after a four-year residence there, admits that his initial intention was to write a pamphlet that would dissuade English people from emigrating to America. Holmes expanded the pamphlet to such an extent that he produced a full-length book, whereas the underlying intention remained unchanged. Likewise, Frances Trollope seems to imply that disclosing the unpleasant truth about America is her mission and expresses her readiness to face the consequences of her frankness, considering America to be a virtually personal antagonist:

> All the freedom enjoyed in America, beyond what is enjoyed in England, is enjoyed solely by the disorderly at the expense of the orderly; and were I a stout knight, either of the sword or of the pen, I would fearlessly throw down my gauntlet, and challenge the whole Republic to prove the contrary; but being, as I am, a feeble looker on, with a needle for my spear, and "I talk" for my device, I must be contented with the power of stating the fact, perfectly certain that I will be contradicted by one loud shout from Maine to Georgia. (62)

The appeal of the narratives written by British travelers is confirmed by the fact that such texts greatly inspired negative depictions of the United States in works of fiction published by authors who had never visited America (Brightfield 311–312). Probably the best proof that English travelogues considerably influenced collective consciousness was the declaration made by Basil Hall, a former captain of the Royal Navy, in the preface to his *Travels in North America, In the Years 1827 and 1828* (1829), wherein he says that he wanted to see America for himself, "in order to ascertain, by personal inspection, how far the sentiments prevalent in England with respect to that country were correct or otherwise." Moreover, he admits that he refrained from reading accounts by authors who had traveled there before him so that he could make his own independent judgments (i).[7]

The most direct American attempt to examine the "literary animosity" between America and England is Washington Irving's short essay "English Writers on America" from *The Sketch Book* (1820), published prior to the English accounts discussed above in response to "an elaborate ethnography of the early US Republic" (Chandler 89) that English writers had produced in the years following the Napoleonic Wars. The writer opens his sketch with an emphasis on the unprecedented scale of British misconceptions about America that spread as a result of false depictions of the distant country in travel books. He feels confused about and appalled at such a state of things because he is convinced that there is not any ground for the uncompromising critique of America by English travelers. First, Irving suggests that the possible explanation of this literary conflict should be sought in the very nature of the specific class of travelers who come to America; they are mostly tradesmen, adventurers, agents and so on, while it is statesmen and philosophers who would be able to appreciate America, "a country in which one of the greatest political experiments in the history of the world is now performing" (53). Importantly, such a classification of travelers indicates that those who visit America and then accuse Americans of bad manners lack sophistication and knowledge themselves. Thus, Irving recognizes not only their ill-will, but also their ignorance. However, if the worrying issue that Irving addresses concerned only quite a large, but essentially harmless, circle of individuals, who betray the "weakness of mind that indulges absurd expectations" and "produces petulance in disappointment" (54), the writer perhaps would not have felt compelled to respond to their pronouncements. What truly disturbs Irving is that English editors and publishers, who are known for their scrupulousness in selecting materials for publication, bring out travel accounts of America without any discrimination whatsoever. Therefore, there must be some deeper reason why British travelers create stark misrepresentations of America, publishers publish their books, and readers willingly believe them.

Irving stresses the detriment that unfavorable literary depictions can cause to America: "Over no nation does the press hold a more absolute control that over the people of America, for the universal education of the poorest makes every individual a reader." He discerns in contemporary writing symptoms of the political struggle for power at the time of the diminishing of English worldwide influences: "The present friendship of America may be of but little moment to her; but the future destinies of that country do not admit of a doubt; over those of England there lower some shadows of uncertainty"; "in all our rivalships with England, we are the rising and the gaining party." He goes on to say that America should prove its superiority to the "old countries" in renouncing national prejudices, "contracted in rude and ignorant ages, when nations knew but little of each other, and looked beyond their own boundaries with distrust and hostility" (57–61). Interestingly, James Chandler writes that Irving exaggerated the scale of the literary conflict: "Irving's...suggestion that English writers on America were uniformly hostile at the time is ultimately misleading. For a good deal of the anti-American animosity that existed in the post-Waterloo years was as heated as it was precisely because other English writers on America were depicting it in excessively attractive terms" (93–94). According to the critic, the issue at stake was English immigration to America, the consequences of which was not easy to predict and thus exacerbated the tension between England and America.

The conclusion of "English Writers on America," where Irving declares that: "We may thus place England before us as a perpetual volume of reference, wherein are recorded sound deductions from ages of experience; and while we avoid the errors and absurdities which may have crept into the page, we may draw thence golden maxims of practical wisdom" (61), in many ways, prefigures the design of Ralph Waldo Emerson's *English Traits*. Emerson's book is a cognitive as well as a discursive project in which the author transcends the boundaries of the established literary convention precisely in order to demonstrate the profundity of his insights into the essence of the English character; in other words, he creates a discourse that allows him to avoid the traps of superficiality and one-sidedness. He produces a hybrid text, with narrative passages, describing his second English journey, visibly outnumbered by essayistic considerations of the eponymous subject. In Ahmed M. Metwalli's words, *English Traits* "is actually more an essay in cultural anthropology dealing with ideas and institutions than a travel book of itinerant wonderings and recorded experiences" (70). It can be said that Emerson ascribes merely an auxiliary function to the traditional narrative core of the travelogue. The arrangement of chapters in the book and the method of titling them—some exemplary titles are: "Race," "Ability," "Manners," "Truth"—mirror the composition of Emerson's books of essays. Likewise, the tone of *English Traits* echoes that of his essays and lectures. There are chapters that relatively conform to the narrative rules of travel writing, especially at the beginning, where Emerson describes his arrival in England and recounts his acquaintance with famous English men-of-letters, and at the end, where he relates his trip to Stonehenge. Interestingly, the parts depicting Emerson's meetings with great English writers evoke his recollections from the first visit to England; in consequence, they introduce temporal ambivalence into the narrative frame of *English Traits*. Additionally, the book ends with a speech that Emerson delivered in Manchester, a token of his appreciation for oral forms of expression. It is also worth adding that some chapters, for example "Cockayne," "Aristocracy," or "Universities," sound as if Emerson employed social satire in them. In a word, the book is "an omnium-gatherum," as Joel Porte calls it ("Problem of Emerson" 66). Critics usually regard compositional incoherence as a major structural flaw of Emerson's book; Philip L. Nicoloff, the author of a book-length monograph on *English Traits*, thus comments on its structure:

> [E]ven the chapters within the "core" often lacked sufficient coherence and integration. Many of them had the old shoveled-together quality, were without adequate transitions, and contained paragraphs which might more properly have been transferred to other positions in the book. Actually, the chief unifying element in the book was an impetuous style which by its very velocity and energy carried the reader across many deserts of jumbled and seemingly directionless observations. (35)

In turn, Kenneth Marc Harris points to the correspondence between the inconclusiveness of Emerson's remarks and the book's structural inconsistency: "in place of conclusions *English Traits* offers a tangle of ambiguities. And the confusion, which I believe is partly contrived, not only emerges from the substance but extends to the very structure of the book" (143). It would be worth considering if there exists any possibility of justifying Emerson's "directionless observations"; as a matter of fact, the most tangible explanation of structural inconsistencies is that *English Traits* functions as a discursive laboratory that allows the writer to test different ways of speaking about nation. In consequence, the flawed, one might say—uncertain, composition parallels the ambivalence of Emerson's project of constructing the discourse of another nation instead of his own.

The composition of *English Traits* does not reflect the chronology of Emerson's journey. The writer rejects the logic of linearity, which seems to be inherent in the activity of travel due to the very fact that the traveler moves from place to place in a given territory, and that a journey has a beginning and an end. In travel writing, the activity and the narrative mutually determine their limits. Unlike English authors of travel accounts, Emerson seeks a way to avoid such limitations, because he intends to convey truths about the English the significance of which should not be diminished by the passage of time, the changeability of space, or the narrative finitude. The travelogue in *English Traits* constitutes a sediment, surfacing here and there in the essayistic prose; such reduction of the travelogue enhances the validity of Emerson's observations concerning the formation of the English character. At the same time, however fragmentary, the elements of the travelogue are indispensable; while the generic paradigm of travel writing is reworked in a reductive way, its presence in the text serves to legitimize Emerson's views. He gives his text the form reminding the reader about the author's firsthand knowledge of the country and the nation, with personal overtones appearing in chapter II, "Voyage to England," and Chapters XVI and XVII, "Stonehenge" and "Personal." Probably, the central paradox of *English Traits* is that at times it encourages the reader to remember about the author's textual position as a traveler, while at other times it erases this very memory and elicits the reader's appreciation for hard facts, grounded in scientific or quasi-scientific theories and discoveries. This dialectic of memory and forgetfulness corresponds not only with the presence and absence of the travelogue frame, but also with the presence and absence of America in Emerson's account. All in all, Emerson needs, so to speak, the immediate authority of the traveler, who witnesses and experiences things, to enhance his authority as a scholar. He thus skillfully combines the authority deriving from the external reality and the authority substantiated by discourse.

According to William W. Stowe, the structure of *English Traits* reveals Emerson's intention that "his book will be an appreciation as well as a critique of his gracious host country" (97). Critics usually consider the alteration of tone in successive essays in *English Traits* as a key to Emerson's method of structuring. Sealts and Stowe see Chapter X, "Wealth," as pivotal, because, for the first time in the book, the writer presents here a deepened and sustained critique of English manners and establishments (Sealts 225, Stowe 97). The preceding parts of the book "offer a generally favorable view of the English, reflecting opinions Emerson had formed while lecturing in provincial cities and coming to know members of the industrious middle class" (Sealts 225). What facilitates the transition toward criticism is a thematic shift from the discussion of the well-balanced life of smaller communities to the depiction of the restless existence in industrialized areas. Sealts claims that Emerson structured *English Traits* carefully (225–226): thus, the first four chapters briefly recount the circumstances of Emerson's journey and survey the geographical conditions of England, the next five chapters show English achievements in an unequivocally positive light, then comes the transitional chapter on wealth, followed by another five chapters, oscillating between praise and criticism. In these chapters, criticism appears to prevail over praise for the simple reason that it signifies a new stylistic and conceptual quality in the text. The concluding four chapters, distinguished by structural and generic diversity, recover the travelogue frame ("Stonehenge" relates one of Emerson's most important trips) as well as extend the plane of generalizations. Accordingly, the overall conception underlying the structure of *English Traits* consists in a balanced depiction of English assets and drawbacks.

Given Emerson's reductive treatment of the travelogue, it is interesting to take a look at how what may be called "facts of travel" have been incorporated into the narrative of *English Traits*. Above all, such facts, informing the reader about the journey and the writer's impressions, are imperceptibly woven into rather than manifestly present in the text. Emerson hints at his activities as a traveler in single sentences placed in longish passages; while particular hints can be easily overlooked, taken together they perform a crucial work on the reader's memory. The passage quoted below, from the chapter entitled "Religion," illustrates how smoothly Emerson incorporates facts of travel into his essayistic prose, how skillfully he combines such narrative strands with a different generic form onto which they have been grafted, and, finally, how easily he shifts from the content determined by temporal and spatial circumstances to musings transcending historical boundaries:

> In seeing old castles and cathedrals, I sometimes say, as to-day, in front of Dundee Church tower, which is eight hundred years old, "this was built by another and a better race than any that now look on it." And, plainly, there has been great power of sentiment at work in this island, of which these buildings are the proofs: as volcanic basalts show the work of fire which has been extinguished for ages. England felt the full heat of Christianity which fermented Europe, and drew, like the chemistry of fire, a firm line between barbarism and culture. The power of the religious sentiment put an end to human sacrifices, checked appetite, inspired the crusades, inspired resistance to tyrants, inspired self-respect, set bounds to serfdom and slavery, founded liberty, created the religious architecture. (*Essays and Lectures* 883)

It is impossible to reconstruct Emerson's itinerary or to determine which events, expeditions, or encounters during his stay in England were of utmost personal significance to him, perhaps with the exception of the trip to Stonehenge in the company of Thomas Carlyle. Emerson often provides crucial background information as if in passing, as if incidentally, while such information is often necessary for the understanding of his diagnosis: "I happened to arrive in England at the moment of a commercial crisis. But it was evident, that, let who will fail, England will not. These people have sat there a thousand years, and here will continue to sit" (824).

Certainly, Emerson's presentation of the facts of travel is closely connected with his self-fashioning as the narrator. In travel accounts, generally, the creation of the narrator-traveler is a key to the transaction between the perception of reality and the textual representation of that reality. The correspondence between the activities of traveling and narrating seems to guarantee the equivalence of experience and representation. In *English Traits*, Emerson withdraws into the background of the text. The status of his manifestly subjective observations can be judged from the fact that he reserves one chapter out of nineteen for typically personal considerations, as the meaningful title of this chapter—"Personal"—clearly indicates. It can be said that "the personal" is designated here as the subtext, unlike in more conventional travelogues where the author's own impressions and conclusions constitute the essential content. Concomitantly, the very act of writing bestows on the traveler a public function, turning him into a guide, which is a role entertained by Emerson; indeed, he emerges from the book as more of a guide than a traveler, a guide in history, manners, national sentiments, though rather not in space, which is the province of the ordinary traveler. Therefore, even though Emerson reduces the personal aspect of his work, he can strengthen his position as a controlling and legitimating presence.

Emerson's book illustrates a certain dilemma that writers of travel accounts invariably face: namely, how to balance the authority of the text and the authority of the writer. The confluence of these two areas of negotiating the authority is rather illusory; Eric J. Leed writes about an interesting and symptomatic practice that became common among travelers in the era of scientific travel and which consisted in keeping two travel journals, "one in which to record events and experiences in the sequence of their occurrence, and the other for organizing all knowledge of a place or region in an encyclopedic fashion" (186). This is perhaps the most striking evidence of the precautions that writers take in order to curb their own intrusiveness and to conceal their idiosyncrasies, which would threaten to ruin the trustworthiness of their accounts. The excess of personal information may undermine the cognitive value of a travel book, nevertheless the author is the constitutive element of the genre, for the simple reason that he decides about where he goes, whom he meets, and so on, that is about the very content of the literary work. In *English Traits*, Emerson's voice comes as if from beyond the text. While reducing or completely renouncing his authority in those textual domains in which the traveler's authority is usually most firmly anchored, he seeks ways of reaffirming it in other spheres.

Eric J. Leed, in his book on the history of travel and tourism, states that textual authority in the travelogue derives from direct observation; in fact, one subchapter in Leed's book is entitled "The Authority of the Eye." The critic writes: "Implicit in this concept of the eye as direct channel to the world are the superiority of direct experience to book learning and the high valuation placed upon books containing an author's experience, observations, information in contrast to those that simply stored, rearranged, or promulgated information derived from other books" (183). Leed discusses a breakthrough in the thinking about the purposes of travel and about the qualifications of the traveler that took place in the Renaissance and was connected with the rise of scientific travel: "No longer the bearer of fabulous gifts, the teller of exotic or monstrous tales, the truthful traveler was recognized as one who corrected errors, who admitted the limits of the observational perspective and the partiality of personal experience" (183). In the sixteenth and seventeenth centuries, travel writing was primarily a way of producing and accumulating knowledge: "The journey, from the Renaissance on, became a structured and highly elaborate method of appropriating the world as information; the most privileged official motive of travel became to see and know the world, to record it, to assemble a complete and detailed picture of it" (188). The eighteenth century witnessed the loosening of scientific strictures in travel writing as a result of the emergence of landscape painting that had a crucial influence on the rules of literary representation: "In the eighteenth century, the ban on subjectivity in valid travel reports was lifted, and the travel writer was allowed and even encouraged to make use of elevated sentiments and profound raptures in the description of landscape. These developments brought about the romantic, subjective travel report" (186). In his presentation of the historical development of travel writing, Leed stresses the existence of the tension between allegedly objective observations and recognizably personal additions. The presence of such a tension is detectable in *English Traits*, where Emerson seems to reacknowledge and recover the prerogatives of preromantic, scientific travel writing and to live up to his own idea of what Leed calls "the truthful traveler." Critics concur that falsification, an immediate result of fictionalization, has always been a powerful temptation for travel writers. For example, Leed, elsewhere in his book, observes that one of the primary functions of travel literature was to convey knowledge of other worlds, and this is why there existed "the characteristic double-bind of the traveler whose truths are uttered in a climate of non-belief" (106–107). Accordingly, the conventions of objectivity, imposed on travel accounts in the sixteenth and seventeenth centuries, could be perceived as an attempt to prevent contamination by fictional elements. Susan Bassnett compares travel writers to mapmakers and translators, saying that "[t]he works they create are part of a process of manipulation that shapes and conditions our attitudes to other cultures while purporting to be something else." In the case of travel writers, this manipulation consists in "their position[ing] themselves in relation to their point of origin in a culture and the context they are describing" (99). In turn, Christopher Mulvey talks about the tendency of nineteenth-century British and American travel writers to give their narratives a certain fictive coloring: "Travelers are said to be great liars. The prefaces of nineteenth-century travel books abound with noble reasons for crossing the Atlantic though in fact their authors were often motivated by rather meaner considerations" (*Anglo-American Landscapes* 4).

For Emerson, truthfulness conditions the text's authority and accounts for its power of appeal. The most recognizable sign of Emerson's striving for truthfulness and objectivity is the scholarly air that he sustains throughout the text. He aims to verify and reorder the state of knowledge about England, and, for this reason, his own feelings and perceptions should not be allowed to play a crucial role. Emerson's success as an author depends on his ability to conceal the fact that what he presents in *English Traits* is, precisely, his own idea of the condition of England. The result of such a positioning of the author is that, for example, when Emerson says that "England is aghast at the disclosure of her fraud, in the adulteration of food, of drugs, and of almost every fabric in her mills and shops; finding that milk will not nourish, nor sugar sweeten, nor bread satisfy, nor pepper bite the tongue, nor glue stick. In true England all is false and forged" (857–858), it should be assumed that this is not, by any means, the author's arbitrary opinion, but, conversely, the essence of truth, possibly the kind of truth that no one has stated previously.

It goes without saying that the travel writer inevitably represents his own culture, no matter if he manifestly supports or denounces cultural prejudice; neither Dickens nor Emerson are exceptions in this respect. However, the difference is that Emerson invents a literary form which makes his political allegiance less obvious; for the author of *English Traits*, this may an effective response to the forms of travelogue developed by English travel writers and the views spread through this generic medium.

It has already been mentioned that a characteristic aspect of Emerson's treatment of the author-traveler persona is the role of a guide that he takes on. In a sense, every traveler becomes a guide, addressing his book mostly to those who have never been to the places that he visited. This is a necessary, but an insufficient criterion for recognizing a guide. The qualities and prerequisites that the guide must absolutely possess are knowledge and intention; in addition, he needs discourse and convention to convey his ideas. It is important that the guide's insight can even be greater than that of local inhabitants, which is, indeed, Emerson's aspiration. In *English Traits*, there are passages that sound as if they came from a guidebook:

> In evidence of the wealth amassed by ancient families, the traveler is shown the palaces of Piccadilly, Burlington House, Devonshire House, Lansdowne House in Berkshire Square, and, lower down in the city, a few noble houses which still withstand in all their amplitude the enforcement of streets. The Duke of Bedford includes or included a mile square in the heart of London, where the British Museum, once Montague House, now stands, and the land occupied by Woburn Square, Bedford Square, Russell Square. The Marquise of Westminster built within a few years the series of squares called Belgravia. Stafford House is the noblest palace in London. Northumberland House holds its place by Charing Cross. Chesterfield House remains in Audley Street. Sion House and Holland House are in the suburbs. But most of the historical houses are masked or lost in the modern uses to which trade or charity has converted them. A multitude of town palaces contain inestimable galleries of art. (864–865)

The opening sentence of this passage contains an interesting discursive hint: the phrase "the traveler is shown the palaces" can be seen as a replacement for the phrase "I have been shown the palaces." Consequently, such an apparently minor discursive modification completely alters the angle of perception, facilitating the writer's transformation from a stranger into a guide. The binarism, involving the ignorant visitor and the experienced guide, enhances the privileged status of verifiable knowledge in the text. Emerson evokes this opposition and resolves it much to his own advantage. Namely, he emphasizes his central role as a guide not only in exploring English geography, which is a lesser concern, but primarily in examining all major areas of English life, such as economy, religion, history, politics, social organization, and so on. The visible difference between Emerson and English travel-writers is that the American author wants to sound like an insider, closely scrutinizing the English character, while his English counterparts make explicit their position as outsiders in America.

Emerson's continuous negotiation of textual authority gives him freedom to construct a rather subversive presentation of the eponymous English traits, without threatening to disclose his revisionist intentions. He simultaneously replicates and undoes English colonial rhetoric when he locates the sources of the greatness of England where hardly anybody would look for them. One of the most intriguing themes in *English Traits* is the depiction of the English character as a hybrid in the chapter entitled "Race." For instance, Emerson extols the intellectual as well as the physical potential of what he calls the English "race" ("The English, at present day, have great vigor of body and endurance.... I suppose a hundred English taken at random out of the street would weigh a fourth more, than so many Americans", 801). Studying the historical lineage of the English, Emerson probes their Nordic heritage, which he considers to be a factor explaining their unlimited potential at the present moment. He concludes that the unique strength of the English temperament is due to the mixture of the best qualities of several nations. Characteristically, Emerson formulates this observation not as his own thesis, but as an attestation to an existing truth; the unquestionable colonial authority on whom the author of *English Traits* relies for support in this matter is Daniel Defoe himself: "Defoe said in his wrath, 'The Englishman was the mud of all races'" (794). Furthermore, given the strong rhetorical effect of Defoe's statement, Emerson's utterance turns out to be reasonably balanced in its rhetoric. What Defoe sees as implicitly offensive in the English character, Emerson recognizes as one the great advantages of the most powerful "race": "The English derive their pedigree from such a range of nationalities, that there needs sea-room and land-room to unfold the varieties of talent and character. Perhaps the ocean serves as a galvanic battery to distribute acids at one pole, and alkalies at the other" (794). When Emerson identifies inherent "racial" hybridity as a major factor determining the history of England, he offers a reinterpretation of British colonization, no longer perceived as a political project, but as a virtually biological necessity. Elsewhere in "Race," he writes that "The two sexes are co-present in the English mind" (802), and substantiates this thesis with arguments concerning the behavior of Englishmen during wartime and in its aftermath: "They are rather manly than warlike. When the war is over, the mask falls from the affectionate and domestic tastes, which make them women in kindness" (802). However, in his search for the roots of English hybridity, nowhere else does Emerson go further and, in fact, make his intention more explicit, than in the passage describing the affinities between the English and animals:

> I suppose, the dogs and horses must be thanked for the fact, that the men have muscles almost as tough and supple as their own. If in every efficient man, there is first a fine animal, in the English race it is of the best breed, a wealthy, juicy, broad-chested creature, steeped in ale and good cheer, and a little overloaded by his flesh. Men of animal nature rely, like animals, on their instincts. The Englishman associates well with dogs and horses. His attachment to the horse arises from the courage and address required to manage it. The horse finds out who is afraid of it, and does not disguise his opinion. (804)

Observations similar to this tongue-in-cheek remark foreshadow Emerson's serious critiques that appear in the latter part of the book.

Sealts claims that "Emerson's severe strictures on English religion and literature demand special attention, for they lie at the very heart of his evaluation of materialistic nineteenth-century society in both England and America" (226). However, a narrow view of Emerson's critique as focused on materialism and its devastating consequences obviates the recognition of *English Traits* as a text that reflects tensions between two countries and nations with a common historical legacy. Emerson demythologizes England, envisaged as a historical, social, and discursive monolith, discovering various fissures in it. Describing the rhetoric employed in *English Traits*, Stowe observes that the writer moves "rapidly back and forth between widely admired features of English life and character and their often negative social and moral implications, making his critical point again and again through argument, example, and metaphor" (94). The insight into the contradictions of English society enables Emerson "to create a dynamic rhetorical strategy for his text." Importantly,

Stowe implies that the construction of the discourse about England brings Emerson closer to the invention of the discourse about America:

> The central purpose of *English Traits* is to use England's familiar, native otherness as a foil against which to construct a reasonable independence and define a reasonable, even an "ideal" American identity by demonstrating the important ways in which English and American life and thought both complement and contradict each other. (92)

The part of *English Traits* that best illustrates Emerson's rhetorical method described by Stowe comprises chapters ten to fifteen: "Wealth," "Aristocracy," "Universities," "Religion," and "The 'Times.'" For example, in "Wealth," Emerson contends that economic changes in England have liberated the spirit of self-reliance in men. The Englishman "has passion for independence" and "believes that every man must take care of himself, and has himself to thank, if he do not mend his condition" (851). Here, the writer considers a generally commendable feature, which he discovers in the English cast of the mind, a feature very much in keeping with his own program of individual independence and initiative, and then he immediately suggests, albeit in a very subtle manner, the limiting influence of certain economic habits and practices:

> The Crystal Palace is not considered honest until it pays;—no matter how much convenience, beauty, or éclat, it must be self-supporting. They are contented with slower steamers, as long as they know that swifter boats lose money. They proceed logically by the double method of labor and thrift. Every household exhibits an exact economy, and nothing of that uncalculated headlong expenditure which families use in America. If they cannot pay, they do not buy; for they have no presumption of better fortunes next year, as our people have; and they say without shame, I cannot afford it. (851)

On the surface, there is nothing negative about the strict economic views and attitudes that prevail among the English; on the contrary, they are rather exemplary. Emerson builds ambivalent rhetoric to stress the ambivalence of English habits: he enumerates details that suggest a certain one-sidedness of the English experience and obscure a broader view of the English, as if at their own wish. Emerson's ambiguous recognition of the praiseworthy English traits, which are almost imperceptibly tinged with the grotesque, slightly resembles Frances Trollope's hesitant, conditional acknowledgment of the beauty of America and of the achievements of its inhabitants. The difference is that the former author glosses over his political motivation. Occasionally, expressions of praise for the English are followed by ironic remarks, slight exaggerations, half-serious overstatements, which instantly lessen the appeal of eulogies. One of the recurrent observations made by Emerson concerns the tendency of the English to misconceive desirable values and fall into excesses: "The ambition to create value evokes every kind of ability, government becomes a manufacturing corporation, and every house a mill. The headlong bias to utility will let no talent lie in a napkin,—if possible, will teach spiders to weave silk stockings" (852). However, Emerson admits that while English wealth often results in some kind of abuse, it is the major factor behind the nation's imperial power: "The wealth of London determines prices all over the globe" (855). Symptomatically, even though the writer confesses that "I much prefer the condition of an English gentleman of the better class, to that of any potentate in Europe" (856), he remembers about the permanence of social divisions and concludes his considerations of English wealth on an utterly pessimistic note: "not the aims of a manly life, but the means of meeting certain ponderous expense, is that which is to be considered by a youth in England emerging from his minority. A large family is reckoned a misfortune. And it is a consolation in the death of the young, that a source of expense is closed" (859). In the like vein, in the chapter "Universities," Emerson criticizes, among others, the mistaken economic policy of Oxford University whose authorities have taken measures to prevent poorer students from entering there. The author of *English Traits* predicts that such a policy will result in an inevitable dwindling of teaching standards and, subsequently, in a general intellectual impoverishment of English people. If the intellectual impoverishment is still to come, spiritual life in England, as Emerson indicates in "Religion," is already exceptionally shallow, with the Anglican Church as nothing but a mere institutional establishment, whose "instinct is hostile to all change in politics, literature, or social arts"; "If you let it alone, it will let you alone" (888). On the whole, the drawback of the English character that particularly strikes Emerson is the narrowness of perspective, evident in how reluctantly English people engage in initiatives that bring benefits other than material as well as in how drastically they have limited the scope of values that they cherish.

What corresponds very closely to Emerson's critique of the collapse of dignified mores in England is his assessment of English literature.

In the chapter on "Literature," one finds a clear corrective intention. The writer observes that English literature gives expression to the mind which, from the very beginning, was distinguished by "a strong common sense," "a rude strength newly applied to thought, as of sailors and soldiers who had lately learned to read" (893). Accordingly, "Chaucer's hard painting of his Canterbury pilgrims satisfies the senses," while Swift "describes his fictitious persons, as if for the police." In general, the English character is "common sense inspired" (894). Thus, Emerson turns a particular feature of the constitution of the English temperament, which in the chapter on "Race" he recognized as a vital asset, into a drawback, or at least a limitation. The writer to whom he pays the most attention in "Literature" is Francis Bacon, whose scientific treatises he dismisses as totally worthless, but whose idealistic inclinations he appreciates as a rare virtue. In a sense, Emerson sees himself as one who can do justice to Bacon, being free from the English bias toward "practical skill" (903). Interestingly, his elaborate appreciation of Bacon contrasts with his dismissive remarks about contemporary writers, such as Dickens, who is "local and temporary in his tints and style, and local in his aims," Bulwer, who "appeals to the worldly ambition of the student" and produces romances that "fan these low flames," and Thackeray, who convinces his readers that "we must renounce ideals, and accept London" (900). Assuredly, none of them deserves the acclaim that they now enjoy. In such pronouncements, Emerson may be half-mockingly dubbing British critics' tendentious remarks about the dubious achievement of American writers.

Apparently, Emerson believes that his comments on English economy, religion, literature and so on, sound convincing as long as he maintains the appearance of not arguing any special American cause; hence, his authorial self-fashioning is directly connected with the presentation of America in *English Traits*. The presence of America in the text is inconspicuous, partly as a result of the withdrawal of the traveler-narrator into the background of the text. Of course, Emerson does treat America as a frame of reference, but he avoids extending the comparative scope of his book or diversifies comparative allusions; for that matter, France is mentioned as often as America, and sometimes Germany furnishes a relevant reference. The distinctive characteristics of all these nations constitute a natural background for the scrutiny of English qualities. Indeed, the presence of America in the text should be, precisely, natural. If America became a central subject in the book, the whole discursive and political design underlying *English Traits* would be threatened. This design consists in working out a coherent discourse about the English nation that would instruct Emerson as to how to create an equally consistent discourse about America and Americans. The secondary role of America as a theme in Emerson's book attests that the discourse about his own country and nation exists in his work only, so to speak, in an embryonic form. Analogically to "The American Scholar," *English Traits* concerns itself with America as a promise, and not as a fulfillment of a promise.

English Traits projects Emerson's familiar view that America is on the eve of its greatness; however, the most important sign of the rising power of America is the decline of England. It seems characteristic of Emerson that he analyzes the negative aspects of the present situation of England before attempting to formulate the positive program for America's future. This program never acquires a complete shape because it is defined in negative terms; in other words, using the case of England, Emerson shows what America *should not* be. In *English Traits*, he remarks that he came to England at the time when the country was going through a serious economic crisis; but there is much more at stake than economic difficulties, no matter how severe. England has reached a critical phase after which, as Emerson prophesies, it will never be the global power that it still remains. London still constitutes the center of the world, having become an idea synonymous with the English imperial project: "The nation sits in the immense city they have builded, a London extended into every man's mind, though he live in Van Dieman's Land or Capetown" (815). Earlier in the book, Emerson writes: "if we visit London, the present time is the best time, as some signs portend that it has reached its highest point. It is observed that the English interest is a little less within a few years; and hence the impression that the British power has culminated, is in solstice, or already declining" (785). This admittedly casual remark about why it is time to visit London has truly apocalyptic implications for the English, implications conveyed through such suggestive and disturbing concepts as "culmination," "solstice," and "decline," appearing in succession in the quoted passage.[8] Phyllis Cole writes that for Emerson, America "was a new England and an anti-England" (85); while Cole is certainly right, her two meaningful notions defining America in relation to England should be seen as pointing not to simultaneous states, but to a desired process that necessarily begins with the recognition of English errors and vices.

Emerson discerns portentous symptoms of the decline of England in the degeneration of English manners. The chapter entitled

"Aristocracy" abounds in examples of a low moral condition of the British ruling classes:

> [G]aming, racing, drinking and mistresses, bring them down, and the democrat can still gather scandals, if he will. Dismal anecdotes abound, verifying the gossip of the last generation of dukes served by bailiffs with all their plate in pawn; of great lords living by the showing of their houses; and of an old man wheeled in his chair from room to room, whilst his chambers are exhibited to the visitor for money; of ruined dukes, and earls living in exile for debt. (871)

Reading such words, the reader cannot help wondering about how it was at all possible for such base people to build an empire. It is important to notice that this passage illustrates Emerson's method of establishing the perspective of perception and the basis for assessment, the method that admittedly excels the narrative strategies employed by English travel writers. The English who write about America make sure that they speak on behalf of their nation, whereas Emerson can be the spokesman for English people as well as for Americans. However bitter and disappointed he sounds, he does not limit his observations to sheer criticism, but he indicates which spheres of the English life should be reformed. Emerson evokes a tone of worry and indignation, not condescension, therefore it can be said that he is more understanding toward England than British travelers are toward America. His understanding, in turn, legitimates his unobtrusively American terms of judgment and his categorical enunciations, just like the one found in the chapter on "Religion": "Their religion is a quotation; their church is a doll; and any examination is interdicted with screams of terror. In good company, you expect them to laugh at the fanaticism of the vulgar; but they do not; they are the vulgar" (887).

In contrast with English travelers, Emerson more easily talks about certain similarities between America and England or about processes that were begun in England and are continued in America. In "Race," he estimates the population of the English "race" and says that the English should be counted together with Americans. In a sense, he imagines America as a more perfect version of England: "England tends to accumulate her liberals in America, and her conservatives at London" (794). As a matter of fact, this statement provides a good illustration of Emerson's logic of contradiction, because it implies both commonality and divergence. Undoubtedly, the most meaningful metaphor by means of which Emerson defines the relation between England and America is that of parent and child:

> I surely know, that, as soon as I return to Massachusetts, I shall lapse at once into the feeling, which the geography of America inevitably inspires, that we play the game with immense advantage; that there and not here is the seat and center of the British race; and that no skill or activity can long compete with the prodigious natural advantages of that country, in the hands of the same race; and that England, an old and exhausted island, must one day be contented, like other parents, to be strong in her children. But this was a proposition which no Englishman of whatever condition can easily entertain. (916)

The metaphor strongly suggests that the parent country is reluctant to yield to the expansive energy of the young one. Consequently, the natural course of events whereby the younger generation peacefully replaces the older is disturbed by a strong hint of antagonism. Nevertheless, Emerson's metaphor does allow for the possibility of some kind of reconciliation, unlike, for instance, Nathaniel Hawthorne's figure of hopelessly tangled roots in his sketch "Consular Experiences" from the volume *Our Old Home* (1863):

> When our forefathers left the old home, they pulled up many of their roots, but trailed along with them others, which were never snapt asunder by the tug of such a lengthening distance, nor have been torn out of the original soil by the violence of subsequent struggles, nor severed by the edge of the sword. Even so late as these days, they remain entangled with our heart-strings, and might often have influenced our national cause like the tiller-ropes of a ship, if the rough gripe of England had been capable of managing so sensitive a kind of machinery. It has required nothing less than the boorishness, the stolidity, the self-sufficiency, the contemptuous jealousy, the half-sagacity, invariably blind of one eye and often distorted of the other, that characterize this strange people, to compel us to be a great nation in our own right, instead of continuing virtually, if not in name, a province of their small island. What pains did they take to shake us off, and have ever since taken to keep us wide apart from them! (14–15)

In the light of enunciations like Hawthorne's, wherein England is a force that provokes rather than inspires America, it only becomes apparent that, all in all, Emerson's America is bound to remain dependent even in its future greatness, which will derive directly from the passing greatness of England. *English Traits* shows Emerson preoccupied with justifications for his idea of America, as if he were unable to take his country and his nation for what they are. In his book *Semiologies of Travel*, David Scott writes: "Travel writing is a paradox in that it is a rite of passage both to the *real*—that is to an epistemic system different from that of the writer and which thus provokes a profound re-assessment of experience and values— and to the *ideal*—that is to the world of renewed and heightened meaning" (6). However, *English Traits* demonstrates that "the ideal" can signify the unattainable or inexpressible "heightened meaning," whether it refers to private ideas or public visions. One of the most memorable statements made by Emerson with respect to England is that it "may be the best of actual nations but is far from the best imaginable nation" (908). It can be easily guessed that America is destined to be "the best imaginable nation"; paradoxically, this is a troubling rather than a reassuring prospect for America and for Emerson, because once America becomes "the best actual nation" it will face the danger of forfeiting its promise. This is why America should remain, precisely, imaginable. Richard Bridgman comments on Emerson's "suppressed doubt about the true potentialities of mankind" ("Greenough" 485); indeed, the writer expresses his incertitude as to the directions that the human kind has followed, but the primary reason for this may be that his confidence in America staggers or has never really boomed. Emerson does not have a consistent vision of America, therefore he cannot work out a consistent discourse about his country and nation and he still needs auxiliary concepts by means of which he tries to define his America. In 1837, Emerson felt more at home with the notion of "Man Complete" than that of "the American scholar," twenty years later, he wrote more easily about England than about America. In *English Traits*, postcolonial critique functions as a substitute for a thorough depiction of America's past entanglements and future possibilities. *English Traits*, more than any other text composed by Emerson, makes one think about what the author of "Self-Reliance" *did not write*; namely, the absent core of his oeuvre is a book on "American traits." Hypothetically, such a book would provide some kind of closure for Emerson's writing, the closure that the writer puts off until his vision of America becomes crystallized, which never happens. All in all, *English Traits* is yet another text by Emerson that shows him on the threshold of vision and on the threshold of discourse. In one of the opening chapters of *Democracy in America* (1835–1840), Alexis de

Tocqueville states: "If we carefully examine the social and political state of America, after having studied its history, we shall remain perfectly convinced that not an opinion, not a custom, not a law, I may even say not an event, is upon record which the origin of that people will not explain" (vol.1, 14). This is the kind of conviction that Emerson concomitantly desires and fears.

Chapter 3

Emerson, New England, and the Rhetoric of Expansion

Between January 1843 and January 1844, Ralph Waldo Emerson toured several American cities: Baltimore, Philadelphia, New York, and Providence, and delivered a series of lectures that focused on the history, character, manners, and current developments of New England. Of the five lectures, one did not survive. A comprehensive, two-volume anthology *The Later Lectures of Ralph Waldo Emerson*, edited by Ronald A. Bosco and Joel Myerson, includes the following titles in the *New England* series: "The Genius and National Character of the Anglo-Saxon Race," "The Trade of New England," "New England: Genius, Manners, and Customs," and "New England: Recent Literary and Spiritual Influences" (vol. 1, 3–70). Nancy Craig Simmons thus characterizes these lectures: "Profoundly New England-centric and self-consciously 'American,' they are rooted in a specific place and organized chronologically as well as topically.... Also, they seem much less 'transcendental' and more contemporary, more worldly, and more directly critical of contemporary culture than the lectures from the first decade of his career" (53). Shortly after the first presentation of the *New England* lectures, in February 1844, Emerson read a lecture entitled "The Young American" to the Mercantile Library Association in Boston. Interestingly, "The Young American" appears to be a follow-up to the *New England* lectures, as it reveals evident thematic connections with them, and at the same time, in the light of Emerson's earlier observations on the character of New England, it can be seen as a complementary, if not altogether corrective, statement made by the writer.

Among the concerns shared by the *New England* lectures and "The Young American," there is the significance of trade in Emerson's native region and in the country at large, but the subject is thematized in markedly different ways; thus, in the former depiction of New England, trade is shown as an international activity in which Emerson's compatriots play a primary role, whereas in the latter, it becomes a strictly domestic endeavor. The modification of the writer's rhetoric to be observed here can be described in terms of meaningful shifts in style, focus, and emphasis: from concreteness to abstraction, from historical contingency to divine ordinance, and from epistemological explanations to ontological deliberations. In other words, while thematic connections remain visible, the varying terms of the presentation of New England in Emerson's writings in the early and mid-1840s signify rhetorical and political ambiguities. In the opening part of "The Young American," the author, in quite a familiar fashion, declares that he is concerned with America alone and speaks dismissively about Europe: "America is beginning to assert itself to the sense and the imagination of her children, and Europe is receding in the same degree" (*Essays and Lectures* 213). This national assertiveness manifests itself, among others, as "[the] rage for road building is beneficent for America, where vast distance is so main a consideration in our domestic politics and trade" (213). As Michael H. Cowan has noted, "newness, large scale, rapid motion, and heterogeneity...were potentially dramatic metaphors by which one could explore symbolically the various possible meanings of America" (41). Needless to say, what helped to conceive of those "possible meanings of America" were the emergent forms of public discourse. This chapter argues that the modifications in Emerson's rhetoric in the mid-1840s illustrate his attempts to address the issue of American expansionism and to incorporate this appealing ideology into his own conceptual and esthetic frame.

Emerson composed the *New England* lectures and "The Young American" at the time when the idea of Manifest Destiny was gaining currency and when the American expansionist policy was about to assume the most drastic forms. Frederick Merk writes that Manifest Destiny signified "expansion, prearranged by Heaven, over an area not clearly defined. In some minds it meant expansion over the region to the Pacific; in others, over the American continent; in others, over the hemisphere." Merk adds that while Manifest Destiny was not altogether a new idea at the dawn of the mid-nineteenth century expansion, its earlier versions had never had a comparable power of appeal, and it was only by the mid-1840s that the number of advocates of Manifest Destiny became so big as to give rise to a movement (24). In the words of the historian Bradford Perkins, the period between 1845 and 1848 marked "the greatest surge of territorial expansionism in the nation's history, one that won Texan annexation, the vast conquests of a war with Mexico, and clear title to areas in the Northwest previously challenged by Britain" (175). President James K. Polk, who came into office in 1845, made the following declaration in his speech justifying the annexation of Texas and the acquisition of Oregon: "It is confidently believed that our system may be safely extended to the utmost bounds of our territorial limits, and that as it shall be extended the bonds of our Union, so far from being weakened, will become stronger" (qtd. in Paterson 257). Perkins observes that the successful expansionist projects awakened in the nation new expectations and, in no lesser degree, new fantasies: "Some Americans talked of all of Mexico, of Yucatan and Cuba and Nicaragua, of Hawai and Okinawa, even—this was the pet project of Matthew Maury, the great oceanographer and proslavery imperialist—of a hemispheric empire reaching as far as Brazil" (175). Of course, many such expansionist plans, at times indeed preposterous, could not be pursued, but the very fact that they had been articulated and introduced into the public debate attests to the imaginative appeal of the recent land acquisitions in Emerson's time.

Perkins discusses several symptomatic factors that led to the strengthening of American expansionism in the mid- nineteenth century. First, he sees it as a manifestation of the rivalry between the Democrats and the Whigs; namely, expansion was a Democratic project aimed at undermining the position of the Whigs, especially in the slave states, through spreading the influence of the Democrats in the new territories. Second, the historian claims that expansionism reflected the convictions prevalent in the reform era, when Americans believed that they had established a social system that possessed certain redeeming qualities, and they felt the urge to carry its blessings to all the areas within their reach, in the first place those that had been long subjected to despotic rule. Third, and most obviously, Perkins speaks of the great economic value of the new lands: "Prime land, mineral resources, access to commercial routes—these and other material interests attracted expansionists." The new territories would become the home for all those who would come to America to build its greatness: "expansion seemed necessary to assure the nation's future" (178). It should also be remembered that, in the American public debate, the notions of greatness, future, and destiny, have featured prominently from the Puritan times and that the mid-nineteenth-century rhetoric of expansion was a relevant way to articulate such concerns.

It goes without saying that American expansionism of the 1840s was a culmination of earlier processes. Thomas R. Hietala argues that Manifest Destiny was part of the legacy of Jeffersonian agrarianism: "American farms raised good republican citizens as well as corn, cotton, and wheat: cultivated fields produced virtuous, cultivated people" (262); the idea of the role of the land in the shaping of the nation was later developed by President Andrew Jackson and his followers, who "exalted the pioneer as the epitome of the common man, and...celebrated American expansion as an integral part of their mission to obtain a better nation and a better world based on individual freedom, liberalized international trade, and peaceful coexistence" (Hietala 257). In turn, Reginald Horsman points to a surge of Anglo-Saxon racism in the 1830s; in particular, the proponents of Anglo-Saxon domination, understood as a sign of the divine will, looked down on Mexicans who "were a mixed inferior race with considerable Indian and some black blood" ("Anglo-Saxon" 267). Obviously, such views were reiterated with great strength during the annexation of Texas.

Frederick Merk admits that there is not any statistical method that would enable one to assess the appeal of Manifest Destiny, all the same, he puts emphasis on two phenomena indicative of the scale of influence: one is the number of journals and newspapers that articulated and boosted expansionist ambitions, the other is the number of congressional speeches delivered by the supporters of Manifest Destiny and devoted to this political cause. Thus, most of the journals that voiced the strongest advocacy of the expansionist policy were published in the northeastern and northwestern regions of America. New York was the place where a variety of journals and dailies appeared, either openly expounding the continental expansion or moderately supporting this political direction (moderation usually characterized independent press). For example, the *Democratic Review*, where John L. O'Sullivan published his influential editorials, was based in New York. In New England, the main cities of Massachusetts, Connecticut, and New Hampshire had journals devoted to Manifest Destiny, and so did the biggest cities in the midwestern states like Ohio, Indiana, and Illinois. Merk adds that the advocates in the East were more focused on the tenets of the doctrine, while those in the West called for immediate actions and demanded immediate results. The debates over territorial acquisitions showed that the combative spirit undoubtedly prevailed in the latter group. In the south there were numerous politicians, reformers, and editors who opposed the northern project of continentalism, but there was a general agreement about the expansion over those territories where the southern system could be spread; that is why the annexation of Texas had many supporters in the South. Merk concludes that in spite of divergent definitions of the scope of expansion, "[i]n every section of the Union, and at every level of intelligence, believers in the doctrine of Manifest Destiny were...found" (35–40).

Attempts at contextualizing Emerson's writing in relation to the ideology of expansionism represent a recent tendency in Emerson scholarship[1]; the most extensive critical treatment of the subject can be found in Chris Fresonke's book *West of Emerson. The Design of Manifest Destiny*, published in 2003. Fresonke examines the correspondences between Emerson's selected texts from the 1830s—in particular his lectures on natural history and his groundbreaking essay *Nature*—and the exploration accounts of the western territories written by Lewis and Clark, Zebulon Pike, Stephen Long, and William Emory. Fresonke's key concept, recognized as a common theme in the explorers' narratives and Emerson's lectures and essays, is "the design argument," a well-entrenched philosophical as well as a theological assumption that "from the manifest design of the world, we can infer the presence of a designer" (3), which she further defines as "the tendency of thought that reads aesthetic qualities and divine volition in the orderly appearance of the world" (4).

In tracing the history of "the design argument," Fresonke mentions briefly Aristotle's and Thomas Aquinas's doctrines of teleology as its original sources, and stresses its functional importance during the Enlightenment and its appreciation by the Romantics, who saw a connection between "the design argument" and the power of human intuition insofar as the latter probed and confirmed what the former presupposed. She adds that "the design argument" became a permanent element of the U.S. political discourse in the 1820s, "particularized as the argument of America's manifest destiny." Fresonke writes: "Design is the key to the attempts to make nature, particularly in the Wild West, look American. Americans, who always believe more easily in God than in America, like to perform sacraments of landscape, transubstantiating the West into a national-theological proof, a region that proves we exist" (5). The critic juxtaposes Emerson's reinterpretation of "the design argument" to President Andrew Jackson's rather crude use of it; namely, the president and his supporters believed that each endeavor to expand the territory enhanced the national glory and, accordingly, provided the justification for further expansion. In Fresonke's formulation, Emerson refined the ruthless Jacksonian credo that "conquest makes nature belong more to us" into "conquest makes us belong to nature" (122). Thus, she observes that:

> Emerson's habit of conflating America with nature…is a strategic use of teleology (or, the argument from design), one that insists that America be used, as nature is used, but underscoring the extent to which both of them use us. Our nationalism is, it seems, a bequest from nature, a cognitive faculty that makes possible our mastering of the world—while encouraging at the same time, in lesser men, merely Annexations and Purchases. (124)

Fresonke concludes that "Emerson's corrective to Jackson was to see design without brutal conquest, or fulfilled promise without repugnant political programs like Cherokee removal and the Mexican War" (128).

A very interesting discussion of the ways in which the expansionist rhetoric manifests itself in Emerson's writing can be found in Jenine Abboushi Dallal's article entitled "American Imperialism UnManifest: Emerson's 'Inquest' and Cultural Regeneration" from 2001. To begin with, Dallal states that "[a]t its height in the nineteenth century, expansionism was represented as an abstract, tautological, and domestic process, not a corporeal encounter with rivals over land," and goes on to say that the resulting discourse was "disembodied," which essentially means that it served as "the rhetorical circumvention of expansionism." Perhaps the most puzzling idea appearing in this explanation of the character of American expansionism is that it was "tautological"; this idea has to do with the fact that the United States was a settler society and, unlike the European imperial societies, in its expansionist doctrine and activity, it did not necessarily define the hostile or barbarian Other whose subjugation, in the name of the blessings of civilized life, would help to justify the conquest. Americans primarily wanted to acquire new land; therefore, the removal of Indians from that land was a corollary rather than an aim. Hence, as Dallal observes, "both nineteenth-century discourse and most twentieth-century historiography implicitly relegate the high era of expansion to the domain of diplomacy with European powers, separate from Indian removal and extermination" (50). Accordingly, "[t]he [European] empire organizes the encounter between colonizer and colonized, Christian and heathen, the civilized and the barbaric. In contrast, U.S. expansion organizes the encounter of the United States with itself—its own destiny; the ideology admits no dialectic and no Other, which accounts for the rhetoric's self-referentiality and opacity" (54). Dallal remarks that whenever Emerson's rhetoric touches upon the question of expansion, it reflects the "tautological" and "disembodied" discourse:

> Emerson's dismissal of the "particular occasions & methods" of expansion suggests a belief that ends justify the means. Yet to read his words literally, the building blocks of empire are not current "methods," such as annexation, but the vital force of the "strong" race. The dialectics of cause and effect or means and ends are internalized, displaced from history onto a national self: hence, by this logic, local events and long-term history are objectively unrelated. This disconnection is signaled by erasure. Emerson consistently argues in his writings that the sordid facts of history—wars, slavery, the conquest and subjugation of one race by another—disappear when perceived on a grand scale. (56)

Discursive disembodiment, understood as the evasion of the primary subject, enables "the internalization of conflict" (59). It is interesting to notice that Emerson's figuration of expansion, as described by Dallal, symptomatically corresponds to the metaphorization of colonial dependence in "The American Scholar" and "Self-Reliance" in that it escapes the immediate, disquieting political context.

There are several reasons why the *New England* lectures and "The Young American" offer an interesting perspective on Emerson's shaping of the rhetoric of expansion. First of all, his way of negotiating the regional and the national appears to be of crucial significance insofar as it allows him to present expansion in somewhat reductive terms, which is as an endeavor particular for New England, without really undermining the scale of this project. The regional view of expansion leads to a certain ambivalence, because it problematizes the agency of the nation as a whole. Second, Emerson's extended focus on the subject of New England trade seems to illustrate what Dallal recognizes as a rhetorical way of circumventing expansion; namely, trade can be a factor directly dynamizing territorial conquest, but it can be, as well, a phenomenon accompanying expansionist activities in important but coincidental ways. Third, these texts reveal Emerson's preoccupation with the idea of land, the idea that he infuses with certain transcendentalist notions, and which, at the same time, he uses to reconsider the political and economic issues of the day. Taken together, the *New England* lectures and "The Young American" illustrate the functioning of Emersonian dichotomies, the stylistic and conceptual quality described by Julie Ellison:

> It is most clearly manifest, perhaps, in his use of abstract words, especially...terms evocative of philosophical discourse. In Emerson's journals and essays, idealism, mind, soul, intellect, Reason—terms which designate abstracting thought—appear in a setting of conflict aimed at their opposites: materialism, body, nature, Understanding. In order to represent conflict verbally, Emerson speaks of men and aspects of himself as personified abstractions....Terms like idealism and materialism, soul and nature, poet and skeptic, behave like figures borrowed from allegory. They are images of virtues, vices, or other invisible attributes engaged in actions, primarily contests and conquests. (160–161)

Ellison looks at Emerson's dichotomous imaginings as essentially oppositional; however, it seems that, in the writer's discourse, contrasting notions may entail complementarity, given that Emersonian dualities result from imaginative reinventions rather than from direct observations.

The *New England* lectures are characterized by a notably matter-of-fact tone; Emerson writes about causal historical processes as well as about social and cultural conditions of New England. Appropriately enough, he opens the first lecture with remarks on the Puritan ancestry of contemporary New Englanders and introduces a crucial idea of the inseparability of "the love of Religion and the love of Commerce" (9) at the foundation of the Puritan colonies. Later on, this theme is reformulated in "The Young American." In "The Genius and National Character of the Anglo-Saxon Race," Emerson talks about the changes in the religious life of New England that had taken place in the course of time, and while he praises the distinct and heightened form of spirituality that evolved in his native parts, he calls the faith that had substantiated it "antique" (11), which implies the existence of disparate ways of understanding the role of religion in the past and the present. Furthermore, such a historical view of the manifestations of religious attitudes in New England entails the differentiation of religious and secular concerns, the differentiation highlighted in the *New England* lectures, but meaningfully absent from "The Young American," where the idea of sanctity informs his observations about the expansive spirit of the age. In the lectures, Emerson appreciates "the old religion" as much as he embraces the mode of skepticism, resulting from "a love of philosophy" and "an impatience of words." This mixture of sentiments, particular for New

England, makes the writer name his region, in oxymoronic terms, "a most religious infidel" (14). He is impressed with how much New Englanders have achieved thanks to their education: "The universality of an elementary education in New England is her praise and her power in the whole world" (15). At the same time, he implies that the region is still the land of pioneers, and sees, in its social organization, two groups that have the greatest influence on the quality of life: farmers and traders. Accordingly, in "The Anglo-Saxon Race," he envisages the farmer whose "employments...isolate him every day and drive him into some remote meadow or wood lot to spend the entire day in solitary labor" (14). In "The Trade of New England," he adds: "Farming in New England is a cold and surly business: no Arcadian affair, no piping shepherds, no dancing milkmaids, but a hard tug and an incessant care" (22), and "In New England, we have little that can be called heroic farming: no invention, no generalship, no humanity, but drudge follows drudge" (23). The point is that, in Emerson's descriptions, the conditions of New England determine the most representative national experiences, which give Americans good reasons to feel proud of where they belong; it is the land of the most accomplished intellectual leaders, the busiest traders, and the most indefatigable farmers.

The way Emerson talks about the farmer's labor creates the impression of the materiality of the land, which is epitomized in the image of the "frozen soil": "Men who have often turned the frozen soil into corn and wheaten cakes will never feel that terror of starvation which overpowers an inhabitant of cities" (24). In fact, this statement shows how literal Emerson can be in his writing. His limited use of metaphoric figurations in the *New England* lectures harmonizes with his preoccupation with daily, down-to-earth affairs. The materiality of the land is reiterated in the passages that depict tangible space, for instance: "This broad district of rural New England lies there, rough with aboriginal forests, towering into granite peaks, sinking into deep valleys, watered with sounding streams which form rich alluvial bottoms" (26). Such epithets as "rough," "towering," "sinking," "watered," and "sounding" engage the writer's as well as the reader's senses, becoming a suggestive substitution for the direct experience of being in the midst of the landscape, which should be seen, felt, and heard. The scenery of New England fills Emerson with rapture and, concomitantly, makes him feel alert, because the harsh conditions of the life and work there may have a degrading influence on the people and damage their moral sense. It is also worth noticing that, in the *New England* lectures, Emerson's idea of the land is quite utilitarian, and it usually appears in reference to farming. Given the amount of attention Emerson pays first to farming and then to commerce, it can be said that the lectures are visibly concerned with the professionalization of the regional life. Departing from the concreteness of the *New England* lectures, "The Young American" illustrates the process whereby the "abstract" and "disembodied" rhetoric of expansion, to use Dallal's terms, takes shape. Above all, the latter text depicts the land in such a way as to disregard its material qualities. Such a representation has to do with the broadening of perspective from New England to the whole American continent, and indeed, the whole globe: "Columbus alleged as a reason for seeking a continent in the West, that the harmony of nature required a great tract of land in the western hemisphere, to balance the known extent of land in the eastern" (214). New England still features quite prominently in "The Young American," especially in its concluding part, as the home of the elect populace, while the New Englander is typified in the eponymous figure of the Young American. The evaporation of materiality is occasioned, among others, by the disappearance of distances that have been "annihilated" as a result of the building of railroads. Another consequence of the development of the new means of transport is the leveling down of all sorts of distinctions: "when, as now, the locomotive and the steamboat, like enormous shuttles, shoot every day across the thousand various threads of national dissent and employment...an hourly assimilation goes forward, and there is no danger that local peculiarities and hostilities should be preserved" (213). Here, Emerson talks implicitly about a positive homogenization of the American experience, which has been removed from the factual sphere of local diversities, dismissed as "peculiarities and hostilities," into the figurative sphere of unifying national emblems, such as the locomotive and the steamboat "shoot[ing]...the thousand various threads." Emerson adds that "An unlooked for consequence of the railroad, is the increased acquaintance it has given the American people with the boundless resources of their own soil" (213). Predictably, the resources are there for a purpose; Emerson presupposes that the prospect of using the resources is conditioned by natural circumstances, and not by sheer human necessity. In the light of this idea, the phrase "[a]n unlooked for consequence" appears to be particularly meaningful, as it suggests that the agency of Americans is stimulated by outside factors. Another phrase that is worth pointing out is the assertive statement of the possession of "their own soil."

In the *New England* lectures, the land is depicted as neutral toward man and, at times, as capable of resisting human endeavors; this view changes in "The Young American," where Emerson uses the key concept of "inviting" which alone helps to link his literary language with the rhetoric of expansion. Emerson writes: "The habit of living in the presence of these invitations of natural wealth is not inoperative"; and: "Meantime, with cheap land, and the pacific disposition of the people, every thing invites to the arts of agriculture, of gardening and domestic architecture" (215). Symptomatically, there emerges a double understanding of what the land represents. On the one hand, it embodies an economic value, which is expressed by means of a rather dismissive term "cheap land"; later on in the text, Emerson makes an equally reductive utterance: "The land,—travel a whole day together,—looks poverty-stricken, and the buildings plain and poor" (216). On the other hand, the land appears to be an idea, an abstraction, rendered in the above quote by means of the vague phrase "every thing," connoting both immensity and immateriality. The most essential difference between these two notions of land has to do with value; thus, the land that exists as a physical entity has relatively low value, as it is "cheap," while the land that can be embraced and explored by the spirit or the imagination—whatever names Emerson has for this special faculty—represents the true value. As a result, in "The Young American," the notion of value operates primarily on the level of metaphor, for the simple reason that it is divorced from the rules of economy. The very idea of the boundless land renders irrelevant all typical economic estimates. In metaphorizing value, Emerson's text moves toward the general figuration of the sphere of economy, and this rhetorical strategy fulfils a crucial ideological function insofar as it completely denies the unrelenting economic motivation that underlay the expansionist project.

The Emersonian figure of the Young American, reflecting the desire for the embodiment of a particular idea of America, can perhaps be seen as an avatar of what Wai-chee Dimock calls "the proprietary self" in her seminal book on Melville entitled *Empire for Liberty*. She describes the rhetorical and conceptual process whereby this entity emerged:

> There was an obvious and problematic discrepancy between land as indivisible body and land as highly divisible commodity, between land as a changeless order of organic permanence and land as an ever-fluctuating exchange value on the market. In the rhetoric of commerce, however, that discrepancy was harmonized in yet another reconstituted entity, an even more powerful use of personification. This new entity came about through the characteristic strategy of splitting and

> reincorporation: by reducing to a part what might otherwise have been seen as an integral whole and, in doing so, at once subordinating and reassimilating that part into a more encompassing order. The nation's corporeal self was thus only part of a larger system of personhood. It had to be united with a human component to make up another integral unit, whose operative logic was not so much the associative logic of contiguous parts as the circulatory logic of the owner and the owned. What resulted was the proprietary self, a figure that assimilated what it owned into a kind of personified economy. (30)

This way of construing selfhood enforced the conviction that "[p]roprietorship is not so much an option as a given, not so much an extrinsic venture as a constitutive relation within the self—the relation between its organic components and its corporate identity." Accordingly, ownership becomes "an ontological provision"; "Human identity emanates from it, revolves around it, and ceaselessly reaffirms it" (31).

The idea of "inviting" signifies a certain kind of intentionality that is inherent in the land and which elicits agency in man. In other words, Emerson envisages expansion as a form of response to the land; consequently, in the sequence of causes and effects that he defines, the land provides the primary cause and the final effect, it determines what happens to it. This point is illustrated by the way in which Emerson talks about characteristic habits that have evolved in America:

> this habit [of living in the presence of these invitations of natural wealth], combined with the moral sentiment which, in the recent years, has interrogated every institution, usage, and law, has naturally given a strong direction to the wishes and aims of active young men to withdraw from cities, and cultivate the soil. This inclination has appeared in the most unlooked for quarters, in men supposed to be absorbed in business, and in those connected with the liberal professions. (214)

First of all, Emerson ascribes great existential significance to habits and indicates that they can become a collective property and a common benefit. In saying that living in specific conditions is itself a habit, he emphasizes the natural principle whereby external conditions shape habits and, more generally, patterns of human behavior. The statement "This inclination has appeared in the most unlooked for quarters" is extremely meaningful, as it suggests that men of various professions were literally taken aback by the self-discovery of a strong and sudden urge to leave everything behind and start cultivating the distant land. Their sense of agency received a powerful stimulus from the outside. Symptomatically, the examination of habits enables Emerson to retain a dual understanding of the land as a physical entity and as a powerful idea:

> Any relation to the land, the habit of tilling it, mining it, or even hunting on it, generates the feeling of patriotism. He who keeps shops on it, or he who merely uses it as a support to his desk and ledger, or to his manufactory, values it less. The vast majority of the people of this country live by the land, and carry its quality.... I think we must regard the *land* as a commanding and increasing power on the citizen, the sanative and Americanizing influence, which promises to disclose new virtues for ages to come. (216–217)

It is not surprising that Emerson considers tilling land, mining, and hunting to be habits rather than just activities; as habits deriving from human nature shaped by the land, they do not require any justification, or, to put it tautologically, they find justification in themselves. Subsequently, Emerson distinguishes those who "keep shops" on the land from those who "live by the land"; this is an apparent contrast that, at first glance, hinges on the differences in professional occupations and pits farming against urban professions. However, the idea of "living by the land" signifies much more than just farming, and it points to the national standard that the people of all backgrounds should share. Jenine Abboushi Dallal insightfully observes that the rhetoric that circumvents expansionism entails "the internalization of conflict" (59). In "The Young American," a brief glimpse of sectional America is overshadowed by the pronouncement that there is "the national mind" and that "we shall yet have an American genius" (216).[2] Additionally, the passage quoted above shows how Emerson's grandiloquent rhetoric yields reductive effects in the presentation of physical entities or phenomena. The writer may be troubled by the intangibility of the land as idea and perhaps he intuitively feels the need for the evidence that it does exist, therefore he searches for its embodied manifestations. He finds such embodiments in Americans, the people who "have grown in the bowers of a paradise" (216). The reductive rhetorical effect revolves precisely around the concept of embodiment: "The Young American" traces the process of the transubstantiation of the land into "manners and opinions."

Expansion can be easily inscribed into Emerson's philosophical doctrine for the simple reason that it functions as a form of transcendence.

The writer essentially equates the land with nature that represents agency as well as has the power to stimulate human agency: "Nature is the noblest engineer, yet uses a grinding economy, working up all that is wasted to-day into to-morrow's creation.... She flung us out in her plenty, but we cannot shed a hair, or a paring of a nail, but instantly she snatches at the shred and appropriates it to the general stock" (218). Nature redeems man in his low condition: "Our condition is like that of the poor wolves" (218), and sanctifies his endeavors. The very fact of expansion provides evidence that man has reached a regenerate state, otherwise all human efforts—the fruits of which can be seen in the present and will be seen in the future—would have failed. In "The Young American," there appear three corresponding, and to some extent synonymous, concepts that firmly anchor this text in Emerson's conceptual frame: genius, destiny, and power. These concepts are associated with nature; they signify its divinity and define the blessings that emanate from nature onto man. For example, Emerson writes: "There is a sublime and friendly Destiny by which the human race is guided" (217); "That Genius has infused itself into nature" (217); "This Genius, or Destiny, is of the sternest administration" (218). If Destiny is the guiding force, it inspires man to expand his realm; and accordingly, if the land invites man, this is when divine ordinance can be fulfilled.

Susan L. Roberson observes that the metaphors of travel, discovery, and mobility recur in Emerson's writing and closely correspond to his idea of self-reliance insofar as they convey the essence of freedom and progress: "the geography of self-reliance...is located both in the external, progressive spatiality of mobility and the open road, and in the inner, private domain of the self, making the self both a pilgrim on a journey to self-reliance and the stabilizing center from which self-reliance emerges" (277). Such an understanding of self-reliance can be easily attuned to imperialist conceptions: "What we might call imperialism Emerson validates as progressive and improving, the material realization of spiritual growth" (280). Roberson concludes:

> [T]he geographies of self-reliance and Manifest Destiny share the positive value of linear movement, the rhetoric and ideology of progress. This shared rhetoric made it easy for nineteenth-century thinkers to praise expansionism as progressive and inevitable at the same time that they suppressed its costs.... Self-reliance, self-cultivation, self-improvement were encouraged by many Americans, even people such as Margaret Fuller, who criticized the extermination of the Indian; Thoreau, who went to jail rather than support a government that

condoned slavery and war; and Emerson, who wrote angrily about the removal of the southern Indians in what became known as the "Trail of Tears," calling it a "crime" and an "outrage" in his open letter to Pres. Martin Van Buren. Even these advocates for the individual repeated the message of Manifest Destiny and the inevitable march forward and onward across the American terrain. (283)

Interestingly, the primary literary material on which Roberson's argument is based, are Emerson's sermons from the 1830s. Generally, Emerson often uses the kind of language that is either manifestly or explicitly religious; for example, in "The Young American," he constructs quasi-religious rhetoric to talk about the benefits of trade: "Trade is an instrument in the hand of that friendly Power which works for us in our own despite. We design it thus and thus; it turns out otherwise and far better. This beneficent tendency, omnipotent without violence, exists and works" (221).

In a sense, Emerson's recognition of trade as a sign of the workings of a divine force suggests that "The Young American" can be seen as a way to reinvent the expansionist rhetoric, especially in comparison with the writer's observations about trade in the *New England* lectures. In "The Trade of New England" and "The Young American," the ways in which Emerson describes trade as a phenomenon and an influence are markedly different, which does not mean that, in the former, he plays down the significance of trade for the development of the region and the country. Quite on the contrary, as the lecture's title indicates, Emerson devotes a lot of attention to the way trade shapes the character of New Englanders; for instance: "Trade flagellates that melancholy temperament into health and contentment by its incessant stimulus" (20). Trade is the formula for success that the people of New England have perfected. Moreover, it is the pride of the region where "The merchant may be taken as the type of the population; the leading and characterizing figure in our society" (28). Emerson talks about the results of the work of farmers and the purposes of the work of traders, stressing their interdependence. He also mentions appreciatively the crucial role of sailors without whose service the very functioning of trade would have been hard to imagine. The writer can be surprisingly concrete when talking about the talents, activities, or responsibilities of the representatives of given professional groups. He discusses the economic conditions with apparent precision: "When he [every person of energy] wishes to go into trade, he finds little difficulty in procuring unlimited credits, for the new state of things in America has accustomed the European as well as the American capitalist to advance goods on the probabilities of talent and success" (35). Characteristically, twice in the course of the lecture, Emerson emphatically points to the detriment that trade can cause to religious sentiments by distracting people's attention from them: "Commerce has no reverence: Prayer and prophecy are irrelevant to its bargain" (37). Therefore he strongly advocates that people should be able to balance professional occupations and spiritual needs and, without much hesitation, he points to the attitudes of New Englanders as exemplary in this respect.

In "The Trade of New England," Emerson makes evident the separateness of the interests and endeavors of different professions, even though he highlights the convergences between them; in "The Young American," conversely, this sense of separateness disappears, and the writer's understanding of the meaning of trade visibly changes. First of all, in the latter text, he describes trade as a factor defining the epoch and says that trade replaced feudalism, just as feudalism had replaced an earlier form of rule: "Feudalism had been good, had broken the power of the kings...but it had grown mischievous, it was time for it to die...Trade was the strong man that broke it down, and raised a new and unknown power in its place. It is a new agent in the world, and one of great function; it is a very intellectual force" (220). Emerson ascribes anthropomorphic qualities to trade ("the strong man") and perceives it as a powerful source of agency. If trade defines the whole epoch, it has a decisive influence on the epistemological horizons and ontological ideas at a given time in history. In "The Trade of New England," Emerson enhances the cognitive value of trade, but it is in "The Young American" that he acknowledges its fundamental ontological significance. Trade predetermines the general existential priorities, limiting the scope of choices for man. Furthermore, it epitomizes historical necessity; by extension, expansion, which is inseparable from trade, appears to be a reflection of historical necessity, too: "Every line of history inspires a confidence that we shall not go far wrong; that things mend. That is the moral of all we learn, that it warrants Hope, the prolific mother of reform" (221). Similarly to Emerson's eulogy of the land, his praise of trade involves a dichotomy of the mundane and the divine. Thus, there is an overtone of disenchantment in Emerson's statement that "This is the good and the evil of trade, that it would put everything into market, talent, beauty, virtue, and man himself" (221); this is a glimpse of trade at its crudest. Emerson touches upon this particular manifestation of trade to signal the disparity between down-to-earth occupations and the workings of divinity; the point is that whatever the writer deems desirable, including trade and expansion seen as spiritual pursuits or national projects, has a secure place in the divine realm. Trade, understood as "an instrument in the hand of that friendly Power" (221), does not really involve exchange, which admittedly lies in the nature of all imaginable forms of trade; this paradox is due to the fact that Emerson pays attention to the accomplishment, rather than to the process, in this way avoiding the need to talk about contingent historical events. Additionally, trade confirms the exceptional American experience; therefore, it calls for an exclusively national context. The *New England* lectures present a completely different view of things. "The Trade of New England" shows a global dimension of the eponymous phenomenon, hence the emphasis on the participation of sailors in the growth of trade. Trade gives worldwide prominence to the writer's native parts: "Behold the result in the cities that line the Atlantic coast from Portland to Savannah: Boston; New York; Philadelphia; Baltimore; and Charleston; new but great, and growing—God only knows to what immense enlargement scarcely two centuries old, yet related by commerce to all the world" (31). Trade helps to establish and sustain connections between places, nations, social, or professional groups. Importantly, Emerson recognizes the essentially cosmopolitan effects of the development of trade: "It destroys patriotism and substitutes cosmopolitanism. It makes peace and keeps peace. The citizens of every nation own property in the territory of every other nation" (32). The main logical continuity that underlies Emerson's argumentation in the *New England* lectures and "The Young American" is the recognition of the fact that trade removes boundaries; perhaps this is why he finds this phenomenon so desirable. In the latter text, while Emerson still makes repeated references to the New England experience, the geographical particulars altogether disappear, albeit the idea of space remains central. Trade comes to signify ubiquity through the figurative association with the land in the metaphor of a plant: "Trade, a plant which grows wherever there is peace, as soon as there is peace, and as long as there is peace" (220). It can be easily surmised that, in "The Young American," trade has nothing to do with cosmopolitanism, and instead of extinguishing patriotism, it boosts this feeling: "the uprise and culmination of the new and anti-feudal power of Commerce, is the political fact of most significance to the American at this hour" (217).

In Emerson's construction of the rhetoric of expansion, the shift in the presentation of land and trade from the tangible to the abstract is characteristically accompanied by the writer's apparent dissociation from current politics, even though he uses ideas taken from the political discourse. In the *New England* lectures, he concentrates on the past and the present, whereas in "The Young American" he looks toward the future, therefore in the former he occasionally sounds critical, for example complaining about the temporary and improvisatory nature of many pursuits undertaken by Americans or about the limited visions of his compatriots ("America is...the country of small adventures, of short plans, of daring risks—not of patience, not of great combinations, not of long, persistent, close-woven schemes demanding the utmost fortitude, temper, faith, and poverty," 53), and in the latter he erases any ground for criticism through the very choice of a prospective outlook. In "The Young American," Emerson enthusiastically declares:

> It seems so easy for America to inspire and express the most expansive and humane spirit; new born, free, healthful, strong, the land of the laborer, of the democrat, of the philanthropist, of the believer, of the saint, she should speak for the human race. It is the country of the Future. From Washington, proverbially the city of magnificent distances, through all its cities, states, and territories, it is a country of beginnings, of projects, of designs and expectations. (217)

This passage perfectly illustrates the writer's rhetorical method that consists in the evasion of the hard facts of American politics and in the concomitant replication of the political discourse. Such discursive correspondences become evident when one compares Emerson's "The Young American" and, for instance, John O Sullivan's famous article "The Great Nation of Futurity," one of the most straightforward statements in favor of the American expansionist policy, published in the *United States Magazine* in 1839. Admittedly, the very title of O'Sullivan's text sounds as if it were in keeping with Emerson's convictions, and so does its content:

> Yes, we are the nation of progress, of individual freedom, of universal enfranchisement. Equality of rights is cynosure of our union of states, the grand exemplar of the correlative equality of individuals; and while truth sheds its effulgence, we cannot retrograde without dissolving the one and subverting the other. We must onward to the fulfilment of our mission—to the entire development of the principle of our organization—freedom of conscience, freedom of person, freedom of trade and business pursuits, universality of freedom and equality. This is our highest destiny, and in nature's eternal, inevitable decree of cause and effect we must accomplish it. All this will be our future history, to establish on earth the moral dignity and salvation of man—the

immutable truth and beneficence of God. For this blessed mission to the nations of the world, which are shut from the life-giving light of truth, has America been chosen; and her high example shall smite unto death the tyranny of kings, hierarchs, and oligarchs and carry the glad tidings of peace and good will where myriads now endure an existence scarcely more enviable than that of beasts of the field. Who, then, can doubt that our country is destined to be *the great nation* of futurity? (9, original italics)

Emerson's "The Young American" echoes a number of observations and postulates made by O'Sullivan. First of all, there is a common idea that America has a mission to fulfill and that nothing will ever prevent the nation from its accomplishment; the true strength of Americans derives first of all from nature's or God's decrees, and second of all from the people's unique qualities. Americans have become agents of progress and avatars of freedom as a result of divine ordinance, which renders the question of political responsibility irrelevant. In the light of the claim that destiny defines the nation's means and ends, it is metaphysics that provides the conceptual and discursive frame for politics. O'Sullivan emphasizes the inevitable future fulfillment of the American project, which will ultimately lead to the revelation of "the immutable truth and beneficence of God." His idea that America has been blessed with an insight into "the life-giving light of truth" converges with Emerson's recognition of expansion as a form of transcendence.

In "The Young American," Emerson distances himself from the crudities of politics, among others, through the critique of the government as an obsolete formation. For instance, he implies that the government has a natural tendency to lag behind, and that the changes in its functioning are facilitated by developments in the spheres of life which it does not really control. Emerson illustrates his point with the observation that the government has been surprised by the dynamic growth of trade: "In consequence of the revolution in the state of society wrought by trade, Government in our times is beginning to wear clumsy and cumbrous appearance" (222). In general, governments are remnants of the feudal system, therefore trade as a factor of historical necessity makes them "insignificant" (221); hence the comparison of the government to "a fossil" (221). The government often fails to perform its tasks, such as "to instruct the ignorant, to supply the poor with work and good guidance" (222); it is interesting to notice how narrowly Emerson defines governmental duties. If the government is a failure even in its most basic functions, it is obvious that it will never overcome its countless limitations. However, Emerson creates a characteristic figuration of the government, one that suits the set of abstract terms to be found in the presentation of expansion. Namely, in a rather peculiar metaphor, he describes the government as "mediation between want and supply," in other words, as a kind of action in which powerful agency becomes manifest: "These rising grounds which command the champaign below, seem to ask for lords, true lords, *land*-lords who understand the land and its uses, and the applicabilities of men, and whose government would be what it should, namely, mediation between want and supply" (224, original italics). As the land necessitates the emergence of the government, this imagined system of rule can be seen as yet another sign that the land provides the impetus for the endeavors of men. What is also important in this passage is the writer's insistence on the idea of possessing land, rhetorically accomplished through the repetition of the word "lords" in differing configurations, as if Emerson aimed to invent a gradation of "*land*-lords." It should also be remembered that the word "lord" has, among others, religious connotations; therefore, it perfectly suits the sermonic quality of Emerson's style.[3] The idea of land-possessing appears in "The Young American" already in the introductory part, where the writer says: "The beautiful continent is ours, state on state, and territory on territory, to the waves of the Pacific sea" (214).

Emerson's metaphor of the government as "mediation between want and supply" is very meaningful, considering the sides involved in this process. Namely, both sides, that is "rising grounds," on the one hand, and "*land*-lords," on the other, represent want and supply at the same time. Emerson presents the following image of the newly arrived people spreading all over the American territory: "A heterogeneous population crowding on all ships from all corners of the world to the great gates of North America, namely Boston, New York, and New Orleans, and thence proceeding inward to the prairie and the mountains" (217).[4] The anxiety of those newly born Americans can be seen as a sign of want and supply, alike. Thus, they strive to benefit from the blessings of the land, which is "the appointed remedy for whatever is false and fantastic in our culture. The continent we inhabit is to be physic and food for our mind, as well as our body" (214). The use of such words as "remedy," "physic," and "food," as well as the use of passive voice, indicates that the land satisfies certain needs. Concomitantly, the land epitomizes "a commanding and increasing power on the citizen" (214), a power to which people are compelled to respond. In other words, the land and the people are subjects on equal terms, and there are two parallel directions of influence between them.

The disparity between the tangible reality and its imaginary figuration becomes apparent on the closing pages of "The Young American," where Emerson refers to the experience of New England to characterize the conditions of the present moment and to highlight the divergence between the present and the future. Even though the writer perceives New England as the land with great potential, at the same time he expresses his concern about certain negative tendencies in the American life of which, unfortunately, New Englanders partake: "In America, out of doors all seems a market; in doors, an air-tight stove of conventionalism. Every body who comes into our houses savors of these habits; the men, of the market; the women, of the custom" (226). He goes on to complain that "I find no expression in our state papers or legislative debate, in our lyceums or churches, specially in our newspapers, of a high national feeling, no lofty counsels that rightfully stir the blood" (226). This view of New England—bound up by conventions, self-complacent in the most pejorative sense, overwhelmed with inertia—contrasts sharply with the highly appreciative presentation of the region and its inhabitants in the *New England* lectures. In a self-contradictory fashion, Emerson wonders whether Americans are really destined for grand achievements, given their "sensitiveness to foreign and especially English censure" (228). Moreover, he seems to share the doubts of many of his contemporaries about the course of American history: "to imaginative persons in this country, there is somewhat bare and bald in our short history, and unsettled wilderness" (228). The articulation of the worries about the tendencies that weaken the nation is accompanied by the replacement of the mesmerizing vision of the inviting land by that of "unsettled wilderness."

In the conclusion of "The Young American," there appears an interesting new idea in Emerson's adaptation of the expansionist rhetoric: "the development of our American internal resources, the extension to the utmost of the commercial system, and the appearance of new moral causes which are to modify the state, are giving an aspect of greatness to the Future, which the imagination fears to open" (228). In other words, the thought of the greatness of America inspires the feeling of awe, it paralyzes the imagination, which in Emerson's case is the main, if not the only, domain for expansion. If imagination fails to sustain the individual's and the nation's confidence at such a crucial time, there can be no certainty as to whether Americans will recognize the emanations of the "Genius" and will allow the "Power" to guide them. Emerson closes "The Young American" with the following observation:

> Here stars, here woods, here hills, here animals, here men abound, and the vast tendencies concur of a new order. If only the men are employed in conspiring with the designs of the Spirit who led us hither, and is

leading us still, we shall quickly enough advance out of all hearing of other's censures, out of all regrets of our own, into a new and more excellent social state than history has recorded. (230)

The unwavering conviction, expressed through declarative statements, eventually gives way to a sense of hesitation expressed in the meaningful conditional phrase "if only." If, in "The Young American," Emerson attempts to create his own variant of the rhetoric of expansion, in the conclusion of this address, he assumes a somewhat detached stance. This genuine authorial gesture complicates the recognition of Emerson's political sympathies. However, despite its anchoring in the mid-nineteenth-century American politics, "The Young American" does not really seem to have been meant as a statement of the author's lasting political views. Olaf Hansen writes that Emerson's texts are "exercise[s] in approximation" and the writer "refine[s] and cultivate[s] the art of the correlative argument, the art of circumvention, of hyperbolic rhetoric and a pushing of his own ideas into the shape of narrowing circles" (91). This is definitely true of "The Young American," where the imaginative and discursive process of approximation is aimed at a particular kind of rhetoric—rather than at a particular concept—which shows Emerson's awareness that symbolic linguistic structures not only give substance to political doctrines, but also constitute a primary factor in understanding national and individual experience.

Part II

Henry David Thoreau: The Imperial Imaginary

Chapter 4

Thoreau's Imperial Fantasy: *Walden* versus *Robinson Crusoe*

On the opening pages of *Walden* (1854), Henry David Thoreau declares: "In most books, the *I*, or the first person, is omitted; in this it will be retained; that, in respect to egotism, is the main difference. We commonly do not remember that it is, after all, always the first person that is speaking," and he immediately adds, as if in a tone of excuse: "I should not talk so much about myself if there were anybody else whom I knew as well. Unfortunately, I am confined to this theme by the narrowness of my experience" (325). This is a somewhat precautionary statement, defending the author's unique selfhood and the autonomy of his text through the delineation of interpretative boundaries. However, Thoreau's textual position is inevitably defined by his culture. It is only natural that critics notice the broader implications of his personal perceptions and experiences at Walden Pond and point to the existence of correspondences between the Thoreauvian microcosm and the American national macrocosm. Joan Burbick calls Thoreau's book "a fable of the renewal of culture": "The major activity of *Walden* is to build a house and to cultivate the soil, that is to produce a human culture where health, free labor, and productivity abound" (61). Richard Slotkin sees *Walden* as "an attempt to achieve an American epic—a poem whose images and sequence will recapitulate the experiential and spiritual history of the New World as myth and as personal narrative" (*Regeneration* 537).

In his celebrated book *The Senses of Walden*, Stanley Cavell asserts that the kind of imagery that Thoreau evokes in *Walden* metaphorically describes "a crisis in the nation's life": "the nation too must die down to the root if it is to continue to recognize and to neighbor itself. This is to be expected from the people whose groping for expression produced a literature by producing prophecy" (116). For Cavell, the central metaphor in Thoreau's book that pertains to the national condition is the building of the house; the critic emphasizes its significance as "the general prophecy": "The nation, and the nation's people, have yet to be well made. And that the day is at hand for it to depart from its present constructions is amply shown in its hero's beginning and ending his tale with departures from Walden" (116). It is possible to say that Cavell's meaningful phrase "present constructions" implies two kinds of dialectic: that of the past and the present, and that of the present and the future. The present, indicated for example in the specific duration of the Walden experiment, which stresses the temporary nature of human endeavors, becomes the site wherein the past and the future are continuously negotiated. The essential difference between what there was and what there is to come can be accounted for, precisely, in terms of America's transition from the political status of colony to that of empire.

Frederick Garber observes that Thoreau found himself in a particular historical situation, which was characterized by a strong urge to redefine America's place, especially in relation to Europe. Garber implies that the writer's America, metonymically featuring in his texts as landscape, acquires its meaning through the negation of or opposition to Europe. Thoreau's earliest writings already contain telling comments on non-American landscape, the comments that Garber labels "conventional jingoism" and "amused chauvinism." The writer emerges as an Adamic figure, "looking out from a fresh paradise at the old fallen world." In Thoreau's *Journal*, Garber discovers symptomatic regularities in the descriptions of American and European natural scenery: "In those comparisons European nature always comes up short. It is arid as well as tame, while America is humid, fertile, and primitive" (*Thoreau's Redemptive Imagination* 52).

While Garber's analysis leads to the recognition of Thoreau's postcolonial position, this chapter aims to supplement the assumption that Thoreau shared the postcolonial sentiments of his epoch with a view that his discourse was simultaneously immersed in the rhetoric of empire, whose powerful effect in Thoreau's time was virtually inescapable. Accordingly, this chapter explores Thoreau's construction of the self in *Walden* through a reference to the lasting and appealing colonial topos created in Daniel Defoe's novel *Robinson Crusoe* (1719), the narrative that possessed unique potential to substantiate the British colonial mythology and colonial politics for centuries, indeed, as well as to excite literary imagination on both sides of the Atlantic across history. The primary interpretative clue is John Carlos Rowe's concept of "imperial fantasy," developed in an article on Poe, where the critic writes:

> In "The Journal of Julius Rodman" and "A Tale of the Ragged Mountains," Poe's model for imperial power in North America and India, respectively, is Great Britain, but there is a strange doubling of Great Britain and the United States in these two narratives that works out what I will call Poe's *imperial fantasy*. What Poe imagines in these two fantastic travel narratives is achievable only in and through his own poetic authority vested in the literary author and by no means realizable in what Poe considers the increasingly decadent politics of democracy. Fantastic as such poetic authority may thus remain, it is by no means harmless or trivial; it remains very much a part of the neo-colonial practices that can be traced from the late eighteenth century to the present and are uniquely influential in the development of U.S. imperialism in the same modern period. ("Edgar Allan Poe's Imperial Fantasy" 77, original italics)

Rowe specifically explores Poe's "rhetorical uses of non-European peoples... in relation to late eighteenth-and nineteenth-century imperialism and the discursive practices employed by the imperial powers to rationalize their subjugation" (75). This chapter modifies Rowe's formulation in showing that the presence of imperial fantasy in a text does not necessarily have to correspond closely to the author's political convictions, but may simply reflect the imaginative appeal of imperial projects as well as of narratives on which such projects are founded. The comparison of *Walden* and *Robinson Crusoe* sheds light on the complexity of Thoreau's "personal ideology" and suggests clues to the writer's imaginative method of resolving specific conflicts, for example between wilderness and civilization, admittedly the kind of binarism that was relevant in the American national context no less than in different colonial contexts. The comparison of the heroes and narrators of *Robinson Crusoe* and *Walden*, of their histories and discourses, allows one to examine such parallel aspects of the two works as the construction of value systems, the perception of place, the representation of Otherness, or the shaping of narrative authority. Last but not least, the possibility that Thoreau's Walden experiment, to some extent a reenactment of Robinson's adventure, leads to a better understanding of the performative nature of his self-fashioning and, through the evocation of context, poses questions about the ideological underpinnings of performance.[1]

The most significant question that such a comparative approach to Thoreau's book poses is whether his experiment is, in its essence, Robinsonian or anti-Robinsonian. Of course, there is no unequivocal answer to this question because there is no way to balance the similarities and disparities between the characters, events, or ideas presented in the two narratives. It seems that, on the surface level, the convergence of the texts is to be found in semiotic configurations; both *Robinson Crusoe* and *Walden* depict alienated individuals in the midst of wilderness, so a certain thematic commonality, pertaining mainly to actions determined by the space, simply must exist. Thus, for instance, the protagonists build their own shelters and explore the fauna and flora of their territories. On the other hand, the primary divergence in the literary portrayals of Thoreau and Crusoe would seem to be, in a broad sense, ideological; William H. Bonner enumerates fundamental values that Defoe praises in Crusoe and which Thoreau would never accept: "Crusoe's bland acceptance of money values, of British colonial expansion, and of unquestioned supremacy of Puritan-Christian faith" (96). However, at a closer scrutiny, it turns out that neither is the semiotic analogy so simple, nor the ideological difference so obvious.

In the examination of the similarities and differences between *Robinson Crusoe* and *Walden*, the nuances matter as much as—if not more than—direct parallels or notable oppositions. In relation to the Robinsonian topos, the Walden project is neither a recognizable continuation nor a radical rejection, but a certain form of refinement. To see this, one should try to compare the psychological reactions of the two characters first, rather than the spaces that they shape or the ideologies that they profess. Thus, *Robinson Crusoe* contains recurring insights into the hero's apprehensions, misconceptions, or miscalculations, and emphasizes his determination to resist the paralyzing influence of fear and to rectify the errors he committed. Robinson's initial incertitude and disorientation make his victory over his own weakness and over the surrounding territory even more appealing: "the whole country was my own mere property...I was absolute lord and lawgiver" (236). In turn, Thoreau is never bothered by the kind of doubts that haunt Robinson, and he writes in *Walden* that nature is to him "an answered question":

> After a still winter night I awoke with the impression that some question had been put to me, which I had been endeavoring in vain to answer in my sleep, as what—how—when—where? But there was dawning nature, in whom all creatures live, looking in at my broad

windows with serene and satisfied face, and no question on *her* lips. I awoke to an answered question, to Nature and daylight...Nature puts no question and answers none that we mortals ask. She has long ago taken her resolution. (547)

Apparently, Thoreau tries to obviate the dilemmas that Robinson faces, because they are *no longer* relevant; perhaps—let us speculate—Thoreau at Walden symbolically subscribes to the cultural project brought to a certain stage by Robinson. It is interesting to note, after Cecelia Tichi, that in *Walden*, unlike in *The Maine Woods* (1864), the author erases any signs of hostile nature (167). All in all, both literary characters, though each in his own way, become sovereigns. Therefore, the most important sphere of convergence between *Robinson Crusoe* and *Walden* is the work performed by a culturally determined individual imagination. It must be remembered that Thoreau's book describes an experiment that only a person with a certain historical and intellectual background could embark upon.

A comparison with Defoe's book helps to probe the ambiguity underlying Thoreau's strategies of constructing and expressing the self in *Walden*. Richard J. Schneider points out that the writer's attitude and discourse are characterized by a combination of "confidence and insecurity" and provides the following illustration: "He [Thoreau] seems supremely confident in his own wisdom, but occasionally reveals his insecurity, as in 'The Bean Field' where he admits that some of the seeds of virtue that he planted in himself 'did not come up.' Thus our guide, who seems most of the time to know so clearly where he is going, sometimes becomes one of us and shares our uncertainty" (*"Walden"* 94). A somewhat analogous mixture of utmost self-assertion and disturbing lapses of confidence seems to characterize the colonizer, who does not cherish any doubts as to the vital purpose and historical significance of his mission, but falters in its realization as a result of the mistaken judgment of external factors as well as the exaggerated self-assessment. By all means, this is a far-fetched analogy, at the same time a very intriguing one. Eric J. Sundquist finds in *Walden* the kind of binarism that evokes the most lasting colonial signifiers: "*Walden* has often been taken to be the primary text on the American way of taking up residence, of founding a home in the most basic sense, though it is again and again unsettled by civilized doubts and savage eruptions, that threaten to tear its elegantly labored edifice apart at the seams." In fact, Sundquist implies that Thoreau enacts a fantasy in which "civilized doubts" and "savage eruptions" are necessary elements; in turn, this fantasy is inscribed into an elaborate narrative structure: "What is most unnerving about the book, however, is that despite Thoreau's constant paradigm of simplicity and economy, a more rhetorically ornate volume is hard to imagine." The point is, precisely, that the opposition of civilization and savagery functions within a larger rhetorical design, and the complexity of this theme has, above all, rhetorical character. Accordingly, Sundquist concludes: "*Walden* recounts an experiment in settlement, one that strips itself down to essentials of a sort, but the record finally contains far more showmanship than primitivism" (*Home* 43).

That the figure of Robinson Crusoe was a significant inspiration for Thoreau is evident from *A Week on the Concord and Merrimack Rivers* (1849), where Defoe's book is evoked directly several times. In *Walden*, the allusions to Crusoe are more implicit, and basically they have to do with the use of imagery. For instance, in the chapter "Sounds," Thoreau describes his perceptions:

> I am refreshed and expanded when the freight train rattles past me, and I smell the stores which go dispensing their odors all the way from Long Wharf to Lake Champlain, reminding me of foreign parts, of coral reefs, and Indian oceans, and tropical climes, and the extent of the globe. I feel more like a citizen of the world at the sight of the palm-leaf which will cover so many flaxen New England heads the next summer, the Manilla hemp and cocoanut husks, the old junk, gunny bags, scrap iron, and rusty nails. This carload of torn sails is more legible and interesting now than if they should be wrought into paper and printed books. Who can write so graphically the history of the storms they have weathered as these rents have done? (417)

This passage, illustrating Thoreau's tendency to place himself "in relation to unusually distant markers" (Mendelson 274), expresses his fantasies about far-off lands. He admits that he easily succumbs to certain impulses that have their sources in technological inventions; in any case, "the freight train" is a symbolic "machine in the garden," to mention Leo Marx's crucial trope (*Machine* 190-209). The train "rattl[ing]" past him and "the stores...dispensing their odors" stimulate a sensory reaction, which, in turn, triggers off Thoreau's imaginary vision of "coral reefs" and "tropical climes." The natural surroundings in the area of Walden and in the fantasy about "foreign parts" bear the marks of the intrusion of civilization. Symptomatically, when Thoreau, in his imagination, wanders off to the tropical expanses, he has the requisite belongings of a civilized man with him, even though he talks dismissively about such possessions as "the old junk." Paradoxically, the temporary imaginary erasure of civilization is accompanied by an implicit re-acknowledgement of its permanence and validity.

The echoes of the Robinsonian topos sometimes appear in *Walden* in rather unexpected contexts, thus confirming the imaginative appeal of Defoe's narrative and the rhetorical accomplishment of Thoreau's text. The chapter "Economy" contains, among others, Thoreau's memorable deliberations about fashion, which manifestly defies the principles of self-sufficiency. The writer's assessment of people who go to great lengths to keep up with the times and therefore willingly make fools of themselves is, indeed, uncompromising: "The head monkey at Paris puts on a traveller's cap, and all the monkeys in America do the same" (342). Astounded by the recent tendencies in fashion, he remarks: "I think that it cannot be maintained that dressing has in this or any other country risen to the dignity of an art. At present men make shift to wear what they can get. Like shipwrecked sailors, they put on what they can find on the beach, and at a little distance, whether of space or time, laugh at each other's masquerade" (343). The simile evoking "shipwrecked sailors," who collect things scattered on the beach, is somewhat out of place, but purposefully so: it suggests the sorry consequences of a preposterous fashion. Indeed, it would be difficult to imagine two groups of people that differ from each other more starkly than shipwrecks do from dandies: the former stand for self-sufficiency in the face of severe scarcity, while the latter embody excess that virtually becomes a form of self-mockery. In other words, the simile is antithetical and yields the effect of caricature. At the same time, the whole idea attests to Thoreau's recognition of the enormous appeal of a shipwreck's story, which not only incites fantasies, but also substantiates serious postulates.

William H. Bonner, in his monograph on Thoreau's use of naval imagery, points to a variety of parallels between Thoreau and Defoe, ranging from stylistic solutions to psychological interests:

> It is...tempting to think he [Thoreau] might be mimicking Defoe. He overloads his account. Starting with only a few tools, he prepares life down to the essentials that Robinson was forced to begin with: the clearing of the land; the cultivation of a garden, including the various kinds of seeds he uses, which crops succeed, which fail; the construction of a house; the exact amount of such things as boards, nails, hinges, screws, and one thousand old bricks. The early chapters overwhelm us with details. This is precisely Defoe's trick. Other parallels are: the cutting of timber, the salvage of iron, wood and brick from other, disused structures; careful selection of the homesite; the

difficulties of making pots, baking bread, etc. Piece by piece their houses are displayed as they go up. (98–99)

However, such analogies, revolving around the formation of personal economy, conceal a fundamental difference in the circumstances that compel Robinson on a desert island and Thoreau at Walden to define their economic principles: the former is completely separated from the community and thus from its economic practices, whereas the latter withdraws from his social environment, but does not renounce his economic connections with it. The Walden experiment is a reformatory project that shows a certain existential alternative, this is why there is so much of performance in it, with economy incorporated in Thoreau's spectacle. Paradoxically, Thoreau would probably envy Robinson, this proto-colonizer, the decisiveness with which Defoe's protagonist talks about the illusory value of money and other symbolic means of exchange: "I had not the least advantage by it or benefit from it [about thirty-six pounds sterling]; but there it lay in a drawer and grew mouldy with the damp of the cave in the wet season; and if I had had the drawer full of diamonds, it had been the same case; and they had been of no manner of value to me because of no use" (129–130). Interestingly, in a sense, this is a redeeming condition for Robinson; thus, having in the end settled down on his flourishing estate in Brazil, he ponders: "and indeed, I had more care upon my head now than I had in my silent state of life in the island, where I wanted nothing but what I had, and had nothing but what I wanted" (279). This pronouncement sounds very much like a Thoreauvian credo, highlighting the utopian quality of Thoreau's project. Michael T. Gilmore rightly observes that the author of *Walden* does not delude himself about the possibility of a total withdrawal from the systems of exchange: "He recognizes...the obsolescence of his program as a *literal* antidote to the ills of market civilization" (298). However, Thoreau does not fall into despair over such a state of things, and he readily uses economic arguments to demonstrate that his project is workable.

Bonner points to several analogies in the construction of the protagonists in Defoe's and Thoreau's texts. First, the heroes of both *Robinson Crusoe* and *Walden* write journals, although their self-narratives differ markedly in thematic and stylistic terms: the former's is a "a mariner's log" and concentrates on "fact and event," the latter's emerges as "a repository of his finest thinking and acutest observation." Second, in their solitude, both men brood over the essentials of life and contemplate the place of man in the universe: "Crusoe's meditations led him to Divine Providence; Thoreau's to God-like man.

Crusoe was driven to religious essentials; Thoreau to essentials of the human spirit." Third, Robinson and Thoreau confront not only the new surroundings, but also their own selves; as Bonner laconically puts it, "Each has much to say about exploring the inner sea." Fourth, both characters are faced with "the idea of getting back to the primitive source of things" (98–100). All in all, Robinson and Crusoe are portrayed in situations that help to probe the narrative mechanism whereby activities or circumstances can be seen as constructs of the literary imagination.

The eponymous protagonist of *Robinson Crusoe* is guided by ultimate utilitarianism in his actions as much as in his utterances, that is in his role as a character, occupying a space, and in his function as a teller, constructing a discourse. He is attentive to details and strives to acknowledge every event, of major or minor importance, that sheds light on his conditions. The parts where he relates his actions outnumber the parts where he expresses and analyzes his doubts or apprehensions. He continuously seeks causal connections in the surrounding world, even if he sometimes ascribes certain happenings to divine ordinance. Importantly, Robinson does not indulge in fantasies that would threaten to disturb the routine he has so painstakingly worked out. The best illustration of a possible detriment caused by fantasies to one's peace of mind is Robinson's reaction to the mysterious footprint discovered in the sand: "nor is it possible to describe how many various shapes affrighted imagination represented things to me in; how many wild ideas were found every moment in my fancy, and what strange, unaccountable whimsies came into my thoughts by the way" (152–153). For Robinson, fantasy signifies the inexplicable, whereas for Thoreau, it offers a clue to mysteries and reconciles the elusive with the tangible. Therefore Thoreau can say with utmost conviction that: "I have always endeavored to acquire strict business habits; they are indispensable to every man. If your trade is with the Celestial Empire, then some small counting house on the coast, in some Salem harbor, will be fixture enough" (338). The imaginary topography of "the Celestial Empire" and the real topography of "some Salem harbor" smoothly merge; the point is that Thoreau selects and shapes the content of his fantasies, defining the scope of experience as well as enhancing the possibilities of self-expression and self-creation.

The way Thoreau envisages himself in some passages clearly attests that his fantasy is infused with imperial images or notions:

> To oversee all the details yourself in person; to be at once pilot and captain, and owner and underwriter; to buy and sell and keep the

accounts; to read every letter received, and write or read every letter sent; to superintend the discharge of imports night and day; to be upon many parts of the coast almost at the same time;—often the richest fright will be discharged upon a Jersey shore;—to be your own telegraph, unweariedly sweeping the horizon, speaking all passing vessels bound coastwise; to keep up a steady dispatch of commodities for the supply of such a distant and exorbitant market; to keep yourself informed of the state of the markets, prospects of war and peace everywhere, and anticipate the tendencies of trade and civilization,—taking advantage of the results of all exploring expeditions, using new passages and all improvements in navigation; charts to be studied, the position of reefs and new lights and buoys to be ascertained, and ever, and ever, the logarithmic tables to be corrected, for by the error of some calculator the vessel often splits upon a rock that should have reached a friendly pier—there is the untold fate of La Perouse;—universal science to be kept pace with, studying the lives of all great discoverers and navigators, great adventurers and merchants, from Hanno and the Phoenicians down to our day; in fine, account of stock to be taken from time to time, to know how you stand. (338–339)

This passage clearly shows that, as Haskell S. Springer points out, "the sea, the ship, the voyage, as public facts and personal symbols, provide Thoreau a syntax of figurative expression" (84). Despite the elaborate rhetoric of this passage and despite its metaphorical overtones, the writer's self-projection seems to be very concrete, due to the accumulation of mutually complementary ideas. In Defoe's work, Robinson perceives details that constitute larger configurations and therefore should be closely connected with one another; analogically, he makes sure that activities have been presented in proper sequences. His sense of order depends on his ability to control perception. Thoreau as narrator, by contrast, is extremely selective in his choice of objects, activities, and ideas for presentation or discussion; moreover, he talks about what he experiences as often as about what he imagines. Robinson constantly faces adverse circumstances, therefore however confident he feels, his doubts and worries about his condition are never fully dispersed. As a consequence, he is not predisposed to the wanderings of the mind that would threaten to weaken his vigilance. His discourse reflects his alertness. Thoreau has a much greater influence on the circumstances he confronts; all in all, with Walden located quite close to Concord, he can easily walk to the town whenever he longs for human company. One may conjecture that, for Thoreau, the pond and the forest are far less of a mystery than the island is for Robinson. Thoreau's gestures and enunciations are well thought-through. In his imagination, he carefully arranges his surroundings, then he meticulously shapes his discourse. The effect of rhetorical excess partly results from Thoreau's self-confidence, while Robinson's discursive discipline counteracts his lingering disorientation. On the whole, Robinson functions in the realm of potentiality, Thoreau in the sphere of fantasy.

Both Robinson and Thoreau are products of the age of individualism. In his seminal study of the eighteenth-century English novel, Iann Watt describes Robinson's individualism as "economic." For example, the critic stresses Robinson's eagerness for bookkeeping, which, in a broader sense, corresponds to the necessity to organize the life on the island in accordance with "individual contractual relationships" (66). The protagonist of *Walden* undoubtedly differs from Robinson in his view of economic prerogatives, however, what Watt says about the roots of Crusoe's individualism is also true about Thoreau. The critic observes that individualism flourishes in a society that presupposes the individual's independence from other people's influence, on the one hand, and from "past modes of thought and action denoted by the word 'tradition,'" on the other:

> The existence of such a society, in turn, obviously depends on a special type of economic and political organization and on an appropriate ideology; more specifically, on an economic and political organization which allows its members a very wide range of choices in their actions, and on an ideology primarily based, not on the tradition of the past, but on the autonomy of the individual, irrespective of his particular social status or personal capacity. (62)

Watt concludes that "it is appropriate that the tradition of the novel should begin with a work that annihilated the relationships of the traditional social order, and thus drew attention to the opportunity and the need of building up a network of personal relationships on a new and conscious pattern" (96). Characteristically, both Robinson and Thoreau withdraw from what Watt calls "the traditional social order"; the former, craving for adventure and eager to prove his self-reliance, embarks on a sea voyage against his father's wish, which loosens his family ties, and eventually he becomes completely separated from his background, whereas the latter symbolically suspends his contacts with society, moving to a secluded place. Additionally, they both invent new "personal relationships," which are characterized by a higher level of self-consciousness because of the limited frequency of meeting other people. It is interesting to notice that in Defoe's and

Thoreau's books the presentation of inter-human relations has to do with the invention of Otherness.

The construction of Otherness in *Robinson Crusoe* and *Walden* is connected with the semiotic aspect of positioning of the self in relation to the surroundings. The representation of space in Defoe's narrative is characterized by the existence of a concentric structure, with the eponymous hero as the central presence, dwelling at a place meaningfully called "the fortress." The fortress functions as an extension of Robinson's self and helps to assuage his solipsistic predicament. In the beginning, the shipwreck carefully selects the place for his would-be home: "In search of a place proper for this, I found a little plain on the side of a rising hill, whose front towards this little plain was steep as a house-side, so that nothing could come down upon me from the top" (62). He makes sure that the location shelters him from disagreeable climatic conditions as well as prevents human intrusion. Upon deciding where to put up his tent, Robinson performs a symbolic act of delineating the boundary of the fortress: "Before I set up my tent, I drew a half circle before the hollow place, which took in about ten yards in its semidiameter from the rock, and twenty yards in its diameter, from its beginning and ending" (62). The island, to which Robinson lays his claim, constitutes the outer circle in this spatial configuration. It is worth noticing that Robinson, until when Man Friday joins him, is the only permanent inhabitant of the island, which is occasionally visited by cannibals with their prisoners. Robinson watches the shore, where he confronts Otherness; accordingly, the shore is the contact zone (the traditional colonial topos whereby natives meet European visitors on the seashore is thus reversed, perhaps signifying a more advanced stage of colonization). There are two possibilities of what happens to the Other on Robinson's island: the Other either leaves or is forced to leave the island, relegated beyond the frontiers of the hero's domain, or stays with Robinson, unconditionally accepting his sovereignty, which is precisely Man Friday's lot. The fact that Man Friday accompanies Robinson during his journey to Europe ultimately confirms his utter subjugation.

Thoreau chooses to live at a place that seems to be devoid of territorial boundaries, although the fact that a railway runs near his dwelling place suggests that this "sojourner in wilderness" needs some reminder that boundaries do exist. Indeed, the very first sentence of *Walden* contains information about the topography evoked in the book: "When I wrote the following pages, or rather the bulk of them, I lived alone, in the woods, a mile from any neighbor, in a house which I had built myself, on the shore of Walden Pond, in Concord, Massachusetts, and earned my living by the labor of my hands only" (325). Thoreau declares that he could live practically anywhere in the Concord woods: "Wherever I sat, there I might live, and the landscape radiated from me accordingly.... I discovered many a site for a house not likely to be soon improved, which some might have thought too far from the village, but to my eyes the village was too far from it" (387). His thorough knowledge of the area is a sign that he has "colonized" it, even if for strictly personal reasons and purposes. It is also symptomatic that Thoreau buys somebody else's house, the Hollowell place, takes it to pieces, transports it to the shore of Walden, and erects it there anew, reaffirming the symbolic importance of the act of settlement. The house in the wilderness, built from the materials recovered from civilization, just as in *Robinson Crusoe*, becomes Thoreau's outpost, which is very much in tune with the imperial fantasy. The act of moving to the wilderness is essential for the project of expansion. In Thoreau's case, one should rather talk about the expansion carried out by the mind, although the intellectual activity involves the exploration of physical space.

Walden can perhaps be seen as an example of what David E. Nye calls "the technological foundation story." Essentially, the narratives of technological foundation depicted the processes of community-building on newly acquired territories, and thus they complemented the narratives of regeneration through violence. As Nye puts it, in foundation stories, the "dramatic action focuses on transforming an uninhabited, unknown, abstract space into a technologically defined place," or in other words, on "creating society by applying new technologies to the physical world." The invariable feature of the narratives of technological foundation was the attribution of important symbolic senses to certain man-made objects of general use that, in specific ways, corresponded to the successive stages in the establishment of human settlements in what used to be the wilderness. Nye mentions the following objects and constructions that acquired such symbolic significance: "the axe, used to create the log cabin and the clearing; the mill, the center of new communities; canals and railroad, used to open western lands to settlement; irrigation, which converted worthless desert into lush farmland." Characteristically, because of their causal and sequential logic, the narratives of technological foundation helped to understand history as well as destiny, providing the inhabitants of new settlements in particular, and the whole nation in general, with a sense of being anchored in the past and of having a great task to accomplish in the present or the future (3-4). Thoreau's log-house is certainly a sign of the technological transformation of uninhabited space and of the writer's link with the community.[2] The boundless space depicted in *Walden* belongs to Thoreau as much as to the Other, therefore unlike Robinson, who rigorously defines the conditions for appropriating the Other, Thoreau readily embraces Otherness. And yet, one can notice Thoreau's inclination to write about the people whom he encounters in terms of how they differ from him; for that matter, the Irish farmers, Thoreau's closest neighbors, appear to be a different category of humans. Evidently, he is in the vanguard, the Irish farmers lag behind.[3] The difference between Thoreau's and Robinson's perceptions of Otherness manifests itself in how the two characters read signs of alien presence in their territories. One of the most memorable passages in *Robinson Crusoe* describes the hero's terror at the sight of a "naked" human footprint on the beach:

> It happened one day about noon, going towards my boat, I was exceedingly surprised with the print of a man's naked foot on the shore, which was very plain to be seen in the sand. I stood like one thunderstruck, or as if I had seen an apparition; I listened, I looked round me, I could hear nothing, nor see anything; I went up to a rising ground to look for there; I went up the shore and down the shore, but it was all one, I could see no other impression but that one; I went to it again to see if there were any more, and to observe if it might not be my fancy; but there was no room for that, for there was exactly the very print of a foot, toes, heel, and every part of a foot; how it came thither I knew not, nor could in the least imagine. (152)

As Antonio Ballesteron González comments on this famous passage, Robinson "is frightened to death by the fact that the elusive human being is *an-other*, possibly a black man, perhaps a cannibal.... Language betrays Crusoe's colonial ideology: a native becomes a more frightful menace for him than the Devil himself" (91). By contrast, having discovered the signs of alien presence at his place, Thoreau expresses a sort of complacency about the easiness with which he identifies the category of visitors:

> When I return to my house I find that visitors have been there and left their cards, either a bunch of flowers, or a wreath of evergreen, or a name in pencil on a yellow walnut leaf or a chip. They who come rarely to the woods take some little piece of the forest into their hands to play with by the way, which they leave, either intentionally or accidentally. One has peeled a willow wand, woven it into a ring, and dropped it on

my table. I could always tell if visitors had called in my absence, either by the bended twigs or grass, or the print of their shoes, and generally of what sex or age or quality they were by some slight trace left, as a flower dropped or a bunch of grass plucked and thrown away, even as far off as the railroad, half a mile distant, or by the lingering odor of a cigar or pipe. Nay, I was frequently notified of the passage of a traveller along the highway sixty rods off by the scent of his pipe. (425)

The two passages quoted reveal an interesting analogy in employing the motif of intrusion upon the hero's territorial domain. Apparently, Thoreau welcomes such intrusion and finds satisfaction in having unknown guests, yet he immediately emphasizes his solitary condition, using colonial references: "But for the most part it is as solitary where I live as on the prairies. It is as much Asia or Africa as New England" (426). This is a meaningful comparison: the colonizer must learn to endure solitude to persist in his endeavor, while Thoreau, in a somewhat similar vein, regards solitude as an essential personal condition.

The protagonists of *Robinson Crusoe* and *Walden* find themselves, as it were, in specific cognitive situations; in this respect, Robinson seems to be in an underprivileged position, because, when confronted with the footprint, he sees the menace of an overwhelming signifier with no clear signified, which is why the sign has a monstrous quality, whereas Thoreau easily matches signifiers and signifieds, even though he often relies on surmises or presuppositions. The fact that both texts contain the motif of encountering the Other as a sign and not as a tangible presence is of primary significance insofar as it implies the privileging of the narrator as an observer and, consequently, as a subject of cognition. In Defoe's book, the natives remain unaware of Robinson's presence until he attacks them—he defeats them thanks to his knowledge and their ignorance. Thoreau uses a more subtle strategy so as to ascertain the narrative and cognitive authority: namely, he contrasts himself with those "who come rarely to the woods," have childish habits, and leave traces, allowing him to learn about them much more than they have found out about him. He talks about them in a patronizing manner, just as Robinson talks about Man Friday.

In *Walden*, Thoreau creates, so to speak, a particular human topography, which is half-real, half-imaginary, and which comprises individuals, groups of people, and imagined beings. An important part of this human landscape is the community of Concord, the narrator's townsmen, present in the narrative from the very beginning, though apparently removed from it. *Walden* is memorable for many passages wherein Thoreau, in a preacher-like manner, instructs readers about the essentials of life, especially in the opening and longest chapter "Economy." Thoreau talks about the mistaken priorities of his "neighbors," who are enslaved by labor and possessions, yet it is thanks to such people that *Walden* was published, if we trust Thoreau's words. At the very beginning of the book, Thoreau admits that he felt encouraged to publish his account by the inquiries of his townsmen; thus, it is not surprising that he identifies them as his readers: "I should not obtrude my affairs so much on the notice of my readers if very particular inquiries had not been made by my townsmen concerning my mode of life" (325), thus pointing to the affinities between himself and the people of Concord.

In spite of Thoreau's critique of the habits of his townspeople, it is the community of Concord that provides the writer with his cultural anchoring, the background necessary for a safe meditation about the savage. Notwithstanding a thorough redefinition of the savage in *Walden*, this very idea remains a colonial invention. In a sense, the abstract notion of the savage is subordinated to Thoreau's communal convictions, because the writer's purpose is to help his countrymen to reform their lives through suggesting to them a model of conduct embodied by the savage. The savage is a projection: a set of features, of virtues and talents, a frame of reference, but never a being from the physical world. Thoreau proceeds with his discussion on a safe level of generalization and in a tone of utmost conviction: "The customs of some savage nations might, perchance, be profitably imitated by us" (376). The eulogy of the imaginary skills and experiences of the savage illustrates Thoreau's characteristic method of reconciling opposites and of reaffirming hierarchies that have just been undermined: "The civilized man is a more experienced and wiser savage" (354). In fact, this idea can be easily inscribed into a broader cultural and historical context; as Kerwin Lee Klein writes: "Universal history avoided 'cultural relativism' by imagining savage and civil life as sequences in a cosmic drama rather than radically opposed alternatives" (246).

Whether the savage is a living creature, like in *Robinson Crusoe*, or an abstraction, like in *Walden*, he requires a proper measure of control. At the beginning of the chapter "Higher Laws," Thoreau writes:

> Once or twice, however, while I lived at the pond, I found myself ranging the woods, like a half-starved hound, with a strange abandonment, seeking some kind of venison which I might devour, and no morsel

could have been too savage for me. The wildest scenes had become unaccountably familiar. I found in myself, and still find, an instinct toward a higher, or, as it is named, spiritual life, as do most men, and another toward a primitive rank and savage one, and I reverence them both. I love the wild not less than the good...I like sometimes to take rank hold on life and spend my day more as the animals do. (490)

In spite of Thoreau's insistence that he cherishes equal reverence for "spiritual" and "savage" life, the discovery of the savage in himself is a truly disturbing experience. The passage contains several indications that such a state requires alertness and control. First, Thoreau says that his berserk behavior occurred only incidentally, "once or twice" during the whole two-year stay at Walden. This condition is unique and terrifying, not natural and desired. Second, contrary to the contention that he readily embraced the savage in him, the utterance "I found myself ranging the woods" implies that during such bouts Thoreau experienced a kind of split in his self. Third, the very rhetoric of the passage, with the change of tone and the sequential use of images, facilitates discursive control; namely, the bloodthirsty "hound" roaming the woods for venison gives way to a complacent individual who likes to spend a day "as the animals do" from time to time. Thoreau's confession here is an act of self-purification. His redefinitions of the savage Other testify to his determination to incorporate this concept into his intellectual frame. Interestingly, Thoreau leaves aside the traditional binarism of savagery versus civilization, and conceives of two more relevant binary structures, that is spirituality versus savagery and good versus wildness. In this way, the perception of the savage becomes a moral concern. Subsequently, it is not that spirituality smoothly merges with savagery, or good with wildness; rather, it is that spirituality sanctifies savagery. Thoreau tends to encode contradictory messages in his statements; for example, later in "Higher Laws," where he ponders the discovery of "an animal in us," the animal represents sensual experience, which arouses the narrator's fear of monstrosity:

> We are conscious of an animal in us, which awakens in proportion as our higher nature slumbers. It is reptile and sensual, and perhaps cannot be wholly expelled; like the worms which, even in life and health, occupy our bodies. Possibly we may withdraw from it, but never change its nature. I fear that it may enjoy a certain health of its own; that we may be well, yet no pure. The other day I picked up a lower jaw of a hog, with white and sound teeth and tusks, which suggested that there was an animal health and vigor distinct from the spiritual. (497)

No wonder, Thoreau comes to regard control as imperative: "Yet the spirit can for the time pervade and control every member and function of the body, and transmute what in form is the grossest sensuality into purity and devotion" (497).

Thoreau's sense of inner duality is symptomatically reflected in his recollections of the meetings with a Canadian woodchopper in the chapter "Visitors." On the one hand, the narrator sees the Canadian as an embodiment of self-reliance, on the other, he is struck by the inordinate presence of "the animal" in the man. The account of Thoreau's encounters with the Canadian implies that *Walden* is, indeed, a rhetorical experiment in constructing Otherness. Thoreau devotes about four pages to the presentation of the Canadian, which is a notable proportion for the author-narrator who is so self-conscious and so digressive. The woodchopper is introduced as an alien in a double sense: a half-mythical being, "a true Homeric or Pephlagonian man" (437), and a foreigner. Significantly, Thoreau refuses to reveal his name: "he had so suitable and poetic a name that I am sorry I cannot print it here" (437), which emphasizes the chopper's alien status.[4] The man speaks to Thoreau in Canadian French or English with a strong accent, as if his linguistic skills remained undeveloped. On the whole, Thoreau entertains doubts about the Canadian's intellectual development: "I did not know whether he was as wise as Shakespeare or as simply ignorant as a child, whether to suspect him of a fine poetic consciousness or of stupidity" (440). The writer and the woodchopper share a passion for Homer. On one occasion, the latter asks the former to translate a passage from the ancient poet's work; recounting this episode, Thoreau points to himself as the knowledgeable instructor. All in all, in writing about the woodchopper, Thoreau recognizes his own authoritative position: "To him Homer was a great writer, though what his writing was about he did not know" (437–438); "Wiser men were demigods to him" (440). Thoreau envisages himself as, precisely, a "demigod." The Canadian woodchopper's inferiority results directly from his alleged status as a colonized subject: "He had been instructed only in that innocent and ineffectual way in which Catholic priests teach other aborigines, by which the pupil is never educated to the degree of consciousness, but to the degree of trust and reverence, and a child is not made a man, but kept a child" (439).

In describing the woodchopper, Thoreau relies on the notions he explores in "Higher Laws," such as spiritual life. It is important to notice that for him satisfactory spiritual life, supposedly like his own, is impossible to reconcile with simpler modes of existence. Accordingly,

Thoreau admits that "Yet I never, by any maneuvering, could get him to take the spiritual view of things; the highest that he appeared to conceive of was a simple expediency, such as you might expect an animal to appreciate" (441–442). It is interesting to mention that Frederick Garber compares the Canadian to Caliban, "natural man in a pastoral landscape, an image of an earlier state in a largely pastoral book" (*Thoreau's Fable* 180). Thoreau sees the woodchopper's utter indifference to "spiritual" pursuits as a sufficient justification for the fact that it is he, the writer, who exclusively benefits from this acquaintance through acquisition of knowledge. Not only does he learn a lot about the man's disposition and behavior, but also, as a result of the conversations with the Canadian, he takes a fresh view of ideas and happenings, such as various reformatory undertakings, assessed by the interlocutor. Symptomatically, their conversations are not exchanges, strictly speaking, but rather resemble interrogations, with Thoreau asking questions and the Canadian providing answers. In the end, Thoreau leaves the Canadian in an unredeemed condition; it cannot really be determined whether the writer believes that the chopper does not need any redeeming guidance or regards the task of redeeming him as pointless: "there might be men of genius in the lowest grades of life, however permanently humble and illiterate, who take their own view always, or do not pretend to see it at all, who are as bottomless even as Walden Pond was thought to be, though they may be dark and muddy" (442).[5]

Similarly to Thoreau's Canadian woodchopper, Defoe's Man Friday is also a man "of genius in the lowest grades of life." It is interesting that Robinson more willingly acknowledges Man Friday's intellectual capacity than Thoreau does the Canadian's mental potential, perhaps because the relationship between the characters in Defoe's novel is less ambivalent than the encounter depicted in *Walden*. Obviously, it is Robinson who decides about the limits of Man Friday's cognition and instructs him in matters that he deems most crucial. Their relationship, in essence, entails enslavement, which Defoe veils as Friday's affectionate devotion to Robinson. The Canadian woodchopper remains something of an enigma for Thoreau, while Man Friday becomes increasingly "transparent" in Robinson's eyes, especially after he has acquired his master's language. Despite evident differences, there are important analogies between Robinson and Thoreau with regard to how they build their narrative authority. Thus, they both claim the privilege of naming others, although Thoreau paradoxically manifests his right to do so in not disclosing the Canadian's name, as if he were interested in him as a human type, rather than as a unique person. In turn, Robinson decides what the native's new name will be, without ever bothering to ask him what his original name was. Thoreau uses sophisticated narrative strategies to express his personal refinement and to justify his claim to authority; Robinson produces a matter-of-fact account, where the hierarchy of values is clear, for a similar purpose. Another noteworthy analogy is the fact that the protagonists of *Robinson Crusoe* and *Walden* acquire further knowledge of themselves from the encounters with Otherness; thus, Thoreau begins to see certain notions and phenomena in a new light, and Robinson learns to probe religious questions more consciously, which is necessitated by Friday's curiosity: "I really informed and instructed myself in many things that either I did not know or had not fully considered before, but which occurred naturally to my mind upon searching into them for the information of this poor savage" (216). It goes without saying that in expanding their own selves through contacts with the Other, the narrators of *Robinson Crusoe* and *Walden* do not allow the Other to undermine their self-confidence.

The dialectic of intuition and knowledge, fundamental in American transcendentalism, turns out to be something of a dilemma in *Walden*, analogically to the corresponding dialectic of sensuality and spirituality. The chapter entitled "The Pond in Winter" evokes the memorable picture of the fishermen coming to fish in Walden:

> Early in the morning, while all things are crisp with frost, men come with fishing reels and slender lunch, and let down their fine lines through the snowy field to take pickerel and perch; wild men, who instinctively follow other fashions and trust other authorities than their townsmen, and by their goings and comings stitch towns together in parts where else they would be ripped. They sit and eat their luncheon in stout fear-naughts on the dry oak leaves on the shore, as wise in natural lore as the citizen is in artificial. They never consulted with books, and know and can tell much less than they have done. The things which they practise are said not yet to be known. Here is one fishing for pickerel with grown perch for bait....His life itself passes deeper in Nature than the studies of the naturalist penetrate; himself the subject for the naturalist....Such a man has some right to fish, and I love to see Nature carried out in him. (547–548)

Thoreau presents himself simultaneously as an insider and an outsider. He and the fishermen inhabit the same environment, therefore he is an insider by virtue of contiguity. However, his description of the fishermen's activities seems to imply that, more often than not, when Thoreau watches them, he himself remains unseen: "When I strolled around the pond in misty weather I was sometimes amused by the primitive mode which some ruder fishermen had adopted" (548). He takes immense delight in watching the fishermen; the more spontaneously or instinctively the men behave, the more strongly they stimulate his curiosity and fascination. In his eyes, primitivism is much of a performance. His admiration for the fishermen's skills and talents does not mean that he wishes to possess similar abilities. Thoreau, an observer and admirer, is closer to the naturalist than to the fisherman. The naturalist is one of the roles that he temporarily assumes in order to better fulfill his pioneering mission: "The future inhabitants of this region, wherever they may place their houses, may be sure that they have been anticipated" (387). It is in such statements that Thoreau's imperial fantasy acquires a recognizable rhetorical form.

Thoreau's method of self-presentation in *Walden* can be analyzed in the light of pastoralism, which underlay political and aesthetic visions of the United States in the writer's time. In his article "Pastoralism in America," Leo Marx claims that pastoralism, which emerged in the ancient Near East, flourished in Europe during the Renaissance, and developed in America toward the end of the eighteenth and into the nineteenth century, constituted and still constitutes a major intellectual impulse for American thinkers. The pastoral mode, both in its ancient and modern version, foregrounds a particular spatial structure, which is present in the works of a number of nineteenth-century American writers, including Thoreau. This spatial configuration is tripartite and comprises the natural expanses, the urban area, and the borderland between them. The borderland is the province of the shepherd or herdsman, the central figure in a pastoral landscape. As Marx puts it, the shepherd is a "liminal figure," oscillating between "the realm of organized society and the realm of nature." In fact, the shepherd represents contrasting values because, on the one hand, "seen against the background of the wilderness, he appears to be a representative of a complex, hierarchal, urban society," while on the other, "seen... against the background of the settled community with its ordered, sophisticated ways and its power, he appears to epitomize the virtues of a simple, unworldly life disengaged from civilization." It is not surprising that Thoreau appears in Marx's discussion as an emblematic figure: "he [the shepherd] is independent, self-sufficient and, like Henry Thoreau or the rugged western hero of American mythology, a man singularly endowed with the qualities needed to endure long periods of solitude, discomfort, deprivation." The borderland between the wild and the urban territory is the area of mediation: "To mediate in this context means, quite literally, to resolve the root tension between civilization and nature by living in the borderland between them. The mediation is two-directional. In the earliest documents there are instances of a shepherd helping to effect the passage of people moving either to or from the organized community." Marx adds that the tension between civilization and nature manifests itself as the feeling of anxiety and that the borderland space enables the sufferer to regain balance and composure (43). Lawrence Buell thus accounts for the prominence of pastoral imaginings in colonial discourse:

> The Renaissance invention of Europe's new worlds under the sign of pastoral... set all the following in motion: it held out the prospect that the never-never lands of pastoral might truly be located in actual somewheres; it helped energize quests, both selfish and unselfish, to map and understand those territories; and it thereby helped ensure a future interplay between projective fantasy and responsiveness to actual environments in which pastoral thinking both energized environmental perception and organized that perception into schemas. New world pastoral thus offered both to filter the vision of those enchanted by it and to stimulate them to question metropolitan culture itself (even while participating in it). (*Environmental Imagination* 54)

Likewise, in her well-known discussion of the tradition of colonizing America in discourse through attributing feminine qualities to the landscape, Annette Kolodny claims that the familiar image of America as "Eden, Paradise, the Golden Age, and the idyllic garden" (6) evolved from the European literary pastoral: "Beautiful, indeed, that wilderness appeared—but also dark, uncharted, and prowled by howling beasts. In a sense, to make the new continent Woman was already to civilize it a bit, casting the stamp of human relations upon what was otherwise unknown and untamed" (9).

Thoreau's role as a pastoral mediator is rather ambivalent. On the one hand, if he has any redeeming influence on his townsmen at all, it is exercised as if *ex post*, that is after his return to civilization, the act ultimately confirmed by the appearance of the book. On the other, his account of the meetings with the woodchopper suggests that Thoreau does not pay much heed to the innermost feelings of the people whose temperaments had been shaped as a result of their complete immersion in the world of nature. Added to this, the spatial configuration in *Walden* markedly differs from the traditional pastoral structure insofar as the wilderness where Thoreau finds his place is surrounded by civilized territories and, in fact, it is more of a projection, thus functioning as a sort of stage upon which he performs his spectacle.[6] Laura Dassow Walls writes: "The act of taking up Walden into a symbolic system meant making it into a social fact, a new word in the language. By thus making it mobile he took it from its own orbit and put it in his own, sending the pond, like the pastoral valley he saw going by on the Fitchburg Railroad, whirling off and away to Boston" (*Seeing* 164). It takes a person with a particular background to conceive of and enact such a pastoral spectacle. Moreover, the whole performance is intended for the audience accepting the existential standards determined by the achievements of civilization. All in all, the evocation of pastoral ideas confirms the writer's attachment to a well-entrenched cultural mode. Just like Robinson on the desert island, Thoreau on Walden finds himself in an unusual situation that elicits in him a variety of responses, a number of which can be seen as emblematic of the imperial culture that shaped him.

Chapter 5

The Politics of the Genre: Exploration and Ethnography in *The Maine Woods*

In "Ktaadn," the first part of Henry David Thoreau's *The Maine Woods* (1864), there appears an interesting reference to Robinson Crusoe:

> At one place we were startled by seeing, on a little sandy shelf by the side of the stream, the fresh print of a man's foot, and for a moment realized how Robinson Crusoe felt in a similar case; but at last we remembered that we had struck this stream on our way up, though we could not have told where, and one had descended into the ravine for a drink. (643)

Thoreau describes his own and his companions' reaction as a characteristic sequence, with an initial sense of confusion and apprehension immediately followed by a recovery of certainty and confidence. Thus, the mountainous expanses of Maine become the scenery where the writer, in the company of guides, reaffirms his cultural legacy and personal identity. This process of self-assertion is inscribed into a pattern of repetition and change: the myth of Robinson Crusoe does not have its original relevance, but it still retains a great power of appeal and serves as an instantly recognizable frame of reference. The discovery of the print of a human foot triggers off a reenactment of the imperial fantasy about the confrontation with the Other. However, unlike in *Walden*, where the use of the Robinsonian topos can be seen as a major structuring principle and an indication of the text's ideological entanglements, in *The Maine Woods*, the single allusion to Robinson Crusoe constitutes a symptomatic, albeit seemingly marginal, element of an account of exploration. Accordingly, the thrust of argument in this chapter concerns the ways in which, in the latter text, Thoreau employs the narrative form that had played a significant role in the historical development of the colonial discourse in general and which functioned as one of the literary means of expressing American imperial aspirations in the first half of the nineteenth century in particular. Obviously, the writer's use of the paradigm of exploration narrative in the three personal accounts included in *The Maine Woods* is justified by the circumstances described in these texts, but at the same time it reflects the esthetic as much as ideological factors that helped to shape Thoreau's sensibility as a writer and underpinned his imaginative constructions.

Thoreau's writings were launched into an extensive textual environment wherein accounts of exploration were a frequent and popular form, which strengthened the link between literary discourse and political rhetoric. The first half of the nineteenth century witnessed a proliferation of exploration and travel narratives, whose authors usually, more or less openly, endorsed the political project of expansion. Importantly, the appearance of a multitude of thematically related texts entailed the recognition of a variety of reasons why the American nation was destined for expansion; in consequence, as Eric J. Sundquist observes: "The ideas of liberty, originality, wilderness, moral health, and national mission became intertwined, not always exactly equivalent nonetheless provoking constant associations with one another" (*Empire* 17). The texts about expeditions to the territories of strategic importance in the economic and political sense, for example the Rocky Mountains, the areas along the Mississippi and Missouri rivers, California, and Oregon, were appearing alongside the accounts of journeys to places onto which the readers with unrestrained imagination might have wished to extend the imperial domain, even if such wishes had little, if anything, to do with political feasibility. For example, from the 1830s through the 1850s, a number of texts were published that presented the explorations of the Arctic region or the most distant parts of the Pacific Ocean. Such texts provided literary writers with attractive and convincing structural solutions, patterns of plot-building, thematic inspirations, methods of characterization. It is important to notice that the American teams of explorers often included scientists who wrote reports on their findings, thus codifying the cognitive value of the endeavors that, as a rule, resulted from political motivation in the broad sense; those scientists who participated in expeditions to the uncharted territories usually represented such academic disciplines as ornithology, entomology, zoology, botany, geology, and ethnology. Sundquist writes: "The classifying of vast quantities of both natural phenomena and alien human customs thus often tended to blur into a combined scientific, diplomatic, and economic enterprise that worked in service of political and cultural hegemony." The critic adds that "whereas personal journals often recorded the mundane, frequently harsh details of the journey west, public documents, typically uniting scientific observation and imaginative projection, better revealed national identity" (*Empire* 24). Symptomatically, the narrative structure of Thoreau's *The Maine Woods* hinges on a combination of the two narrative forms discussed by Sundquist: the personal journal and the scientific report, which implies a question about the writer's ways of relating selfhood to nationhood.

The objectives that the organizers and participants of exploring expeditions wanted to achieve determined their roles as reflected in the accounts that they produced. Thoreau's narrative positions in *The Maine Woods* can be defined through a reference to the role models emerging from the reports written by explorers. As Ning Yu points out: "Although Thoreau did not carry out the westward project he planned with his brother, he vicariously experienced the excitement of discovery through reading the reports, memoirs, and travelogues written either by or about the explorers and adventurers" (117). John Aldrich Christie estimates that Thoreau read narratives of exploration at an impressive pace of 8,849 pages a year and meaningfully calls the effect that such accounts had on the writer "influence 'by saturation'" (45, 247). In essence, Thoreau envisages himself as a successor of those who had come to the woods of Maine to chart this territory; in mentioning their names and achievements, Thoreau suggests that there is a continuity between the earlier expeditions and his own. As an explorer, he reacknowledges his cultural background because through the contact with the land and its native inhabitants he learns about how the familiar forms of social and cultural life differ from those that are altogether alien to him; the awareness of difference makes him see clearly where he belongs. Having reached what appears to be the fringes of civilization, he becomes a witness as well as an agent of progress. In particular, he describes the natural circumstances that accelerate or hinder progress; for example, he puts emphasis on the harsh conditions of travel and on the necessity to overcome countless obstacles encountered by him and his companions, thus expressing not only the excitement that accompanied the movement forward through the dense woods, but also the readiness for sacrifice, which is invariably essential for successful exploration. Thoreau praises the achievements of explorers as much as he appreciates the work done by scientists who have been involved in exploring expeditions, and he treats the accomplishment of the latter group as a model for his own pursuits. In *The Maine Woods*, the writer's strategy of self-fashioning that entails the highlighting of his passion for science does not really arouse surprise, as it repeats the author's presentation of himself as a naturalist in the earlier books. Thoreau admits that one of his aims during the expeditions to the woods of Maine was to study closely the unique local flora. In stylistic terms, the shifts from the perspective of an explorer to that of a scientist manifest themselves in the sequential arrangement of narrative relations and botanical descriptions. Moreover, in his botanical discourse, Thoreau frequently resorts to enumerations of the specimens of the flora particular for a given place; such systematizations reveal his intention to extend the existing body of knowledge. It should be added that scientific observations appear much more often in the second and third parts of *The Maine Woods*—"Chesuncook" and "The Allegash and East Branch"—than in the first part, as if "Ktaadn" presented the circumstances of acquiring the experience necessary for conducting research in a territory that virtually resists the human cognitive attempts. Last but not least, Thoreau assumes the role of an ethnographer, studying the ways of the natives. His observations about the Indians are in tune with his remarks about the land, thus indicating that the people are an emanation of their habitat, the idea that certainly mirrors the view of the indigene as encoded in colonial discourse. In any case, Thoreau's self-presentation as simultaneously an explorer, a naturalist and an ethnographer evidently attests to his will to knowledge.

Thoreau's double focus on the exploration of the place and the encounter with the natives corresponds to the principal thematic interests and generic patterns that, according to Gordon M. Sayre, emerged at the outset of the colonization of America by the British and the French and informed a variety of discourses about the continent and its inhabitants through the nineteenth century until the strengthening of anthropology as a scientific discipline. Sayre claims that from the time of the appearance of the first narratives of European settlement and exploration onward they combined two genres: travel narrative and ethnographic description: "In these texts two different ways of looking at the American land and native cultures, though in many respects epistemologically incompatible, were brought together in a formal hybrid that persisted for centuries" (79). Importantly, the mixing together of two genres that explicitly dealt with the parallel processes of cognition served to enhance the authority of the writer and, by extension, the primacy of the culture that had shaped his outlook. Sayre adds that this hybrid generic form "organized partial knowledge so as to make it appear complete, and to enable colonials to impose a sense of order and control over the land and the Indians." Furthermore, the critic describes the genre, in Foucauldian terms, as discourse, that is "an intellectual or theoretical construct that served practical ends in the administration of colonial power" (79). Sayre distinguishes two kinds of dialectic underlying the texts that merged exploration narrative with ethnographic study; one has to do with the authority of the writer which, in travel accounts, derived from empiricism, rooted in rational philosophy and bourgeois individualism, and in ethnography from "Europeans' sense of cultural universality," whereas the other concerns the different ways of presenting the indigenous peoples and is not genre-specific. Namely, there were two discernible tendencies in the depictions of Native Americans: they were seen either as the semblances of Europeans, such a view having been grounded in the biblical genealogy of the human kind, or as embodiments of the qualities that radically opposed the features shared by Europeans. Sayre calls these two respective methods of portraying the indigene "substitution" and "negation" (80–81). The presentation of American Indians in *The Maine Woods* seems to oscillate between these two models.

Sayre gives several reasons why authors of exploration narratives included in their texts, descriptions of native customs or of the fauna and the flora. First of all, they aimed to counteract the skepticism with which they expected that their books would be received, and thus they provided the kind of textual evidence that made the readers feel they participated in the process of "a cultural construction of identity and difference," the process itself sustained by accounts of exploration. Second, the incorporation of the details regarding the life of the natives or the geographical specificity allowed writers to transcend the generic limitations of the travelogue. Ethnographic discourse substantiated "an extrapolation from what one *did* see to what one *would* see behind the curtain of trees if one went in there"; "From the limited perspective of an explorer in the wilderness, it enabled a shift to the speculative power of a scholar in the library." In other words, the use of ethnographic discourse resulted in a more efficient codification of knowledge acquired by explorers in the course of their activities. Third, the combination of travel and ethnography reflected the general logic of the colonial enterprise: "the blank space on a map could be claimed only after it had been circumscribed by the exploration of rivers, lakes, coasts or mountains" (111–114).

In Thoreau's *The Maine Woods*, the combination of exploration narrative and ethnographic study is reflected in the variations of theme and focus across the three parts of the whole that were composed in different periods: "Ktaadn," "Chesuncook," and "The Allegash and East Branch" relate the writer's three expeditions to the New England mountainous woodland in 1846, 1853, and 1857, respectively. The first two parts were originally delivered as lectures and then published in journals, while the third appeared first in the posthumous edition of *The Maine Woods* in 1864. For understandable reasons, *The Maine Woods* as a whole is characterized by noticeable thematic and stylistic modifications in comparison with Thoreau's earlier volumes. As Richard J. Schneider points out, "Ktaadn" resembles *A Week on the Concord and Merrimack Rivers* and *Walden* "in that it records Thoreau's attempts to extend his experiment with primitive life from the tame beauty of the pond to the actual wilderness and to explore the extreme boundaries of life." The critic also notes that "Ktaadn" is richer in symbolic associations than the other two parts, with "the climbing of the mountain as a central symbolic episode." In turn, "Chesuncook" is "less philosophical than 'Ktaadn,' and focuses more on narration, description of the wilderness, and characterization, particularly of Joe Aitteon." Additionally, in the second essay, Thoreau is "less the wide-eyed tourist and more the trained observer." Finally, "The Allegash and East Branch" is "more journalistic in tone," with "descriptions of the wilderness [that] are less poetic and more scientific" (*Henry David Thoreau* 77–78). When read alongside Sayre's discussion of exploration and ethnography, Schneider's remarks about the differences between the consecutive parts of Thoreau's book seem to imply that the primary narrative development across the three essays consists in a movement from exploration toward ethnography, especially that the last part features Joe Polis, Thoreau's most memorable Indian character. It should be mentioned that this shift toward the examination of manners and customs, judged on the basis of Polis's behavior, is not accompanied by any attempt at authorial self-effacement, unlike in those ethnographic texts where the authors strove to enhance the veracity of the account at the expense of the removal of the author into the background. In Schneider's words, "The Allegash and East Branch" "gives the fullest view of him [Thoreau] actually fronting the facts of the wilderness in survival situations—fighting mosquitoes, shooting rapids, and agonizing over a lost companion. It is a Thoreau we see as fully nowhere else in his writings" (78). The writer's central presence in his text has to do with the fact that, for him, being an ethnographer is more of an imaginary role than a public function.

The fundamental significance of imagination in Thoreau's self-fashioning in *The Maine Woods* perhaps is less evident than in *Walden* because the writer tries to adhere closely to facts. This factual quality influences the use of imagery and the rules of self-presentation, in the end contributing to the overall literary effect. For example, in one of the opening paragraphs, Thoreau makes sure to place his first journey to the woods of Maine in a sequence of expeditions to this area of New England: "Ktaadn...was first ascended by white men in 1804. It was visited by Professor J. W. Bailey of West Point in 1836; by Dr. Charles T. Jackson, the State Geologist in 1837; and by two young men from Boston in 1845" (593). He puts himself in the same line with those earlier explorers; in a way, their discoveries and experiences predetermine his own aims and expectations. He follows in their footsteps in a double sense: by going to the places they had previously visited and by intending to write a personal account: "All these have given accounts of their expeditions. Since I was there, two or three other parties have made the excursion, and told their stories" (593). Thus, exploration and narration turn out to be interconnected activities; the former necessarily entails the latter. Later on in "Ktaadn," Thoreau quotes a remark by the assistant state geologist about a place that he himself is just about to see. The writer appears to have a particular appreciation for the Report on the Geology of Maine, dating from 1838, to which he refers in both "Chesuncook" and "The Allegash and East Branch" (675, 727). Even if such references are not very frequent in the whole text, they are sufficient to strengthen the impression of Thoreau's cultural allegiance.

The inclusion into the text of the factual evidence regarding the previous ventures into the primeval forests of New England attests that Thoreau sets out on his expeditions with the utmost awareness of the legacy that has been transmitted to him and which he will subsequently pass over to others. In other words, he remembers not only about those who preceded him, but also about those who will come after him; accordingly, at one point in "Ktaadn," in the description of the route that he and his companions covered during one day, he enumerates the names of lakes, streams, and waterfalls, and defines distances with notable precision "for the benefit of future tourists" (626). Apart from its practical aspect, Thoreau's idea of exploration as a continuous enterprise has a mythologizing function, as the writer inscribes the history of the expeditions in the state of Maine among the lasting effects of the discovery of America. In one of the concluding passages in "Ktaadn," he writes:

> I am reminded by my journey how exceedingly new this country still is. You have only to travel for a few days into the interior and back parts even of many of the old States, to come to that very America which the Northmen, and Cabot, and Gosnold, and Smith, and Raleigh visited. If Columbus was the first to discover the island, Americus Vespucius and Cabot, and the Puritans, and we their descendants, have discovered only the shores of America. While the republic has already acquired a history world-wide, America is still unsettled and unexplored. Like the English in New Holland, we live only on the shores of a continent even yet, and hardly know where the rivers come from which float our navy. The very timber and boards and shingles of which our houses are made, grew but yesterday in a wilderness where the Indian still hunts and the moose runs wild. New York has her wilderness within her own borders; and though the sailors of Europe are familiar with the soundings of her Hudson, and Fulton long since invented the steamboat on its waters, an Indian is still necessary to guide her scientific men to its headwaters in the Adirondac country. (654)

It is interesting to notice that the acknowledgments of the historic achievements of discoverers, explorers, and scientists open and close Thoreau's narrative in "Ktaadn," providing a thematic frame in the first part of *The Maine Woods*. The writer sees himself as kin to a West Point professor or a state geologist, on the one hand, and to Columbus, Vespucci, Raleigh, Smith, and the Puritans, on the other. The great endeavor initiated by Columbus and continued by those who followed him is far from completion, despite the centuries that had elapsed since the discovery of America. Thoreau even indicates that the development of the American political system has proceeded at a much faster pace than the settlement of the country. There are still many important tasks to be undertaken, individually or collectively, because such are the demands of history, which produced great figures like Christopher Columbus and John Smith. In the conclusion of "Ktaadn," there appears a symptomatic shift in narrative perspective from the first-person singular to the first-person plural, signifying the convergence of individual and national prerogatives. America, with its boundless, unpopulated spaces resembles "a desolate island, and No-man's Land" (654). Admittedly, such figurative verbal constructions yield a disturbing effect in suggesting that America still has not overcome its unredeemed condition. It is thus understandable that Thoreau feels an urge to take action so as to change the desolate territories. In his view, the events and processes marking the course of the continental expansion give a misleading impression of its completion: "We have advanced by leaps to the Pacific, and left many a lesser Oregon and California unexplored behind us" (655). The very last sentence of "Ktaadn" reads: "Twelve miles in the rear, twelve miles of railroad, are Orono and the Indian Island, the home of the Penobscot tribe, and then commence the bateau and the canoe, and the military road; and sixty miles above, the country is virtually unmapped and unexplored, and there still waves the virgin forest of the New World" (655). The scenery in the midst of which Thoreau finds himself is the threshold of the New World. Probably it would be difficult to find another passage in his writings that would evoke stronger associations with the imagery representative of colonial discourse.

Thoreau's self-identification as a figure in a succession of historical discoverers and local explorers implies that he shares crucial features with these distinguished individuals. These features are, among others, heroism, endurance, determination, self-confidence, and physical strength. The necessity to confront the dark, hostile, impenetrable, and inaccessible nature elicits such qualities in a certain category of men into which Thoreau includes himself. *The Maine Woods*, more than any other of his texts, is literally concerned with survival, hence the recurring descriptions of the obstacles the writer and his companions overcame or the hardships they endured. As several critics have pointed out, *The Maine Woods* and *Walden* differ considerably with respect to the depiction of nature insofar as in the former text, to quote Schneider, nature "inspires not only reverence but fear—fear of perhaps being unable to transcend the physical to achieve spiritual meaning" (*Henry David Thoreau* 86). For example, in "Ktaadn," Thoreau highlights the moment of entering the dense woods, of passing from the familiar to the unknown world; the men in the expedition feel exceedingly energized: "The evergreen woods had a decidedly sweet and bracing fragrance; the air was a sort of diet-drink, and we walked on buoyantly in Indian file, stretching our legs" (603). Possibly, their excitement has been aroused by the concomitance of diving into the wilderness and remaining in the proximity of civilized settlements. However, their invigoration and possible bravura would have disastrous consequences, if the men were to forget that "Here...one could no longer accuse institutions and society, but must front the true source of evil" (603). When they visit the last farm on their route, they hear a story about how the owners had recently lost their sheep, killed by the wolves. Thoreau immediately comprehends the true meaning of this occurrence: "This realized the old fables of the wolves and sheep, and convinced me that that ancient hostility still existed" (613–614). Thoreau often writes about particular places on the itinerary in the way suggesting that those places cause a hindrance to human activities, such as putting up a tent or collecting firewood, and thus resist man's will. It is as if he ascribed specific intentions to the wild nature, as a rule, intentions opposing the human plan.

In his descriptions of the wilderness in "Ktaadn," Thoreau repeatedly uses such words as "grim," "savage," "desolate"; the positive terms of presentation do not really balance the negative ones. It seems that this kind of discourse about American spaces harks back to the rhetoric that was established in the age of great discoveries. Robert Lawson-Peebles claims that Christopher Columbus and Amerigo Vespucci, in their relations from voyages to America, created two varieties of rhetoric in order to capture the spatial particularity of the new land. On the one hand, Columbus perceived America as "Otro Mundo," on the other, Vespucci saw it as "terra nuoua"; accordingly, the former defined it in terms of otherness, and the latter in terms of newness. Columbus relied on a plethora of misconceptions that he wanted to confirm, while Vespucci hoped to find empirical evidence that would give him solid knowledge. Lawson-Peebles calls these two rhetorical strategies "negation" and "novelty," respectively, and says that they signify "an integral instability in the relation of text and terrain." He suggests that the boundless American space extends beyond the grasp of imagination, or at best furnishes the observer with "a cornucopia of unrelated images." As a result, "if American space both encourages and defeats the imagination, it encourages and defeats the linguistic structures through which the imagination expresses itself." Lawson-Peebles concludes that: "The rhetorics of novelty and negation, because they are based on a structure of rejection, are ultimately nihilistic. They can offer no positive way in which to construct a relationship between the text and whatever may lie outside it" (12–13). In *The Maine Woods*, Thoreau's use of the rhetoric of negation becomes visible when he resorts to the dialectic of the familiar and the strange, emphasizing the deceptiveness of agreeable appearances that feed the perceptions of space. Characteristically, certain spaces become familiar to Thoreau by virtue of yielding to the demands of his literary discourse; other spaces, however, remain utterly strange and inexpressible to him and virtually force him to admit the irrelevance of linguistic representation: "Here was no man's garden, but the unhandselled globe. It was not lawn, nor pasture, nor mead, nor woodland, nor lea, nor arable, nor waste-land" (645).

In his construction of what John S. Pipkin call "fragmented geographies" (542), Thoreau employs the rhetoric of negation as well as the rhetoric of novelty, which is best seen on the example of two descriptions of the Maine wilderness on the last pages of "Ktaadn." The first description suits the rhetorical model of negation:

> What is most striking in the Maine wilderness is the continuousness of the forest, with fewer open intervals or glades than you had imagined. Except the few burnt-lands, the narrow intervals on the rivers, the bare tops of the high mountains, and the lakes and streams, the forest is uninterrupted. It is even more grim and wild than you had anticipated, a damp and intricate wilderness, in the spring everywhere wet and miry. The aspect of the country, indeed, is universally stern and savage, excepting the distant views of the forest from hills, and the lake prospects, which are mild and civilizing in a degree. (653)

Lawson-Peebles's explication of the rhetoric of negation is applicable here, as this passage constantly refers to the observer's expectations and preconceptions, which are emphasized in the comparative constructions "than you had imagined" and "than you had anticipated." In one of the sentences that follow Thoreau writes: "The lakes are something which you are unprepared for" (653). The epistemological impasse is exacerbated by the condition of the body which, exposed to the emissions of the surroundings, receives unpleasant sensations. Thoreau identifies certain spatial emblems of the observer's cultural background so as to put stress on the difference between where the observer comes from and where he has come to: "These are not the artificial forests of an English king,—a royal preserve merely. Here prevail no forest laws but those of nature" (653). In fact, this is a very meaningful association: it can be read as an ironic comment on the English ways, but nevertheless it points to a factor that determines, to some extent, the mindset of the American explorer. This passage echoes all the spatial descriptions in *The Maine Woods* substantiating Thoreau's idea that, as Bob Pepperman Taylor puts it, "[a]t its very wildest, nature is no place for people. Beneath, or rather above, the benign nature Thoreau so commonly praises is an awesome, beautiful, 'titanic,' and radically inhuman core to the natural world." Taylor further argues that the writer's perspective on the wilderness in *The Maine Woods* evolves in such a way as to eventually harmonize with his pastoral longings: "that wilderness is less the central home for our civilization, a place in which to live, like Adam, in abundance and youthful pleasure, than it is a periphery that supplies the pastoral center with its necessities" (40–41).

In the passage that follows, the rhetoric of negation is replaced by the rhetoric of novelty:

> It is a country full of evergreen trees, of mossy silver birches and watery maples, the ground dotted with insipid, small, red berries, and strewn with damp and moss-grown rocks,—a country diversified with innumerable lakes and rapid streams, peopled with trout and various species of *leucisci*, with salmon, shad and pickerel, and other fishes; the forest resounding at rare intervals with the note of the chicadee, the blue-jay, and the woodpecker, the scream of the fishhawk and the eagle, the laugh of the loon, and the whistle of ducks along the solitary streams; at night, with the hooting of owls and howling of wolves; in summer, swarming with myriads of black flies and mosquitoes, more formidable than wolves to the white man. Such is the home of the moose, the bear, the caribou, the wolf, the beaver, and the Indian. Who shall describe the inexpressible tenderness and immortal life of the grim forest, where Nature, though it be mid-winter, is ever in her spring, where the moss-grown and decaying trees are not old, but seem to enjoy a perpetual youth; and blissful, innocent Nature, like a serene infant, is too happy to make a noise, except by a few tinkling, lisping birds and trickling rills? (653)

While in the earlier passage Thoreau sanctions the observer's expectations, here he removes the traces of the observer's perspective altogether; what matters now is the possibility of expression. Characteristically, expression turns out to be a hopeless task: "Who shall describe the inexpressible tenderness and immortal life of the grim forest...?" This question leaves the subject unidentified, as if Thoreau did not want to owe up that this is precisely the dilemma he is facing. His rhetorically accomplished style veils the inconsistencies and contradictions that defer the shaping of a linguistic descriptive formula and, in consequence, prevent him from ordering the surroundings in discursive terms. Importantly, the style also glosses over the writer's mood of "desperate disturbance" (Blair and Trowbridge 511). Thoreau's perspective permanently shifts, as when a broad, panoramic view of "a country full of evergreen trees" is immediately followed by a kind of close-up of "the ground dotted with...berries." It seems that the writer acts on an urge to collect as much data as the circumstances permit, hence his neighboring enumerations of tree species and fish species. There is a possibility that sensory impressions will cause disorientation, because the visual stimuli (the elements of the landscape) do not converge with auditory sensations (the noises made by different kinds of birds).

Thoreau says what happens in the Maine woods "at night" only to add what happens there "in summer," thus mixing up, as if in haste, two incompatible temporal contexts. He names several different sounds made by birds, and thus particular for the natural environment (the note, the scream, the laugh, the whistle), and then asserts that "Nature...is too happy to make a noise"; "a few tinkling, lisping birds" suddenly become insignificant. Eventually, decay signifies "a perpetual youth." The passage signals the existence of a number of linguistic possibilities, but none of these possibilities is fully realized. A comprehensive description of the wilderness sinks into the ambivalence of changing perspectives, divergent temporal sequences, varied evidence of the senses, and, last but not least, literal and figurative linguistic constructions. David R. Foster writes: "In his quest to understand the landscape that surrounded him, Thoreau became a historian of nature, using a diverse range of clues in the natural world as well as human records to reconstruct landscape and forest history" (184). The conclusion of "Ktaadn" shows Thoreau at a moment of crisis when all such clues have proven to be of no avail: "What lurks at the very quick of shifting experiences of landscape cannot be seized upon in, patterned, and limned in any particular way... In Thoreauvian space the world of 'mirage' does not yield at last to one more deceptively stable mirage, but rather to what remains imagistically volatile" (Abrams 250).

The stylistic modifications introduced in "Chesuncook" and "The Allegash and East Branch" can be seen as a sign of Thoreau's determination to overcome the impasse of representation. Among the most characteristic passages to be found in the second and third parts of *The Maine Woods*, there are catalogues naming the specimens of the local flora. Moreover, Thoreau wrote an appendix where he categorized, according to the size, the plants growing in the forests of Maine, listed the bird species the specimens of which he had seen during the last expedition, enumerated the items of clothing and equipment indispensable for successful exploration, and finally included a short dictionary of Indian words, mainly names of places, plants, and animals. At one point in "Chesuncook," Thoreau enumerates a few rare plants that grow in abundance in certain areas of the New England forests: "Labrador tea, Kalmia glauca, Canada blueberry... Clintonia and Linnaea borealis, which last a lumberer called a *moxon*, creeping snowberry, painted trillium, large-flowered bellwort, etc." (663). Interestingly, all these plants with fancy names have sprouted by a railway, in other words at a place transformed by man. Thus, the passage echoes the notion, present already in "Ktaadn," that human influence can affect positively the natural environment insofar as people know how to stimulate the land to make it yield rich crops. In a sense, the mushrooming of rare plants precisely "between the rails" (663) is a by-product of man's interference into nature. The effort to transform nature parallels the effort to describe it. It goes without saying that catalogues entail a gesture of linguistic appropriation that empowers the writer-explorer-scientist in relation to the object of examination.

In Thoreau's account, the transformation of the wilderness into an agreeable and productive terrain is seen as an inevitable process, triggered off by the arrival of the "civilized man":

> The civilized man not only clears the land permanently to a great extent, and cultivates open fields, but he tames and cultivates to a certain extent the forest itself. By his mere presence, almost, he changes the nature of the trees as no other creature does. The sun and air, and perhaps fire, have been introduced, and grain raised where it stands. It has lost its wild, damp, and shaggy look, the countless fallen and decaying trees are gone, and consequently that thick coat of moss which lived on them is gone too. (708)

Elsewhere in "Chesuncook," the writer predicts that immigration will considerably accelerate the development of the country: "Here immigration is a tide which may ebb when it has swept away the pines; there it is not a tide but an inundation, and roads and other improvements come steadily rushing after" (687). In general, throughout *The Maine Woods* there recur the musings about the fruitful merging of the forms of natural life and the creations of civilized life. For example, the places that have been changed by men, like clearings with log-houses, have an ornamental function in the larger surroundings. Thoreau's respect for the work of the pioneers whose settlements mark his itinerary is reflected in very detailed descriptions of their houses; such houses are a lasting sign of the unimaginable effort that the pioneers made against all odds. Man-made architecture—not only modest farmhouses, but also lofty, sophisticated buildings—harmonizes with the natural environment. Thoreau describes an intriguing fantasy he had on returning once at night to the camp in the forest:

> Being in this dreamy state which the moonlight enhanced, I did not clearly discern the shore, but seemed, most of the time, to be floating through ornamental grounds,—for I associated the fir-tops with such scenes;—very high up some Broadway, and beneath or between their tops, I thought I saw an endless succession of porticos and columns,

cornices and facades, verandas and churches. I did not merely fancy this, but in my drowsy state such was the illusion. I fairly lost myself in sleep several times, still dreaming of that architecture, and the nobility that dwelt behind and might issue from it [.] (682) [1]

Interestingly, what brings Thoreau back to full consciousness is the sound made by an Indian guide to attract a moose.

Admittedly, the domestic setting, whether real or imaginary, has a soothing effect on Thoreau. As Richard Bridgman points out, "Thoreau's feelings of insecurity in the backwoods may help to explain why, whenever he came to a settlement, no matter how small, his language always posited an urban growth to come"; "Tedious, complacent, materialistic as it might be, the domesticity of a town had protective features attractive to Thoreau" (*Dark Thoreau* 217). In contrast with *Walden*, where the writer examines the activities betokening of the human inclination toward excess and exaggeration (in the chapter "Economy"), in *The Maine Woods* he concentrates on those activities that are associated with order, balance, and permanence. In particular, the work of the pioneers who founded farms in far-off places shows the benefits coming from a wise use of the natural resources. The unique skill that farmers possess is the ability to accommodate their needs and plans to the process of the regeneration of nature. In this respect, they stand in opposition to lumbermen who use the resources in an excessive, and therefore abusive, manner, thus making regeneration impossible. Importantly, the wise use of the land and its resources is a sign of the human control over nature; for Thoreau, such control is a positive state and should be maintained. Moreover, he claims that Americans have a national interest in preserving nature in its entire richness. "Chesuncook" ends with the following rhetorical question: "Why should not we, who have renounced the king's authority, have our national preserves...in which the bear and the panther, and some even of the hunter race, may still exist...not for idle sport or food, but for inspiration and our own true re-creation?" (712). Thoreau's construction of the natural imagery echoes the spatial imaginings characteristic of colonial discourse; as Thomas Hallock observes: "Images of nature, which suggested how the land should be used, presumed to establish a grounds for possession where little existed" (8).

It is worth mentioning that there is a crucial difference between "Ktaadn" and the later parts of *The Maine Woods* with regard to the presentation of the attempts at subjugating nature, and thus accomplishing the acts of will. In the former narrative, Thoreau reminisces about the time when he and his companions found themselves in "a savage and dreary scenery," where they camped for the night. The place was exceptionally damp, and they feared they would not light a fire, but they eventually did: "but fire prevailed at last, and blazed here, too, like a good citizen of the world" (639). Here, nature is a powerful and resistant force, symbolically challenged by man in small gestures only. The dissimilarity between "Ktaadn," on the one hand, and "Chesuncook" and "The Allegash and East Branch," on the other, is striking, indeed, as the latter parts depict nature that is literally at the mercy of man. Toward the end of "Chesuncook," Thoreau writes in a tone of anxiety and bitter irony: "They have lately, as I hear, invented a machine for chopping up huckleberry-bushes fine, and so converting them into fuel!—bushes which, for fruit alone, are worth all the pear-trees in the country many times over.... At this rate, we shall all be obliged to let our beards grow at least, if only to hide the nakedness of the land and make a sylvan appearance" (710). In turn, in "The Allegash and East Branch," he compares cutting down a tree to murdering a person (769). He is appalled at the unfathomable brutality with which Americans sometimes treat nature: "The Anglo-American can indeed cut down, and grub up all this waving forest, and make a stump speech, and vote for Buchanan on its ruins" (769).

Thoreau's constant oscillation between the elation at the spiritual value of nature and the fear of the evil residing there, as well as between the need to control nature and the indignation at its abusive exploitation, account for the characteristic ambivalence of the writer's attitude. A specific subject that illustrates this ambivalence and which constitutes a primary theme in *The Maine Woods* is hunting. In his discussion of Thoreau's literary preoccupation with hunting, Thomas L. Altherr states that "[h]is published works and private journals reflect much intellectual anguish over the question of killing animals and much elation about that killing as an affirmation of man's connections to nature." Hunting was "an activity which both stimulated and disturbed his moral notions about environmental confrontation between man and animal" (345). In "Chesuncook," Thoreau admits: "Though I had not come a-hunting, and felt some compunctions about accompanying the hunters, I wished to see a moose near at hand, and was not sorry to learn how the Indian managed to kill one" (667). This statement carries an implication that the desire "to see a moose near at hand"—and obviously the only way to satisfy it was to kill one—prevails over the initial doubts or qualms. Thoreau thinks of himself as "reporter or chaplain to hunters" (667). The point is that exploration as a serious and difficult enterprise involves a certain division of responsibilities: there are tasks to be carried out by hunters, "reporters," "chaplains," and others. Thoreau and the hunters have mutual interests, therefore he manifests his solidarity with them by taking his own gun with him: "the chaplain has been known to carry a gun himself" (667). Altherr focuses mainly on Thoreau's journals where references to hunting are quite frequent and illustrate differing reactions on the writer's part. On the whole, Thoreau responded with curiosity to the news that hunts would be organized in his surroundings, accepted specimens of the local fauna as gifts from hunters, spoke of hunting as an act of mythical significance, and perceived it as a sign of romantic sensitivity. At the same time, he "found much repulsiveness, much impurity, much coarseness of motive in hunting" and "questioned the morality of humans killing and ingesting animals, or selling their pelts for a few pennies" (Altherr 348–355).

The ambivalence that marks Thoreau's understanding of nature may be taken to imply that the writer found the discourse of empire appealing and inspiring, while he did not support the imperial political plans of his nation. In *The Maine Woods*, there are certain themes, tropes, and kinds of imagery that echo the traditional colonialist presumptions. First of all, Thoreau believes that he has made a modest contribution to the history of the exploration of America, the process initiated by the great discoverers whose names he mentions with reverence. Just as he has benefited from the accounts written by earlier explorers, he hopes that those who will follow him into the woods of Maine will find his testimony useful; therefore it can be said that there is a notion of a service to be done, or a mission to be accomplished, underlying his writerly effort. Unlike *Walden*, which is centered on the idea of man's unity with nature, *The Maine Woods* combines this idea with the opposite concept of confronting and subjugating nature. Symptomatically, this confrontation is ultimately motivated less by the human intention than by the external conditions. Such an idea of necessity evidently derives from the colonial discourse that often justified the imperial rule in terms of the progressive historical change. Furthermore, Thoreau believes that human presence can have a redeeming effect on the wilderness, and he describes the settlements of pioneers-farmers as the emblems of great achievement. In general, he talks about exploration and settlement in heroic terms, emphasizing the sacrifices that the pursuit of these goals inevitably entails.[2] Alongside the theme of the confrontation with nature, attuned to the generic pattern of the narrative of exploration, another subject that illustrates Thoreau's use of the American discourse of empire, with its colonialist underpinnings, is the encounter with the natives. Again, *Walden* can serve as a contrasting point of reference; namely, in that book, Thoreau repeatedly talks about the aborigine as an avatar of balanced existence. The aborigine is an abstraction, a projection of the writer's longings, desires, beliefs, and sentiments, therefore he can afford to idealize this figure. In *The Maine Woods*, conversely, the Indians are living beings, and the encounters with them provoke Thoreau to express a mixture of sincere respect with prejudice and suspicion, and thus to reveal racial preconceptions shared by his contemporaries and sustained by the ethnographic literature of the day. With the tangible presence of the indigene, the wilderness in *The Maine Woods*, unlike in *Walden*, becomes a "zone of contest": "a territory whose contours are sketched as overlappings rather than boundaries, a terrain of mediations and equally of confrontations" (Jehlen, "Why Did the Europeans" 55).

The earliest important critical discussion of Thoreau's depictions of Native Americans is a chapter in Albert Keiser's book *The Indian in American Literature*, originally published in 1933. The meaningful title of the chapter—"Thoreau—Friend of the Native"—clearly indicates that Keiser subscribes to the romantic understanding of the writer's view of Indians. The critic observes:

> With his instinctive love of the native, Thoreau deplores that some poets and historians have spoken slightingly of the Indian as a race so low and brutish that it hardly deserved to be remembered. And in writing their histories of this country, they have in a hostile manner disposed of what they looked upon as the refuse of humanity which littered and defiled the shore and the interior. Such a historian, though he may profess more humanity than the trapper, the mountain man, or the gold digger who shoots down a native as a wild beast, really exhibits and practices a similar inhumanity to him, the only difference being that he wields a pen instead of a rifle. (218)

Keiser takes Thoreau's brave convictions at face value: "Granted that the natives are wild men, they are nevertheless much more like ourselves than unlike." He adds that Thoreau examined all the historical traces of the Indian presence and despaired over the moral and material degradation that the natives sometimes experienced. Kaiser concludes: "The influence of the Indian in Thoreau's life is so deep and thoroughgoing as to color his whole existence"; "The reticence and the stoicism of the native ingrained themselves in the very fiber of his being as he moved about the ancient hunting-grounds of the vanished tribes, pondering the destiny, and gathering the sacred remains of the former possessors of the soil" (228, 231).

More recent criticism on Thoreau's presentation of Native Americans visibly departs from Kaiser's misconceived, if well-meant, considerations and emphasizes the ways in which the writer's discourse reproduced the dominant racialized notions.[3] In principle, such criticism is indebted to Robert F. Sayre's pioneering, book-length study *Thoreau and the American Indians* (1977). Sayre claims that the primary conceptual framework into which Thoreau's imaginings about Indians should be inscribed is savagism, "the complex of theories about Indians held by nearly all Americans in Thoreau's time" (3). Savagism highlighted a variety of deficiencies that characterized the representatives of the indigenous race. It defined the Indian as a hunter, strong and self-reliant, as much as cruel and cunning; it juxtaposed hunting to farming, with the latter occupation signifying a more advanced stage of development. In general, according to the assumptions of savagism, Indians were incapable of any kind of development, hence they were often perceived as childlike. In confrontation with white Americans, Indians were the weaker party and as such they were "doomed to extinction" (Sayre 6). In other words, savagism explained the prognosticated extinction of the indigene as a manifestation of the law of historical process. Sayre demonstrates that savagism was a typical point of departure in Thoreau's studies of American Indians, even if he broke its conventions. In any case, the fact remains that racial stereotypes are present in Thoreau's writings, and that *The Maine Woods* in particular contains a number of examples of the stereotyped thinking about Native Americans. If the category of race signifies, as Dana D. Nelson puts it, "the arbitrary enforcement and institutionalization of Anglo superiority in United States history" (*Word in Black* 21), this is what underlies, to a notable extent, the mindset emerging from Thoreau's account of the Maine Woods. Klaus Lubbers states that "[e]ven Thoreau's frequent, if scattered, tokens of transcultural sympathy failed to puncture the ideological balloon that his writings as a whole helped to inflate" (71). In turn, Lynda Frost writes that for Thoreau the Indian is "a rhetorical rather than material figure" (24), and accordingly, the writer "keeps the Indian person at arm's length, ignoring the historical conditions that have shaped and continue to shape tribal life and culture in his attempts to find a prehistoric ideal" (41). Finally, Philip F. Gura calls the Thoreau of *The Maine Woods* "a budding, sometimes fumbling, anthropologist" who "[p]rior to his actual encounters with the tribes...labored under the romantic burden placed on 'savages' at least since the time of Rousseau." Gura believes, though, that *The Maine Woods* attests to Thoreau's "gradually increasing sensitivity to the natives he sought to understand" (241).

142   THE POSTCOLONIAL AND IMPERIAL EXPERIENCE

Toward the conclusion of "Ktaadn," the part that contains comparatively fewer observations about the life of the natives than "Chesuncook" and "The Allegash and East Branch," there appear two characteristic depictions of the American Indian, the one presenting a particular individual, the other an imaginary figure. The former is a portrayal of Thoreau's acquaintance, Louis Neptune; the writer says that, when seen from a distance, Neptune and his companions, wearing "broad-brimmed hats and overcoats with broad capes," could be mistaken for Quakers or "fashionable gentlemen the morning after a spree" (651). However: "Met face to face, these Indians in their native woods looked like the sinister and slouching fellows whom you meet picking up strings and paper in the streets of a city" (651).[4] Thoreau thus comes to a sad conclusion that Neptune and his people have reached such a state of degradation that makes them indistinguishable from the lowest urban classes. Apparently, in the writer's view, the ultimate moral and material degradation erases racial difference; this is the kind of conviction that arises at the intersection of the prejudices of the colonizer and of the capitalist.[5] His unflattering impressions of the Indians often result from the negative verification of his earlier ideas, in a word—from his disappointment. He went to the woods of Maine with a strong belief that the natives had a particular bond with nature that made them a unique category of humans, and this belief was irreversibly undermined by the Indians who were anything but proud, noble, and honest. Even those natives whom Thoreau respected sometimes aroused his confusion or suspicion. In his description of Neptune and the others, he symptomatically adheres to the familiar social context of the city life, which completely dispels the aura of the uncanny about the Indians. He further implies that not only is their appearance bizarre, but also their character weak; if white people bear partial responsibility for the degradation of the natives, the latter are to blame for not having resisted the detrimental influence.

Thoreau's tone changes immediately when he begins to write about what he imagines instead of what he witnesses; namely, he envisages "a primitive man":

> Thus a man shall lead his life away here on the edge of the wilderness, on Indian Millinocket stream, in a new world, far in the dark of the continent, and have a flute to play at evening here, while his strains echo to the stars, amid the howling of the wolves; shall live, as it were, in the primitive age of the world, a primitive man...In a bark vessel sewn with the roots of the spruce, with hornbeam paddles, he dips

his way along. He is but dim and misty to me, obscured by the aeons that lie between the bark canoe and the batteau. He builds no house of logs, but a wigwam of skins. He eats no hot bread and sweet cake, but musquash and moose-meat and the fat of bears. He glides up the Millinocket and is lost to my sight, as a more distant and misty cloud is seen flitting by behind a nearer, and is lost in space. So he goes about his destiny, the red face of man. (652)

Thoreau evokes the image of the vanishing native who epitomizes the "destiny" of "the red face of man." The writer and the "primitive man" inhabit two different temporalities that have intersected: "he shall spend a sunny day, and in this century be my contemporary" (652); the question arises as to what will happen when "this century" comes to an end. Importantly, the Indian's temporality is defined in the contradictory terms of the past and the future, while "this century" belongs to Thoreau, and the Indian is only a guest in this temporal realm. It is as if the Indian were placed outside the margins of the measurable or perceivable time. Moreover, Thoreau infuses spatial concepts with temporal significance, as distance in space enhances distance in time. The figurative constructions of time serve to highlight the opposition of permanence versus impermanence, the latter characterizing the natural ways of American Indians, who build wigwams instead of log-houses. The antithetical statements about habitation and eating manners echo the theory of savagism and establish a hierarchy where log-houses and hot bread function as signifiers of cultural superiority. The "dim and misty" image of the Indian engages the narrator's senses, especially his sight, and stimulates his imperative of cognition; dimness implies that there is something about the "primitive man" that remains beyond the observer's field of vision and beyond the grasp of his mind. This epistemological deficiency, however, does not threaten Thoreau's privileged position because once the natives have vanished—which is bound to happen—the knowledge of their ways of existence will have limited relevance. Helen Carr writes: "By the mid-nineteenth century, the idea of the Indian closeness to the natural world was another confirmation that Indians were backward failures in the evolutionary process, and must disappear along with the buffalo and the forest from whom they could scarcely be distinguished" (67). Indeed, in *The Maine Woods*, there is an evident correspondence between the irreversibility of the transformation of the natural environment and the inevitability of the gradual disappearance of the "primitive" race. In "Chesuncook," Thoreau even suggests that Indians have been partly to blame for the aggravation of the threat of their own extinction, because together with white hunters they have abused the wilderness by killing great numbers of animals: "What a coarse and imperfect use Indians and hunters make of Nature! No wonder that their race is so soon exterminated" (684). He discerns a strange solidarity between the hunters and the natives in their proclivity for destruction, but only the latter will suffer the consequences of the wrongs committed. Finally, "The Allegash and East Branch" begins on a note attuned to the theme of the vanishing American: Thoreau recalls his first meeting with Joe Polis, a Penobscot Indian who becomes a central character later in the narrative. He admits that the first words he heard from Polis made him think of "that strange remoteness in which the Indian ever dwells" (713), as if his would-be guide, and by extension Native Americans generally, were out of touch with the present moment.

Renée L. Bergland claims that the American literary discourse in the eighteenth and nineteenth centuries often projects Native Americans as ghostly beings: "When European Americans speak of Native Americans, they always use the language of ghostliness. They call Indians demons, apparitions, shapes, specters, or ghosts. They insist that Indians are able to appear and disappear suddenly and mysteriously, and also that they are ultimately doomed to vanish." The quality of ghostliness is connected with the theme of dispossession that recurs in the descriptions of the experiences of the natives and points to the discursive strategy employed by white writers whereby Indians were removed from the American land and transferred to the American imagination. Bergland observes that the prominence of the theme of haunting expresses "a dynamic of repression." In other words, Indians stand for unsuccessful repression of "our fears and our horrors": "Ghostly Indians present us with the possibility of vanishing ourselves, being swallowed up into another's discourse, another's imagination. When ghostly Indian figures haunt the white American imagination, they serve as constant reminders of the fragility of national identity." According to Bergland, the model of colonial relations determines the formation of modern subjectivity at the root of which there lies the awareness of America's historical break with Europe: "American nationalist subjectivity internalizes the colonial relation, but, since the nation was established by denying the validity of colonialism, American subjects repress this interiorized colonialism far more deeply than do Europeans." America originated as a European colony only to become an imperial power not long after gaining independence; both these historical facts evoke national shame, because they undermine the founding myth of "the denial of colonialism." In a sense, American Indians are seen as dependent and independent at the same time, and this self-contradictory view attests to "a continuing attempt to repress the colonial structure of America without giving it up." The reason why such a construction of nationhood should not be renounced is that it provides a formula for power relations that the majority of Americans of European background would wish to sustain (2–14).

While the notion of Indian ghostliness discloses a sense of anxiety on the part of white Americans, resulting from their ambiguous history as concomitantly a colonized and a colonizing nation, it nevertheless remains a reflection of the racial cliché that the natives were bound to vanish. The relevance of this belief for Thoreau finds expression in the differing styles he employs to talk about the course of Indian history and the present symptoms of its continuity. The aforementioned musing about "a primitive man" "in the primitive age of the world" from the conclusion of "Ktaadn" aims at mythologizing American Indians through the emphasis on their containment in the times long gone. The mythical aborigine is a figure of absence, and this absence accounts for Thoreau's respect for such an imaginary being as much as for his use of lofty language. Conversely, Thoreau's reactions to living Indians are based on a mixture of positive and negative impressions, with the latter eventually prevailing. His personal experiences from contacts with the natives strengthen his conviction as to the inevitability of their extermination:

> This afternoon's experience suggested to me how base or coarse are the motives which commonly carry men into the wilderness. The explorers and lumberers generally are all hirelings, paid so much a day for their labor, and as such they have no more love for wild nature than woodsawyers have for forests. Other white men and Indians who come here are for the most part hunters, whose object is to slay as many moose and other wild animals as possible. But, pray, could not one spend some weeks or years in the solitude of thus vast wilderness with other employments than these,—employments perfectly sweet and innocent and ennobling? For one that comes with a pencil to sketch or sing, a thousand come with an axe or rifle. What a coarse and imperfect use Indians make of Nature! No wonder that their race is so soon exterminated. I already, and for weeks afterward, felt my nature the coarser for this part of my woodland experience, and was reminded that our life should be lived as tenderly and daintily as one would pluck a flower. (683–684)

Thoreau's train of thought is meaningful here: a pronouncement, which begins as a biter accusation of white people who, driven by greed, abuse the wilderness, ends as an assertion of the Indians' responsibility for the forthcoming destruction of their own race. Even though the whites and the natives share the guilt for the degradation of the land's natural wealth, only the latter will face the tragic consequences of this. Moreover, the preservation of the wilderness depends on the awareness, attitude, and activity of the civilized man who knows how to live "tenderly and daintily." In spite of the writer's manifest detachment, in this passage, from hunters and lumberers, there is an ominous similarity between the results of the hunters' use of rifles or the lumberers' use of axes and of Thoreau's use of the pen. Namely, in identifying himself as the true defender of the wilderness and, by extension, in lessening the analogous role of the indigenous inhabitants, he implies that Indians in fact have become redundant.

Thoreau does not cherish any profound sentiments for American Indians unless they live up to the model aboriginal figure of his own invention, which they usually do not, therefore he reveals his prejudices quite freely. For example, he recalls a situation when he and his companions were to decide whether they would spend the night at a camp of the lumberers or at a nearby camp of the Indians. Thoreau was not excited about either possibility because the lumberers as much as the Indians emitted very foul smell; in the end, he found the Indian smell more tolerable (694). Elsewhere, he writes about a visit to a big Indian settlement and stresses the natives' indifference to the necessity of tilling land: "very little land was cultivated, but an abundance of weeds, indigenous and naturalized; more introduced weeds than useful vegetables, as the Indian is said to cultivate the vices rather than the virtues of the white man" (704). Interestingly, Thoreau admits that the place was cleaner than similar Irish establishments. The recurrent comparisons of the natives to urban delinquents, poor farmers, or smelly lumberers, disempower the aborigine by way of making them appear to be part and parcel of Thoreau's familiar universe. The association of the natives with the lower social classes assuages the writer's apprehensions aroused in the course of his encounters with the Indians. Suffice it to say that on several occasions he suspects Indians of lying to him; he thus points to their treacherous character. The alleged ill will of Native Americans manifests itself most strikingly in their use of the white man's language for malicious purposes, which chagrins Thoreau utterly, because in his scholarly pursuits he cannot rely fully on the evidence provided by those Indians who have engaged in communication with him. Apart from the persistent fear that Indians deceive him, Thoreau admits to specific fears elicited in him by the circumstances. The best example is the fear of the natives' latent cannibalism, inspired by the tales he heard from two Indians who accompanied him during the expedition to Chesunkcook (696). The opposite of the treacherous native is the infantile Indian. In "The Allegash and East Branch," Thoreau extensively describes the manner of behavior of Joe Polis of the Penobscot tribe, one of the most memorable figures of Indians in American romantic literature; among others, the writer recalls Polis singing what he called "a Latin song": "His singing carried me back to the period of the discovery of America, to San Salvador and the Incas, when Europeans first encountered the simple faith of the Indians. There was, indeed, a beautiful simplicity about it; nothing of the dark and savage, only the mild and infantile" (730). The Indian begins to sing after he has wrapped himself up in a blanket for the night, thus he resembles a child in a cradle; the impression of his childishness is further enhanced by the fact that he pronounces the allegedly Latin words very indistinctly, as if he were gibbering. The vision of the discovery and conquest of America that comes to Thoreau's mind when he hears the song suggests that there is a connection between the distant past and the present moment, in particular that the infantile condition of the Indian reflects the legacy of the great discoveries. Indeed, the onset of the European exploration of America inaugurated the common history of indigenous tribes and white people, the process of the increasing dependence of the former upon the latter. There is something grotesque about Polis singing an utterly incomprehensible Latin song, but it is precisely this grotesque quality that constitutes a sort of measure of the colonizer's interference with indigenous culture. It is also interesting to notice that, in Thoreau's words, Polis's song expresses "[t]he sentiments of humility and reverence" (730). It is as if the Indian's humility elicited Thoreau's kindliness toward him. In any case, words like "humility" and "reverence" conjure up a cultural hierarchy; it is only too obvious to say which parties have been placed in it in *The Maine Woods*.

The deceitful Indian and the infantile Indian embody extreme features that highlight the divergence between the ways of the natives and the standards of existence in Thoreau's cultural environment. However, the sense of fundamental racial difference surfaces not only in the parts of *The Maine Woods*, where the writer shows the indigene in an unfavorable light, but also in those parts where he speaks of them in a tone of appreciation. Typically, Thoreau admires their unique ability to rely on instinct and intuition, which accounts for their special bond with nature:

> It appeared as if the sources of information were so various that he did not give a distinct, conscious attention to any one, and so could not readily refer to any when questioned about it, but he found his way very much as an animal does. Perhaps what is commonly called instinct in the animal, in this case is merely a sharpened and educated sense. Often, when an Indian says, "I don't know," in regard to the route he is to take, he does not mean what a white man would by those words, for his Indian instinct may tell him still as much as the most confident white man knows. He does not carry things in his head, nor remember the route exactly, like a white man, but relies on himself at the moment. Not having experienced the need of the sort of knowledge, all labelled and arranged, he has not acquired it. (735)

Thoreau implies that civilized people have a lot to learn from Indians: "Nature must have made a lot of revelations to them which are still secrets to us" (731). The question arises as to whether he really wants to be *like* a native; it seems that the desire that underlies his statement of respect for Indians can be articulated, but must not be fulfilled. Essentially, its fulfillment would erase some of the crucial differences between the races and threaten to destabilize the hierarchy that grants Thoreau a privileged status as a subject of cognition in relation to the object. All in all, in "Chesuncook," the writer admits that one of his personal aims during the expedition was ethnographic examination: "I narrowly watched his motions, and listened attentively to his observations, for we had employed an Indian mainly that I might have an opportunity to study his ways" (664–665).

As a self-appointed ethnographer, Thoreau relies primarily on his personal observations of Indians; in "Chesuncook" he looks closely at Joe Aitteon and in "The Allegash and East Branch" at Joe Polis, paying attention to the ways they move, work, speak, sing, use weapons, find paths, navigate boats, and so on. Specific sequences of the text in the second and third part of *The Maine Woods* could perhaps be seen as elements of case studies, given their focus on either of the two Indian characters. It goes without saying that if Thoreau treats his ethnographic investigation seriously, he must carry it past individualized depictions of his native companions so as to arrive at valid generalizations. However, Thoreau does not make general inferences too often, and when he does they are based on his own perceptions (e.g., "He [Aitteon], and Indians generally, with whom I have talked, are not able to describe dimensions or distances in our own measures with any accuracy"; 693), on testimonies made by other people whose expertise purports to be unquestionable (e.g., "The white hunter had told me that the Indians were not good shots, because they were excited"; 798), or on presumably existing ethnographic evidence (e.g., "Simple races, as savages, do not climb mountains,—their tops are sacred and mysterious tracts never visited by them. Pamola is always angry with those who climb to the summit of Ktaadn"; 641). The limited scope of generalizations has to do with the fact that Thoreau's Indian is surrounded by a mythical aura whose imaginary quality does not really harmonize with the apparent concreteness of the results of ethnographic study, even if such results possess their own indelible imaginative aspect. Furthermore, far-reaching ethnographic conclusions should derive from the examination of collective existence rather than of individual manners, while Thoreau's insights into the tribal life are quite infrequent for the simple reason that there were very few Indian villages on his itinerary, and he did not spend much time inside native communities. Importantly, this marginal interest in the conditions of the aboriginal collective existence entails the presentation of Indians as alienated from their communities. One could therefore risk a thesis that in its subtext *The Maine Woods* touches upon the process of the dissolution of tribal structures.

Symptomatically, one of Thoreau's particular interests in his study of American Indians is their language to which he reacts with a mixture of apprehension and fascination:

> There can be no more startling evidence of their being a distinct and comparatively aboriginal race, than to hear this unaltered Indian language, which the white man cannot speak nor understand. We may suspect change and deterioration in almost every other particular, but the language which is so wholly unintelligible to us. It took me by surprise, though I had found so many arrow-heads, and convinced that the Indian was not the invention of historians and poets. It was a purely wild and primitive American sound, as much as the barking of a *chickaree*, and I could not understand a syllable of it; but Paugus, had he been there, would have understood it. These Abenakis gossiped, laughed, and jested, in the language in which Eliot's Indian Bible is written, the language which has been spoken in New England who shall say how long? These were the sounds that issued from the wigwams of this country before Columbus was born; they have not yet died away; and, with remarkably few exceptions, the language of their fathers is still copious enough for them. I felt that I stood, or rather lay, as near to the primitive man of America, that night, as any of its discoverers ever did. (697)

This passage adequately reflects Thoreau's varied impressions and associations evoked by the sound of the aboriginal language. On the one hand, the language spoken by the natives provides "startling evidence" of racial difference and it delimits the territory that lies beyond the white man's capacity for scrutiny. While all other manifestations of Indian existence undergo "change and deterioration," possibly because of the influence of civilized people, the language turns out to be the true stronghold of the native tradition and, ultimately, a site of resistance. The awareness that there exist the spheres of the indigenous life that evade the white man's control stimulates the imperative to find means of executing such control, this is why Thoreau mentions the circumstances in which the Indian language would be made intelligible. On the other hand, the writer is fascinated with the Indian expression, because it gives him a sense of closeness to "the primitive man of America" and to historical discoverers. He mythologizes the vanishing native as much as he does his individual endeavor: the Indian language opens up a unique temporality where Thoreau resides together with Columbus and others.

The mixture of fascination and apprehension in Thoreau's perception of American Indians can be seen as indicative of the extent in which his personal perspective had been influenced by the American imperial design, since in his encounters with the natives as physical, and not imagined, beings, he invariably asserts his difference from them, thus explicitly designating them as Others and implicitly acknowledging his cultural allegiances. The fact that Thoreau was inevitably exposed to the ideology of expansionism and that his work reflects its impact on his way of thinking does not mean that he supported the political solutions propagated by ideology. However, when it comes to understanding Thoreau's approach to the American land and the native inhabitants, his dissenting political views matter far less than his imaginative, narrative constructions. The ideology of empire reached the minds of Americans through diverse channels, including the models of literary creation, such as the travel narrative, which, in Erick Cheyfitz's words, "establishes the verbal *forms* of conquest in their social, cultural, political, and economic aspects" (205, original italics). While Thoreau's manifest views departed radically from the prevailing political postulates to the point of opposing them, his literary constructions harmonized, in significant ways, with the tropes found in a huge body of writing that, in his time, was at the actual or virtual service of the American empire.

Part III

Walt Whitman: The National Trajectory

CHAPTER 6

POSTCOLONIAL WHITMAN: THE
POET AND THE NATION IN THE 1855
PREFACE TO *LEAVES OF GRASS*

Walt Whitman's Preface to the first edition of *Leaves of Grass* is a text manifestly highlighting the bond between esthetics and politics. This programmatic statement, expressing Whitman's utmost self-confidence as well as his faith in compatriots, has a double focus: poetry and nation. These two central concepts are figuratively combined in the opening part of the Preface where Whitman writes: "The Americans of all nations at any time upon the earth have probably the fullest poetical nature. The United States themselves are essentially the greatest poem" (5). In other words, poetry constitutes the core of and, concomitantly, finds its own final sanction in the American sense of nationhood, as if poetry nourished the nation as well as received its own nourishment from the nation. Accordingly, the poet—or more precisely "the great poet"—inevitably becomes the spokesman for the nation and accepts this ennobling and empowering responsibility with enthusiasm. Poetry, so to speak, is both substance and metaphor, it confronts the tangible reality and exists in the imagination. Exactly the same can be said about the nation. Therefore it comes as no surprise that these two ideas appear in Whitman's Preface in various conceptual configurations, allowing him to explore multiple dimensions of the American experience. Thus, he moves smoothly from space to time to habits to politics, in a way collecting the constitutive elements of American nationhood. This chapter is concerned with the nation as a rhetorical construction in the prefatory part of *Leaves of Grass* and with the way Whitman envisages his nation's hold on the reality of the historical moment whose imaginative horizon is determined, at least in part, by the awareness of the colonial legacy of America. The other primary focus is the ambivalence underlying Whitman's definition of the poet's role in the nation. This ambivalence expresses itself as a dialectic of integration and separation; as Edward Whitley remarks, "In the 1855 edition of *Leaves of Grass Whitman* crafted a poetic persona that functioned as a representative national figure and as an outsider on the fringes of national society" (463).[1] In the twentieth century, an analogous kind of dialectic keeps recurring in the debates over the place of the postcolonial intellectual in relation to his people.

The specific issue addressed in this article concerns the possible postcolonial implications of Whitman's 1855 Preface and, by extension, of his poetic project in general. There are several crucial aspects of Whitman's writing that postcolonial criticism helps illuminate. First, the poet's very intention to define American nationhood is meaningful; as the authors of the *Key Concepts in Post-Colonial Studies* put it, the nation "is an extremely contentious site, on which ideas of self-determination and freedom, of identity and unity, collide with ideas of suppression and force, of domination and exclusion" (Ashcroft, Griffiths, and Tiffin 151). They also emphasize the fact that the ways of understanding national priorities were instrumental in the establishment of colonizing projects as well as in the emergence of the forms of anticolonial resistance (154). It is interesting to notice that, in Whitman's view, the American nation is firmly consolidated, primarily around the ideology of freedom, while at the same time it still needs special guidance from poetry. Consequently, poetry serves as a vehicle for further national consolidation. What is more, the presence of great poets is a sign of the nation's maturity; the poet's independence, which is the necessary attribute of his greatness, provides a mirror for the nation's independence. Second, Whitman's musings on the role of the American poet yield interesting analogies to the pronouncements of the revolutionary intellectuals who emerged in the era of decolonization in the twentieth-century. For Whitman, just like for Franz Fanon, the major criterion of assessing the significance of art is the way art reflects or enhances the sense of nationhood. Third, one of the central subjects of Whitman's Preface is freedom and the political development that it conditions. Paradoxically, the notable frequency with which the poet talks about freedom or liberty makes one suspect that this fundamental American value is in some way threatened, and that Whitman wants to give it a stronger anchoring in language, as if words were to enchant historical contingencies. Fourth, while stressing the unity of all Americans, their dynamic commonality, he essentially envisages them as a hybrid nation, in a symptomatic way combining the idea of ethnic hybridity with the notions of class stratification and territorial diversity.

It must be emphasized that postcolonial theory should be used in the study of nineteenth-century American literature cautiously, because in this particular field, postcolonialism, which is a historicizing critical method, may involve interpretative procedures disregarding history and producing far-fetched or anachronistic conclusions. The reading of Whitman's postcoloniality, presented here, corresponds to Walter Grünzweig's nuanced view of Whitman's imperialism in the light of Michael Hardt's and Antonio Negri's analysis of "Empire." Grünzweig writes:

> I am arguing here that Whitman's poetry does constitute a version of imperialism but that its lyrical representation points beyond the repressive nature of this social and cultural formation in the sense that Hardt's and Negri's 'Empire' does.... Although this is not a historical reading of texts published almost one and a half centuries before the emergence of the term 'Empire' in this [Hardt's and Negri's] sense, it is neither ahistorical nor antihistorical. Rather than as a pseudomimetic reflection of an 'external reality,' Whitman's poetry can be read as a *simulation* of a speeded-up development of a globalizing world. In his poetry, he was examining the consequences of processes he saw by modeling them in his poetry—much like the future behavior of substances and products is studied by subjecting them to conditions simulating long term use. (156)

It goes without saying that there is hardly any ground for direct comparisons between the political situation of the United States many decades after gaining independence and the condition of the newly established postcolonial states in the twentieth century. However, where such parallels do exist is the sphere of rhetoric, because the discussions of the formation and progress of the nation are usually conducted on a more general level, transcending immediate temporal boundaries.

Grünzweig's article partially illustrates an important historicist tendency in recent Whitman scholarship, most visibly present in Betsy Erkkila's criticism, to consider his writing in the context of American imperialism of the mid-nineteenth century. In her article "Whitman and American Empire," Erkkila discusses evident imperialist overtones in Whitman's journalism before 1855, wherein he endorsed the doctrine of Manifest Destiny and, in particular, expressed his support for the Mexican war. She claims that "the expansionist political policies Whitman advocated in his journalism on Texas annexation, the Mexican war, and westward expansion become the very ground of the expansive and bound-breaking persona who emerges in the 1855 *Leaves of Grass*." She highlights the abundance of the metaphors of "size, space, superiority, conquest, and mastery" in the preface and points to Whitman's construction of "a poetics of national and ultimately global expansion" (60). Thus, Erkkila concludes:

> What Whitman's 1855 preface suggests, finally, is not Frederick Jackson Turner's idea of the ways in which the frontier influenced the development of American character and institutions, but rather the ways in which the representation of the "other" in Whitman's poetic economy—whether as the West, nature, the Indians, Mexico, the People, the soul itself—is meant to serve the 'jealous and passionate instinct of American—and specifically imperial—policies and "standards." (61)

What this chapter postulates by no means contests, but rather complements, critical insights like those formulated by Erkkila; basically, the aim here is to uncover, as it were, the deeper sediment of Whitman's political rhetoric and to demonstrate that the great paradox of Whitman's writing, and indeed of numerous other works of nineteenth-century American literature from Charles Brockden Brown to Henry James, hinges on the coexistence of postcolonial and imperial discursive strands. It is worth citing the historian Walter LaFeber who writes that from the early nineteenth century onward decolonization was part and parcel of the American imperialist project insofar as the American authorities often supported decolonization of the territories that were still controlled by the European powers in order to take over such control (24–29).

A useful tool to explore Whitman's understanding of nationhood is Benedict Anderson's celebrated definition of the nation as an "imagined community." According to Anderson, imagination plays a fundamental role in people's perception of where they belong insofar as a representative of a given nation can never know all other fellow-members, and yet he believes that he and they constitute a communion. Thus, the notion of "community" signifies "a deep horizontal comradeship" (7), which appears to be very much in keeping with Whitman's view of the American nation. However, Anderson adds that the nation, in principle, is imagined as "inherently limited," and this means that there do exist boundaries "beyond which lie other nations." As he puts it laconically, "[n]o nation imagines itself coterminous with mankind" (7). Anderson's description of the nature of "imagined communities" seems to imply that the psychological process whereby an individual identifies with the nation involves the collective unconscious. In Whitman's works, this process of self-identification takes place at a heightened level of consciousness. His Americans are more aware of where they belong because of shared affections; as Peter Coviello observes, "For Whitman, nationality consists not in legal compulsion or geographical happenstance but in the specifically affective attachments that somehow tie together people who have never seen one another, who live in different climates, come from different cultures, and harbor wildly different needs and aspirations" (87). The poet's responsibility is to help the people imagine themselves as a nation; in other words, the poet channels the feelings that unite people and gives direction to the processes of individual and collective identity formation.

It is possible that, in his figuration of the Americans *en masse* as capable of transcending all sorts of boundaries, Whitman interrogates the European understanding of the nation, especially in the light of the fact that this concept has its roots in European history. Namely, as Anderson observes, the concept of the nation came into existence in the course of three parallel processes that eventually, in the eighteenth century, radically changed the ways of thinking about ontology. The first such process was the disintegration of the religious community. Traditionally, religion helped people to define their place in the world through the identification with a virtually boundless group of believers: "All great classical communities conceived of themselves as cosmically central, through the medium of a sacred language linked to the superterrestrial order of power" (13). The common "sacred" language, even though it could have been available only to the chosen ones, like Latin was in Christendom, obviated the need to recognize the territorial boundaries of communities. What accelerated the dissolution of the religious community was, on the one hand, the exploration of the non-European world, which brought about the awareness that boundaries and different forms of culture did exist, and, on the other, the dwindling significance of the sacred language, as the circle of its users drastically narrowed down. The second process was the collapse of "the dynastic realm." Essentially, at the time of the rule of dynasties, state sovereignty was concentrated in the monarch, and, as a consequence, his subjects defined their identity in relation to the hierarchy the top of which was occupied by the ruler. The third process was the changing apprehension of time; Anderson talks about the "homogeneous empty time" in which "simultaneity is, as it were, transverse, cross-time, marked not by prefiguring and fulfillment, but by temporal coincidence" (24). It is tempting to think that Whitman challenges the exclusionary European ideas underlying the recognition of the horizons of nations.

However, Europe is a subject that never finds full articulation in the Preface, while it lurks behind some of Whitman's most significant considerations presented there, for instance those concerning the American nation's sense of temporality, or rather the sense of temporality that the poet ascribes to this nation. It is well-known that Whitman perceives time as the merging of past, present, and future: "Past, present and future are not disjoned but joined" (13). This insistence on temporal unity may conceal the possibility that time is a factor causing the poet's anxiety and disturbing the nation's integrity, which is visible in the rhetorical constructions Whitman uses to talk about the past. In fact, the Preface begins on a note of disquiet: "America does not repel the past or what it has produced under its forms or amid other politics or the idea of castes or the old religions" (5). It seems that the entire semantic potential of this opening statement resides in the word "repel," which immediately entails the question why America should repel its past. In other words, the very beginning of the Preface sounds like an argument against certain preconceived notions about the American condition as well as like a justification of the nation's heretofore hampered progress "amid other politics." As Robert Weisbuch puts it, "Whitman essentially shucks history.... [His] anxiety of earliness is such that the past is to be known only so that it can be avoided" (*Atlantic Double-Cross* 103). Whitman's temporal dialectic that involves the time "before" and the time "after" enables him to gloss over historical contingency through making an instant leap from "before" to "after" and through identifying the emergence of the great poet as the breakthrough. This shift is reflected, in the opening paragraph of the Preface, in the prophecy of the approach of "the stalwart and wellshaped heir" (5), the prophecy that immediately becomes materialized as Whitman's theme. Nevertheless, the past haunts the poet in the image of "the corpse" (5)—which Lawrence Buell reads as the figure of Europe ("Postcolonial Anxiety" 203)—indeed an extraordinary metaphor in a text brimming with positive meanings. Weisbuch indicates that Whitman considers the American tendency to look to Europe for models as a symptom of "death wish" (*Atlantic Double-Cross* 93). The metaphor of putrefaction recurs later in the Preface when Whitman talks about the dead being dragged out of their coffins to testify before the living: "Rise and walk before me that I may realize you" (13). The poet's subjectivity—and thus the subjectivity of the nation of which the poet is a delegate—is reaffirmed in a situation that involves a violent manifestation of power.

Violence appears in Whitman's vision as an index of physicality. In one of his self-reviews published after the appearance of the first *Leaves of Grass*, Whitman equates word and movement as forces that constitute the poet: "Every move of him has the free play of the muscle of one who never knew what it was to feel that he stood in the presence of a superior. Every word that falls from his mouth shows silent disdain and defiance of the old theories and forms" (Price, ed., 9).[2] In general, movement is a central idea in Whitman's writing, which is not surprising, given his declaration that he is "a poet of the body." Movement is crucial for the perception of space and for the sense of being in space; consequently, it has a formative influence on the individual mind in enhancing the awareness of sharing the territory with others. Whitman thus speaks of himself in the review: "He appears in his poems surrounded by women and children, and by young men, and by common objects and qualities. He gives to each just what belongs to it, neither more nor less. The person nearest him, that person he ushers hand in hand with himself" (10). It is understandable that the body becomes an appropriate metaphor of the nation: "He makes audacious and *native* use of his own body and soul" (Price, ed., 9, emphasis added). Significantly, Whitman depicts the process of nation-*building* as a performance of the body no less than of the imagination. In the aforementioned self-commentary, he asserts that: "We shall start an athletic and defiant literature" (9). The epithet "athletic" perfectly renders the ideology that informs Whitman's poetic works. It is interesting to see the correspondence between Whitman's idea of the poet who aims to shape and strengthen the physical and intellectual qualities of the nation, and Antonio Gramsci's notion of the intellectual who participates in the formation of social class, the process that involves "muscular-nervous effort":

> The problem of creating a new stratum of intellectuals consists...in the critical elaboration of the intellectual activity that exists in everyone at a certain degree of development, modifying its relationship with the muscular-nervous effort towards a new equilibrium, and ensuring that the muscular-nervous effort itself, in so far as it is an element of a general practical activity, which is perpetually innovating the physical

and social world, becomes the foundation of a new and integral conception of the world. (141)

Gramsci makes a distinction between the traditional intellectual and the organic intellectual: the former, "vulgarized type," "is given by the man of letters, the philosopher, the artist," the latter is exemplified by a person who performs the complex functions of "constructor, organizer, 'permanent persuader'" (141–142).[3] This is precisely how Whitman envisages his guiding role; he aspires to be "the seedsman" and "the culture healer," to quote Kenneth M. Price's meaningful terms (*Whitman and Tradition* 12).

The poet's attitude is marked by defiance; characteristically, defiance is not only an individual propensity translated into a political agenda, but also an essential component of the esthetic program around which the poet wants to unify the whole nation. Whitman readily talks about the significance of defiance for artistic creation: "Of the traits of the brotherhood of writers savans musicians inventors and artists nothing is finer than silent defiance advancing from new free forms" (14). The desirable qualities that he finds in art—and apart from defiance these are freedom and newness—are immediately acknowledged in the nation. In the literary domain, defiance becomes synonymous with independence; Whitman writes: "The fluency and ornaments of the finest poem or music or orations or recitations are not independent but dependent" (11). The transitory stage of art, manifesting itself in the persistence of inadequate, obsolete forms, corresponds to the transition that the nation is undergoing. Whitman wants to make absolutely sure that Americans will follow the proper course, hence his insistence on the poet's guiding role. To some extent, Whitman's assessment of the development of the American nation corresponds to Emerson's view of it, as expressed in "The American Scholar" where the author famously says: "We have listened too long to the courtly muses of Europe" (70), as if suggesting that many still do. Concomitantly, Whitman's concreteness implies that his determination to take part in the shaping of the nation is much stronger than Emerson's.

The variegated new nation is not yet free from lasting divisions that are a shameful legacy of history and must finally be overcome. When defining the poet's prerogatives, Whitman writes "a bard is to be commensurate with a people" (7) and constructs a catalogue naming the places where Americans live and the varieties of people who inhabit different locations. The kaleidoscopic view of America and Americans contrasts sharply with the view evoked later in a corresponding context concerning the poet's duties: "the attitude of the great poets is to cheer up slaves and horrify despots" (17). Taken together, the figurations of the elated poet watching the blooming nation and the belligerent poet confronting despots shed light on the process of the nation's transition. In the quoted passage, slavery not only evokes a familiar pressing problem, but it also functions as a general metaphor of the loss of liberty:

> Liberty relies upon itself, invites no one, promises nothing, sits in calmness and light, is positive and composed, and knows not discouragement. The battle rages with many a loud alarm and frequent advance and retreat....the enemy triumphs....the prison, the handcuffs, the iron necklace and anklet, the scaffold, garrote and leadballs do their work....the cause is asleep....the strong throats are choked with their own blood....the young men drop their eyelashes toward the ground when they pass each other....and is liberty gone out of that place? No never. When liberty goes it is not the first to go nor the second or third to go...it waits for all the rest to go...it is the last....(17)

Whitman's poetic authority derives from his ability to see or anticipate the threats, whether coming from the outside or resulting from the young nation's vulnerability, and to navigate his compatriots safely through such threats.

A possible threat to the national integrity is the language that Americans inherited from the colonizer. As Whitman himself remarks in a short essay entitled "Slang in America" (published in 1885, but written much earlier): "the United States inherit by far their most precious possession—the language they talk and write—from the Old World, under and out of its feudal institutes" (1165).[4] In his definition, slang is a vibrant and anarchic form of language that instantly counteracts the linguistic structures from which it has deviated as well as the social structures that sustain the dominant norms of language. Whitman illustrates his point with a reference to Shakespeare's plays that feature characters of extremely varied backgrounds, from kings to clowns, and show how the language of the lowly excels the language of the mighty in its liveliness, flexibility, and inventiveness. In addition, slang signifies the new in language, supplanting whatever has become obsolete in it, which is only a very natural process. Characteristically, prior to his considerations about the power of slang, Whitman clearly ascertains that English in itself is an appropriate way of expression for Americans due to its richness. Thus, the first sentence of the essay reads: "View'd, freely, the English language is the accretion and growth of every dialect, race and range of time, and is both the free and compacted composition of all" (1165). It is therefore very much in keeping with Whitman's convictions to claim, as Jonathan Arac does, "that the 'crealization' of American English is what produces its difference from the English that served as the standard of literary language" (49). Interestingly, the postcolonial critic Ismail S. Talib, in his recent book *The Language of Postcolonial Literatures*, apparently plays down the significance of Whitman's linguistic innovations, saying that it is difficult to determine what is so specifically American about them and that the alleged "'American' quality" of Whitman's poetry is a matter of "spirit" rather than language (50).

In an article on the symbolic importance of Whitman's innovative discourse, Wai Chee Dimock contrasts syntax and semantics on the grounds that they establish conflicting guidelines in the ways languageusers construe meanings of utterances. Employing Noam Chomsky's theory of linguistics, the critic argues that Whitman privileges syntax over semantics because syntax, governed by the principles of "substitutability and interchangeability" is "the wellspring of language, its source of perpetual renewal and perpetual regularity" ("Whitman, Syntax" 65–66). Dimock further observes that, in Chomsky's terms, linguistic competence as an innate capacity, at least to some extent, defends the individual against the threats that come from the outside and which can be generally labeled "political" (67). In turn, such threats can be linked to semantics insofar as semantics functions as a vehicle for memory. Notwithstanding the fact that memory consists in "the transposition of seriality into simultaneity" and constitutes "a field of spatial latitude rather than temporal extension" (73), it performs its work on language, leaving in words an impure sediment: "prior usages might have left behind memories of their passing, accumulated nuances and inflections that make it impossible for words to be quite innocent, quite neutral, quite pristine, impossible for them to begin unencumbered" (76). It goes without saying that Whitman's aim is, precisely, to recover the innocent and pristine quality of words so that they may "begin unencumbered."[5]

As if Whitman were not completely confident that the new combinations of words, constructions of sentences, or compositions of paragraphs could ultimately speak for themselves, in the preface to *Leaves of Grass* he readily comes up with an ideological explanation why, in his own words, "[t]he English language befriends the grand American expression" (25).[6] The initial conditional recognition of English as "brawny *enough* and limber and full *enough*" (25; italics mine) is immediately replaced by its full embrace: "It is the powerful language of resistance."

Characteristically, what follows is a meaningful addition that "it is the dialect of common sense" (25).[7] In this way, Whitman puts an equation mark between resistance and common sense. Essentially, his insistence on the absolute necessity to be resistant has to do with his acute awareness of the permanence of hierarchical structures. Poetry is meant to counteract such structures: "The American bard shall delineate no class of persons nor one or two out of the strata of interest nor love most nor truth most nor the soul most nor the body most.... and not be for the eastern states more than the western or the northern states more than the southern" (15). It is, as if, resistance were for Whitman primarily a preventive measure. His poet is proud and enthusiastic as much as he is alert. Accordingly, it is only understandable that Whitman reminds Americans how much they have to lose: "When the memories of the old martyrs are faded utterly away.... when the large names of patriots are laughed at in the public halls from the lips of the orators.... when the boys are no more christened after the same but christened after tyrants and traitors instead" (17). It is important to note that there is a discernible apocalyptic undertone in this passage, suggesting the possibility of the Americans' fall into an unredeemed condition.

Whitman's view of the nation could be described, in E J. Hobsbawm's terms, as "revolutionary-democratic," which essentially means that for the author of *Leaves of Grass* the nation should be equated, first of all, with the people, and only second of all, with the state. Hobsbawm's discussion of the concepts of nation revolves around the formula "state = nation = people"; thus, what characterizes the "nation-people" is "the common interest against particular interests, the common good against privilege" (20). Such nation-defining factors as "ethnicity, common language, religion, territory and common historical memories" (20), providing the foundation for the nation-state, are of lesser significance for the nation-people. Hobsbawm also adds that the existence of the nation-state is inextricably connected with the establishment of political entities, such as the parliament, the government, and so on. While the concept of the nation-people is central in the preface to *Leaves of Grass*, that of the nation-state is also present there. For one thing, Whitman talks about the American land, highlighting its richness. For another, he emphasizes the potential of the English language to express the revolutionary achievement of America: "It is the chosen tongue to express growth faith self-esteem freedom justice equality friendliness amplitude prudence decision and courage" (25). Both territory and language help define the nation-state. However, perhaps the best illustration of how the idea of the nation-state is treated in the Preface is Whitman's assertion that the poet excels the president as the natural authority: "Their Presidents shall not be their common referee so much as their poets shall" (8). The remark about the limited power of the presidents in contrast with the great authority embodied by the poets is very telling because it implies that the two groups compete for national leadership. Daniel Aaron writes about certain ambiguities underlying Whitman's respect for the Founding Fathers. One the one hand, from his early childhood he was exposed to and himself keenly embraced the patriotic legacy of the Founding Fathers, after whom some of his brothers had been named, though he unconditionally revered only George Washington. On the other hand, with the passage of time, he came to believe that the political project initiated by the Founding Fathers had been corrupted by their narrow-minded successors (47–48). As Betsy Erkkila puts it: "Whitman came of age at a time when the racial, sexual, economic, and class contradictions that were left unresolved at the time of the nation's founding were beginning to tear the American union apart at the seams" ("Public Love" 118–119). Aaron points out that "Whitman never devoted a whole poem or substantial prose work to the Constitution or to the men who designed and defended it and agitated for its adoption" (49). Even if, as Mitchell Meltzer persuasively argues, "the constitutional poetics," the essence of which is "a secular revelation," informs the works of most of the writers of the American Renaissance (1–6), in Whitman's writings, it translates itself into a "spirit" that is felt rather than into a tangible theme. References to the time of the struggle for independence or to the historical figures from that time are easier to find in Whitman's journalism than in his poetry, as if he were hesitant to fully incorporate the Revolution and its aftermath into the poetic vision of the birth of the nation. In the preface, the presence of the legacy of the Revolution is a far cry from ostensible; the line that reads: "the haughty defiance of '76, and the war and peace and formation of the constitution" (8) appears in a long catalogue that deprives the events named of any hierarchical significance among the many other developments mentioned. Furthermore, "political liberty" becomes an absolute value in itself, free from any contextual contingency. In Whitman's assessment, the fundamental difference between the poet and the politician is that the former is ready to renounce his selfhood for the sake of the nation, while the latter never forgets about self-interest. It is also interesting to see that the historical religious origins of America are hardly acknowledged in Whitman's poetic discourse. This should not be surprising, given Whitman's intention to inextricably connect the religious and political roots of his nation with its poetic beginnings. Great poetry must contain both religion and politics, this is why his own poetry is so infused with religious and political meanings. At the same time, without poetry, politics and religion are useless endeavors.

The text that most directly expresses Whitman's disenchantment with American politics is "The Eighteenth Presidency," a political tract of sorts, which was composed in 1856, but saw print as late as 1928. This text was inspired by the immediate political situation, namely by the announcement that James Buchanan of Pennsylvania and Millard Filmore of New York would be running for presidency, the news that aroused Whitman's utmost indignation since he saw both politicians as embodiments of the worst corruption on the congressional and governmental level.[8] It is symptomatic that such two different texts as the preface to *Leaves of Grass* and "The Eighteenth Presidency!" were written within the time span of more or less one year. They contain contrasting visions of America, and yet Whitman's recognizable rhetoric and imagery serve as links between them and provoke one to think about how the two visions are related. Essentially, "The Eighteenth Presidency!" as a text with a more dubious, but still discernible, mythopoeic intention, sheds light on the immense work of imagination that Whitman performs in the preface. In the opening part of "The Eighteenth Presidency!," Whitman meaningfully divides history into the time before and after "the American era": "Before the American era, the programme of classes of a nation read thus, first the king, second the noblemen and gentry, third the great mass of mechanics, farmers, men following the water, and all laboring persons" (1307). To Whitman's chagrin, the change that had taken place during "the American era" had not been radical enough. The symptom of the unfinished transformation is that American politicians have conserved quasi-colonial structures of hegemony, heavily reminiscent of feudalism: "The sixteenth and seventeenth terms of the American Presidency have shown that the villainy and shallowness of great rulers are just as eligible to these states as to any foreign despotism, kingdom, or empire—there is not a bit of difference" (1310). There runs a deep divide between those who are in power and benefit from it and those who do not participate in power, especially the power represented by institutions. This division perhaps resembles the one between the colonizers and the colonized, with the exception that Whitman's "American young men" are "a different superior race" (1314), fully confident in their strength and cherishing the insurgent spirit in themselves. Interestingly, just as he does in the preface, Whitman evokes the imagery of bodily putrefaction for the figurative representation of shameful social deeds or political practices. Thus, having formulated the question: "Whence then do these nominating dictators of America year after year start out?," Whitman immediately answers: "from political hearses, and from the coffins inside, and from the shrouds inside of the coffins; from the tumors and abscesses of the land; from the skeletons and skulls in the vaults of the federal almshouses; from the running sores of the great cities" (1313). The transposition of the metaphor of decay from the transnational context in the Preface to the national in "The Eighteenth Presidency!" implies that Whitman finds a broad range of uses for the kind of imagery that first appeared in his anticolonial discourse.

In the 1855 Preface to *Leaves of Grass* as well as in "The Eighteenth Presidency!," Whitman's assertiveness borders on aggressiveness. In the Preface, this is visible not only in the figurative image of the dead removed forcibly from their coffins, but also in the militant tone of some passages:

> He [the poet] is the equalizer of his age and land...In war he is the most deadly force of the war. Who recruits him recruits horse and foot...he fetches parks of artillery the best that engineer ever knew. If the time becomes slothful and heavy he knows how to arouse it...he can make every word he speaks draw blood...He is no arguer...he is judgment. He judges not as the judge judges but as the sun falling around a helpless thing...Now he has passed that way see after him! there is not left any vestige of despair or misanthropy or cunning or exclusiveness or the ignominy of a nativity or color or delusion of hell or the necessity of hell....and no man thenceforward shall be degraded for ignorance or weakness or sin. (9–10)

In his essay "On National Culture," Franz Fanon describes different tones that appear in literary art produced at the time of the political transition from colonial dependence to liberation and which correspond to the stages in the development of national consciousness: "The lament first makes the indictment; and then it makes an appeal. In the period that follows, the words of command are heard" (*Wretched* 239). In other words, the achievement of liberation is reflected in the literary discourse in the replacement of the tone of lament by the tone of command. This change is critical for the shaping of national literature because it marks the emergence of what Fanon meaningfully calls the "literature of combat":

> This may be properly called a literature of combat, in the sense that it calls on all the people to fight for their existence as a nation. It

is a literature of combat because it moulds the national consciousness, giving it form and contours and flinging open before it new and boundless horizons; it is the literature of combat because it assumes responsibility, and because it is the will to liberty expressed in terms of time and space. (240)

Within Fanon's conceptual framework, the Preface to the *Leaves of Grass* can be seen as an example of the literature of combat. In Whitman's view, combativeness is one of the inalienable qualities of the great poet. First, the poet takes up fight whenever the circumstances demand this from him; second, he is a relentless judge claiming unlimited power; finally, he is named the conqueror: "The presence of the greatest poet conquers not parleying or struggling or any prepared attempts" (10). Whitman emphasizes the necessity for the poet to remain active at all times; indeed, he believes that the poet's constant eagerness to take action justifies his aspiration to become a national leader. To put it briefly, action functions as a primary criterion of verification; this is precisely what Fanon postulates in his essay: "The colonized man who writes for his people ought to use the past with the intention of opening the future, as an invitation to action and a basis for hope. But to ensure that hope and to give it form, he must take part in action and throw himself body and soul into the national struggle" (232). Notwithstanding the self-evident and innumerable differences between Whitman's and Fanon's political circumstances, the ways the two writers talk about the significance of literature for national liberation are so convergent that Fanon's pronouncements about the literature unifying the nation around a common cause, opening "boundless horizons," and assuming "responsibility" sound as if they echoed Whitman's enunciations.

It seems that the centrality of the poet in Whitman's Preface corresponds to the focus on the intellectual in Fanon's essay, especially that for the latter the intellectual and the artist are, to a great extent, interchangeable categories. Importantly, Fanon implies that it is not at all obvious that the nation's priorities and the intellectual's prerogatives should meet, even though the intellectual aims to produce art which is meant to serve the national progress and to express the national spirit. This is a more general issue in postcolonial theory; as Rumina Sethi points out:

> The requirements of a modern state and the aspirations of the masses are hardly compatible with a nostalgic retreat into culture. This is very relevant in anti-colonial struggles where a culturally imagined unification must work side by side with mass mobilization, the primary motive

being the establishment of an independent nation-state. The emerging nation-state, consequently, witnesses rapid appropriation of workers, peasants, minorities, and the lower orders, and enlists their participation.... [T]he intelligentsia remains separate from the subaltern, and the field of writing or rhetoric from the field of political action, although nationalist ideology tends to cover up its differences. (5)

Albert Memmi diagnoses a somewhat analogous problem in his recent book *Decolonization and the Decolonized*, in the chapters that have meaningful titles "The Failure of the Intellectuals" and "Cultural Lethargy," wherein he discusses the local intellectuals' inability to confront the existing despotic Muslim states (30–36, 40–44). Generally, the pivotal point of such discussions is the artist's or the intellectual's alienation. Franz Fanon observes that misjudgment or misunderstanding often underpin the esthetic forms that emerge on the eve of national liberation. Furthermore, he delineates those fields of artistic production in which native artists tend to wrongly locate their interest; for example, he regards the exploration of folklore as one of the most mistaken ideas about national art. In a tone of warning, he says that the intellectual easily deludes himself that the perpetuation of customs by means of art instantly creates a strong bond between the artist and the people. In fact, art which is an extension of folklore barely touches the surface of problems faced by the nation. Such art is banal and reductive; accordingly, it becomes anachronistic already at the moment of creation. As Fanon tellingly puts it: "Culture has never the translucidity of custom; it abhors all simplification. In its essence it is opposed to custom, for custom is always the deterioration of culture." Indeed, the intellectual who attaches himself to customs not only goes against "the current of history," but also "oppose[s]...[his] own people." Tradition possesses a dynamic quality that allows it to evolve with the course of history; custom is static and, ultimately, regressive. Fanon adds that the intellectual who stands in the vanguard during the struggle for independence may become temporarily separated from his people and later may strive to return to them through art which is a form of ingratiation (223–224). In his reading of "On National Culture," Imre Szeman rightly observes that

> Fanon commonly ascribes only two positions to intellectuals: either they are nativists, 'hypnotized' by the 'mummified fragments' of the 'dead-husk of culture'...or they have been seduced into mimicking the colonizer's national culture. Both of these positions distance the

intellectual from the national culture...that is being forged through the process of national liberation. (36)

In any case, apart from the complications involved in the creation of native art, what Fanon examines is a certain state of insularity. The dilemma of the poet's alienation is suggested in the Preface to *Leaves of Grass*, though never fully articulated. Whitman's grandiloquent rhetoric forecloses the space for the articulation of disturbance. However, on the one hand, Whitman says that "the genius of the United States" is best expressed in "the common people" (5–6) and "The American poets are to enclose old and new for America is the race of races. Of them a bard is to be commensurate with a people" (6–7), while on the other, he implies that the great poet lives, as if, both in and outside the nation:

> The greatest poet hardly knows pettiness or triviality. If he breathes into any thing that was before thought small it dilates with the grandeur and life of the universe. He is a seer....he is individual...he is complete in himself....the others are as good as he, only he sees it, and they do not. He is not one of the chorus...he does not stop for any regulation...he is the president of regulation. What the eyesight does to the rest he does to the rest. Who knows the curious mystery of the eyesight? The other senses corroborate themselves, but this is removed from any proof but its own and foreruns the identities of the spiritual world. (10)

It is true that, as James Dougherty remarks, in this passage Whitman stresses "the poet's visionary power to discern the marvelous in the commonplace" and recognizes eyesight as "the ideal symbol of his faith and the favored medium by which the poet discovers the path between reality and his own soul, and communicates it to folks" (22–23). But it is also true that Whitman declares here the poet's ultimate autonomy, if not altogether separateness: "he is complete in himself." Dougherty further argues that "Whitman here claims (as had Emerson) that this discernment is not the poet's unique gift but rather a power common to all men and women—active in the poet, latent in them but capable of developing if stimulated by a true egalitarian poet" (22). However, the opposite is not completely impossible; namely, the poet may possess a special gift that the people do not have: "the others are as good as he, only he sees it and *they do not*" (emphasis added). In the figurative sense, the poet is blessed with sight, while the people are afflicted with a kind of blindness, which corresponds with Emerson's diagnosis in "Self-Reliance": "Well, most men have bound their eyes with one or another handkerchief, and attached themselves to some one of these communities of opinion" (*Essays and Lectures* 264). In effect, eyesight as a symbol of insight may well be a very undemocratic gift. It is also worth adding that the above-quoted passage from the Preface illustrates the way Whitman gropes for words and metaphors when he says that the poet "is not one of the chorus." The word "chorus" has negative associations, whereas the word "people" evokes positive ones; the point is that the two concepts to some extent coincide, but the former lacks any anchoring in the political discourse and can be safely used. Such metaphoric shifts temporarily dislodge the immediate social or political context and contribute to the Preface's internal dynamics.

Whitman's assertion that the great poet is "individual" and "complete in himself" echoes Emerson's idea of self-reliance. Interestingly, unlike his transcendentalist mentor, Whitman continually strives to connect art and politics, the spheres between which Emerson discerns a kind of discrepancy. Emerson wants to see universal issues and typically American concerns as not necessarily overlapping, therefore he does not invest in his idea of the poet all those national notions that Whitman invests in his. In his essay "The Poet," Emerson thus describes the province of poetry: "The poet...represents beauty. He is a sovereign, and stands on the centre. For the world is not painted, or adorned, but is from the beginning beautiful; and God has not made some beautiful things, but Beauty is the creator of the universe" (*Essays and Lectures* 449). In the genealogy of poetry thus delineated, beauty comes before anything else, in particular before the nation. Accordingly, the ultimate nature of beauty casts doubt on the use of the national criteria in judging poetry. Emerson can only marvel at the appeal of the national emblems: "See the power of national emblems. Some stars, lilies, leopards, a crescent, a lion, an eagle, or other figure, which came into credit God knows why, on an old rag of bunting...shall make the blood tingle under the rudest, or the most conventional exterior" (454). He treats national interests in a rather dismissive way in the concluding part of "The Poet," where, on the one hand, he acknowledges the need for true American poetry, saying "Yet America is a poem in our eyes" (465)— though the word "yet" immediately undermines the appeal of the statement—and on the other, he admits that the qualities necessary for poetic greatness are, in general, extremely rare, so they are rare among Americans, too, and that he himself is not "wise enough for a national criticism" (466).

Whitman's insistence that the great poet be "complete in himself" thus involves a contradiction, since he primarily envisages the poet as part of the collective self. As Graham Clarke points out with regard to "Song of Myself"—but the comment perfectly applies to the Preface—it is "a celebratory text of the poet *as* America. It fuses together the self and its vision through the prophetic voice of the poet whose 'speech' redeems and sanctifies the nationhood on which its prophecy is based." The rhetoric does not allow for any "[i]ntrospection and doubt [that] would cut into its rhythms, disturbing the achieved surface sheen" (79). Paradoxically, then, notwithstanding Whitman's endlessly reiterated individualism, what threatens to undermine the power of his appeal are excessive personal imprints. Clarke indicates that the constant feature of Whitman's writing is "the speaking (singing) voice...always 'afoot' with its 'vision.'" More often than not, the voice is the only trace of the person. The critic makes an interesting point, saying that the poet's personhood may acquire a more distinct shape only when the prophecy becomes tangible: "It [the voice] can only be given a specific location in Walt Whitman...once the definitive terms of the poem's continental and prophetic claims have been established" (80). The Preface's underlying dialectic revolves around the conditions under which the poet's should be (in)distinguishable from the nation. Evidently, the voice is what marks the poet out; in other words, the poet's voice always comes before the voice of the nation, determining its forms of self-articulation. In consequence, the poet's voice, which facilitates the national consolidation, precludes his own complete merging with the nation. Assuredly, such a state can be called, after Kerry C. Larson, "Whitman's drama of consensus" (xiii–xiv).

Whitman is determined to create an inextricable link between the national and the universal; for him, being the American poet means being the poet "of the kosmos" (18). Indeed, this is the sign of the poet's greatness:

> As the attitudes of the poets of the kosmos concentrate in the real body and soul and in the pleasure of things they possess the superiority of genuineness over all fiction and romance. As they emit themselves facts are showered over with light.... the daylight is lit with more volatile light.... also the deep between the setting and rising sun goes deeper many fold. Each precise object or condition or combination or process exhibits a beauty.... the multiplication table its—old age its—the carpenter's trade its—the grand opera its.... the hugehulled cleanshaped New-York clipper at sea under steam or full sail gleams with unmatched beauty.... the American circles and large harmonies of government gleam with theirs.... and the commonest definite intentions and actions with theirs. The poets of the kosmos advance

through all interpositions and coverings and turmoils and stratagems to first principles. (18)

There is no arguing that, as Michael Sowder puts it, "Whitman tended to include the entire world in his vision of an America-like, spiritual democracy replacing monarchies, old religions, and worn-out conventions throughout the world" and that the use of America as a metonymy of that vision "had chauvinistic and imperialist connotations" (96). Surprisingly, Whitman's global visions turn out to possess very interesting hidden meanings when tentatively treated as enunciations of, so to speak, the postcolonial subject. Thus, in the Preface to *Leaves of Grass*, poetry emerges as a province wherein the nation asserts its subjectivity through a contribution to the achievement of the human kind. This desire may result from the fear of self-containment or from the impulse to forget, since, in a grand poetic project, it is a prospect that matters and not a memory. And while Whitman undoubtedly participates in the construction of the rhetoric of modern imperialism, he also dismantles the enduring rhetoric that had helped sustain the structures of colonial dependence for centuries.

It is interesting to notice that some of the most crucial postulates that Whitman made in the Preface appear a hundred years later, albeit totally independently from *Leaves of Grass*, in the writings of one of the leaders of the liberation movement in Africa, Amilcar Cabral (1924–1973). Indeed, in "National Liberation and Culture," Cabral comes up with the ideas that sound as if they were borrowed from Whitman: "we can say that the accomplishments of the African genius in economic, political, social and cultural domains, despite the inhospitable character of the environment, are epic—comparable to the major historical examples of the greatness of man" (61). "Genius" and "greatness" are notions used by both Whitman and Cabral, and although in both cases they have national or quasi-national qualifiers: "the African genius" and "the genius of the United States," they essentially transcend the national, territorial, or temporal boundaries that the colonialist discourse was meant to sustain. As Emerson's essay "The Poet" demonstrates, "genius" and "greatness" are transnational categories. Such categories help to assert the identity of the nation and to immediately reach beyond the possible limits of the national. Cabral further says that "it is important to be conscious of the value of African cultures in the framework of universal civilization" (62). It must be stressed that the notion of "universal civilization," which Whitman would supposedly acknowledge, preoccupies twentieth-century writers who come from former colonies, for example English-Caribbean V. S. Naipaul or French-Lebanese Amin Maalouf. Cabral insists that it is important "to compare this value [of African cultures] not with a view of deciding its superiority or inferiority, but in order to determine, in the general framework of the struggle for progress, what contribution African culture has made or can make, and what are the contributions it can or must receive from elsewhere" (62). Analogically to Whitman, Cabral sees national progress as a vector of general progress. It seems that this considerable convergence in Whitman's and Cabral's ideas has to do with their personal assessments of the stage of national development. First of all, they both examine the situation when there exists a growing confidence in the sovereignty and potential of the liberated nation, hence the crystallization of culture, the empowerment of the people, and the growth of economy. Characteristically, Franz Fanon who takes a much more precarious view of contemporary global politics talks about the deep-rooted antagonism between Africa and the West, concluding that a common destiny belongs only to African nations. In any case, it is possible that the cosmopolitanism, however vague, encoded in Whitman's writing at least slightly redeems his endorsement of imperialism.

It is ironic that, on the one hand, the ability to help shape universal civilization turns out to be a possible defining feature of a liberated nation and, on the other, universality was a central idea in the hegemonic discourses of European empires. The authors of the *Key Concepts in Post-Colonial Studies* observe that the insistence on the fundamental commonality of human experience and achievement that transcends specific social, economic, geographical, or cultural conditions was a significant discursive means of strengthening colonial domination for the simple reason that the colonizer's culture was perceived as tantamount to universal civilization. In consequence, universal civilization provided the ideal desired by the colonized; it was precisely this psychological mechanism of desire on the part of the colonized that made colonial hegemony such a lasting phenomenon, the symptoms of which would be visible for a long time after liberation (Ashcroft, Griffiths, and Tiffin 235–236). Whereas Fanon disproves the vested notion of universality, Cabral redefines it; the latter strategy appears to be Whitman's choice. Basically, such a redefinition consists in replacing the idea of universal civilization as a monolithic structure with a single source with the idea of a sum-total of multiple contributions with their own unique origins. The sources of such contributions should remain identifiable even though they become common property or common heritage. It is worth noticing that Whitman envisages "the poets of the kosmos" reaching "first principles" (18) and, in this way, he introduces the notion of tracing the origins of things. Additionally, the poet is "the equalizer of his age and land" (9) not only on his native grounds:

> Men and women and the earth and all upon it are simply to be taken as they are, and the investigation of their past and present and future shall be unintermitted and shall be done with perfect candor. Upon this basis philosophy speculates ever looking toward the poet, ever regarding the eternal tendencies of all toward happiness never inconsistent with what is clear to the senses and to the soul. For the eternal tendencies of all toward happiness make the only point of sane philosophy. (16)

Poetry is the art that disregards divisions, boundaries or hierarchies: "A great poem is for ages and ages in common and for all degrees and complexions and all departments and sects and for a woman as much as for a man and a man as much as for a woman" (24). One can risk a thesis that in Whitman's Preface the double bind between the postcolonial discourse and the imperialist one is reflected in the shifts from general considerations, wherein he acknowledges human beings as equals in all respects, to particular observations about America, in which his own nation invariably, and hence naturally, occupies the vanguard.

Whitman conceives of a literary and political project that enables him to embrace all Americans, even if, as M. Wynn Thomas points out: "Behind his startling innovations in style, form, and subject there lay in part a social imperative—a deep but unacknowledged need to deny the disturbing divisions that were evident in the world around him" (20). According to Whitman, the formative moment in the history of the American nation is the integration of all the peoples who inhabit the entire territory; importantly, this process of consolidation is instigated or at least accelerated by the power of the poet's word:

> To him [the poet] enter the essences of the real things and past and present events—of the enormous diversity of temperature and agriculture and mines—the tribes of red aborigines—the weather-beaten vessels entering new ports or making landings on rocky coasts—the first settlements north or south—the rapid stature and muscle—the haughty defiance of '76, and the war and peace and formation of the constitution...the union always surrounded by blatherers and always calm and impregnable—the perpetual coming of immigrants—the warfhem'd

cities and superior marine—the unsurveyed interior—the loghouses and clearings and wild animals and hunters and trappers....the free commerce—the fisheries and whaling and gold-digging—the endless gestation of new states—the convening of Congress every December, the members duly coming up from all climates and the uttermost parts....the noble character of the young mechanics and of all free American workmen and workwomen....the general ardor and friendliness and enterprise—the perfect equality of the female with the male....the large amativeness—the fluid movement of the population—the factories and mercantile life and laborsaving machinery—the Yankee swap—the New-York firemen and the target excursion—the southern plantation life—the character of the northeast and the northwest and of the northwest and southwest—slavery and the tremulous spreading of hands to protect it and, and the stern opposition to it which shall never cease till it ceases or the speaking of tongues and the moving of lips cease. For such the expression of the American poet is to be transcendent and new. (7–8)

Evidently, Whitman envisages Americans as a diverse nation in every possible sense, first of all recognizing its hybridity, which seems to stand in opposition to the exclusionary European imaginings. Thus the American nation comprises three races that are acknowledged in the order reflecting the mythologized origins of America: first "the tribes of red aborigines," then the first settlers and the waves of immigrants who came later, populating ever new territories, and finally black slaves. The diversity also results from territorial differences and social stratification, the latter presented as a rather neutral phenomenon. Last but not least, there is a touch of androgyny in the nation. Elrid Herrington observes that "[i]n registering the diversity of his nation, he [Whitman] is one of few nineteenth-century writers with a sense of the continent of 'America' as part of the identity of the 'United States'" (128).

Whitman's vision of the formation of the nation, constructed in the form of an extended catalogue, closes the sequence of visions that depict the successive stages in the emergence of the land and the nation and which employ the same stylistic pattern of cataloguing. The sequence begins with an all-encompassing view of the land:

> Mississippi with annual freshets and changing chutes, Missouri and Columbia and Ohio and Saint Lawrence with the falls and beautiful masculine Hudson, do not embouchure into him. The blue breadth over the inland sea of Virginia and Maryland and the sea off Massachusetts and Maine and over Manhattan bay and over Champlain and Erie and over Ontario and Huron and Michigan and Superior, and over

the Texan and Mexican and Floridian and Cuban seas and over the seas off California and Oregon, is not tallied by the blue breadth of the waters below more than the breadth of above and below is tallied by him. (7)

In this passage, the space of the nation acquires concrete contours as the geographical names possess a certain material quality, signifying something that can be seen and experienced and that exists within the poet's grasp: "He spans between them also from east to west and reflects what is between them" (7). Most significantly, it is the poet who performs the act of naming—"of mastery and transfiguration," to quote Tenney Nathanson (30)—even though he uses well-known names. The linguistic act helps to constitute what Anthony D. Smith calls "ethnoscape," "the poetic landscape [which is] an intrinsic part of the character, history and destiny of the culture community, to be commemorated regularly and defended at all costs" (151). The names in Whitman's catalogues create the permanent bond between the nation and the space therefore it is necessary that they undergo a kind of purification in the ritual of repetition. The geographical enumeration is followed by two other catalogues that further enhance the impression of the tangibility of the space inhabited by the nation and that illustrate how different planes of the nation's existence become interconnected. In one of the catalogues, Whitman enumerates the names of trees: "pine and cedar and hemlock and liveoak and locust and chestnut and cypress, and hickory and limetree and cottonwood and tuliptree and cactus and wildvine and tamarind and persimmon" (7), in the other the names of bird species: "wildpigeon and highhold and orchard-oriole and coot and surf-duck and redshouldered-hawk and fish-hawk and white-ibis and Indian-hen and cat-owl and water pheasant and qua-bird and pied-sheldrake and blackbird and mockingbird and buzzard and condor and night-heron and eagle" (7). Both catalogues strengthen the sense of the uniqueness and divinity of America. In his poetic discourse, Whitman reenacts the creation, with the poet as the one who calls rivers, mountains, plains, trees, birds and, finally, people into existence.

The correspondences between Whitman's description of the emerging land and nation and the biblical story of the creation of the world and man clearly indicate that he aims to mythologize America as the new country and the new nation without any historical burden. In fact, some critics have rightly pointed out that Whitman mythologizes the present or even the future; for instance, Biancamaria Tedeschini Lalli characterizes his mythologizing project in the following way: "the mythopoeic direction of a sense of present as history, American history *par excellence*, which translates directly America as history in the present tense: that is America as the place and time where the future becomes present" (21). The question regarding America before the great poet appeared and renamed the land and the people loses all relevance. Characteristically, as Tedeschini Lalli suggests, Whitman annuls this question by means of the very syntactic structure of the Preface that is written in the present tense. In the second paragraph, he defines the moment of the nation's emergence with the word "here," repeated several times in the anaphoric openings of successive sentences. "Here" is a spatial concept that entails a particular sense of temporality: here and now. Whitman readily acknowledges personal history: "To him the hereditary countenance descends both mother's and father's" (7), and concomitantly, he talks quite dismissively of what may be called general history, reflected in the European historical legacy: "Let the age and wars of other nations be chanted and their eras and characters be illustrated and that finish the verse" (8). Whitman's longing for a new beginning attests that what Lawrence Buell calls "postcolonial anxiety" ("Postcolonial Anxiety" 196) was a major factor behind the shaping of the American intellectual horizon in the mid-nineteenth century.

Chapter 7

Passage to (More Than) India: The Poetics and Politics of Whitman's Textualization of the Orient

This chapter examines the rhetorical construction of the Orient in Walt Whitman's 1871 poem "Passage to India." The interest in the Orient became noticeable in American intellectual life in the mid-eighteenth century and, not surprisingly, flourished in the Romantic era. Such writers as Edgar Allan Poe, Ralph Waldo Emerson, Henry David Thoreau, or Walt Whitman found important inspirations in Eastern philosophy, religion, and literature; in this respect, "Passage to India" is definitely one of the most prominent literary testimonies. Beongcheon Yu, in his book on nineteenth-century American writers' fascination with the Orient, argues that the American perception of the Orient differed from the European, of course in the positive sense, and thus characterizes American writers' view of the Orient: "What was unique about their response...was the total absence of literary exoticism and cultural dilettantism. At once existential and mythical, they responded to the Orient as a mandate of history, as a matter of birthright" (22). This chapter offers a polemic with such unequivocal critical assessments. Taking issue with the opinions that "Passage to India" "is, above all, the fervent expression of a deep-seated religious faith.... There is no point in trying to x-ray the poem for hidden motives; it must be read for what it is, for what Whitman wanted it to be" (Asselineau 87), the chapter aims to prove that, in the poem, Whitman constructs a subtext of Western imperialism, and yet he eventually casts doubt on the political priorities of the imperial project he himself endorses. Therefore, many arguments in this reading are substantiated by Edward Said's observations from his seminal work *Orientalism*.

"Passage to India," the text characterized by critics as "the most important poem in the 1871 edition [of *The Leaves of Grass*]" (Allen 135) and as "the last of Whitman's major poems on the grand scale" (Justin Kaplan 338), is symptomatic of the poet's use of colonial imagery, but simultaneously it raises a plethora of other issues, which preoccupied Whitman throughout his writing career. He explores the spiritual wealth of India and concomitantly extols the completion of the expansion in the American territory, and these two crucial interests become intertwined with each other within a broader vision of time and history. "Passage to India" shows Whitman, to use Ezra Greenspan's phrase, as "the writer in search of connection" (223). On the one hand, there are familiar "connections" known from the earlier editions of *Leaves of Grass* that Whitman, now a mature and experienced man, still truly desires and readily embraces, but there are also those that have gone wrong or have not been established at all, at times giving Whitman a pretext to express or at least imply his dissatisfaction with and his worry about the dubious advantages coming from the fulfillment of America's potential. In other words, the vision he has adhered to is no longer flawless.

Traditionally, "Passage to India" has been considered as yet another manifestation of Whitman's belief in the progress of the human kind, in the unity of races, in the merging of people's past and present achievements on their way to the future. Van Wyck Brooks's remark, stated in his book *The Times of Melville and Whitman*, which came out toward the end of the first half of the twentieth century, serves as a good illustration of this traditional view:

> In "Passage to India" he returned to this past and its mysteries and splendors in an effort to conceive the ideal world of the future, imagining a humanity born again in the union of all that was spiritual in the East with all the materialism of the West that was truly enlightened. America and its poetry, he felt, must merge with the past of Asia and Europe, and Americans should hospitably receive and complete the work of older civilizations and change their small scale to the largest and proudest. (189)

It seems that in the case of many critics, the passage of time and, more particularly, the growing skepticism and suspiciousness of late twentieth-century philosophy and literary theory have not eroded their conviction of Whitman's confidence and ingenuousness, the conviction which they share with Brooks. A noteworthy difference would be that contemporary optimistically-inclined critics of Whitman's later poetry do not repeat Brooks's rather odd and, indeed, compromisingly evaluative remark about the "small scale" of "older civilizations." Otherwise, even if critics detect some ambivalent rhetorical or thematic solutions in "Passage to India," they end up talking about "the deepest affirmation of Whitman's brave soul" (Warren, "Whitman's Postwar Poetry" 63). Wilson Allen writes: "Having always been fascinated by the history of the human race and its long upward journey through the cycles of evolution, Whitman now sees these events as symbols and spiritual prophesies"; he goes on to say that "with the lyric inspiration of his pre-war poems, he sketches the history of the race, saluting the restless soul of man, which has explored the continents and founded the civilizations" (135). Harold Aspiz focuses on the implications of Whitman's treatment of the theme of death in the poem:

> "Passage to India" commemorates the persona's imagined "outlet preparation" for "another grade" of existence as he readies to seek the mysterious God who will be his equal, his companion, his lover, and his ultimate Self. Thus the poem that begins by praising mechanical progress becomes a paean to spiritual progress and the ennobling state of death. (212)

Finally, one of Whitman's biographers writes: "The material civilization of the nineteenth century, its deep disease cured, was to evolve into a grand spiritual civilization in which 'Nature and Man shall be disjoin'd and diffused no more'" (Justin Kaplan 339).

However, other critics have attempted to trace the ambiguities of literary representation in Whitman's postwar poetry, in general, and in "Passage to India," in particular. These critics talk about the poet's shock caused by the Civil War, his skepticism about the more radical forms of social involvement, or his "conservative stance" (Reynolds, "Introduction" 11). Larzer Ziff observes that after the war Whitman came to perceive the American nation as a mass, which did not mean "the crowds on city streets nor the gatherings in the barn at husking time, but an imperial political entity." According to Ziff, the poet saw Americans as "a race of races destined to regenerate humanity, not, as Emerson had it, by providing models of individual man released from the prejudices of history could do, but as a swarming collectivity" (244). Importantly, Ziff's critical discourse counters the statements that favor the unconditional recognition of

Whitman's oeuvre as a national mythology. John P. McWilliams sees Whitman's postwar poetry as a "panegyric" that is "based on cultural symbols" and moves away from "celebrating the life force in all things" (230). A good example of such a cultural symbol certainly is Christopher Columbus to whom the poet alludes in several later poems. In her discussion of Whitman's portrayals of the great discoverer, Agnieszka Salska regards "Passage to India" as "a turning point poem" that reflects the author's disturbance over his inability to comprehend the American reality and to locate his own experience in it. She claims that whereas Whitman's celebration of the modern achievements echoes the nationalist interests from his early poetry, "Passage to India" is structured around a marked transition from the eulogy of civilization to the desire of a more spiritual vision. The Whitman persona not only "leaves the civilization behind", he does not "insist on the company of the reader or disciple in this ultimate journey." Salska concludes that instead of reconciling opposites, like material versus spiritual existence, the speaker simply abandons such a binary perspective ("Whitman's Columbus" 61). Finally, the biographer Jerome Loving thus expounds the paradox of Whitman's complicated political consciousness: "In 'Passage to India' the focus is on democracy, which must and will transcend its shortcomings but probably only (for now at least) by going beyond the material and the moral" (333).

Salska and Loving suggest the presence of political tensions underpinning "Passage to India," however no detailed analysis of this aspect of the poem's textual complication has been proposed so far, while there are articles on the problematic structure of Whitman's text, the most notable of which is probably "Passage to Less than India: Structure and Meaning in Whitman's 'Passage to India'" by Arthur Golden. Essentially, the author concentrates on the structural inconsistencies resulting from the fact that Whitman incorporated into the poem three shorter pieces, which, in Golden's opinion, disrupt the thematic unity and undermine the temporal order. Whereas it must be admitted that the critic's observations broaden our knowledge of, specifically, the history of the poem's composition, he seems to disregard the significance of structural inconsistencies for the political significance (1095–1103). Characteristically, James Perrin Warren, who accuses Golden of a kind of formalist myopia and develops a counter-thesis that all disparate elements of the poem add to its essence ("Whitman's Postwar Poetry" 55), similarly to Golden, hardly touches upon the political subtext. Finally, it is worth mentioning a comment by Hyatt H. Waggoner, who considers "Passage to India" "a failed visionary poem," in which "the vagueness of its celebration of the 'myths and fables of eld'" contrasts visibly with "the specific clarity of the imagery drawn from the present" (60–62). There are several discussions of the ideological significance of Whitman's construction of space in "Passage to India," constituting the closest critical context for the present thrust of argument. For example, Eric Wertheimer points out that "Whitman makes odd choices about history, for there is a strangely Columbus-like failure to recognize the New World as something geographical and historical, as well as new and different, in his dual constructions of personal identity and national community"; the critic considers this failure to be a sign of "a broader cultural loss that is related to the assumption of imperial hegemony on the part of the United States" (162). In Wertheimer's view, Whitman's India "is a destination without verifying content; the world before us—India despite the evidence—merely confirms the world desired and sought for" (180). Malini Johar Schueller claims that Whitman's depiction of the Orient shows the political currency of the American myth of innocence:

> Whitman's discourse on the Far Eastern Orient employs a strategic language of political innocence. While the writers of Algerian Orientalism embodied the nation as manly and virtuous, and while Near Eastern Orientalists embodied it through the archaeologist/explorer/missionary with the power to define, Whitman makes his poetic persona, as representative of an expanding United States, simply a strong, earthy male with an omnivorous appetite and a desire to embrace all. He is an innocent striding the world. Whitman projects his poetic persona, whose palms cover continents, as a nonchalant, amative self, and he presents this persona as representative of his contemporary United States; in relation to this amative self, the Asian Orient appears most regularly as mother. But while the imperialistic implications of this loving, embracing self are clear, the very idea of the nation as a lover necessitates us viewing it as a subject that necessarily derives its identity from interaction with the other. (181)

John R. Eperjesi also emphasizes Whitman's involvement with the U.S. imperialism as evinced in "Passage to India" which "appears to be directly committed to the commercialization and striation of Pacific space, to enacting, at the level of imagination, the time and space compression upon which political and economic expansion depends" (52).

This chapter highlights the interrelationship between the structure, rhetoric, and politics in "Passage to India," and examines the ideological implications of the geographical configurations evoked in the poem. The shifts from metonymy to metaphor are indicative of Whitman's suspension between the American imperial project, which he supports, and his personal doubts as to its means and ends. Accordingly, it is this intimate sense of division that makes Whitman recede into the vagueness of the final vision, presented in the three concluding stanzas of the poem. This transition can also be seen in the competition between scientific and religious discourses used in the text, or in the employment and subsequent abandonment of the textualization of geographical space.

"Passage to India" consists of nine parts, which can be subdivided into three clusters. Each cluster comprises a shorter prelude and two longer parts. The function of preludes should be ascribed to Parts 1, 4, and 7, as they signal the ideas to be probed in Parts 2 and 3, 5 and 6, 8 and 9, respectively. Part 1 lists the achievements that provided the occasion for the composition of the poem, and it also introduces one of the crucial motifs that is the recognition of the past as a direct cause of all later developments. Part 2 expresses the speaker's rapture over the new opportunities that are due to the opening of the passage to India, while Part 3 depicts the panorama of America, the grasp of which is now possible after the completion of the Pacific Railroad. This first cluster is, evidently, the most occasional; the further Whitman proceeds, the less specific he becomes about the particular historical moment he finds himself in. Part 4, which mentions "[s]truggles of many captains, tales of many a sailor dead" and "[t]he plans, the voyages again, the expeditions" (533), as well as the two consecutive sections anchor the greatest achievements and inventions of the day: the Suez Canal, the Pacific Railroad, and the Transatlantic Cable, in a broader historical background. For example, the speaker sees a continuity between Vasco da Gama and Ferdinand Lesseps; as he discovers more such affinities, established across time, the task he sets himself is to incorporate such series of continuities into a single, harmonious vision. Subsequently, in Parts 5 and 6 the speaker creates the foundation for the discourse that foregrounds continuity, instead of multiple continuities, and glosses over possible chasms. The pivotal point in the poem seems to be the conclusion of Part 6, in which Columbus is addressed and recognized as "the chief histrion," a man of vision, who was rewarded for his discoveries with "misfortunes, columniators... dejection, poverty, death" (536). Part 7 opens the "spiritual cluster"; in this one and the two parts that follow, the speaker extensively converses with his soul, which, albeit invoked from the very beginning, has been one of many concerns so far. Now, as the speaker intends to embark on a "Passage to more than India" (539), his soul turns out to be his only companion. Paradoxically, then, the poem ends with a hint of escapism.

As Whitman himself admitted in his notebook and as critics interested in the poem usually point out, "Passage to India" was inspired by the idea of evolution. James Perrin Warren claims that the poem owes its coherence to the theme of evolution and supports his opinion with quotes from Whitman's notebook: "Whitman focuses on the analogy between 'the long chain of endless development and growth in the physical world' and 'in the ethereal world an endless spiritual procession of growth'" ("Whitman's Postwar Poetry" 55). The poet shared his contemporaries' interest in and appreciation of scientific novelties, Darwin's theory of evolution being among them. He wrote an essay entitled "Darwinism—(Then Furthermore)" wherein he recognized Darwin's theses as a sound scientific theory, although there was a note of caution detectable in his considerations: "In due time the Evolution theory will have to abate its vehemence, cannot be allowed to dominate every thing else, and will have to take its place as a segment of the circle" (1060). Characteristically, Whitman goes on to talk about America, democracy, and the poet in the age of "dazzling novelties" (1061), which probably attests to a certain monological tendency in Whitman's writings. However varied experiences Whitman aspires to embrace, however many people he considers himself a spokesman for, he definitely privileges his own outlook and his own voice. "Darwinism—(Then Furthermore)" also illustrates the eclectic quality of Whitman's poetry and prose, which is easily traceable in "Passage to India." The poet's tendency to combine divergent areas is emphasized in Erkkila's observation: "The return to these myths and fables [of India] becomes the basis for a poetic and essentially religious rereading of Darwin" (*Political Poet* 268). Erkkila also talks about another inspiration for "Passage to India"—Hegelianism:

> "Passage to India"…is structured around a series of trinities: Past / Present / Future, Time / Space / Death, Man / Nature / God, Ancient / Medieval / Modern, Asia / Europe / America, Train / Cable / Telegraph, Explorer / Inventor / Poet. These trinities are rooted in what Whitman called the "triplicate process" of Hegelian evolution: "First the Positive, then the Negative, then the product of the mediation between them; from which product the process is repeated and so goes on without end."…This "triplicate process" of history is the poem's organizing principle and thematic focus. (265)

Darwinism and Hegelianism determine the terms for the embracement of the Orient—Whitman talks not only about India, but also mentions Africa, China, Persia, and Arabia—in the poet's vision. These two systems of thought enable Whitman to solve a certain temporal dilemma, namely how to reconcile two opposite notions of time: linearity and cyclicity. While there is ample textual evidence, for instance in "Song of Myself," that Whitman believes in the essentially cyclic nature of time, "Passage to India" gives testimony to his faith in measurable technological progress, as he praises the grand achievements of his epoch, which marks the moment of culmination in a linear movement of time. Darwinism, by all means, accords with such a perspective of assessing progress. In the light of Darwinism, ancient civilizations epitomize what had existed before the emergence of America, and thus they represent a less advanced stage of development. Such a view inevitably implies civilizational difference and resulting hierarchies. In fact, as Edward Said demonstrates in *Orientalism*, Darwinism produced a particular offshoot, "second-order Darwinism," which served to confirm the theses about "Oriental backwardness, degeneracy, and inequality with the West" (206). Perhaps suspecting the existence of such traps, Whitman discovers valuable guidelines about the positioning of the Orient in Hegelianism. Therefore, while Darwinism remains the formula for imagining technological progress, Hegelianism underpins the idea that the communion of civilizations is to be attained, which crowns the entire historical progress of the human kind.

Edward Said's categorization of nineteenth-century European writers who ventured to describe the Orient sheds light on Whitman's strategy of constructing the speaker as the figure of authority. Said discusses three such categories. One is the type of "the writer who intends to use his residence for the specific task of providing professional Orientalism with scientific material, who considers his residence a form of scientific observation." The next category includes writers "who intend...the same purpose but are less willing to sacrifice the eccentricity and style of [their] individual consciousness to impersonal Orientalist definitions." Finally, the third category, to which Whitman belongs, is reserved for those writers "for whom a real or metaphorical trip to the Orient is the fulfillment of some deeply felt and urgent project." Said adds that a text produced by an author representing the last group, is "built on a personal aesthetic, fed and informed by the project" (157–158). The critic claims that despite the evident differences, the three categories of writers reveal crucial features in common:

For example, works in all three categories rely upon the sheer egoistic powers of the European consciousness at their center. In all cases the Orient is *for* the European observer.... Moreover, certain motifs recur consistently in all three types. The Orient as a place of pilgrimage is one; so too is the vision of Orient as spectacle, or *tableau vivant*. Every work on the Orient in these categories tries to characterize the place, of course, but what is of greater interest is the extent to which the work's internal structure is in some measure synonymous with a comprehensive interpretation (or an attempt at it) of the Orient. Most of the time, not surprisingly, this interpretation is a form of Romantic restructuring of the Orient, a re-vision of it, which restores it redemptively to the present. Every interpretation, every structure created for the Orient, then, is a reinterpretation, a rebuilding of it. (158)

Part 2 of "Passage to India" provides a good illustration of Whitman's reinvention and reinterpretation of the Orient. First of all, the switch from Part 1 to Part 2 represents a transition from temporal: "The Past—the dark unfathom'd retrospect! /...The past—the infinite greatness of the past!" (531), to spatial imagery. Agnieszka Salska asserts that "Translating movement in time into movement in space to show their essential equivalences is Whitman's persistent practice" (*Poetry of Central Consciousness* 116). However, Michel Foucault problematizes such an assumption, usually taken for granted by most Whitman critics: "For all those who confuse history with the old schemes of evolution, living continuity, organic development, the progress of consciousness or the project of existence, the use of spatial terms seems to have the air of anti-history." Rejecting such a belief, Foucault points out that "The spatialising description of discursive realities gives on to the analysis of the related effects of power" (70–71). In other words, temporal representations seem to conceal the mechanisms of power, whereas spatial depictions allow one to trace such mechanisms. In any case, this is how Whitman perceives India and what associations he ascribes to it in Part 2:

> But myths and fables of eld, Asia's, Africa's fables,
> The far darting beams of the spirit, the unloos'd dreams,
> The deep diving bibles and legends,
> The daring plots of the poets, the elder religions;
> O you temples fairer than lilies pour'd over by the rising sun!
> O you fables spurning the known, eluding the hold of the
>   known, mounting to heaven!
> You lofty and dazzling towers, pinnacled, red as roses,
>   burnish'd with gold!

> Towers of fables immortal fashion'd from mortal dreams!
> You too I welcome and fully the same as the rest!
> You too with joy I sing. (531)

Thus, Whitman recognizes three principal emblems of India: its literature, religion, and architecture, and they have one important feature in common, which is a textual quality. The religion is to be appropriated through the texts it had inspired; not incidentally, Whitman mentions "the daring plots of the poets" and "the elder religions in the same line." The speaker's rapture over the wealth of Indian architecture resembles admiration for a literary work, hence the appearance of the architectural-textual metaphor "towers of fables." Emphasizing both metaphoric and metonymic links between literature, religion, and architecture and projecting these three domains as the signs of India, the speaker reductively generalizes the scope of Oriental achievements; or perhaps simply glosses over his ignorance. India functions here as an archive and, accordingly, a promise of knowledge to be acquired. The speaker feels excitement about the existence of the "fables spurning the known, eluding the hold of the / known," and his enthusiasm can be traced back to the prospect of unraveling the mysteries of the fables. If so, his motivation is reminiscent of that which explorers, his predecessors, admittedly shared. At the very beginning of Part 2, the speaker declares: "Eclaircise the myths Asiatic, the primitive fables" (531), thereby announcing a certain cognitive project. Whitman uses here the word "primitive," which does not have a pejorative sense, but adequately captures the Romantic benign penchant for that which is old and exotic. In Part 2 of "Passage to India," clearly a poem about unity and transcendence, the speaker juxtaposes the scientific achievements of the Western civilization ("Not you alone proud truths of the world, / Nor you alone ye facts of modern science," 531) to the arts and religion of India. In this way, he designates two separate realms: the Occident and the Orient standing for *techne* and *poiesis*, respectively, two opposing systems of values, structured in relation to each other around the question of power. In the confrontation of *techne* and *poiesis*, the domination of the former becomes evident, and yet the latter has the power to challenge and even destabilize *techne*. It is possible that this part of Part 2 contains an implicit critique of American materialism, which reflects the "proud truths of the world."

Postcolonial theory has problematized the idea of place and space in discourse and highlighted "the very complex interaction of language, history and environment." The awareness of space, which is so fundamental a factor in the formation of identity, often remains, so to speak, dormant until colonial intervention and the appearance of a new authoritative signifying system that replaces the traditional terms of defining space. In the colonial context, the interference of the colonizer's discourse "radically disrupts the primary modes of…representation by separating 'space' from 'place.'" Importantly, this dominant discourse emphasizes a sense of dislocation not only in the colonizer who, *ex definitione*, is displaced, but above all in the colonized who finds the old ways of speaking about the place inappropriate, which is a sign of his subjugation. There opens "a gap between 'experienced' place and the descriptions the language provides." This perception of place is connected with the revolutionary changes in the measurement of time, the turning point in the history of which was the invention of the mechanical clock, an instrument facilitating the universalization of the European calendar. If time was to be measured in the same way across distant regions, there was a need for a spatial entity corresponding to it: "Locales become shaped by social influences quite distant from them, such as spatial technologies, colonizing languages, or, indeed, the very conception that those languages came to transmit." Thus, while the idea of space signifies discursive imposition, because of its connection with universalized time, the notion of place can suggest resistance, as it implies the specificity of territorial as well as linguistic experience. In postcolonialism, the theory of place "does not propose a simple separation between the 'place' named and described in language and some 'real' place inaccessible, but rather indicates that in some sense place *is* language, something in constant flux, a discourse in process" (Ashcroft, Griffiths, and Tiffin, *Key Concepts* 178–182).

Indeed, India emerges from Whitman's poem as a space, rather than as a place. Its literary, religious, and architectural (it is worth noting the diverse contexts mediating the representation of India in Whitman's text) landscapes are devoid of distinct hallmarks, or, more accurately, they contain so many attractions that it is next to impossible to distinguish one from another. Whitman treats Indian literary works, architectural wonders, and milestones of religious legacy collectively, speaking about them in plural only. Thus, the reader is faced with "myths," "fables," "dreams," "bibles," "legends," "plots," "poets," "religions," "temples," "lilies," and "towers." It is true that he speaks about the achievements of the West in plural, too ("proud truths," "facts of modern science"), but he has named the greatest successes of his civilization in Part 1: "In the Old World the east the Suez canal, / The New by its mighty railroad spann'd, / The seas inlaid with eloquent gentle wires" (531). Additionally, Whitman's description of his imaginary India differs starkly from the depiction of the tangible American landscape, with recognizable mountains, rivers, plains, which comes in Part 3. Whitman presents India in such a way as to make it suit his vision and purpose, he does not need any verification of his opinions and expectations. Quite on the contrary, he might fear verification. Therefore, the speaker identifies his soul as the only reliable companion during the voyage to India; in other words, it is in his own experience, at the same time unique and symptomatic of a certain cultural legacy, that Whitman finds the foundation for the idea of the Orient. Characteristically, the way Whitman envisages India owes a lot to the discourse on the Orient that men-of-letters as well as scientists from Europe and America created in the nineteenth century.

Whitman's insistence on the significance of myths in Part 2 also deserves some comment. The speaker's rapture over the myths of India as a vital part of its historical legacy conceals a utilitarian intention in the reference to myths. The characteristics of myths have a crucial function in the structural and metatextual plane of "Passage to India"; namely, myth serves as a model for combining the past and the present, which is one of Whitman's goals in the poem. Richard Slotkin, in his explanation of the myth-making process, describes it as an act of translation of history into myth, with the dissolution of the clear distinction between the past and the present as the primary consequence of such an operation: "The past is made metaphorically equivalent to the present; and the present appears simply as a repetition of persistently recurring structures identified with the past" (*Fatal Environment* 24). In the light of this observation, the correspondence between the function of myth and Whitman's structuring of the poem seems to be self-evident. Myths are also important for the imperial ideology that informs "Passage to India." Defined by Slotkin as "stories drawn from history, that have acquired through usage over many generations a symbolizing function that is central to the cultural functioning of the society that produced them" (16), myths constitute an area for the production of knowledge. Thus the study of myths is a metanarrative process, which produces their allegories and displaces the source versions. As Slotkin remarks: "The original mythology is a kind of net in which new materials will be caught: but when a fish comes along too big for the net to comprehend, the net must either stretch or break, be cast aside or repaired on a new scale" (23).

In the book entitled *Myth and Literature in the American Renaissance*, Robert D. Richardson stresses Whitman's ambivalent attitude toward myth and argues that the poet "wanted to supplant the old 'objective' mythological religions with a new 'subjective' religion of humanity that was populist, nationalist, and almost the sort of revolutionary religion that Michelet championed in France." Contrasting Whitman, who "wished to disavow the terminology of myth" in the project of "replacing old myths with new ideologies," with Thoreau, who was a devoted and disinterested student and admirer of myths, Richardson seems to suggest that Whitman's treatment of myths was instrumental and sometimes even manipulative. The critic claims that the poet may have felt bound up by myth, which determined the limits of his freedom, artistic and other, because myth "was in some fundamental way opposed to modern reality." Whitman juxtaposes "poems of myths" to "poems of realities," and his preference is for the latter. Richardson adds that the poet's "rejection of myth" results from his indebtedness to the thought of the Enlightenment, for instance to Thomas Paine's political and religious ideas (138–148). Significantly, Richardson alludes to Part 2 of "Passage to India" and offers the following explication of the fragment about India's myths:

> Eclaircise means, and meant at the time, to clear up, not simply to clarify. The difference is slight, but indicative of Whitman's essentially patronizing inclusion of myth. The above lines are Whitman's most appreciative of myth, but the undercurrent of the lines still suggests that the proud truths of the world and the facts of modern science and the urgent call of the present will combine to carry man past myth, however fair or too-much-loved. (147)

In Part 6 of "Passage to India," one finds a passage echoing the praise of India from Part 2 and, concomitantly, modifying the perspective of looking at it:

> Lo soul, the retrospect brought forward,
> The old, most populous, wealthiest of earth's lands,
> The stream of the Indus and the Ganges and their many
>   affluents
> (I my shores of America walking to-day behold, resuming all,)
> The tale of Alexander on his warlike marches suddenly
>   dying
> On one side China and on the other side Persia and Arabia,
> To the south the great seas and the play of Bengal,
> The flowing literatures, tremendous epics, religions, castes,

> Old occult Brahma interminably far back, the tender and
> junior Buddha,
> Central and southern empires and all their belongings,
> possessors,
> The wars of Tamerlane, the reign of Aurungzebe,
> The traders, rulers, explorers, Moslems, Venetians,
> Byzantium, the Arabs, Portuguese,
> The first travelers famous yet, Marco Polo, Batouta the
> Moor,
> Doubts to be solv'd, the map incognita, blanks to be fill'd,
> The foot of man unstayed, the hands never at rest,
> Thyself O soul that will not brook a challenge. (536)

Albeit now admittedly the projection of the mind of the speaker, who walks the "shores of America," the Orient appears more tangible in comparison with its vistas from Part 2 due to the introduction of elements of the discourse of geography: "the streams of the Indus and the Ganges," "to the south...the bay of Bengal," "central and southern empires." Added to this, the speaker's vision now becomes expanded, embracing China, Persia, and Arabia, as if India were just an introductory stage from which he begins to explore the Asian expanses. Symptomatically, "The flowing literatures, tremendous epics, religions, castes, / Old occult Brahma...the tender...Buddha" are squeezed into only two lines. In a sense, Part 2 and Part 6 describe two consecutive stages of the exploration of the Orient, with a noticeable transition from aesthetic appreciation to scientific examination and, in more general terms, from the acquisition of knowledge to the exercise of influence. The latter, while not expressed directly, is implicitly signaled by the increasing geographical precision. As Michel Foucault demonstrates, the use of the discourse of geography almost inevitably produces political signifiers:

> *Territory* is no doubt a geographical notion, but it's first of all a juridico-political one: the area controlled by a certain kind of power. *Field* is an economico-juridical notion. *Displacement*: what displaces itself is an army, a squadron, a population. *Domain* is a juridico-political notion. *Soil* is a historico-political notion. *Region* is a fiscal, administrative, military notion. *Horizon* is a pictorial, but also a strategic notion. (68)

In the above-quoted passage from Part 6, having shifted his attention from Oriental literature, architecture, and religion to geography, Whitman foregrounds one particular aspect of the geographical perspective—exploration. After a puzzling catalogue that mixes up geographical, economic, historical, and demographic concepts: "The traders, rulers, explorers, Moslems, Venetians, / Byzantium, the Arabs, Portuguese," whose function is, possibly, analogical to that of smokescreen, the speaker proceeds to talk about the legacy of "the first travelers famous yet." In discursive terms, the subject of exploration constitutes the meeting ground between history and geography. This theme also facilitates the shift from myth to history, or, more specifically, from Oriental myths to Western history. In fact, as the poem unfolds, the significance of local myths seems to diminish; they are charming in their multitude, and that is about all one can say about them.

Definitely, the most important shift to be found if one compares Parts 2 and 6, the shift that is vital for understanding Whitman's strategy of textualizing the Orient, is from reading in Part 2 to writing in Part 6. Namely, Whitman acknowledges the need to undertake the task of mapmaking: "Doubts to be solv'd, the map incognita, blanks to be fill'd," admitting his cognitive limitations and announcing his determination to overcome them through the use of passive voice. Drawing a map is an activity preceding or accompanying the claiming of the land, because the land undergoes an imaginary adaptation to the criteria of description alien to the native inhabitants, whose experience, let us add, Whitman invariably depicts in collective terms as that of nations, peoples, religious groups, in contradistinction from American experience, epitomized by the speaker as an individual being. Maps of a certain territory and its linguistic descriptions complement one another, forming one thematic archive. Maps offer an arbitrary visual representation of the land, an effect not to be accomplished in writing, while written accounts supplement maps with relevant information difficult or impossible to render graphically. Finally, if we treat territory as a text, in the sense that it is open to certain readerly and writerly procedures, we must notice that a written description of the land, an account of exploration, a map, a dictionary of the native language or local dialect, all belong to the realm of metatext.

Having acknowledged the importance of filling in the blanks on the maps of distant places, the speaker turns out to be much more at ease when it comes to mapping out America, which perhaps attests to his wavering confidence in his own idea of the Orient. Part 3 illustrates this aspect of Whitman's poetic discourse in "Passage to India." This part consists of three stanzas, containing, successively, seven, seventeen, and three lines. The first stanza offers a glimpse of the ceremony of the opening of the Suez Canal, the second presents the speaker admiring American landscapes from the train, and the third, placed in parentheses, contains an address to Columbus. The speaker appears hesitant and lacking in self-assurance in his description of the ceremony, and it is only in the portrayal of the American landscape that he feels reassured about his project. Although in the second line of the part the Suez Canal and the Pacific Railroad are named "tableaus twain" (532), on the textual level the balance in their importance seems somewhat disturbed as a result of the difference in the proportions of their respective descriptions. Perhaps the speaker does not wish to engage in speculation; however, in the context of Whitman's poetry, frequently relying on speculation disguised as prophecy, such reticence is, indeed, surprising. Added to this, the concluding sections of "Passage to India" become increasingly speculative, too. On the other hand, the speaker may intuitively fear the specific political consequences of the opening of the canal, which, as James A. Fields demonstrates, were very serious (385–388).[1] The speaker's admiration for the American landscape corresponds to his trust in the American political system, and the Pacific Railroad, which cuts across the continent, emerges as a symbol of the ultimate harmony of American geography and politics as well as of the inevitability of the democratizing movement in and outside America. Against the backdrop of this perception of his native land, it only becomes more apparent that Whitman subscribes to a certain discursive mode of fashioning the Orient:

> In the system of knowledge about the Orient, the Orient is less a place than a *topos*, a set of references, a congeries of characteristics, that seems to have its origin in a quotation, or a fragment of a text, or a citation from someone's work on the Orient, or some bit of previous imagining, or an amalgam of all these. Direct observations or circumstantial descriptions of the Orient are the fictions presented by writing on the Orient, yet invariably these are totally secondary to systematic tasks of another sort. (Said 177)

Part 3 evokes the impression that the description of the ceremony is inspired by a photograph, while the speaker's knowledge of America comes from firsthand experience. Interestingly, he is concerned about the precision of his view of America, as if the text were to pass the test of verisimilitude, whereas similar constraints do not apply to the Orient. In consequence, he constructs two differing epistemological discourses to prove that he feels equally at home on his native soil and in distant India, China, and Arabia.

The crucial difference between the depictions of the Orient in Parts 2 and 6 and that of America lies not only in the varying thematic focus, but also in the dynamic quality of the latter and a comparatively static character of the former. When the speaker talks about the Orient, he limits himself to the enumeration of its emblems, places, historical events; by contrast, American vistas have their distinguishing marks and evoke in the speaker a very strong sense of "being there," rhetorically expressed by means of anaphoric and strongly personal phrases like "I see," "I hear," "I cross," "I scan" (532–533). From the speaker's point of view, the American landscape, "the grandest scenery in the world" (532), perpetually changes, and, in turn, the Oriental landscape, whether literary, architectural, religious, or, finally, geographical, resembles a mosaic, in which he discerns only the bolder contours and is satisfied with this, because he feels he has enough time to probe this hardly mutable scenery. As a result, the American expanses surprise him and arouse his delight as much as, if not more than, the Oriental landscape. Edward Said recognizes a certain static quality that characterizes the depictions of the Orient in the discourse of Orientalism; this discursive feature derives from the tension between "narrative" and "vision." There exists a very strong holistic tendency in Orientalism: "The Orientalist surveys the Orient from above, with the aim of getting hold of the whole sprawling panorama before him—culture, religion, mind, history." If such is the Orientalist's goal, the only perspective from which to pursue it is a set of "schematic and efficient" categories. Said writes: "since it is more or less assumed that no Oriental can know himself the way an Orientalist can, any vision of the Orient ultimately comes to rely for its coherence and force on the person, institution, or discourse whose property it is," and stresses the "fundamentally conservative" character of such knowledge and the vision that stems from it (239). Said concludes that:

> A vision therefore is static, just as the scientific categories informing late-nineteenth-century Orientalism are static: there is no recourse beyond "the Semites" or "the Oriental mind"; these are final terminals holding every variety of Oriental behavior within a general view of the whole field. As a discipline, as a profession, as specialized language or discourse, Orientalism is staked upon the permanence of the whole Orient, for without 'the Orient' there can be no consistent, intelligible, and articulated knowledge called "Orientalism." (239)

The descriptions of the Orient and America in Parts 2, 3, and 6 can serve as illustrations of Whitman's privileging of metonymy over metaphor, the feature emphasized by several critics, for example C Carroll Hollis and David Simpson. In fact, Hollis's observation turns out to be extremely appropriate in the light of Said's considerations: "metonymy tends to remind us of what we already know; metaphor of what we do not know or had not thought of until that moment" (203). It can be theorized that in the discourse of Orientalism metonymy would confirm the validity of the Orientalist's knowledge and his ability to render the Orient adequately in linguistic terms, while metaphor, on the contrary, would testify to certain shortcomings in the discourse that does not satisfactorily translate the Oriental reality into words and calls for metaphoric enhancement. In other words, metonymy would be characteristic of a more advanced stage of Orientalism. Of course, the use of metaphor is fully justified, but it must be well-controlled, for instance through the codification of figurative tropes.

David Simpson, in turn, claims that metonymy suits Whitman's democratic project, because it stabilizes the relationship between the poet and the reader, both of whom feature prominently in Whitman's poetry, the former as a guide and a prophet, the latter as a modern equivalent of everyman. Namely, metonymy eliminates the effect of surprise that could arouse a sense of inferiority in the reader. By contrast, the use of metaphor has often been referred to as an antidemocratic criterion of assessing poetic "greatness." In the postcolonial context, one more aspect of metaphor is crucial: this trope revolves around the question of "integration and difference." Metonymy, as Simpson characterizes it, "is the trope of self-sufficient independence" (191). The critic draws the following political implications of the reliance on metonymy as a way of reconciling contradictions:

> Only when the 'other' is recognized as having different needs or interests do we worry over the consequences of our actions or words; only when it is admitted that there is a debate, and that our words might have a persuasive effect within it, do we concern ourselves about not publishing contradictions. Whitman's capacity to remain totally unaware of any difference between self and other marks him out as the voice of manifest destiny, and of the most confident period of nationalist enthusiasm. Whitman's compliance with this ideological schema also makes him in some sense its victim; for the acceptance of contradiction is also a covert admission of the ineffectuality of the poet's language. It is hard not to suspect that there is a level at which Whitman makes a virtue of necessity. (192)

Indeed, if we agree that Whitman articulates the "needs and interests" of fellow Americans, we also have to admit that he has difficulty in embracing these in the ephemeral Oriental "other."

Whitman advocates something like enlightened imperialism, believing in the universal ethic common to all human beings. He envisages the creation of a geographical and spiritual domain, however odd this may sound, after all existing frontiers have been transcended. This is an imperial project, as in this world without frontiers there is a power that controls common well-being and justice-for-all. America, represented by its explorers, scientists, missionaries, and, perhaps most importantly, poets, is the leader and instructor. Although in "Passage to India" Whitman does not talk directly about the leading role of America on the global scale, there are enough hints, both textual (the method of describing the American landscape) and factual, that this is how he sees the political configuration in the world. The representation of the Pacific Railroad, the symbol of expansion as well as of democratic leveling, is symptomatic in this respect. The event of its establishment, which has primarily national significance, is placed on the same scale of importance as the Atlantic Cable and the Suez Canal, both signifying political change that transcends national interests. Just as the Pacific Railroad facilitates further democratization of America, the cable and the canal help to democratize Asia and Africa. In a sense, in America, history comes into being sooner than elsewhere, therefore what happens there foreshadows what will take place in other parts of the world, so America is the nation to be treated as a model.

If "Passage to India" does not contain an explicit statement of Whitman's belief in the mission of America, "Democratic Vistas," which is, to some extent, a companion prose text, also published in 1871, throws more light on the matter. In the opening of the essay, Whitman ponders the differences between Europe and America, which is a meaningful coupling, and Asia:

> If a man were asked, for instance, the distinctive points contrasting modern European and American political and other life with the old Asiatic cultus, as lingering—bequeathed yet in China and Turkey, he might find the amount of them in John Stuart Mill's profound essay on Liberty in the future, where he demands two main constituents, or sub-strata, for a truly grand nationality—1st, a large variety of character—and 2nd, full play for human nature to expand itself in numberless and even conflicting directions. (929)

There are two features of Whitman's discourse to be pointed out in this introductory passage in "Democratic Vistas." One is the recognition of the achievement that America shares with Europe. The other is the designation of the emblems of living in the West and in the Orient: in the former, it is the "political" life, while in the latter it is the "cultus." Analogically to "Passage to India," "Democratic Vistas" associates America, and for a time also Europe, with modernity and Asia with whatever the word "old" stands for, which can be seen as an evaluative discursive operation. Symptomatically, in the second paragraph, Europe disappears from the stage:

> Sole among nationalities, these States have assumed the task to put in forms of lasting power and practicality, on areas of amplitude rivaling the operations of the physical kosmos, the moral political speculations of ages, long, long deferr'd, the democratic republican principle, and the theory of development, and perfection by voluntary standards, and self-reliance. (929)

In "Passage to India" and "Democratic Vistas," Whitman persistently refers to America as the "New World," thus instantly establishing a chronology in which both Europe and Asia represent an earlier stage in the history of the human kind.

The reason for the reductive treatment of the Orient in "Passage to India" can be Whitman's belief in a predetermined course of events, in which the East had already played its vital role. The opening of the Suez Canal is a crucial moment, perhaps a turning point, in God's larger design, this view being evident from the speaker's recognition of explorers as God's agents: "You captains, voyagers, explorers.../ You not for trade or transportation only, / But in God's name" (532). Needless to say, such an association harks back to the very beginning of colonization. Whitman's poetic discourse highlights the inevitability of the developments witnessed by the speaker and his contemporaries:

> Passage to India!
> Lo, soul, seest thou not God's purpose from the first?
> The earth to be spann'd, connected by network,
> The races, neighbors, to marry and be given in marriage,
> The oceans to be cross'd, the distant brought near,
> The lands to be welded together. (532)

Whitman persistently uses passive constructions in this passage, as if the earth and whatever it bears were creations whose existence must be explained and sanctioned through their incorporation into some purposeful design. If one wonders who is to carry out such a grand design, the answer comes in the next stanza, wherein the speaker pays tribute to "captains," "voyagers," "explorers," "engineers," "architects," and "machinists." The use of passive voice indicates a very important characteristic of the vision presented in "Passage to India": the limited, if any, possibility of choice on the part of those who are to be united with others, as if the speaker took too many things about them as well as about his own kind for granted and did not really care about what they think about such a prospect. The succession of stanzas evokes a sense of ambivalence: for instance, the address to the soul: "seest thou not God's purpose from the first?" which sounds like a self-admonition by a most ardent supporter of the vision. The central ambivalence, however, hinges on the presence and absence of agency, on the possibility of choice and its lack. The speaker talks about "races, neighbors, to marry and be given in marriage." The juxtaposition that emerges from this statement is one between a deliberate action and a passive acceptance of another party's action. Russell Goodman writes: "There is clearly an element of willed action in the Romantic idea of marrying self and world. Marriage itself is an act requiring a choice, a commitment of partners to it" (23). In the world depicted in "Passage to India," there is a party that does not have much choice, and whose commitment is taken for granted.

The explorers on whose behalf the poet in Whitman's poem speaks are embodiments of agency. The speaker does not bother about the recognition of agency in the Orient, as if Eastern myths and legends or architectural wonders had been mysteriously deprived of their makers or people who perpetuated them. This presence of agency on the one side, and its absence on the other, explains the direction of the conquest, no matter how hard Whitman himself might have tried to dilute the idea of conquest by infusing it with purportedly spiritual significance. Whether intentionally or not, he confirms the Eurocentric conviction of the natural supremacy of Western civilization that shaped individuals who were curious and eager to explore distant lands. Furthermore, European curiosity was often considered as a crucial justification of conquests. In "Passage to India," the idea of Western superiority manifests itself in the appreciation of ancient achievements, now that less and less separates nations and cultures.

The absence of nameable agency in the Orient is connected with silence, with the drastic circumscription of the sphere for the other's linguistic utterance. Explorers, voyagers, engineers, and so on, whom the poem extols, have found their spokesman in the figure of the poet-speaker, who very clearly sees his place in God's design:

> After the seas are all cross'd, (as they seem already cross'd,)
> After the great captains and engineers have accomplish'd
>   their work,
> After the noble inventors, after the scientists, the chemist,
>   the geologist, ethnologist,
> Finally shall come the poet worthy that name,
> The true son of god shall come singing his songs.
>
> Then not your deed only, O voyagers, O scientists and
> inventors, shall be justified,
> All these hearts as of fretted children shall be sooth'd,
> All affection shall be fully responded to, the secret shall be
>   told,
> All these separations and gaps shall be taken up and hook'd
>   and link'd together
> The whole earth, this cold, impassive, voiceless earth shall
>   be completely justified,
> Trinities divine shall be gloriously accomplish'd and
>   compacted by the true son of God, the poet,
> (He shall indeed pass the straits and conquer the mountains,
> He shall double the cape of Good Hope to some purpose,)
> Nature and Man shall be disjoin'd and diffused no more,
> The true son shall absolutely fuse them. (534–535)

Whitman is very specific about the representatives of different disciplines or occupations who have participated in the exploration of the Orient. The poet continues, completes, sanctions, and refines the achievements of those who came before him. He is an explorer in the realm of language, and his activity marks the final stage of exploration, which remains unfinished until the poet has bestowed on it its lasting signified. In this respect, then, the poet performs a strictly political function.

Exploration, whether geographical or spiritual, constitutes a pivotal theme in Whitman's text; references to this phenomenon or process recur in most parts of the poem and, possibly, sound like a sort of thematic refrain; here are some examples: Part 2: "You captains, voyagers, explorers" (532); Part 4: "The plans, the voyages again, the expeditions" (533); Part 5: "the captains and engineers.../ the noble inventors" (534); Part 6: "traders, rulers, explorers" (536). Thanks to the effect of parallelism, this central theme facilitates the transition from the presentation of tangible deeds to the meditation of a spiritual journey, from "Passage to India" to "Passage to more than India" (539) in the concluding Part 9. Indeed, in the end, the poet-speaker embarks on the exploration of "primal thought" (537). The total abandonment of the distinct tone that dominates the first six parts makes one suspect that the speaker's imperial self-confidence may have been a pose. His certitude dwindles as he enters the realm of the unnameable and the unpredictable and faces "aged fierce enigmas" (539), the realm where both his imagination and discourse fall short. He briefly regains his confidence in Part 9, as he recognizes the contours of places that, no matter how distant, can be located in the tangible universe: "O sun and moon and all you stars! Sirius and Jupiter! / Passage to you!" (539).

Another important transition to be found toward the conclusion of the poem signifies a change from metonymic to metaphoric representation. As Parts 1 to 6 illustrate, the initial shift from metaphor to metonymy can be associated with the urge for acquisition, whether territorial, economic, aesthetic, or discursive. Additionally, as this transition results in turning the less-known (rather than the unknown) into the well-know, it strengthens the speaker's cognitive position. In turn, the closing journey metaphor raises doubts, which even the speaker entertains, about the possibility of fully comprehending ideas, therefore it signals a contrasting shift from the known to the unknown. This change in the quality of poetic discourse has profound consequences for the form of political discourse in the poem. In the conclusion, the speaker relinquishes his imperial pretensions and announces a spiritual search for an untainted vision. Apparently, he does not want this final vision to undergo the test of political pragmatism, and thus he turns out to contradict himself, in the light of his earlier, unequivocally political enunciations. Hence his ultimate yearning for the union with his own soul, instead of with the past and present explorers. An analogy that lends itself as a possible explanation for such a radical change of priorities is a bankruptcy of the political vision in a newly liberated, postcolonial nation. The history of such countries often proves that the project of building up a new political structure is the purest, most convincing as well as most intellectually, emotionally, and spiritually stimulating before it becomes reality, that is while it still remains in the sphere of potentiality, in other words on the eve of liberation. Subsequently, everyday challenges inevitably and mercilessly verify the ideal vision; its utter degradation is not infrequent at all. If such correspondence is relevant for the understanding of American history, it reveals a central paradox of America's historical legacy, namely that the imperial zeal may have been inspired by the lingering awareness of the colonial past.

Not surprisingly, the poet-speaker chooses Columbus as his patron. Betsy Erkkila offers the following comment on the role that Whitman ascribes to Columbus:

> With his "pious beaming eyes," Whitman's Columbus is both an explorer and a religious prophet; as an emblem of America (Columbia) he is also the initiator of the democratic phase in history. Erasing the more sordid facts of commerce and conquest that impelled Columbus's quest, Whitman mythologizes Columbus as the "chief histrion" of the democratic history that culminated in the year 1869 with the realization of his dream of a passage to India....
> Columbus is, in effect, a figure of the poet of *Leaves of Grass*, planting the seeds of a democratic golden world that, like the dream of a passage to India and a world in round, might bloom in some future transformation of vision into history. (*Political Poet* 270)

Erkkila points to Whitman's omission of some rather shameful facts of Columbus's expedition and adequately defines the discoverer's function as a prophet, yet she seems to treat Columbus's position in Whitman's dialectic too unequivocally. As Agnieszka Salska indicates, numerous ambiguities underlie the fashioning of the figure of Columbus in "Passage to India" ("Whitman's Columbus"). Indeed, the speaker and his great predecessor are not only leading participants in the historic democratic experiment, they also share the ability to realize or to predict much more than others are capable of comprehending. In a tone of bitterness, the speaker mentions the misunderstandings that Columbus eventually faced, "his dejection, poverty, death" (536). By far, the most important feature that the speaker and Columbus have in common is their faithfulness to the visions that they cherish, as if a vision alone mattered infinitely more than the possibility of making it come true. Oddly enough, what can save the vision is the balance between progress and a kind of regression; this regression is perhaps hard to pinpoint, because Whitman disguises it as a return to primary experience:

> O soul, repressless, I with thee and thou with me,
> Thy circumnavigation of the world begin,
> Of man, the voyage of his mind's return,
> To reason's early paradise,
> Back, back to wisdom's birth, to innocent intuitions,
> Again with fair creation. (537)

In the conclusion of the poem, the signification of the word "India" extends, with India becoming the threshold of the "beyond." This reinvention of India can be associated with redemptive regression. In a sense, following an apparently Hegelian formula, Whitman makes a full circle and reclaims India, which he has previously thoroughly codified in such a way as to place it firmly within the imperial design, which at times looks like a private endeavor and at other times like a strictly political project to be carried out with America at its center. The process of retrieving "more than India" is ushered in by the linguistic shift from the concrete discourses of geography, history, science, to the far less concrete, though no less appealing, religious discourse. This is an escapist gesture, which may imply, as some critics have remarked, that by the 1870s Whitman's enthusiasm about the rapidly changing American reality noticeably dwindled. The concluding shift in Whitman's poetic discourse testifies to the ultimate paradox that he searches for the final sanction and a permanent foundation for a possibly flawed imperial project whose completion, in fact, he increasingly fears.

Conclusion: Representative Men

Ralph Waldo Emerson, Henry David Thoreau, and Walt Whitman developed the idea of the historical uniqueness of the American experience through constructing epitomes of the distinguishing national qualities. The three writers portray literary protagonists who are "representative Americans," to paraphrase the title of Emerson's book of essays. The notion of representativeness is crucial for understanding the conceptual strategy and the rhetorical process whereby the individual condition translates itself into the national situation. It goes without saying that representativeness is semantically connected with the concept of representation: the former suggests ideological function, the latter—aesthetic possibilities. In the works of Emerson, Thoreau, and Whitman, the ideological significance of the protagonist is strongly correlated with the choice of literary means, such as generic patterns, figurative constructions, narrative methods, the uses of topoi, or the configurations of imagery. The three writers—albeit Thoreau perhaps less evidently—envisage their representative Americans at a special moment in history, marked by great hope as much as by lingering apprehensions. The delegate of the nation is eager to act, and at the same time fears some kind of paralysis. Indeed, agency is his essential prerequisite—agency that defines his selfhood and also, importantly, becomes a gauge of the nation's progress. He knows he has a great potential to be fulfilled in the future, but in order to make the most of it, he must free himself from the entanglements of the past, hence the memorable declarations of historical caesuras in Emerson and Whitman. This dichotomy in the literary construction of the nation's representative reflects the fundamental nineteenth-century American dialectic: the concomitance of the colonial legacy and the imperial prospect.

In her seminal book *American Incarnation*, Myra Jehlen writes that the European settler who becomes an American begins to perceive himself in opposition to where he comes from, but in the end, he creates a domain modeled on the one he abandoned:

> The European immigrant who became an American saw himself not as entering a better society, but as leaving society altogether. And in the

reconciled natural civilization that once and for all transcended the old world's successive dialectical compromises, he assumed a natural, therefore absolute and not politically disputable, dominion. As insurgencies are successful when, after having displaced the established group, they finally replace it, this new natural ruler completed the liberal revolution by succeeding to, precisely, the landed status of his aristocratic forebears. (5)

This logic behind the emergence of the "American incarnation" seems to correspond to a kind of continuity of the process of colonization insofar as the colonizing efforts of the Europeans were, in the course of time, followed by the expansionist endeavors undertaken by Americans. There are two lines of events—and two bodies of discourses—which permanently intersect with each other, creating what might be called historical nodes. In turn, the existence of such nodes accounts for the unique place of America in history, the concern shared by Emerson, Thoreau, and Whitman.

The anticolonial rejection of the European imperial rule gradually leads to the fruition of the American project of expansion. Emerson seems to have recognized this time of national transition with utmost percipience. His American scholar is primarily motivated by the yearning for a radical change, which symptomatically implies that the present state of things is still largely governed by the mistaken ideas of the past. The key to the understanding of these wrong ideas is the notion of dependence, serving as a foil for the figurative representations of the scholar's qualities. In essence, the American scholar must not allow others to do the thinking for him and eventually to destroy his creative potential, no matter how powerful the structures of authority around him appear to be. In other words, in order to achieve self-fulfillment and to act as a representative man, he must overcome a certain syndrome, all the more menacing because of the degree of habitualization it has reached. The defining aspect of this syndrome—let us call it postcolonial—is timidity, a common feature that has resulted in the overwhelming state of self-renunciation, diagnosed by Emerson. The scholar retains utmost caution because the danger of slipping back into the former condition of dependence looms large. Paradoxically enough, the threat of regression is itself a stimulus for him to act with greater awareness and commitment. The scholar's primary task is to subvert well-entrenched ideas, including cultural hierarchies. The mechanism of such subversive work becomes visible in *English Traits* where the narrator possesses scholarly qualifications and therefore can easily be related to the eponymous figure in Emerson's early lecture. *English Traits* develops the discourse eroding the models of cultural superiority and inferiority. The point is, however, that such models are still taken for granted, which means that the postcolonial syndrome, identified in "The American Scholar," continues to affect the Emersonian representative American and, by extension, the people whom he represents.

Perhaps the Emersonian scholar feels somewhat stuck at a moment in history—when the European rule approaches the phase of eclipse, and America sees its chance more and more clearly—because, despite his brave pronouncements, he does not take steps that would be radical enough. In this respect, he is contrasted with Whitman's poet, as depicted in the Preface to the first edition of *Leaves of Grass*, a truly revolutionary figure. The difference between the ways Emerson and Whitman perceive America's postcolonial situation is that the former emphasizes the need to put an end to the lingering epoch, while the latter announces the beginning of a new one. This difference appears to be slight, but in fact it is fundamental: in a sense, Whitman's vision opens where Emerson's has found its closure. Whitman's poet embarks on a revolutionary project because this is the effectual way to overcome the state of dependence. As Albert Memmi puts it in his classic study *The Colonizer and the Colonized*:

> [R]evolt is the only way out of the colonial situation, and the colonized realizes it sooner or later. His condition is absolute and cries for an absolute solution; a break and not a compromise.... The colonial situation, by its own internal inevitability, brings on revolt. For the colonial condition cannot be adjusted to; like an iron collar, it can only be broken. (127–128)

Memmi emphasizes the indispensable solidarity of the colonized in their struggle with the colonizer and recognizes religion as the main cementing force: "religion is...an extraordinary place of communion for the whole group. The colonized, his leaders and intellectuals, his traditionalists and liberals, all classes of society, can meet there, reinforce their bonds, verify and re-create their unity" (133). The unity of American people of diverse backgrounds is the central vision of the nation conveyed in Whitman's Preface, with poetry—necessarily carrying religious senses—as the space for communion.

Similarly to Emerson, Thoreau often relies on the metaphors of dependence as a way to reinforce his argument about proper existence. However, in the case of Thoreau's representative man, that is the explorer, the postcolonial situation is much more difficult to recognize in comparison with Emerson's scholar and Whitman's poet, who both can be seen as epitomes of the national development as prognosticated by the two writers. Admittedly, the Emersonian figures of the scholar and the young American, on the one hand, and Whitman's poet of the Preface and the poet of "Passage to India", on the other, exist in historical situations that differ visibly and which, therefore, constitute a measure of the nation's progress. In Thoreau's writing, the parallelism between the protagonist and the nation is less obvious, since the transformation of the explorer-persona rather has to do with the changing prisms of perception than with political recognitions. Nevertheless, Thoreau's personal project of exploration begins on an impulse that can be called anticolonial, in a figurative sense. In the opening part of *Walden*, Thoreau speaks critically about the wrongness of social norms and hierarchies of values, using the metaphor of slavery. His undertaking begins with a refusal to function within the society where blind attachment to common ideas and individual possessions is a standard, if not a virtue. Importantly, he thus describes a state where mimicry governs the human outlook. It would be perhaps too far-fetched to consider Thoreau's assessment of the destructive mechanisms of social life to be an expression of his involvement with the American colonial legacy, but his reliance on the figurations of dependence is by no means incidental.

In general, in comparison with Emerson's and Whitman's writing, Thoreau's work is much more difficult to fit into the dichotomous ideological context where postcolonial anxiety and expansionist zeal are coexistent phenomena. Apparently, Thoreau formulates postulates that resound with overt national significance less often than Emerson and Whitman. Of course, this does not mean that the ideological concerns shared, to a notable extent, by the two latter writers were altogether strange to the author of *Walden*, for the simple reason that they were inescapable. Thoreau's work illustrates the degree of influence that culture exerts on its representatives, which manifests itself, for instance, in his employment of tropes and topoi harmonizing with the literary representations of the American imperial design. Even if Thoreau opposed the U.S. expansionist policy, most famously in "Civil Disobedience," he used the narrative structures—both themes and genres—which originated from the rhetoric of empire. In fact, when read together, *Walden* and *The Maine Woods* show an interesting development of Thoreau's explorer-persona, who first undertakes a project that, albeit grounded in imperial fantasy, has a reformatory aim devoid of any endorsement for the empire, and then embarks on a mission that is perfectly in keeping with the logic of American expansionism. The two texts also provide the evidence of the evolution of

Thoreau's personal mythology of discovery toward the acknowledgment of the convergence of his efforts and the historical achievements of great explorers. Just like Thoreau's explorer, Emerson's young American is a representative man shaped by imperial culture. Characteristically, the Emersonian figure seems to express the author's ambivalence about American expansionism. This ambivalence has to do with a kind of double filtering of expansionist ideas: first of all, Emerson translates national interests into regional ones, as the young American is necessarily a New Englander. Predictably enough, the writer claims that New England has played a special role in the nation's development because it has always been in the lead and it is only natural that it remain the leader. In consequence, in redefining American expansionism as an endeavor carried out by New Englanders, Emerson takes a reductive view of the dominant politics. The reason for this may be that, on the one hand, he feels a pressure to consider issues of utmost political importance, and on the other, he is uncertain of the outcome of these issues. Emerson's ambivalence toward the empire is further enhanced by the shift to figurative constructions, with a simultaneous replacement of political ideas by philosophical and quasi-religious categories.

Whitman's portrayal of the poet as an imperial figure has to do with the poetic strategy of the oscillation between the reality that is perceived and the reality that is invented, between tangible political doctrines and imaginary political designs, between local happenings and global processes. In an imperial gesture, the poet establishes bonds with and between individuals, communities, races, nations, traditions, religions, et cetera; he thus interrogates the existing cultural and political hierarchies; and, in the end, unequivocally points to himself as the one who decides about the true hierarchies. It goes without saying that Whitman identifies himself with the American nation as much as he does with the entire human kind, therefore he carries with him the national legacy wherever his imagination takes him. The closeness between individuals ultimately guarantees that general equality will remain a fundamental principle. However, the poet can be categorical, which clearly suggests that the one to whom he speaks does not really have any choice but to accept the course of events triggered off by the coming of the poet. Whitman implies the continuous nature of American expansionism; in other words, once the continental expansion has been completed the annexation of "other shores"—as he puts it in the 1860 poem "Starting from Paumanok" (186)—will be a natural and logical corollary.

Notes

Introduction

1. Anne McClintock offers a thorough discussion of the "treacherousness" of postcolonialism in her seminal article "The Angel of Progress: Pitfalls of the Term 'Post-Colonialism.'"
2. In the original version, Buell's article was reprinted in the anthology *American Literature, American Culture*, ed. Gordon Hutner.
3. A very little-known pioneering attempt to situate the American Renaissance in the context of postcolonial literatures, albeit conducted without any use of postcolonial critical terms, is a book by Joseph Jones called *Radical Cousins: Nineteenth-Century American and Australian Writers* (1976). It preceded Buell's article by a decade and a half.
4. The studies in question are: Anna Brickhouse, *Transamerican Literary Relations and the Nineteenth-Century Public Sphere* (2004); Sean X. Goudie, *Creole America. The West Indies and the Formation of Literature and Culture in the New Republic* (2006); George B. Handley, *New World Poetics. Nature and the Adamic Imagination of Whitman, Neruda, and Walcott* (2007).

1 Figures of Dependence: Exploring the Postcolonial in Emerson's Selected Texts

1. The influence of poststructuralism on postcolonialism, of which Bhabha's writing is so good an illustration, is discussed by Simon Gikandi in an article "Poststructuralism and postcolonial discourse," in *The Cambridge Companion to Postcolonial Literary Studies*, ed. Neil Lazarus, 97–119.
2. Leon Chai elucidates Emerson's idea of the connection between history, consciousness and experience: "For Emerson...the problem of historical knowledge is resolved by equating that knowledge with states of consciousness. An epoch constitutes the equivalent of a state of mind or consciousness. To 'know' an epoch is therefore to experience that state of mind. In this sense, historical knowledge does not

consist of a concrete content... but rather of a mode of perceiving and experiencing. A given emotional coloration, a given mood or sense of what things signify in relation to the way we live—this is Emerson's notion of 'historicity,' of various historical epochs and the passage from one to another" (255).

3. In this important article, Burkholder argues that the figurative structure of "The American Scholar" conveys Emerson's understanding of the economic crisis of 1837: "Inherent in the crisis of that summer [1837], Emerson saw the potential obliteration of accepted social, political, and economic systems. For those dislocated by the accompanying chaos of this actual and causal bankruptcy, Emerson offered the theory of 'The American Scholar' that in its subversive asocial and apolitical idealism—its emphasis on self-trust, its advocacy of the severing of cultural and familial ties, its redefinition of traditional concepts of success and democracy—serves as a potent political commentary" (53).

4. It is interesting to mention that Buell removed most of the quoted passage from a revised version of the article published in the anthology *Postcolonial Theory and the United States: Race, Ethnicity, and Literature*, ed. Amritjit Singh and Peter Schmidt.

5. Eduardo Cadava rightly notices that Emerson often refers to political issues by means of analogies. The critic writes: "The analogy then becomes a means to see the way in which Emerson addresses a contemporary events in terms of the history that both precedes and follows it. It may, therefore, serve as an important key to any evaluation of what we might wish to call his 'political' strategy" (180).

6. Kenneth S. Sacks claims that Emerson's conceptual shift from "the American scholar" to "Man Thinking" was an attempt to dissociate liberty from institutional entanglements: "Emerson did not call for the establishment of a scholar with any political characteristics. That vision would become as stultifying as the established literatures he attacked in this very speech. In referring to the American scholar, Emerson fully subverted an established phrase. Used previously with nationalistic and moral overtones, for Emerson it signified freedom from all prescribed culture and convention. The American scholar became Man Thinking—who was no more merely a producer of literature than Socrates had been. And just as Socrates defended and ultimately died for Athenian freedom without ever feeling comfortable with Athenian democracy, Emerson embraced American liberty without feeling beholden to the institutions that supported it" (31).

7. Christopher Newfield discusses the correspondence of the notions of individualism and authoritarianism in Emerson's writing in the light of the mid-nineteenth-century American doctrine of liberalism. See chapter 1 of his book *The Emerson Effect: Individualism and Submission in America* (17–39).

2 BEYOND THE TRAVELER'S TESTIMONY: *ENGLISH TRAITS* AND THE CONSTRUCTION OF POSTCOLONIAL COUNTER-DISCOURSE

1. A selection of reviews of *English Traits*, published in both America and England, can be found in *Emerson and Thoreau: The Contemporary Reviews*, ed. Joel Myerson (256–283). The most exhaustive presentation of the reception of Emerson's book is Robert E. Burkholder's "The Contemporary Reception of *English Traits*" in *Emerson: Centenary Essays*, ed. Joel Myerson (156–172). William J. Sowder discusses the general reception of Emerson's writing in England in his book *Emerson's Impact on the British Isles and Canada*.

2. Discussions of *English Traits* are not very frequent in the existing body of Emerson scholarship; however, the recent years seem to have witnessed a growing interest in this text. Literary scholars, who write on *English Traits* nowadays usually, and understandably, focus on Emerson's notion of race. Exemplary critical articles are Susan Castillo's "'The best of nations'? Race and Imperial Destinies in Emerson's *English Traits*" (2004), and Christopher Hanlon's "'The old race are all gone': Transatlantic Bloodlines and English Traits" (2007).

3. For example, Barbara Korte emphasizes the influence of travel accounts on adventure novels that enjoyed immense popularity in Victorian England. See the chapter "Travel Writing in the Nineteenth Century" of her book *English Travel Writing from Pilgrimages to Postcolonial Explorations*.

4. J. Hillis Miller claims that journeying in the United States was quite a distressing experience for Dickens, who was "constantly exposed to the scrutiny of crowds and strangers" (469), and his depiction of America reflected his psychological reactions: "He saved his sense of himself by converting his experience into his consciousness of that experience. He saw the world now as though it were reflected in a mirror or projected in a 'magic lantern.' He saw it as comedy, as emptied appearance. When this reversal had been performed, the people who had before endangered his sense of himself with their looks were now inanimate objects in human shape, mechanically endowed with motion, gesture, and speech. The America that Dickens now experienced existed for no one except himself. The shared social reality within which Americans lived, a reality created by their acceptance of certain conventions and ways of speaking, was lightened, unsubstantiated, made into a kind of brittle façade by Dickens's oblique perception of it, by his continual transformation of it into something it was not" (470). Dickens's continuing concern with America is discussed by Robert B. Heilman in "The New World in Charles Dickens's Writings. Part One."

5. Helen Heineman comments on the symptomatic easiness with which Frances Trollope switches from broad generalizations to particular situations and the other way round: "This rapid progression from

a broad, over-all view to an almost myopically close one is a characteristic movement in *Domestic Manners*. The particulars of the scene are so well delineated that the reader gives credence to the subsequent generalizations"; "[T]he generalizations are forceful because Mrs. Trollope wears well the cloak of authority. She is the expert among travelers, dogmatically making ex cathedra judgments on any number of American subjects—even on the merit of American peaches"; "Frances Trollope in the New World" (550). The historical background for Trollope's book is presented by Heineman in another article, "'Starving in that Land of Plenty.'"
6. J. Martin Evans writes that in Dickens's *American Notes* and *Martin Chuzzlewit*: "America was represented...neither as a paradise nor as a wilderness, but as a wilderness masquerading as a paradise. In Dickens' eyes this country was evidently a vast confidence trick perpetrated on the innocent inhabitants of Europe, a deliberate conspiracy to defraud the rest of the world by pretending to be the perfect society that the first explorers believed they had found" (27).
7. Not surprisingly, Hall's book was found offensive by the American reading audience; Downs comments briefly on its reception in America: "Not even the bitter pens of Harriet Martineau and Frances Trollope aroused the wrath and resentment of the American people as did Captain Basil Hall's three-volume account of his travels in the United States and Canada in 1827–1828. He was regarded as an arch traitor to the generous hospitality he and his wife and infant daughter received during their leisurely 10,000 mile tour over most of the know territory of the United States" (55).
8. Laura Dassow Walls thus summarizes Emerson's view of the decline of England: "England now had sunk to the solstice of its power and the senescence of its institutions—university, church, literature, science—and although the old idealism occasionally flickered back into life, the cycle had concluded and could only start anew in another location—say, America. England was finished....England, then, displayed the full cycle of arrested and progressive development, transferred from organic life to civil history, but subject to the same law. It was a sad and noble spectacle (*Emerson's Life in Science* 178). On the other hand, as David M. Robinson observes, Emerson's England appears to be the epitome of the modern condition, in particular of the perils that it entails: "England represented both the undisciplined economic power that was becoming an ever more disturbing condition of modern life and a compelling image of an America to which Emerson was in undeniable ways committed. Whatever its seductions for him, English power nevertheless engaged his oppositional instinct, especially as he considered the cost of the modern industrial economies to the individuals who labor in them. Faced with the daunting, mechanized regularity of English life, he rediscovered ground for the social relevance of self-culture, recognizing a social

world that had become hostile to the individual. England was not merely a rich nation; it was the modern, the future. It was America as Emerson felt it might become" (114).

3 EMERSON, NEW ENGLAND, AND THE RHETORIC OF EXPANSION

1. It is worth mentioning that discussions of the significance of the frontier in Emerson's writing began to appear much earlier; see Ernest Marchand's "Emerson and the Frontier" (1931).
2. Robert Kagan suggests that the talk of the nation's unity under the banners of Manifest Destiny was a characteristic rhetorical strategy that led to glossing over the sectional conflict: "What had emerged in the America of the 1840s was not a unifying spirit of confidence and a consensus on the nation's destiny.... Rather there was a fierce clash between two diametrically opposed visions of that destiny, which in turn produced two distinct foreign policies aimed primarily not at the external world but at each other. Northern foreign policy from the 1840s until the Civil War was focused on the containment and eventual, peaceful extinction of southern slavery. Southern foreign policy centered on breaking through the barriers the North was trying to erect.... For all the talk about 'manifest destiny,' the nation's destiny had become subsumed by sectional destinies. The sectional conflict had turned the United States in on itself, not because Americans were isolationist or introspective but because until the question of slavery was settled, until the question of the national identity was settled, it was impossible to reach a common understanding of the nation's role in the world." Kagan continues: "The concept of manifest destiny, in fact, deliberately skirted the problem, which was why it was so useful. Its advocates tried to argue that expansion itself, whether slave or free-soil, was both in the national interest and part of the American mission to bring enlightenment to the benighted.... The irony was that the notion of manifest destiny, so often viewed as an innovation of this era, actually drew what strength it had from sentiments of an earlier time in American history, before the question of slavery had reared up as an insoluble national conundrum. But by the 1840s it had become absurd, a politician's trick, to talk of America's civilizing mission and the beneficent spread of its political institutions, when southerners insisted that among the blessings they would bring to newly absorbed peoples was slavery" (232–233).
3. Lloyd Rohler claims that the appearance of "The Young American" marks Emerson's arrival at "the formula that would make him one of the most popular lecturers of the time": "By adapting the sermonic format to lectures that embraced social and cultural ideals, using homiletic techniques carefully polished in the pulpit, emphasizing his ethical

appeal, and artfully using appeals to audience self-interest clothed in moral pieties, his lectures became inspirational orations" (53).
4. It is interesting to mention that this observation, as an element of the overall vision presented in "The Young American," glosses over Emerson's prejudiced views. Peter S. Field writes about "a set of racial assumptions about Saxon genius that played perfectly into his [Emerson's] evolving nationalism": The fortune of the Republic, Emerson argued, depended upon these Saxon 'rough riders' who understood the necessity of balancing and keeping at bay the snarling majorities of German, Irish and native millions. The nation's vitality as manifested in its explosive expansion, its commercial might, its democratic institutions, and its suspicious destiny, rested upon the elemental virtues of a young and vital race. Insofar as Emerson's faith in popular government was rooted in his conviction that 'The instinct of the people is right,' his definition of 'the people' necessarily remained highly circumscribed. Only some race had attained a sufficiently advanced culture to be able to compete and survive" (173).

4 Thoreau's Imperial Fantasy: *Walden* versus *Robinson Crusoe*

1. The performative aspect of Thoreau's authorial presentation in Walden has been highlighted by Timothy Melley in his article "Performing Experiments: Materiality and Rhetoric in Thoreau's *Walden*."
2. W. Barksdale Mayard describes the similarities between Thoreau's Walden house and similar architectural constructions of the epoch in "Thoreau's House at Walden."
3. Thoreau's attitude toward the Irish is discussed by Helen Lojek in her article "Thoreau's Bog People."
4. Literary historians have been able to identify the woodchopper's name—Alex Therien.
5. The few critics who discuss Thoreau's encounters with the woodchopper would probably agree with Garber that the Canadian is portrayed as "exemplary natural man," "man of origins...close to a unity of the self" (*Thoreau's Fable* 179). Against such background, Nicholas K. Bromell's examination of Thoreau's ambivalence toward the woodchopper in terms of class difference evidently stands out: "Therien cannot be explained...by the conventional antebellum categories of 'manual' and 'mental,' 'animal' and 'spiritual,' 'body' and 'mind.' His thought is 'immersed in his animal life'—that is, it is bound up with and inseparable from the sensuous life of his body...because he cannot be explained by these categories, Therien cannot be represented in a discourse that is predicated on them; his mind produces little that 'can be reported.' Indeed, this 'muddy' (opaque) and 'bottomless' (unfathomable) worker is resistant even to self-representation in literary texts....To put himself,

or his 'thoughts' in writing would be, for Therien, a kind of suicide. His fear suggests that the essence of his identity as a manual laborer is not only resistant to the conventions of writing... but is actually threatened by writing: 'it would kill him.' The fully embodied life of this laboring woodsman, so attractive to Thoreau, is apparently unrepresentable, either by the laborer himself or by others" (225).

6. Robert Sattelmeyer gives an interesting account of how the area around Walden looked at the time of Thoreau's experiment: "As for the pristine character of Walden Pond and its surroundings, it needs to be recalled that Concord was the first inland town the English established, in 1635. Thus, the area had been subject to pressures of settlement and cultivation and environmental change by Europeans and their descendants for over two hundred years by the time Thoreau moved to the pond. The landscape of Concord in the 1840 and 1850s was an agricultural one, dominated by tillage and pastures and cutover areas, with only about 10 percent of the area in forest. In fact, 1850 was the historic low point of forest coverage in Concord: it had been steadily decreasing since initial settlement, and has been increasing steadily ever since, as agricultural lands were abandoned and gradually reverted to forest" (241).

5 The Politics of the Genre: Exploration and Ethnography in *The Maine Woods*

1. This passage can be seen as an example of Thoreau's construction of urban imagery. In his discussion of *Walden*, Robert Fanuzzi demonstrates that "Thoreau creates what urbanists call a development history for the imagination, accounting for the creation of avowedly figural forms by the same changes in social morphology that were transforming the built and unbuilt landscape of eastern Massachusetts into centers in subsidiaries of an equally new social form, the urban-industrial complex" (322).

2. The inclusion of historiographic and mythographic structures within the narrative frame of *The Maine Woods* can be seen as an attempt, on Thoreau's part, to create what David Arnold calls an "environmentalist paradigm." Arnold writes: "The environmentalist paradigm provides us with a distinctive model for understanding and explaining the human past. It does not represent nature in the abstract, as an ecosystem apart from, or devoid of, human influence and intelligence. On the contrary, it is frankly anthropocentric, seeing in nature a reflection or a cause of the human condition, whether physical, social or moral. It arises from a widely held and historically enduring belief that a significant relationship exists between what is conventionally referred to... as 'man' and 'nature,' and that this relationship influences the character of individual societies and the course of their histories" (10).

3. Reginald Horsman discusses such notions extensively in his book *Race and Manifest Destiny. The Origins of American Anglo-Saxonism* (1981).
4. In this passage, admittedly, Thoreau presents himself as one who gazes at the native, and this position is highlighted by a change in perspective: first he looks at the Indians from a distance and then has them at an arm's reach, verifying an earlier impression of them. Predictably enough, in this way, Thoreau assumes an authoritative position in relation to the natives. Rey Chow claims that: "Watching is theoretically defined as the primary agency of violence, an act that pierces the other, who inhabits the place of the passive victim on display.... [T]he image is what has been devastated, left bare, and left behind by aggression" (123). The "devastation" of the image, described by Chow, evidently corresponds to the alleged degradation of the native that Thoreau talks about.
5. Dana D. Nelson describes the figurative mechanism whereby the Indian serves to externalize the ambivalences of capitalism: "the Indian stands, in an increasingly loaded way in the nineteenth-century United States, for the 'communist' antithesis/supplement to capitalism. That is to say, Thoreau's naïve Indian...is a necessary symbol that supplements the logic of capitalism, making a way for the capitalist system and individual capitalist actors to externalize its/their own multiple ambivalences about living inside capitalism. The Indian as savage-savant, whose befuddlement implicitly critiques without challenging the acommunal logic of market relations, holds open a cultural space for white men to voice ambivalence about its destructuring of community and even critique market brutality while disavowing responsibility for that critique by appearing to be strong boosters. It is important to recognize that such disavowal had political ramifications that went well beyond laughing at such supposedly 'silly Indians.' Labeling Indians as enemies of capitalism buttressed white claims to Native lands, provided logic for breaking treaty agreements with indigenous nations, and provided rationales for brutal enforcement of Indian removal that began in the late 1830s. And these actions provided an arena, almost always violent, for the rehearsal of white men's claims to independent, competitive manhood" ("Thoreau" 81–81).

6 POSTCOLONIAL WHITMAN: THE POET AND THE NATION IN THE 1855 PREFACE TO *LEAVES OF GRASS*

1. Robert M. Greenberg problematizes Whitman's textual self-positioning in a similar way; see the chapter "Personalism and Fragmentation in Whitman's *Leaves of Grass* (1855–1860)" his book *Splintered Worlds*.

Fragmentation and the Ideal of Diversity in the Work of Emerson, Melville, Whitman, and Dickinson (121–149). William Pannapacker, in his discussion of the uses of autobiographical modes in the writings by P.T. Barnum, Frederick Douglass, and Walt Whitman, points to the common tendency for these three authors to construct a unique identity and concomitantly to produce a collective voice (10–11).
2. The review entitled "Walt Whitman and His Poems" was published anonymously in the *United States Review*, no. 5, in September 1855.
3. Whitman's "traditional intellectual," like Gramsci's, is much of a "vulgarized type." Whitman satirizes the ways of this class of people in his self-review: "For all our intellectual people, followed by their books, poems, novels, essays, editorials, lectures, tuitions, and criticism, dress by London and Paris modes, receive what is received there, obey the authorities, settle disputes by the old tests, keep out of rain and sun, retreat to the shelter of houses and schools, trim their hair, shave, touch not the earth barefoot, and enter not the sea except in a complete bathing dress. One sees unmistakably genteel persons, travelled, college-learned, used to be served by servants, conversing without heat or vulgarity, supported on chairs, or walking through handsomely-carpeted parlors, or along shelves bearing well-bound volumes, and walls adorned with curtained and collared portraits, and china things, and nick-nacks. But where in American literature is the first show of America?" (8–9).
4. In a recent article, Heidi Kathleen Kim explores Whitman's politics of language in relation to Anglo-Saxonism, which she regards as a cultural factor that considerably shaped the consciousness of mid-nineteenth-century Americans. She claims that Whitman's interest in perpetuating certain Anglo-Saxon qualities through the language of poetry can be linked with the imperial project: "His acclamation of American language and the American race complicates his explicit valorization of English hereditary traits, while his poems celebrating universality cannot entirely erase the impression of the Anglo-Saxon imperial domination" (1).
5. Two most important monographs analyzing Whitman's innovative poetic language are: C. Carroll Hollis's *Language and Style in "Leaves of Grass"* (1983) and James Perrin Warren's *Walt Whitman's Language Experiment* (1990). However, it is Dimock who most thoroughly explores the symbolic senses produced by the very grammar of Whitman's poetic discourse.
6. Tyler Hoffman makes an analogous point in his contribution to *A Companion to Walt Whitman*: "Notably, English does not appeal to Whitman merely on the basis of its phonetic quality—it is not just the sounds that the words make, but the ideological principles that are embodied by words, which are stamped by the native traits of the user of them. This fiction of language is a powerful one, and Whitman

repeatedly reads American English through a political lens, as a sign of the heartiness of the American people, their fierce independence, rugged individualism, and democratic impulses" (362).
7. Whitman further developed his theory of the English language in America in his 1856 essay "America's Mightiest Inheritance."
8. Whitman composed the first *Leaves of Grass* at the time when Americans witnessed a public debate concerning the negative influence of political corruption on language. The worries that a close connection existed between politics and language, to the detriment of the latter, were often expressed by orators and journalists. Thomas Gustafson thus characterizes their anxieties: "For these commentators on language...the American language was falling far short of fulfilling the manifest destiny proclaimed for it by Edward Everett in the early nineteenth century and by Whitman in the preface to *Leaves of Grass*. Instead of becoming the most pure and copious language, it had become glib and oily, debased by Gonerils and Regans—the politicians and other con men—who were willing to speak and purpose not for personal gain. Indeed, in the 1850s and 1860s, the high hopes of John Adams and his son for a renaissance of eloquence in the United States that would be coextensive with the pursuit of liberty, Noah Webster's dream of achieving political harmony through a uniform language, Everett's vision of America overcoming the confusion of Babel, and Whitman's conviction that 'Americans are going to be the most fluent and melodious voiced people in the world—and the most perfect users of words' all seemed to crumble as secondary desires—the desire for riches, for pleasure, for power, and for praise—gained sway over sovereign principles of justice and liberty" (357–358).

7 Passage to (More Than) India: The Poetics and Politics of Whitman's Textualization of the Orient

1. David H. Finnie discusses the American presence in the Middle East in the nineteenth century in his book *Pioneers East. The Early American Experience in the Middle East* (1967).

Bibliography

Aaron, Daniel. "Whitman and the Founding Fathers." *Walt Whitman of Mickle Street: A Centennial Collection.* Ed. Geoffrey M. Sill. 46–53.

Abrams, Robert E. "Image, Object, and Perception in Thoreau's Landscapes: The Development of Anti-Geography." *Nineteenth-Century Literature* 46.2 (September 1991): 245–262.

Afzal-Khan, Fawzia, and Kalpana Seshadri-Crooks, eds. *The Pre-Occupation of Postcolonial Studies.* Durham and London: Duke University Press, 2000.

Allen, Gay Wilson. *The New Walt Whitman Handbook.* New York and London: New York University Press, 1986.

Altherr, Thomas L. "'Chaplain to Hunters': Henry David Thoreau's Ambivalence Toward Hunting." *American Literature* 56.3 (October 1984): 345–361.

Anderson, Benedict. *Imagined Communities: Reflections on the Origin and Spread of Nationalism.* London and New York: Verso, 1996.

Anderson, Quentin. *The Imperial Self: An Essay in American Literary and Cultural History.* New York: Vintage, 1971.

Andrews, William L., ed. *Literary Romanticism in America.* Baton Rouge and London: Louisiana State University Press, 1981.

Appleby, Joyce. *Inheriting the Revolution: The First Generation of Americans.* Cambridge, MA.; and London: The Belknap Press of Harvard University Press, 2000.

Arac, Jonathan. "Whitman and Problems of the Vernacular." *Breaking Bounds: Whitman and American Cultural Studies.* Ed. Betsy Erkkila and Jay Grossman. 44–61.

Arnold, David. *The Problem of Nature: Environment, Culture and European Expansion.* Oxford: Blackwell, 1996.

Ashcroft, Bill, Gareth Griffiths, and Helen Tiffin. *The Empire Writes Back: Theory and Practice in Post-Colonial Literature.* New York and London: Routledge, 1989.

———. *Key Concepts in Post-Colonial Studies.* New York and London: Routledge, 1998.

Ashcroft, Bill, Gareth Griffiths, and Helen Tiffin, eds. *The Post-Colonial Studies Reader.* London and New York: Routledge, 1995.

Aspiz, Harold. *So Long! Walt Whitman's Poetry of Death.* Tuscaloosa and London: The University of Alabama Press, 2004.

Asselineau, Roger. *The Transcendentalist Constant in American Literature.* New York and London: New York University Press, 1980.
Barbour, James, and Thomas Quirk, eds. *Romanticism: Critical Essays in American Literature.* New York and London: Garland Publishing, 1986.
Barker, Francis, and Peter Hulme. "'Nymphs and Reapers Heavily Vanish': The Discursive Con-texts of *The Tempest.*" *New Historicism and Cultural Materialism: A Reader.* Ed. Kiernan Ryan. 125–137.
Bassnett, Susan. *Comparative Literature: A Critical Introduction.* Oxford: Blackwell, 1995.
Bercovitch, Sacvan. *The American Jeremiad.* Madison: University of Wisconsin Press, 1978.
———. "Emerson the Prophet: Romanticism, Puritanism, and Auto-American-Biography." *Emerson: Prophecy, Metamorphosis, and Influence. Selected Papers from the English Institute.* Ed. David Levin. 1–27.
———. *The Rites of Assent: Transformations in the Symbolic Construction of America.* New York and London: Routledge, 1993.
Bercovitch, Sacvan, and Myra Jehlen, eds. *Ideology and Classic American Literature.* Cambridge: Cambridge University Press, 1987.
Bergland, Renée L. *The National Uncanny: Indian Ghosts and American Subjects.* Hanover and London: University Press of New England, 2000.
Bhabha, Homi K. *The Location of Culture.* London and New York: Routledge, 2004.
Bhabha, Homi K., ed. *Nation and Narration.* London and New York: Routledge, 1991.
Białas, Zbigniew, ed. *Aristippus Meets Crusoe: Rethinking the Beach Encounter.* Katowice: University of Silesia Press, 1999.
Blair, John G., and Augustus Trowbridge. "Thoreau on Katahdin." *American Quarterly* 12.4 (Winter 1960): 508–517.
Boehmer, Elleke. *Colonial and Postcolonial Literature: Migrant Metaphors.* Oxford and New York: Oxford University Press, 1995.
Bonner, Willard H. *Harp on the Shore: Thoreau and the Sea.* Ed. George R. Levine. Albany: State University of New York Press, 1985.
Bosco, Ronald A., and Joel Myerson, eds. *Emerson: Bicentennial Essays.* Boston: Massachusetts Historical Society, 2006.
Brickhouse, Anna. *Transamerican Literary Relations and the Nineteenth-Century Public Sphere.* Cambridge: Cambridge University Press, 2004.
Bridgman, Richard. *Dark Thoreau.* Lincoln and London: University of Nebraska Press, 1982.
———"From Greenough to 'Nowhere': Emerson's *English Traits.*" *The New England Quarterly* 59.4 (December 1986): 469–485.
Brightfield, Myron F. "America and the Americans, 1840–1860, as Depicted in English Novels of the Period." *American Literature* 31.3 (November 1959): 309–324.
Bromell, Nicholas K. *By the Sweat of the Brow: Literature and Labor in Antebellum America.* Chicago and London: The University of Chicago Press, 1993.

BIBLIOGRAPHY

Brooks, Van Wyck. *The Times of Melville and Whitman.* E.P. Dutton, 1947 (no place of publication).

Buell, Lawrence. "American Literary Emergence as a Postcolonial Phenomenon." *American Literary History* 4 (1992): 411–442. Reprinted in *American Literature, American Culture.* Ed. Gordon Hutner. 592–612.

———. *Emerson.* Cambridge, MA.; and London: The Belknap Press of Harvard University Press, 2003.

———. "Emerson in His Cultural Context." *Ralph Waldo Emerson: A Collection of Critical Essays.* Ed. Lawrence Buell. 48–60.———. *The Environmental Imagination: Thoreau, Nature Writing, and the Formation of American Culture.* Cambridge, MA.: Belknap Press of Harvard University Press, 1995.

———. *Literary Transcendentalism: Style and Vision in the American Renaissance.* Ithaca and London: Cornell University Press, 1975.

———. *New England Literary Culture: From Revolution through Renaissance.* Cambridge: Cambridge University Press, 1987.

———. "Postcolonial Anxiety in Classic American Literature." *Postcolonial Theory and the United States: Race, Ethnicity, and Literature.* Ed. Amritjit Singh and Peter Schmidt. 196–219.

———. "The Transcendentalists." *Columbia Literary History of the United States.* Ed. Emory Elliott. 364–378.

Buell, Lawrence, ed. *Ralph Waldo Emerson: A Collection of Critical Essays.* Englewood Cliffs: Prentice Hall, 1993.

Burbick, Joan. *Thoreau's Alternative History: Changing Perspectives on Nature, Culture and Language.* Philadelphia: University of Pennsylvania Press, 1987.

Burkholder, Robert E. "The Contemporary Reception of *English Traits*." *Emerson: Centenary Essays.* Ed. Joel Myerson. 156–172.

———"The Radical Emerson: Politics in 'The American Scholar.'" *ESQ: A Journal of The American Renaissance* 34:1–2 (1988): 37–57.

Cabral, Amilcar. "National Liberation and Culture." *Colonial Discourse and Post-Colonial Theory: A Reader.* Ed. Patrick Williams and Laura Chrisman. 53–65.

Cadava, Eduardo. "Emerson and the Climates of Political History." *boundary 2* 21.2 (Summer 1994): 179–219.

Cain, William, ed. *A Historical Guide to Henry David Thoreau.* Oxford: Oxford University Press, 2000.

Camboni, Marina, ed. *Utopia in the Present Tense: Walt Whitman and the Language of the New World.* Rome: Il Calamo, 1994.

Carr, Helen. *Inventing the American Primitive: Politics, Gender and the Representation of Native American Literary Traditions, 1789–1936.* Cork: Cork University Press, 1996.

Castillo, Susan. "'The best of nations'? Race and Imperial Destinies in Emerson's *English Traits*." *Yearbook of English Studies* 34 (2004): 100–111.

Cavell, Stanley. *The Senses of Walden*. Chicago and London: The University of Chicago Press, 1992.
Cayton, Mary Kupiec. *Emerson's Emergence: Self and Society in the Transformation of New England, 1800–1845*. Chapel Hill and London: The University of North Carolina Press, 1989.
Chai, Leon. *The Romantic Foundations of the American Renaissance*. Ithaca and London: Cornell University Press, 1987.
Chandler, James. "Concerning the Influence of America on the Mind: Western Settlements, 'English Writers,' and the Case of US Culture." *American Literary History* 10.1 (Spring 1998): 84–123.
Cheyfitz, Erick. *The Poetics of Imperialism: Translation and Colonization from The Tempest to Tarzan*. Philadelphia: University of Pennsylvania Press, 1997.
Chow, Rey. "Where Have All the Natives Gone?" *Contemporary Postcolonial Theory: A Reader*. Ed. Padmini Mongia. 122–146.
Christie, John Aldrich. *Thoreau as World Traveler*. New York and London: Columbia University Press and American Geographical Society, 1965.
Clarke, Graham. *Walt Whitman: The Poem as Private History*. London: Vision Press; New York: St. Martin's Press, 1991.
Cole, Phyllis. "Emerson, England, and Fate." *Emerson: Prophecy, Metamorphosis, and Influence. Selected Papers from the English Institute*. Ed. David Levin. 83–105.
Conrad, Peter. *Imagining America*. New York: Oxford University Press, 1980.
Coviello, Peter. "Intimate Nationality: Anonymity and Attachment in Whitman." *American Literature* 70.3 (September 2001): 85–119.
Cowan, Michael H. *City of the West: Emerson, America and Urban Metaphor*. New Haven: New Haven and London: Yale University Press, 1967.
Cromphout, Gustaaf Van. "Emerson and the Dialectics of History." *PMLA* 91.1 (January 1976): 54–65.
Dallal, Jenine Abboushi. "American Imperialism UnManifest: Emerson's 'Inquest' and Cultural Regeneration." *American Literature* 73.1 (March 2001): 47–83.
Daniels, Christine, and Michael V. Kennedy, eds. *Negotiated Empires: Centers and Peripheries in the Americas, 1500–1820*. New York and London: Routledge, 2002.
Dauber, Kenneth. "On Not Being Able to Read Emerson, or 'Representative Man.'" *boundary 2* 21.2 (Summer 1994): 220–242.
Defoe, Daniel. *Robinson Crusoe*. Harmondsworth: Penguin Books, 1994.
Dickens, Charles. *American Notes*. London and Glasgow: Collins' Clear-Type Press (no date of publication).
Dimock, Wai-chee. *Empire for Liberty: Melville and the Poetics of Individualism*. Princeton: Princeton University Press, 1989.
———. "Whitman, Syntax, and Political Theory." *Breaking Bounds: Whitman and American Cultural Studies*. Ed. Betsy Erkkila and Jay Grossman. 62–79.

BIBLIOGRAPHY

Dougherty, James. *Walt Whitman and the Citizen's Eye*. Baton Rouge and London: Louisiana University Press, 1993.
Downs, Robert B. *Images of America: Travelers from Abroad in the New World*. Urbana and Chicago: University of Illinois Press, 1987.
Elliott, Emory, ed. *Columbia Literary History of the United States*. New York: Columbia University Press, 1988.
Ellison, Julie. "Aggressive Allegory." *Ralph Waldo Emerson: A Collection of Critical Essays*. Ed. Lawrence Buell. 159–170.
Erkkila, Betsy. "Public Love: Whitman and Political Theory." *Whitman East & West: New Contexts for Reading Walt Whitman*. Ed. Ed Folsom. 115–144.
———. "Whitman and American Empire." *Walt Whitman of Mickle Street: A Centennial Collection*. Ed. Jeffrey M. Sill. 54–69.
———. *Whitman the Political Poet*. New York and Oxford: Oxford University Press, 1989.
Erkkila, Betsy, and Jay Grossman, eds. *Breaking Bounds: Whitman and American Cultural Studies*. New York and Oxford: Oxford University Press, 1996.
Emerson, Ralph Waldo. *Essays and Lectures*. Ed. Joel Porte. New York: The Library of America, 1983.
———. *The Later Lectures of Ralph Waldo Emerson, 1843–1871. Vol. I: 1843–1854. Vol. II: 1855–1871*. Ed. Ronald A. Bosco and Joel Myerson. Athens and London: The University of Georgia Press, 2001.
Eperjesi, John R. *The Imperialist Imaginary: Visions of Asia and the Pacific in American Culture*. Hanover, NH; and London, 2005.
Evans, Martin J. *America: The View From Europe*. New York and London: W.W. Norton, 1979.
Fanon, Frantz. *The Wretched of the Earth*. Trans. Constance Farrington. New York: Grove Press, 1963.
Fanuzzi, Robert. "Thoreau's Urban Imagination." *American Literature* 68.2 (June 1996): 321–346.
Field, James A. Jr. *America and the Mediterranean World, 1776–1882*. Princeton: Princeton University Press, 1969.
Field, Peter S. *Ralph Waldo Emerson: The Making of a Democratic Intellectual*. Lanham, Boulder, New York, Oxford: Rowman and Littlefied, 2002.
Finnie, David H. *Pioneers East: The Early American Experience in the Middle East*. Cambridge, MA: Harvard University Press, 1967.
Folsom, Ed, ed. *Whitman East & West: New Contexts for Reading Walt Whitman*. Iowa City: University of Iowa Press, 2002.
Foster, David R. *Thoreau's Country: Journey Through a Transformed Landscape*. Cambridge, MA; and London: Harvard University Press, 1999.
Foucault, Michel. *Power/Knowledge: Selected Interviews and Other Writings 1972–1977*. Ed. Colin Gordon. Trans. Colin Gordon, Leo Marshall, John Mepham, Kate Soper. New York: Pantheon Books, 1980.
Frank, Albert J. Von. "*Essays: First Series*." *The Cambridge Companion to Ralph Waldo Emerson*. Ed. Joel Porte and Saundra Morris. 106–120.

Fresonke, Kris. *West of Emerson: The Design of Manifest Destiny.* Berkeley, Los Angeles, London: University of California Press, 2003.

Frost, Linda. "'The Red Face of Man,' the Penobscot Indian, and a Conflict of Interest in Thoreau's *Maine Woods.*" *ESQ: A Journal of the American Renaissance* 39.1 (1993): 21–47.

Garber, Frederick. *Thoreau's Redemptive Imagination.* New York: New York University Press, 1977.

———. *Thoreau's Fable of Inscribing.* Princeton: Princeton University Press, 1991.

Gikandi, Simon. "Poststructuralism and Postcolonial Discourse." *The Cambridge Companion to Postcolonial Studies.* Ed. Neil Lazarus. 97–119.

Giles, Paul. *Transatlantic Insurrections. British Culture and the Formation of American Literature, 1730–1860.* Philadelphia: University of Pennsylvania Press, 2001.

Gilmore, Michael T. "*Walden* and the 'Curse of Trade.'" *Ideology and Classic American Literature.* Ed. Sacvan Bercovitch and Myra Jehlen. 293–310.

Ghodes, Clarence. "An American Author as Democrat." *Literary Romanticism in America.* Ed. William L. Andrews. 1–18.

Golden, Arthur. "Passage to Less than India: Structure and Meaning in Whitman's 'Passage to India.'" *PMLA* 88.5 (October 1973): 1095–1103.

González, Antonio Ballesteros. "Looking for Signs of Colonial Otherness: Defoe, H.G.Wells, Conrad." *Aristippus Meets Crusoe: Rethinking the Beach Encounter.* Ed. Zbigniew Białas. 89–103.

Goodman, Russell B. *American Philosophy and the Romantic Tradition.* Cambridge: Cambridge University Press, 1990.

Goudie, Sean X. *Creole America: The West Indies and the Formation of Literature and Culture in the New Republic.* Philadelphia: University of Pennsylvania Press, 2006.

Gramsci, Antonio. *Selections from the Prison Notebooks of Antonio Gramsci.* Ed. and trans. Quentin Hoare and Goeffrey Nowell Smith. London: Electronic Book Co., 2001.

Greenberg, Robert M. *Splintered Worlds: Fragmentation and the Ideal of Diversity in the Work of Emerson, Melville, Whitman, and Dickinson.* Boston: Northeastern University Press, 1993.

Greenspan, Ezra. *Walt Whitman and the Reader.* Cambridge: Cambridge University Press, 1990.

Greenspan, Ezra, ed. *The Cambridge Companion to Walt Whitman.* Cambridge: Cambridge University Press, 1995.

Grünzweig, Walter. "Imperialism." *A Companion to Walt Whitman.* Ed. Donald D. Kummings. 151–163.

Gura, Philip F. *The Crossroads of American History and Literature.* University Park, Penn.: The Pennsylvania State University Press, 1996.

Gura, Philip F., and Joel Myerson, eds. *Critical Essays on American Transcendentalism.* Boston: G.K. Hall, 1982.

Gustafson, Thomas. *Representative Words: Politics, Literature, and the American Language, 1776–1865*. Cambridge: Cambridge University Press, 1992.

Hall, Basil. *Travels in North America, in the Years 1827 and 1828*. Vols. I, II, and III. New York: Arno Press, 1974.

Hallock, Thomas. *From the Fallen Tree: Frontier Narratives, Environmental Politics, and the Roots of a National Pastoral, 1749–1826*. Chapel Hill and London: The University of North Carolina Press, 2003.

Handley, Goerge B. *New World Poetics: Nature and the Adamic Imagination of Whitman, Neruda, and Walcott*. Athens and London: The University of Georgia Press, 2007.

Hanlon, Christopher. "'The Old Race Are All Gone': Transatlantic Bloodlines and English Traits." *American Literary History* 19 (2007): 800–823.

Hansen, Olaf. *Aesthetic Individualism and Practical Intellect: American Allegory in Emerson, Thoreau, Adams and James*. Princeton: Princeton University Press, 1990.

Harris, Kenneth Marc. *Carlyle and Emerson: Their Long Debate*. Cambridge, MA; and London: Harvard University Press, 1978.

Hawthorne, Nathaniel. *Our Old Home and Other Sketches*. Cleveland and New York: The World Syndicate Publishing Company, 1937.

Heilman, Robert B. "The New World in Charles Dickens's Writings. Part One." *Trollopian* 1.3 (September 1946): 25–43.

Heineman, Helen. "Frances Trollope in the New World: *Domestic Manners of the Americans*." *American Quarterly* 21.3 (Autumn 1969): 544–559.

———. "'Starving in that Land of Plenty': New Backgrounds to Frances Trollope's *Domestic Manners of the Americans*." *American Quarterly* 24.5 (December 1972): 643–660.

Herrington, Elrid. "Nation and Identity." *A Companion to Walt Whitman*. Ed. Donald D. Kummings. 122–135.

Hietala, Thomas R. *Manifest Design: Anxious Aggrandizement in Late Jacksonian America*. Ithaca and London: Cornell University Press, 1985.

Hobsbawm, E. J. *Nations and Nationalism since 1780: Programme, Myth, Reality*. Cambridge: Cambridge University Press, 1990.

Hoffman, Michael J. *The Subversive Vision: American Romanticism in Literature*. Port Washington, NY; and London: Kennikat Press, 1972.

Hollis, C. Carroll. *Language and Style in Leaves of Grass*. Baton Rouge and London: Louisiana State University Press, 1983.

Holmes, Isaac. *An Account of the United States of America*. New York: Arno Press, 1974.

Horsman, Reginald. "Anglo-Saxon Racism." *Major Problems in American Foreign Policy: Documents and Essays. Vol. I: To 1914*. Ed. Thomas G. Paterson.

———. *Race and Manifest Destiny: The Origins of American Racial Anglo-Saxonism*. Cambridge, MA, and London: Harvard University Press, 1981.

Hulme, Peter. "Including America." *ARIEL: A Review of International English Literature* 26.1 (January 1995): 117–123.
Hutner, Gordon, ed. *American Literature, American Culture.* New York: Oxford University Press 1999.
Inge, M. Thomas, ed. *A Nineteenth-Century American Reader.* Washington, DC: United States Information Agency, 1995.
Irving, Washington. *The Sketch-Book of Geoffrey Crayon, Gent.* London, Paris, and Melbourne: Cassell and Company, 1897.
Jehlen, Myra. *American Incarnation: The Individual, the Nation, the Continent.* Cambridge, MA, and London: Harvard University Press, 1986.
———. "Why Did the Europeans Cross the Ocean? A Seventeenth-Century Riddle." *Cultures of United States Imperialism.* Ed. Amy Kaplan and Donald Pease. 41–57.
Jones, Joseph. *Radical Cousins: Nineteenth-Century American and Australian Writers.* St. Lucia: University of Queensland Press, 1976.
Kagan, Robert. *Dangerous Nation.* New York: Alfred A. Knopf, 2006.
Kagel, Steven E., ed. *America: Exploration and Travel.* Bowling Green: Bowling Green State University Popular Press, 1979.
Kaplan, Amy. *The Anarchy of Empire in the Making of U.S. Culture.* Cambridge, MA; and London: Harvard University Press, 2002.
Kaplan, Amy, and Donald Pease, eds. *Cultures of United States Imperialism.* Durham and London: Duke University Press, 1993.
Kaplan, Justin. *Walt Whitman: A Life.* New York: Simon and Schuster, 1980.
Kazin, Alfred. *An American Procession: The Major American Writers from 1830–1930—The Crucial Century.* New York: Vintage, 1985.
Keiser, Albert. *The Indian in American Literature.* New York: Octagon Books, 1970 [1933].
Kemp, Mark A. R. "*The Marble Faun* and American Postcolonial Ambivalence." *Modern Fiction Studies* 43.1 (1997): 209–236.
Kennedy, J. Gerald, and Liliane Weissberg, eds. *Romancing the Shadow: Poe and Race.* Oxford: Oxford University Press, 2001.
Kim, Heidi Kathleen. "From Language to Empire: Walt Whitman in the Context of Nineteenth-Century Popular Anglo-Saxonism." *Walt Whitman Quarterly Review* 24.1 (Summer 1996): 1–19.
Klein, Kerwin Lee. *Frontiers of Historical Imagination: Narrating the European Conquest of Native America, 1890–1980.* Berkeley, Los Angeles, London: University of California Press, 1999.
Kolodny, Annette. *The Lay of the Land: Metaphor as Experience and History in American Life and Letters.* Chapel Hill: University of North Carolina Press, 1975.
Korte, Barbara. *English Travel Writing from Pilgrimages to Postcolonial Explorations.* Trans. Catherine Matthias. Houndmills: Macmillan, 2000.
Kummings, Donald D., ed. *A Companion to Walt Whitman.* Malden, MA: Blackwell, 2006.

BIBLIOGRAPHY

LaFeber, Walter. "The American View of Decolonization, 1776–1920: An Ironic Legacy." *The United States and Decolonization: Power and Freedom.* Ed. David Ryan and Victor Pungong. 24–40.

Larson, Kerry. "Individualism and the Place of Understanding in Emerson's Essays." *ELH* 68.4 (Winter 2001): 991–1021.

———. *Whitman's Drama of Consensus.* Chicago and London: The University of Chicago Press, 1988.

Lawson-Peebles, Robert. *Landscape and Written Expression in Revolutionary America: The World Turned Upside Down.* Cambridge: Cambridge University Press, 1988.

Lazarus, Neil, ed. *The Cambridge Companion to Postcolonial Studies.* Cambridge: Cambridge University Press, 2004.

Leed. Eric J. *The Mind of the Traveler: From Gilgamesh to Global Tourism.* New York: Basic Books, 1991.

Levin, David, ed. *Emerson: Prophecy, Metamorphosis, and Influence. Selected Papers from the English Institute.* New York and London: Columbia University Press, 1975.

Lojek, Helen. "Thoreau's Bog People." *The New England Quarterly* 67.2 (June 1994): 279–297.

Loomba, Ania. *Colonialism/Postcolonialism.* London and New York: Routledge, 2000.

Loving, Jerome. *Walt Whitman: The Song of Himself.* Berkeley, Los Angeles, London: University of California Press, 1999.

Lubbers, Klaus. *Born for the Shade: Stereotypes of the Native American in United States Literature and Visual Arts, 1776–1894.* Amsterdam and Atlanta: Rodopi, 1994.

Macdonell, Diane. *Theories of Discourse: An Introduction.* Oxford, UK; and Cambridge, USA: Blackwell, 1993.

McClintock, Anne. "The Angel of Progress: Pitfalls of the Term 'Post-Colonialism.'" *Colonial Discourse and Post-Colonial Theory: A Reader.* Ed. Patrick Williams and Laura Chrisman. 291–304.

McWilliams, John P., Jr. *The American Epic: Transforming the Genre, 1770–1860.* Cambridge: Cambridge University Press, 1989.

Madsen, Deborah L. "Beyond the Commonwealth: Post-Colonialism and American Literature." *Post-Colonial Literatures: Expanding the Canon.* Ed. Deborah L. Madsen. 1–13.

Madsen, Deborah L., ed. *Post-Colonial Literatures: Expanding the Canon.* London and Sterling, Virginia: Pluto Press, 1999.

Marchand, Ernest. "Emerson and the Frontier." *American Literature* 3.2 (May 1931): 149–174.

Marx, Leo. *The Machine in the Garden: Technology and the Pastoral Ideal in America.* London, Oxford, New York: Oxford University Press, 1981.

———. "Pastoralism in America." *Ideology and Classic American Literature.* Ed. Sacvan Bercovitch and Myra Jehlen. 36–69.

Mayard, W. Barksdale. "Thoreau's House at Walden." *The Art Bulletin* 81.2 (June 1999): 303–325.

Melley, Timothy. "Performing Experiments: Materiality and Rhetoric in Thoreau's *Walden*." *ESQ: A Journal of the American Renaissance* 39.4 (1993): 253–277.
Meltzer, Mitchell. *Secular Revelations: The Constitution of the United States and Classic American Literature.* Cambridge, MA; and London: Harvard University Press, 2005.
Memmi, Albert. *The Colonizer and the Colonized.* Trans. Howard Greenfeld. Intr. Jean-Paul Sartre. Aft. Susan Gilson Miller. Boston: Beacon Press, 1991.
———. *Decolonization and the Decolonized.* Trans. Robert Bononno. Minneapolis and London: University of Minnesota Press, 2006.
Mendelson, Donna. "Geographies of Scale: Layers of Self-Locating Associations in *Walden*." *ESQ: A Journal of the American Renaissance* 47.4 (2001): 265–277.
Merk, Frederick. *Manifest Destiny and Mission in American History. A Reinterpretation.* New York: Alfred A. Knopf, 1970.
Metwalli, Ahmed M. "Americans Abroad: The Popular Art of Travel Writing in the Nineteenth Century." *America: Exploration and Travel.* Ed. Steven E. Kagel. 68–82.
Miller, J. Hillis. "The Sources of Dickens's Comic Art: From *American Notes* to *Martin Chuzzlewit*." *Nineteenth-Century Fiction* 24.4, The Charles Dickens Centennial (March 1970): 467–476.
Miller, Perry. "New England's Transcendentalism: Native or Imported?" *Critical Essays on American Transcendentalism.* Ed. Philip F. Gura and Joel Myerson. 387–401.
Mongia, Padmini, ed. *Contemporary Postcolonial Theory: A Reader.* London: Arnold, 1996.
Mulvey, Christopher. *Anglo-American Landscapes: A Study of Nineteenth-Century Anglo-American Travel Literature.* Cambridge: Cambridge University Press, 1983.
———. *Transatlantic Manners: Social Patterns in Nineteenth-Century Anglo-American Travel Writing.* Cambridge: Cambridge University Press, 1990.
Myerson, Joel, ed. *The Cambridge Companion to Henry David Thoreau.* Cambridge: Cambridge University Press, 1999.
Myerson, Joel, ed. *Emerson: Centenary Essays.* Carbondale and Edwardsville: Southern Illinois University Press, 1982.
Myerson, Joel, ed. *Emerson and Thoreau: The Contemporary Reviews.* Cambridge: Cambridge University Press, 1992.
Nathanson, Tenney. *Whitman's Presence: Body, Voice and Writing in Leaves of Grass.* New York and London: New York University Press, 1992.
Nelson, Dana D. "Thoreau, Manhood, and Race: Quiet Desperation versus Representative Isolation." *A Historical Guide to Henry David Thoreau.* Ed. William E. Cain. 61–93.
———. *The Word in Black and White: Reading 'Race' in American Literature, 1638–1867.* New York and Oxford: Oxford University Press, 1992.

Newfield, Christopher. *The Emerson Effect: Individualism and Submission in America.* Chicago and London: The University of Chicago Press, 1996.
Nicoloff, Philip L. *Emerson on Race and History: An Examination of English Traits.* New York: Columbia University Press, 1961.
Nye, David. *America as Second Creation: Technology and Narratives of New Beginnings.* Cambridge, MA; and London: The MIT Press, 2003.
O'Brien, Susie. "The Place of America in the Era of Postcolonial Imperialism." *ARIEL: A Review of International English Studies* 29.2 (April 1998): 159–183.
Onuf, Peter S. "'Empire for Liberty': Center and Peripheries in Postcolonial America." *Negotiated Empires: Centers and Peripheries in the Americas, 1500–1820.* Ed. Christine Daniels and Michael V. Kennedy. 301–317.
O'Sullivan, John L. "The Great Nation of Futurity." *A Nineteenth-Century American Reader.* Ed. M. Thomas Inge. 7–9.
Pannapacker, William. *Revised Lives: Walt Whitman and Nineteenth-Century Authorship.* New York and London: Routledge, 2004.
Paterson, Thomas G., ed. *Major Problems in American Foreign Policy: Documents and Essays. Vol. I: To 1914.* Lexington, MA; and Toronto: D.C. Heath, 1989.
Pease, Donald E. *Visionary Compacts: American Renaissance Writings in Cultural Context.* Madison: The University of Wisconsin Press, 1987.
Perkins, Bradford. *The Cambridge History of American Foreign Relations. Vol. I: The Creation of a Republican Empire, 1776–1865.* Cambridge: Cambridge University Press, 1993.
Piper, Karen. "Post-Colonialism in the United States: Diversity or Hybridity?" *Post-Colonial Literatures: Expanding the Canon.* Ed. Deborah L. Madsen. 14–28.
Pipkin, John S. "Hiding Places: Thoreau's Geographies." *Annals of the Association of American Geographers* 91.3 (September 2001): 527–545.
Porte, Joel. *Consciousness and Culture: Emerson and Thoreau Reviewed.* New Haven and London: Yale University Press, 2004.
———. "The Problem of Emerson." *Romanticism: Critical Essays in American Literature.* Ed. James Barbour and Thomas Quirk. 59–81.
Porte, Joel, ed. *Emerson: Prospect and Retrospect.* Cambridge and London: Harvard University Press, 1982.
Porte, Joel, and Saundra Morris, eds. *The Cambridge Companion to Ralph Waldo Emerson.* Cambridge: Cambridge University Press, 1999.
Powell, Timothy. "Postcolonial Theory in an American Context: A Reading of Martin Delany's *Blake*." *The Pre-Occupation of Postcolonial Studies.* Ed. Fawzia Afzal-Khan and Kalpana Seshadri-Crooks. 346–365.
Pratt, Mary Louise. *Imperial Eyes: Travel Writing and Transculturation.* London: Routledge, 1992.
Price, Kenneth M. *Whitman and Tradition: The Poet in His Century.* New Haven and London: Yale University Press, 1990.
Price, Kenneth, ed. M. *Walt Whitman: The Contemporary Reviews.* Cambridge: Cambridge University Press, 1996.

Reynolds, David S. "Introduction." *A Historical Guide to Walt Whitman*. Ed. David S. Reynolds. 3–14.
———. *Walt Whitman's America: A Cultural Biography*. New York: Alfred A. Knopf, 1995.
Reynolds, David S., ed. *A Historical Guide to Walt Whitman*. New York and Oxford: Oxford University Press, 2000.
Richardson, Robert D., Jr. "Emerson on History." *Emerson: Prospect and Retrospect*. Ed. Joel Porte. 49–64.
———. *Myth and Literature in the American Renaissance*. Bloomington and London: Indiana University Press, 1978.
Roberson, Susan L. "Emerson, Columbus, and the Geography of Self-Reliance. The Example of the Sermons." *Emerson: Bicentennial Essays*. Ed. Ronald A. Bosco and Joel Myerson. 273–288.
Robinson, David M. *Emerson and the Conduct of Life: Pragmatism and Ethical Purpose in the Later Work*. Cambridge: Cambridge University Press, 1993.
Rohler, Lloyd. *Ralph Waldo Emerson: Preacher and Lecturer*. Westport, CT.; and London: Greenwood Press, 1995.
Rowe, John Carlos. *At Emerson's Tomb: The Politics of Classic American Literature*. New York: Columbia University Press, 1997.
———. "Edgar Allan Poe's Imperial Fantasy and the American Frontier." *Romancing the Shadow: Poe and Race*. Ed. J. Gerald Kennedy and Liliane Weissberg. 75–105.
———. *Literary Culture and U.S. Imperialism: From the Revolution to World War II*. Oxford: Oxford University Press, 2000.
———. "Nineteenth-Century United States Literary Culture and Transnationality." *PMLA* 118.1 (January 2003): 78–89.
Rubin, Barry, and Judith Colp Rubin. *Hating America: A History*. Oxford: Oxford University Press, 2004.
Ryan, David, and Victor Pungong, eds. *The United States and Decolonization: Power and Freedom*. Houndmills and London: Macmillan Press, 2000.
Ryan, Kiernan, ed. *New Historicism and Cultural Materialism: A Reader*. London, New York, Sydney, Auckland: Arnold, 1996.
Sacks, Kenneth S. *Understanding Emerson: 'The American Scholar' and His Struggle for Self-Reliance*. Princeton and Oxford: Princeton University Press, 2003.
Said, Edward. *Culture and Imperialism*. London: Chatto and Windus1993.
———*Orientalism*. New York: Vintage, 1994.
Salska, Agnieszka. *The Poetry of Central Consciousness: Whitman and Dickinson*. Lodz: University of Lodz Press, 1982.
———. "Whitman's Columbus: A Paradigm for What Happened to the American Dream." *The American Dream, Past and Present*. Ed. Agnieszka Salska and Paul Wilson. 54–65.
Salska, Agnieszka, and Paul Wilson, eds. *The American Dream, Past and Present*. Lodz: University of Lodz Press, 1994.
Sanborn, Geoffrey. *The Sign of the Cannibal: Melville and the Making of a Postcolonial Reader*. Durham, N.C.: Duke University Press, 1998.

Sattelmeyer, Robert. "Depopulation, Deforestation, and the Actual Walden Pond." *Thoreau's Sense of Place: Essays in American Environmental Writing.* Ed. Richard J. Schneider. 235–243.
Sayre, Gordon M. *Les Sauvages Américains: Representations of Native Americans in French and English Colonial Literature.* Chapel Hill and London: The University of North Carolina Press, 1997.
Sayre, Robert F. *Thoreau and the American Indians.* Princeton: Princeton University Press, 1977.
Schirmeister, Pamela. *Less Legible Meanings: Between Poetry and Philosophy in the Work of Emerson.* Stanford: Stanford University Press, 1999.
Schneider, Richard J. *Henry David Thoreau.* Boston: Twayne, 1987.
———. "Walden." *The Cambridge Companion to Henry David Thoreau.* Ed. Joel Myerson. 92–106.
Schneider, Richard J., ed. *Thoreau's Sense of Place: Essays in American Environmental Writing.* Iowa City: University of Iowa Press, 2000.
Schueller, Malini Johar. *U.S. Orientalisms: Race, Nation, and Gender in Literature, 1790–1890.* Ann Arbor: The University of Michigan Press, 1998.
Scott, David. *Semiologies of Travel: From Gautier to Baudrillard.* Cambridge: Cambridge University Press, 2004.
Sealts, Merton M., Jr. *Emerson on the Scholar.* Columbia and London: University of Missouri Press, 1992.
Sethi, Rumina. *Myths of the Nation: National Identity and Literary Representation.* Oxford: Clarendon Press, 1999.
Sill, Geoffrey M., ed. *Walt Whitman of Mickle Street: A Centennial Collection.* Knoxville: The University of Tennessee Press, 1994.
Simmons, Nancy Craig. "Emerson and His Audiences. The *New England* Lectures, 1843–1844." *Emerson: Bicentennial Essays.* Ed. Ronald A. Bosco and Joel Myerson. 51–85.
Simpson, David. "Destiny Made Manifest: The Styles of Whitman's Poetry." *Nation and Narration.* Ed. Homi K. Bhabha. 177–196.
Singh, Amritjit, and Peter Schmidt. "On the Borders Between U.S. Studies and Postcolonial Theory." *Postcolonial Theory and the United States: Race, Ethnicity, and Literature.* Ed. Amritjit Singh and Peter Schmidt. 3–69.
Singh, Amritjit, and Peter Schmidt, eds. *Postcolonial Theory and the United States: Race, Ethnicity, and Literature.* Jackson: University Press of Mississippi, 2000.
Slotkin, Richard. *The Fatal Environment: The Myth of the Frontier in the Age of Industrialization, 1800–1890.* Middletown: Wesleyan University Press, 1986.
———. *Regeneration through Violence: The Myth of the American Frontier, 1600–1860.* Middletown: Wesleyan University Press, 1973.
Smith, Anthony D. *Myths and Memories of the Nation.* Oxford: Oxford University Press, 1999.
Smith, Wilson, ed. *Essays in American Intellectual History.* Hinsdale, Ill.: The Dryden Press, 1975.

Sowder, Michael. *Whitman's Ecstatic Union: Conversion and Ideology in Leaves of Grass.* New York and London: Routledge, 2005.

Sowder, William J. *Emerson's Impact on the British Isles and Canada.* Charlottesville: The University Press of Virginia, 1966.

Springer, Haskell S. "The Nautical Walden." *The New England Quarterly* 57.1 (March 1984): 84–97.

Stowe, William W. *Going Abroad: European Travel in Nineteenth-Century American Culture.* Princeton: Princeton University Press, 1994.

Sundquist, Eric J. *Empire and Slavery in American Literature 1820–1865.* Jackson: University Press of Mississippi, 2006.

———. *Home as Found. Authority and Genealogy in Nineteenth-Century American Literature.* Baltimore and London: The Johns Hopkins University Press, 1979.

Szeman, Imre. *Zones of Instability: Literature, Postcolonialism, and the Nation.* Baltimore and London: The Johns Hopkins University Press, 2003.

Talib, Ismail S. *The Language of Postcolonial Literatures: An Introduction.* London and New York: Routledge, 2002.

Taylor, Bob Pepperman. *America's Bachelor Uncle: Thoreau and the American Polity.* Lawrence: University Press of Kansas, 1996.

Tedeschini Lalli, Biancamaria. "Utopia in the Present Tense: Walt Whitman and the Language of the New World." *Utopia in the Present Tense: Walt Whitman and the Language of the New World.* Ed. Marina Camboni. 15–33.

Thomas, M. Wynn. *Transatlantic Connections: Whitman U.S., Whitman U.K.* Iowa City: University of Iowa Press, 2005.

Thoreau, Henry David. *A Week on the Concord and Merrimack Rivers. Walden; or, Life in the Woods. The Maine Woods. Cape Cod.* Ed. Robert F. Sayre. New York: The Library of America, 1985.

Tichi, Cecelia. *New World, New Earth: Environmental Reform in American Literature from the Puritans through Whitman.* New Haven and London: Yale University Press, 1979.

Tiffin, Helen. "Post-Colonial Literature and Counter-Discourse." *The Post-Colonial Studies Reader.* Ed. Bill Ashcroft, Gareth Griffiths, and Helen Tiffin. 95–98.

Tocqueville, Alexis de. *Democracy in America.* In Two Volumes with a Critical Appraisal of Each Volume by John Stuart Mill. New York: Schocken Books, 1972.

Trollope, Frances. *Domestic Manners of the Americans.* Ed. John Lauritz Larson. St.James, New York: Brandywine Press, 1993.

Tyler, Hoffman. "Language." *A Companion to Walt Whitman.* Ed. Donald D. Kummings. 361–376.

Waggoner, Hyatt H. *American Visionary Poetry.* Baton Rouge: Louisiana State University Press, 1982.

Walder, Dennis. *Post-Colonial Literatures in English.* History, Language, Theory. Oxford: Blackwell, 1998.

Walls, Laura Dassow. *Emerson's Life in Science: The Culture of Truth.* Ithaca and London: Cornell University Press, 2003.

———. *Seeing New Worlds: Henry David Thoreau and Nineteenth-Century Natural Science*. Madison: The University of Wisconsin Press, 1995.

Warren, James Perrin. "Reading Whitman's Postwar Poetry." *The Cambridge Companion to Walt Whitman*. Ed. Ezra Greenspan. 45–65.

———. *Walt Whitman's Language Experiment*. University Park and London: The Pennsylvania State University Press, 1990.

Watt, Iann. *The Rise of the Novel: Studies in Defoe, Richardson and Fielding*. Harmondsworth: Penguin Books, 1970.

Watts, Edward. *Writing and Postcolonialism in the Early Republic*. Charlottesville and London: University Press of Virginia, 1998.

Webster, Daniel. *The Orations on Bunker Hill Monument, the Character of Washington, and the Landing at Plymouth*. New York, Cincinnati, Chicago: American Book Company, 1894.

Weisbuch, Robert. *Atlantic Double-Cross: American Literature and British Influence in the Age of Emerson*. Chicago and London: The University of Chicago Press, 1986.

———. "Post-Colonial Emerson and the Erasure of Europe." *The Cambridge Companion to Ralph Waldo Emerson*. Ed. Joel Porte and Saundra Morris. 192–217.

Wertheimer, Eric. *Imagined Empires: Incas, Aztecs, and the New World of American Literature, 1771–1876*. Cambridge: Cambridge University Press, 1999.

Whicher, Stephen E. "Emerson's Tragic Sense." *Essays in American Intellectual History*. Ed. Wilson Smith. 223–228.

White, Hayden. *Figural Realism: Studies in the Mimesis Effect*. Baltimore and London: The Johns Hopkins University Press, 1999.

Whitley, Edward. "The First (1855) Edition of *Leaves of Grass*." *A Companion to Walt Whitman*. Ed. Donald D. Kummings. 457–470.

Whitman, Walt. *Complete Poetry and Collected Prose*. Ed. Justin Kaplan. New York: The Library of America, 1982.

Williams, Patrick, and Laura Chrisman, eds. *Colonial Discourse and Post-Colonial Theory: A Reader*. Harlow: Longman, 1994.

Young, Robert C. *Postcolonialism: An Historical Introduction*. Oxford: Blackwell, 2001.

Yu, Beongcheon. *The Great Circle: American Writers and the Orient*. Detroit: Wayne State University, 1983.

Yu, Ning. "Thoreau and the New Geography: The Hydrological Cycle in 'Ktaadn.'" *ESQ: A Journal of the American Renaissance* 40.2 (1994): 113–138.

Ziff, Larzer. *Literary Democracy: The Declaration of Cultural Independence in America*. New York: Viking, 1981.

INDEX

American Renaissance 13–16, 18, 25, 164, 191, 211, 223, 224, 226, 230–232, 235
American Revolution 9, 11, 35

Brackenridge, Hugh Henry 17
Brontë, Charlotte 49
Brown, Charles Brockden 3, 17, 18, 156
Buchanan, James 138, 165
Burton, Richard 54

Cabral, Amilcar 172, 173, 223
Carlyle, Thomas 47, 61, 227
Clark, William 79
class 7, 19, 51, 56, 59, 68, 155, 159, 163, 164, 216, 219
Coetzee, J. M. 49
Coleridge, Samuel Taylor 47
colonial legacy 12, 14, 48, 154, 205, 208
colonialism 4, 5, 6, 11, 12, 16, 42, 144
colonization 4, 10, 13, 15, 16, 20, 31, 35, 40–42, 44, 50, 66, 110, 126, 198, 206
Columbus, Christopher 34, 84, 130, 132, 149, 150, 182–184, 194, 201, 202, 232
conquest 2, 16, 50, 80, 81, 147, 150, 156, 199, 202
Conrad, Joseph 14, 52, 224, 226
Cooper, James Fenimore 15, 33
counter-discourse 21, 49

Darwin, Charles 185

Darwinism 185, 186
decolonization 49, 154, 156
Defoe, Daniel 21, 49, 65, 100, 102–106, 108–110, 113, 117, 224, 226, 235
Robinson Crusoe 21, 99–104, 106, 107, 110–114, 118, 123, 124, 216, 224
dependence 1, 13, 18, 26, 35, 37, 39, 40, 42, 43, 81, 147, 166, 172, 206, 207, 208
Dickens, Charles 14, 52–54, 64, 69, 213, 214, 224, 227, 230

Emerson, Ralph Waldo 1, 2, 15, 17, 19, 20, 21, 23, 25–46, 47–74, 75–96, 160, 169, 170, 172, 179, 181, 205–209, 211–216, 219, 222, 223, 224, 225, 226, 227, 229, 230, 231, 232, 233, 234, 235
"The American Scholar" 15, 20, 26, 32, 36, 37–41, 44, 45, 48, 70, 81, 160, 207, 212, 223, 232
English Traits 20, 21, 47–74, 206, 213, 222, 223, 227, 231
"History" 30–33
New England lectures 75–96
"The Poet" 153, 170, 172, 218, 231, 237
"Self-Reliance" 20, 25, 41–44, 47, 73, 81, 169, 232
"The Young American" 26, 75–96, 215, 216

Emory, William 79, 223, 225
empire 4, 7, 11, 13, 16, 21, 40, 71, 77, 80, 81, 100, 139, 150, 165, 208, 209
ethnic studies 10, 237
ethnography 56, 127, 128, 237
expansion 1, 5, 11–13, 76–81, 84–86, 88, 90, 91, 93–96, 102, 111, 124, 131, 156, 180, 183, 197, 206, 209, 215, 216
expansionism 1, 21, 76–80, 87, 88, 150, 208, 209
exploration 16, 50, 79, 111, 124–130, 135, 138, 139, 147, 157, 168, 192, 193, 200, 201, 208

figuration 25, 39, 43, 81, 85, 93, 94, 157
Filmore, Millard 165
Franklin, Benjamin 16

genre 16, 18, 48, 62, 127

Hall, Basil 55, 214, 227
Hawthorne, Nathaniel 18, 36, 72, 227
Hegelianism 185, 186
hegemony 9, 13–15, 41, 125, 165, 173, 183
Holmes, Isaac 53–55, 227
hybridity 8, 28, 66, 155, 175

ideology 1, 20, 21, 37, 76, 79, 81, 88, 101, 109, 112, 150, 154, 159, 168, 190
imperial fantasy 101, 111, 119, 123, 208
imperialism 1, 4, 5, 6, 8, 11, 12, 16, 21, 40, 88, 101, 155, 172, 173, 179, 183, 197
Indians *see* Native Americans
individualism 109, 127, 171, 212, 220
intertextuality 8

Irving, Washington 17, 33, 56, 57, 228

Jackson, Andrew 78, 79
James, Henry 18, 156

landscape 21, 52, 53, 62, 79, 83, 100, 111, 113, 117, 119, 120, 134, 135, 176, 190, 194, 195, 197, 217
Lewis, Meriwether 79
liberation 6, 13, 16, 26, 37, 40, 166–169, 172, 173, 201
liminality 29, 46
literary canon 9, 10, 34
Long, Stephen 79

Maalouf, Amin 173
Manifest Destiny 2, 12, 76–79, 88, 89, 156, 215, 218, 226, 227, 230
Melville, Herman 15, 17, 85, 180, 219, 223, 224, 226, 232
memory 13, 36, 59, 60, 162, 172
Mexican War 80
Murray, Judith Sargent 17
myth 99, 123, 144, 183, 190, 191, 193

Naipaul, V. S. 14, 173
nation 3, 7, 8, 11–13, 16, 20, 21, 26–30, 39, 47, 51, 56, 58, 59, 68, 70–73, 77, 78, 81, 86, 91–93, 95, 99, 100, 111, 124, 125, 139, 144, 145, 153–161, 163–177, 181, 183, 197, 201, 205–209, 215, 216
nationalism 12, 39, 80, 216
Native Americans 10, 52, 54, 78, 80, 88, 89, 104, 126–128, 130, 131, 134–138, 140–150, 176, 188, 189, 218, 222, 226, 228, 233

Orient 179, 183, 186–188, 190, 192–196, 198–200, 220, 235

Index

Orientalism 4, 180, 183, 186, 195, 196, 232
O'Sullivan, John L. 78, 92, 93, 231

pastoralism 119
Pike, Zebulon 79
Poe, Edgar Allan 101, 179, 232
Polk, James K. 77
postcolonialism 4, 6–11, 13, 17, 18, 155, 189, 211
  in American studies 9, 10, 13
postcoloniality 155

race 19, 47, 60, 65, 66, 71, 72, 78, 81, 88, 92, 137, 140, 141, 143–146, 149, 161, 165, 169, 181, 213, 216, 219
racism 78
representation 2, 8, 9, 14, 16, 18, 20, 28, 29, 61, 62, 84, 101, 110, 132, 135, 155, 156, 165, 181, 189, 193, 197, 201, 205, 216
resistance 4, 8, 13, 32, 45, 60, 150, 154, 162, 163, 189
rhetoric 7, 8, 17, 21, 28, 38, 65–67, 76, 78, 80, 81, 84, 85, 87, 88, 89, 91, 95, 96, 100, 108, 115, 124, 132–134, 155, 156, 165, 168, 169, 171, 172, 183, 208
Rhys, Jean 49
Robinsonian topos 102, 105, 123

savagism 141, 143
science 38, 108, 126, 188, 189, 191, 203, 214
settler colony 7
space 16, 19, 29, 43, 59, 61, 83, 91, 110–112, 120, 128, 132, 135, 143, 156, 159, 176, 183, 184, 187–189, 218
spectacle 106, 121, 187, 214
stereotype 17, 54, 141, 229

Thoreau, Henry David 1, 2, 15, 19, 21, 88, 97, 99–121, 123–150, 179, 191, 205–209, 213, 216–218, 221–227, 229, 230, 231, 233, 234, 235
  "Civil Disobedience" 208
  Journal 100, 101, 223, 226, 230, 235
  The Maine Woods 21, 103, 123–150, 208, 217, 234
  Walden 15, 21, 99–121, 123, 128, 129, 131, 137, 139, 140, 208, 216, 217, 224, 226, 229, 230, 233, 234
  A Week on the Concord and Merrimack Rivers 104, 128, 234
Tocqueville, Alexis de 74, 234
trade 64, 76, 78, 81, 89–93, 107, 108, 171, 198
transatlantic studies 11, 12
transcendentalism 19, 20, 25, 28, 81, 118, 222, 223, 226, 230
translatio studii 15, 37
transnational studies 10, 12
travel writing 14, 21, 48, 50, 51, 55, 58, 59, 62, 63
Trollope, Frances 14, 52, 53, 55, 67, 213, 214, 227, 234
tropology 18
Tyler, Royal 17, 219, 234

Vespucci, Amerigo 130, 132

Watterston, George 17
Webster, Daniel 34–36, 220, 235
Whitman, Walt 1, 2, 15, 19–22, 27, 151, 153–177, 179–203, 205–209, 211, 218–221, 223–235
  "Darwinism—(Then Furthermore)" 185
  "Democratic Vistas" 197, 198

Whitman—*Continued*
  "The Eighteenth Presidency"
    165, 166
  "Passage to India" 22, 179–203,
    208, 226
  Preface to the 1855 edition of
    Leaves of Grass 21,
    153–177, 207,208,
    218, 220

"Slang in America" 161
"Starting from
  Paumanok" 209
wilderness 21, 35, 53, 95, 101,
  102, 110, 111, 119,
  120, 124, 127, 128,
  130–136, 139, 140,
  142–146, 214
Wordsworth, William 47